So here we are, in the northern marches, sitting down and telling lies...

—Yves Meynard, "Foreword"

Every year, two new editors choose the best new writing from Canada's new and established SF writers, from all over the country and from both the anglophone and francophone traditions. This 1996 anthology of Canadian speculative writing, *Tesseracts⁵* contains writing by Natasha Beaulieu (translated by Yves Meynard), Cliff Burns, Mary Choo, Michael Coney, Marlene Dean, Candas Jane Dorsey, Ian Driscoll, Heather Fraser, James Alan Gardner, Tracey Halford, Jan Lars Jensen, Jocko, Sandra Kasturi, Sansoucy Kathenor, Eileen Kernaghan, Michel Martin (translated by Laurent McAllister), Sally McBride, David Nickle, John Park, Francine Pelletier (translated by Howard Scott), Annick Perrot-Bishop (translated by Neil Bishop), Karl Schroeder, Keith Scott, Daniel Sernine (translated by Jean-Louis Trudel), Dale Sproule, Paul Stockton, Peter Such, Jean-Louis Trudel, Élisabeth Vonarburg (translated by Howard Scott), Peter Watts and Andrew Weiner

...almost half of the stories in Tesseracts⁵ are by authors published here for the first time...the future of Canadian speculative fiction has never been brighter...

—Robert Runté, "Afterword"

TESSERACTS ANTHOLOGIES
AVAILABLE FROM TESSERACT BOOKS

Tesseracts (1985)
edited by Judith Merril

Tesseracts² (1987)
edited by Phyllis Gotlieb and
Douglas Barbour

Tesseracts³ (1990)
edited by Candas Jane Dorsey and
Gerry Truscott

Tesseracts⁴ (1992)
edited by Lorna Toolis and Michael
Skeet

Tesseracts^Q (1996) edited by Élisabeth Vonarburg and Jane Brierley

**Tesseracts is now an annual! Each year's volume will announce
the following year's editors and general submission guidelines.
See back pages of this book for ordering details.**

TESSERACTS⁵

THE ANTHOLOGY OF NEW CANADIAN SPECULATIVE FICTION

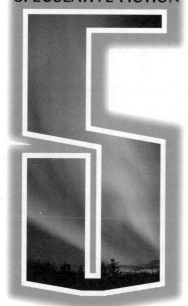

EDITED BY
ROBERT RUNTÉ & YVES MEYNARD

TESSERACT BOOKS
AN IMPRINT OF THE BOOKS COLLECTIVE
EDMONTON
1996

The translation of this book was made possible by a generous grant from the Canada Council. Thanks to the Canada Council Block Grant programme and Alberta Foundation for the Arts for overall publishing support. Thanks to Screaming Colour Inc. (a division of Quality Color Press Inc.), and Kim Smith at Priority Printing.

Cover art copyright ©1996 by David Vereschagin.
Cover design by Gerry Dotto.
Inside design and page set-up by Ike at the Wooden Door, in Toronto and Marlatt (True-Type Fonts) in Word for Windows 6. Printed at Priority Printing, Edmonton, on 50lb. Offset White with softcovers of Cornwall Cover and hardcovers in buckram with Luna Gloss dustjackets.

Published in Canada by Tesseract Books, an imprint of the Books Collective, 214-21, 10405 Jasper Avenue, Edmonton, Alberta, Canada T5J 3S2. Telephone (403) 448 0590. Tesseract Books are distributed in Canada by H.B.Fenn&Co., 34 Nixon Road, Bolton, Ontario L7E 1W2. Ph. 1-800-267-FENN. Mail US orders to press.

Canadian Cataloguing in Publication Data

Tesseracts 5

ISBN 1-895836-26-3 (bound). --ISBN 1-895836-25-5 (pbk.)

1. Science Fiction, Canadian (English) * 2. Canadian fiction (English)--20th century. * 3. Short stories, Canadian (English)*
I. Meynard, Yves II. Runté, Robert. III. Title: Tesseracts five.
PS8323.S3T495 1996   C813'.0876208054   C95-911250-2
PR9197.35.S33T495 1996

TABLE OF CONTENTS

FOREWORD
Yves Meynard

So here we are, in the northern marches, sitting down and telling lies.

And the lies we tell this year are rather dark, and even when we want to make you laugh there's usually something not funny at all behind it.

Because we see things differently, here in the northern marches. Spread out as we are, from one coast to the other, you'd think we would have little in common; I mean, we don't even always use the same language for telling our lies, never mind all the other differences. So it's a myth, right, this idea that we speak with a single voice; it's a lie itself, isn't it?

Maybe. To tell, you'd have to listen to the whole chorus. We can't help you with that: we received over four hundred lies for this book, but we had space for only a few. So you know we biased the book; you know the lies we chose misrepresent the spectrum. And yet, and yet. We see things differently, here in the northern marches. Our lies may pretend to be about the future, but you know that is a lie as well, don't you? Our lies are about the now. And maybe we see things about the present that others tend to miss. From where we stand, perspective is different, you know. Nor do we tell lies the same way here as elsewhere. That is because we've got other models, for one. And then, it's true that sometimes we're afraid of telling lies like they're told elsewhere. We want to remember—we want to believe—that we're different, here in the northern marches.

We've got lies for you, you who like to read that sort of thing. A whole passel of lies, none of which are guaranteed to make you feel better, to soothe your mind, to give you the same comforting stuff you're used to getting. I'm sorry about that.

Actually, no, that's a lie too.

THERE IS A VIOLENCE
Sally McBride

It was a brutal little head on a neck as broad and muscular as an animal's. And yet the eyes in that too-small head held intelligence, of the sort that commands armies. Or that orders the destruction of worlds.

I ran my finger along the top of the skull, over the tight curls of carved stone hair and down the neck.

Bradley gazed possessively at the thing. "Powerful, isn't it?"

The sculpture sat on a tall, gleaming-black pedestal of polished onyx. The onyx column was probably worth more than the green rock of the head, rock that might have come from any second-rate quarry on earth. But the column was mere terrestrial stone; the head came from Raqaaq.

"It seems almost crude," I replied. "Don't you think? But powerful, yes." I drew my finger back and crossed my arms, taking a surprising amount of comfort from the feel of knitted wool.

Brad smiled, rocking back and forth on his heels, his leather boots squeaking slightly. The gallery was empty except for us and the stone head, and a few uncomfortably artsy-looking metal chairs stacked against the back wall. Skylights cast winter sun onto the polished hardwood floor, and lit the pale blue walls into a receding Arctic landscape. The other exhibits from Raqaaq were still being catalogued and prepared for display, but Brad hadn't been able to contain his eagerness to show what he had. He'd always been that way. When we were children, he'd never been able to keep a secret.

"Do you think Rebecca will come?" he asked.

I looked at him and raised my eyebrows. He looked away. Mother was in Germany, involved in some sort of complicated wheeling and dealing of the sort that was the breath of life to her. I doubted she would drop that sort of fun to come back to Toronto for a gallery opening, no matter whose it was or what sort of incredible things were to be shown. And it was a safe bet that Father would be nowhere near. He tended to maintain an equilibric distance from his ex-wife around the planet, via some sort of telepathic warning system of his very own. The last time he'd called me he was in Singapore. No, neither father nor

Rebecca would come.

"She'd only get all political anyway. You don't want that."

Brad winced theatrically. "Oh, god, don't remind me about politics. Anyway, it's all going to hit the fan tomorrow at the opening."

An unselfconscious expression of glee crept over his face, and he brushed his honey-coloured locks back over his broad pale forehead. Brad had always had a yen for the stage—he was certainly pretty enough—and had tried breaking in several times, but was too wealthy to be taken seriously. After a while he had realized he was being allowed to play with the big kids because of all his money, and quietly backed off. I knew it had hurt him more than he wanted to say, but dashing around spending ridiculous amounts on artwork was the next best thing. At least for now.

"Come on," I said. "Let's get away from this thing and get coffee somewhere."

"Don't you want to see all the rest of the stuff? You will not believe what I've got—these people were so warlike it's just. . . well, horrifying. Or splendid, however you want to look at it." He wound his arm into mine and turned me towards the back. "I've taken the whole building till after the show—the things are all spread out under hovering clouds of student types and hairy old profs and all sorts of photographers and so on, they're all busy as bees. It's complete fun."

We passed through a double-wide door at the back into a frigid, high-ceilinged warehouse space lit to brilliance by overhead lights. Electrical cabling looped everywhere, instruments hummed, and people worked, grimly silent.

It didn't look like my idea of fun. Catalytic heaters were going full blast here and there but with little effect. The people working wore heavy sweaters or parkas, and there was a distinct air of subdued tension. Other than a couple of quick glances at us, no one seemed to pay any attention to our entry.

"I can't believe there aren't government people all over. Doesn't this stuff fall under some kind of archaeological treaty or trade ban or some such?"

"I'm sure it will," he said. "But so far, no. Apparently the usual tariffs and reciprocal agreements and interdictions cover the rest of the trade between Raqaaq and Earth, but for some reason there's nothing regarding ancient artifacts like this. It's as if they didn't exist."

We stopped before a complicated whirl of blue metal, designed as a sort of open-work double clam shell. The halogen lights overhead made all its sharp curving edges glitter compellingly. I reached out, intending to tap it with a fingernail and see what sound would come from it, but a man who had been sitting at a terminal, apparently paying no attention to us, suddenly spoke.

"Please don't touch it." He turned in his chair and looked up at us. His nose was red with the cold, and his eyes had dark hollows under them. "You might trigger it, and I'm not quite sure yet how to get it open again."

"Trigger it?" I frowned at the thing. It sat with its base in the remnants of a casing of foamed plastic, in which it must have been shipped. I put my hands behind my back.

"Sue, this is Dr. Tom Miller. Tom, my sister Susan."

Dr. Miller rubbed his hands together. "It's a torture device, as many of the items are. As far as we can tell, everything here either does violence or reminds the viewer of violence. Violence and control. This represents a complete departure from anything we've so far understood about the Raqaa." He sat slumped in his chair, eyeing the clamshell. "We must have more time, Mr. Sundqvist."

Into the gap this meek little wedge had formed rushed everyone else in earshot. A knot of respectful but determined professorial men and women and quiet but obviously overwrought grad students immediately formed around Brad. I left him to sort it out while I looked around the room.

Because I had been alerted, it took me only a few minutes to stop seeing the things as sculptural. And the moment I stopped reading a terrestrial artistic sensibility into their form and grace I could see what they were. What had struck the eye as delightful abstract shapes, reminiscent of a mood or an idea, became claspers, clamps, vises, stretchers hooked and spiny as insects. A frieze of formal shapes in honey-coloured stone became alien creatures being torn apart, lying in chunks along a table. The graceful outline of a four-legged creature like a kneeling horse torqued as I circled it into a cage lined with tiny spines. I looked closer to see that each spine was fed by a hair-thin wire. All the thousands of wires roped together at what would be the hindquarters, if this were actually a horse, to form a silver waterfall of a tail.

What Miller had said was true. This was the trove of a

madman. There was nothing truly sophisticated about the things, nothing to hint at a transcendental meaning wasted on our primitive human minds. The polished metal and colourful stone were debased by the brutal images they had been forced to display.

Perhaps foolishly, I touched a stone sculpture in which a head much like the one I'd first seen gazed down on something that must once have been held in a grasping hand, now broken off. The chipped stone was olive green, densely smooth and fine, and felt icy cold. Nothing happened when I touched it. Disappointing in a way. Perhaps I'd been spoiled by the interactive, high-tech cleverness of other shows I'd attended, whose works demanded a reciprocal display of intelligence. Or at least a response. These demanded nothing, expected nothing but simple captive horror.

I stepped away from the piece and put my hands into the pockets of my trousers. Apparently the researchers were trying to learn as much as they could before the collection was dispersed. Or, more likely, before some agency, human or Raqaa, stepped in and whisked it all away.

What the hell had Brad got hold of? What was he thinking, messing with nasty stuff like this? It didn't seem representative of the Raqaa that humans were coming to know, a reserved and aloof society that seemed all business to the point of boredom. Yes, the show would cause a sensation and probably sell out; yes, he'd be the toast of the artsy crowd for a while. And he'd probably get invitations to parties no normal person would want to attend.

I had started to drift back towards Brad when his voice rose.

"Look, all I want is a provenance disk for each piece, and for you to make sure the things are set so that no one gets tangled up in one of them. How hard could that be? Come on!"

A mutter from Dr. Miller that I couldn't make out.

"Well, you'll just have to pick up the pace," stated Brad. "The lighting people are coming in tomorrow morning, and the actors have to do a run-through. I've got the wheels in motion, Tom, can't you understand that?"

Miller threw up his hands and stalked back to his terminal. I was sure I could hear his teeth grinding from where I stood. Brad looked exasperated but cheery, and was immediately tackled by another in the little cluster around him. I turned away and came face to face with a gangly young man with a wispy beard and a fervid look in his eye.

"You're his sister, right? Ms. Sundqvist?"

"Yes, I am." I kept my hands in my pockets. "Before you say anything, I have to point out that I'm just here on a quick visit, a little tour. I have no influence over my brother."

That wasn't exactly true. I had a lot of influence, as did our parents, but it was subtle and seemed to be the kind that, instead of reining him in, would more likely goad him into doing foolish things. I knew the look Brad would get on his face if I tried to wheedle him into letting these researchers have their way.

"Well, someone has to talk to him," he said. He wiped his nose with the back of a hand that was visibly trembling. "We simply have to have more time. He won't even let us get a TET scanner in here, or any deep holo equipment—nothing. It's *absurd*. Mr. Sundkvist doesn't know what he's got here."

"You're probably right," I said, handing him a tissue. He crushed it distractedly in one hand.

He swallowed and stood breathing heavily for a moment. "Do you realize," he said in a low voice, "that Tom Miller dropped everything to fly in here, probably fucking up his situation in Cairo completely, just so he could work his ass off in these ridiculous conditions? Do you?"

"Look, I—"

"Christ, it's absolutely c-criminal!" His voice was rising. "These artifacts are of incredible value, absolutely fucking—I mean, they're from a world we have virtually no knowledge of...we'll just never—" He stuttered to a stop, his face flaming red. At least he looked warmer now.

"I'm sorry," he said. "We're all tired, frustrated."

"I'll bet you are."

He drew back and narrowed his eyes at me. His chin went up. He'd suddenly remembered the kind of power that goes with wealth like my family has; stupid, crafty power that is capable of utterly reprehensible actions. The idle rich and their trivial minds. Right now he was getting ready to say something carefully vicious and march away.

I held up my hand. "Just a moment, please, Mr...."

"Jordan," he said tightly. "Kenneth Jordan. I was a student of Dr. Miller's a few years ago."

"Mr. Jordan. Believe it or not, I'm on your side. But probably not for the same highly civilized reasons. I just want to keep my little brother out of trouble, and I sense that these things—" I waved my arm, "—mean trouble."

His face had lost its blush of anger. Now he was as pale and hollow-eyed as a teenager who has been up all night doing drugs and is groping around for some kind of upper. He laughed shortly. "You're damned right they're trouble."

With that he wheeled and stalked off. He'd said his piece and he wasn't going to waste any more time on me. I considered following him and pumping him for information, but Brad came up and caught my arm.

We escaped to the outer gallery and put on our coats while Brad complained. "With all the money I'm handing over you'd think they'd be more grateful, damn it. But all I get is demands and thinly veiled threats. Makes me feel like trying one of those contraptions to see if it works."

I wrapped my scarf around my neck and up to my chin. "They do seem terribly serious. Can't you delay things a bit?"

He snorted. "Come on, Sue! I've had the collection here over a week now, and I do want this show to happen." He released the door and we passed through the small foyer to the building exit. More fiddling with locks and codes. "What Miller and the rest don't realize," he continued, "is that I'm actually doing them a favour."

"Oh? How do you figure that?"

"The floodgates will be opened. What I've got here barely scratches the surface, I'm sure of it. Once interest has been aroused there'll be all sorts of stuff coming out of Raqaaq, and these obstructive bastards will be at the head of the line." He shook his head, as an indulgent but irritated father will at a child's unreasonable demands. I knew he was playing a part for me, and probably for himself too; he had no other real motive than the general astonishment he hoped to provoke.

"What have the Raqaa got to say about it?"

"Absolutely nothing," he said smugly as we hurried along the side of the building towards his car, our footsteps creaking in the packed snow. Someone would have to clear the walkway before the opening, or we'd have lawsuits on our hands. No, that's how mother would think, I chided myself. This is Brad's effort; let him worry. He'd got himself in and out of many a sticky situation with a simple flourish of his wit and looks.

"They're ignoring this? They always seem so. . . I don't know, dignified. Reserved. It could be that they don't want their culture displayed."

"They're just being coy. Everyone is dying to know more about them, and a cultural exchange is the perfect way to open up relations."

So now it was a cultural exchange. Next he would anoint himself Goodwill Ambassador for the Earth. I shook my head, taking his arm and squeezing it. "That's my boy. Well, I just hope it comes off the way you want it to."

A small car was approaching along the alley, the whine of its motor dropping in pitch as it slowed to stop beside us. Both doors flew up and two well-bundled people popped out like bread from a toaster, carrying puffs of heated air with them. They looked Filipino, small and dark, a man and a woman alike in height and colouring. They might be husband and wife, or brother and sister as Brad and I were. They squinted against the cold white light and looked us up and down. Then both turned and seemed to let me drop out of their dual consciousness to focus on Brad.

"Mr. Bradley Sundqvist?"

Brad gave them his highly-bred racehorse confronting a butcher's nag look. "I am. What may I do for—"

He wasn't allowed to finish. The woman's small, pretty face went blank, her head dropped back slackly and her mouth fell open. Out of it erupted a voice like hot wind and whipcracks, a sound that made me flinch back against the wall in shock. The heavy, stinging voice said, "Return our property." Her lips didn't move.

A voder implant, somewhere in her slim little throat.

Brad stood his ground. The hood of the woman's jacket fell back, revealing her skin. There was some sort of metal device clinging to her neck like an articulated brace or collar, with projections winding up past her jaw to her temples and into her shiny black hair. Her companion hovered beside her, his hands touching her lightly as if he were teaching her to skate and was solicitously preventing a loss of balance. His bright unblinking eyes looked over her shoulder at us.

"Mr. Sundqvist. Return our property."

I reached for Brad's arm, but he pushed me back behind him quite roughly. I could hear him breathing hard through his nose. The car had pulled its doors primly shut and sat idling.

"Who are you?" demanded Brad.

"We are Raqaa. You have acquired property that is Raqaa."

"That's right, I have. It was purchased from a legitimate trader."

The woman's head came forward and she took a great gasp of air, then it went back again as though she were a sun-worshipper lolling on a beach. The man behind her patted her shoulders, his eyes watering slightly.

"It was purchased illegally," came that boiling voice again. "It will be returned."

With that the woman resumed a normal stance, composed herself with a couple of deep breaths and smiled almost warmly. The man stepped back and clapped his hands together, blowing out puffs of breath. Just two minor functionaries delivering a message.

"Is it always this cold in Canada?" The woman's voice was high and pleasant, with a slight lisp. She huddled into her parka, casually pulling the hood up over her hair and the metal device.

Brad said nothing. I stepped up beside him and clasped his arm. The solidarity of fear. Brad's lips had compressed into a line of stubbornness that I knew well.

The woman held out a little packet. "If you will take this visk and look it over," she said, "everything should be clear."

Both of them bowed as Brad accepted the visk. Then, walking carefully on the snow, the man went around to the driver's side and opened the car, and they were off.

Brad and I looked at each other. "Well," I said as the little car dipped its nose and entered the roadway. "What do we do now?"

Brad scowled at the visk, holding it as if it were a small dish of rancid food. "You will go home, like a good girl. And I'll look at this, I suppose." He snorted. "Imagine, sending their little slaves to deliver this. Who do they think I am?"

I bit my lip, hesitated. "You might have to give it up, sweetie. Who needs this sort of fuss?"

Wrong move. His bravado changed into small-boy craftiness. "Give up? Not without a fight, I won't. People are flying in from Brazil, Japan, for god's sake. I've invested too much into this to be scared off by this sort of crude tactic. I've learned a thing or two from mother, after all."

"Well, I am not going home, not until we look at this. Come on, let's check it out in the car."

So we did. The screen popped up, and a face much like the

carved stone head's appeared and began to speak, the lip movements not matching the english words. Raqaa were not pretty, nor were they fond of chumming around with humans. Their likenesses did not turn up much in the news, nor had heartwarming TV movies featuring our new friends been produced. The small eyes in that bullet head held no glitter of life or personality, nor were there any lines or softnesses to make the Raqaa anything more than a talking lump of muscle.

The stone head in the gallery was a glossy green. The visk showed a being as grey as concrete, something I hadn't expected. Its small, close-set eyes were chilly blue with pin-point pupils. Grey hair clung to its head, looking moist and curly like persian lamb. I took it to be a male. The thick neck flexed as words formed. "This is an interactive visk," it said. "I am able to answer most questions you may have." It continued without further preamble. "The artifacts you have obtained are not for display. They are stolen property. You will return them."

"Yes, your associates mentioned that." Brad said to the screen image, his voice flat. "How is it that you have humans working for you?"

"That is a question I am unable to answer."

"Then tell me why you say the artifacts were stolen. I bought them from a being representing itself as a Raqaa trader."

"That being was not a Raqaa trader. That being encountered a cache of items stolen from Raqaaq in the year 3,157." A line of print appeared at the bottom of the screen translating this as being A.D. 839. "That being sold them to you illegally."

"Just a minute," said Brad stiffly. "I know of no legalities or restrictions regarding such items as the ones I acquired. You can't claim them back now."

"We are prepared to compensate you, Mr. Sundqvist. We will have them back. You will see that they are readied for transport."

The face in the visk display showed no emotion that I could recognize, and after a pause in which no one spoke, the image blinked its little blue eyes and disappeared. Brad snapped the screen down and took the controls of the car, a tight smile on his lips. He engaged the motor and we pulled out.

After a pause, I said, "Well, isn't this fun?" not without irony.

A burst of laughter, and Brad seemed to regain some of his

devil-may-care spirit. It was probably unwise of me to make light of this turn of events, but I could never resist playing my part. I suppose I'm really very much like him. "I wonder what Rebecca would think of all this?"

"Mother?" He snorted and wheeled us expertly into an underground parking lot, neatly cutting off another car and bouncing to a halt in a slot. "She'd tell them where to go, wouldn't she?"

The car plugged itself in officiously, and we headed for coffee.

Presumably Brad spent the next 24 hours making last-minute preparations for his show. I knew, of course, that he would not comply with the Raqaa demand. It simply wasn't in his nature.

I spent the evening alone, fussing with my orchids and wishing...oh, lots of things. That father would call. That I'd suddenly develop a talent for something; that Justin hadn't left. I'm good at worrying at problems that have no solution. I went to bed thinking of Brad and his wavy golden locks.

The next day nothing happened. No more warnings or weird alien pronouncements were forthcoming.

I arrived early for the opening. Brad was there to meet me at the door, his eyes bright and his hair and clothes perfect. He looked, in this little kingdom of pandemonium, like its rogue prince, tall and thin and wearing shades of grey-blue to match his eyes.

"Sue, darling!" He dragged me in and shucked me of my coat, yelling against the noise. Music played and people dashed back and forth in semi-darkness. "You look gorgeous! Didn't you bring anyone? Oh, well, come get some wine. The caterers were early, so the actors are using the gallery to get in costume. Hope you don't mind naked boys. Look out!"

Two burly women trotted by with a ladder. A man, arms full of stick-on lights, brought up the rear.

"I gather we're having victims to liven things up," I yelled. "Are you sure it'll be all right, sweetie?"

"Of course I am. Tom said he thinks everything's inactive. It's mostly sculptures anyway, and they just sit there and look dour. The devices are really pretty simple, just mechanical toys—"

"*Toys*? Brad—"

"Nothing's going to happen! Here, drink this, look pretty

and stay out of the way. Oh, now what?"

Two androgynous youths, a boy and a girl, had run up, shivering in their holographic paint and complaining of the cold.

"Don't worry, it'll warm up soon. Body heat, you know. No, you *can't* put on clothes, your make-up will smear. There's hot coffee in the back." He shooed them away and they turned, pouting, their painted backs and buttocks flickering from naked flesh to blood and bone, and then to vertiginous flashes of moving stars.

More people arrived, obviously friends of Brad's, and he went off to usher them in. Then someone got his ear with a message. He turned and beckoned me over. "It's Mother on the phone," he shouted as a burst of music crashed and died. We slipped into the cavernous space at the back, once occupied by the hapless researchers, now filled with a catering crew and their kitchen, which they had driven right inside. Blessed warmth, and mother's face on the screen. She wasn't smiling.

"Put this on privacy, Bradley, right away. Hi, Sue, you look fabulous. Darlings, I don't have much time. You have to listen to me."

"I really wish you could be here, Rebecca darling, it's such fun—"

Mother's eyes narrowed meaningfully and Brad subsided. She looked distracted, aloof somehow, as though her mind was occupied with many different stratagems all at once, any one of which being more important than the current conversation. In other words, she looked the same as ever. She was dressed as if returning from a formal function, stripping off gloves. Much jewellery was laden on, including an ornate necklace of glimmering metal beads.

"I heard about your show only now, Bradley. I know this will be difficult, but you're going to have to cancel it."

"Cancel it! You're joking. I can't possibly—"

"Cancel it, *now*! Send everyone away, do exactly as the Raqaa tell you, and things should be all right."

"What are you talking about? Mother, do you realize what's at stake here?" He threw up his hands and turned away from the screen, then wheeled back and pointed an angry finger at Rebecca's visage, getting ready to throw a tantrum.

But I'd seen something. Something winding up out of the ornamental necklace and into Mother's hair. I pulled Brad back, my hands cold on his elbow. His muscles were tight as steel springs. "Brad. Brad, look at her. She's wearing one of those Raqaa collars."

He shook off my hand, but he'd heard me. So had she. Brad stood perfectly still as she carefully lifted the coils of formally arranged, honey-blonde hair off her neck. Trails of gleaming gold lay close against her skin, flexing softly as she turned her head. "Yes, Sue, you're right. And Brad, I do know exactly what I'm talking about. The Raqaa do not want their past on display, not to scientists, not to politicians, and most particularly not to collectors of *objets d'art*." She let her hair fall back into place. "You *have* been warned, darling."

Brad found his voice. "What have you done? *What have they done to you?* My god. . . "

Her voice snapped out, "Bradley, don't be a fool. This is your last chance."

"Bastards!" He lunged at the screen and actually punched it, to no avail. The image didn't even flicker. "Fucking bastards!" Mother blinked calmly at him, seemed to listen to a voice only she could hear, then gave us both a pitying look.

I don't know what Brad or I would have said or done next, because suddenly there was a dull crunching noise, the building shook and the door between us and the gallery flew open. A blast of winter air rushed through it, and we abandoned mother's image and ran into the gallery.

A big hole had been punched through the roof, and a circle of starry night glittered overhead. The gallery lay like a glowing little stage filled with throbbing red and yellow lights, echoing with screams and crashes. Something grappled the edge of the roof and ripped it back so forcefully that there was no time for anything to fall on us. What meagre heat the room still held flew up into the night. Electrical sparks crackled and the sprinkler system began fountaining water into the night. The portable lights installed for the show still burned, now knocked askew and wildly spinning.

Something big moved in and blocked off most of the stars overhead. Helmeted soldiers festooned with armaments leapt in from above, landed nimbly on their feet and quickly fanned out across the floor. Two of the actors stood looking up, clinging to each other, almost invisible as their skin flashed stars in the red-lit night. Then they broke and ran.

Several of the soldiers wore canisters at their mid-sections, from which they aimed streams of foam that encased each piece Brad had placed on display. The white, wetly quivering cocoons were lassoed and yanked skywards by filaments extruded from the ship.

A Raqaa, decked in body armour but no helmet, floated down on one of the tendrils to land in the middle of the floor. It stood planted like a statue, small head swivelling on the thick neck as it, or he, watched the action. He spoke rapidly into a hand-held device, apparently giving orders.

Two people had been cut down by some kind of weapon fire and lay shrieking, another had been caught in a foam stream along with one of the displays. I think everyone else managed to escape. From my position huddled in the doorway between the gallery and the back room, I watched the caterers pull out, their mobile kitchen laden with people clinging to its sides.

Brad, who had been crouched beside me, suddenly sprang to his feet swearing, and started to battle his way towards the Raqaa leader. The soldiers paid him no attention; it's my opinion that anyone killed or injured had simply been in the way of the operation. All they wanted was their damned stuff back.

A soldier, looking too small to be frightening, scampered past me to peer into the back room. It was a chimpanzee, decked out in miniature body armour and sporting a silver collar on its hairy neck. On seeing no artifacts there, it screeched at me excitedly through grinning yellow teeth and grabbed at my dress. I drew back. The chimp gave me a look as hot and dangerous as a jungle night, and ran back to join his comrades. Humans, I guess, were not to his taste. Perhaps he held a racial memory of zoos and laboratories and now was getting his revenge.

The lights had stopped spinning, everyone who could get away had vanished, and a dripping winter silence descended on the gallery. I could hear the heavy beating whine of a helicopter approaching, and sirens wailing.

I stood shivering in my party dress. The chaos in the stripped and foam-spattered gallery had resolved itself into a frieze uncannily like one I had seen only yesterday. But this one involved my brother.

The Raqaa had him on his knees in the icy, foam-flecked water that slicked the floor. He was holding Brad by the neck and shaking him. I knew without a doubt that he could have snapped Brad's spine if he'd wanted to, but I guess he didn't.

Then, faster than my eyes could follow, the Raqaa plucked a device from his belt and injected something into Brad's neck. Brad went down instantly, like a puppet whose strings have been cut, and before his head had hit the floor he'd been scooped up and carried off by the chimp. I hadn't realized chimps were so strong.

My brother was gone, just like that.

And that is how I remember the incident that started the war. Or that boosted it into its next stage; after all, the conquest had been going on for quite some time. No one has ever been able to tell me what happened to Brad, not even Mother.

The Raqaa stood watching me while it stowed its various tools and weapons into pouches and loops on its armour. I took a step toward it, intending I don't know what.

It grimaced at me, and after a while I realized it was mimicking a human smile. I stopped about ten feet from it.

"We do not enjoy this sort of action as much as we once would have," it said, without the aid of a voder. "Not as much as the artifacts your brother acquired might have indicated. That, after all, is in our past, when we were barbarians. We do not care to be reminded of our past."

"We. . . we won't all be taken so easily," I said in a pathetically small voice. "Your dirty laundry is out in the open now. We know what you are."

It pulled on the dangling tendril and a coil formed at the bottom. He stepped into it and began to rise.

I stumbled forward, not caring what happened. Anger took me then, anger hotter than any I'd ever felt. I heard myself start to scream and shout like a fishwife. "We never liked you ugly sons of bitches anyway, you're too damned boring, you know that? Do you? Boring, ugly bastards!"

The Raqaa disappeared, drawn up into its ship. In another few seconds the ship took off, silently, a great electric shiver stroking the night and raising every hair on my body.

A helicopter buzzed nervously into the space the ship had vacated and shone a spotlight down on me. I looked away, covering my eyes. But I wasn't crying. I've never cried and I won't start now.

DOMESTIC SLASH AND THRUST
Jan Lars Jensen

1011. Subject carves holiday turkey with Brunhaus Electric Carving Knife, grabs blade, severs muscles in the palm; suffers blood loss, distressed tissue, infection from bacteria transferred from meat.

1012. Subject attempts "precision cut" with Brunhaus knife, cuts off distal phalanx of thumb. Subject's aunt faints at the sight of thumb on plate.

1013. Subject attempts to open milk carton using Brunhaus knife, also cuts open left wrist. Severed radial artery, blood loss, shock.

1014. Subject asks friend to "pass" the Brunhaus knife...

For reasons of privacy, the name of the individual in every case had been substituted with the term "subject." Lausanne knew this, but when scrolling through the list she nonetheless thought of the subject as being one distinct person who had suffered *all* the wounds involving the Brunhaus Electric Carving Knife, yet continued to use it and inflict further damage on himself, his friends, his relatives, his pets. Clumsiness, ineptitude, drowsiness, drunkenness, failure to read the manual. Failure to turn off the knife, failure to avoid hard objects, failure to avoid his fingers. Blood, tissue, bone. By now, she thought, the subject would keep a good ten metres between himself and the knife. Or throw it in the trash.

But no. He kept returning to it, in some composite of a hundred thousand homes he crept into the kitchen and knelt before the cupboard, checking that no one watched as he reached inside with a hand that still smelled of disinfectant until his fingers closed over the treble-clef handle of the Brunhaus Electric.

What makes you such a masochist? she wanted to ask him.

Lausanne pushed away from the desk, chair gliding silently back. "I need a vacation," she said. "White beaches and steel drums..." But she couldn't afford more time away from the case studies than a cup of camomile tea would require.

The staff room looked like a show room. Dishwasher and clothes dryer, bread baker and cappucino maker; they all sat in gleaming rows like concept cars at an auto show, configurations of ivory plastic and bright stainless steel so aggressively *new* that their exact function sometimes eluded Lausanne. Their alienness, however, was curtailed by prominent flourishes of Brunhaus design.

Clashing with the swirled lines and smooth finials this afternoon was someone she'd never before seen. Crew cut, bushy eyebrows, and terrible glasses with a thick black frame—like a concession to safety in a woodshop. He busily dispensed ice cubes from the front of the fridge. A large mound sat in the receptacle tray and he transferred the cubes one by one to the microwave nearby. Lausanne watched as he stacked them inside in precise, measured rows.

"I've given up on ordinary consumers," she announced.

He said nothing, didn't look away from the ice cubes.

"Did you hear me?"

No response.

"Hello...?" She prodded him with her foot. His eyes flickered her way.

"You all right?" she said.

"You're taking me out."

"Out?"

She didn't know what he meant but decided to focus on making tea. Normally she nuked a cup of water in the microwave. A little digging revealed that Brunhaus had provided an ovoid of ivory plastic called a Tea-maker, so new the plastic still smelled, and she pretended to concentrate on its instructions as she continued observing the oddball. When he'd filled the microwave to capacity he gently closed its door and pressed a button on the front display. Maximum heat, the microwave said, and followed with an appropriate hum.

"Sorry," he said. "I'm not used to this."

"Not used to what?"

"This."

"Talking?"

He nodded.

Lausanne shuddered, realizing he must be from Programming. "Why aren't you in your own staff room?"

"Remodeling. Guys in blue coveralls, sawdust, power tools."

"Oh."

"I wasn't being rude before. You were taking me out."

"What do you mean, out?"

"In our staff room we avoid talking to one another. It's courtesy. Programming, you see—" he paddled his hands in a way that didn't clarify what he was saying. "We get into it," he said. "We get into the code. If we divert our attention from programming, well, we slip up. Bugs. Logic errors. Extra work."

She raised her eyebrows and took a chair. Fine. "I guess that's why we have separate staff rooms in the first place."

"I wasn't being rude." He stood and closed his eyes. *"I've given up on ordinary consumers."*

She complimented his recall.

"What caused this crisis?" he said. "What do you do?"

"Product Safety in Design. Supposedly I'm re-imagining the Brunhaus Electric Carving Knife without the tendency to slice off thumbs. I have a database of thousands of cases where people cut themselves, their friends, their relatives, et cetera, with our knife. No amount of exclamation marks in the safety manual can persuade them to use it properly."

"So you've come back to the product."

"I come back to how people use the product. The problem is I can't get a handle on the average user. I can't predict how he thinks. When I try to assimilate my case studies I form an image of him as a reckless idiot."

"Oh, oh, oh," he said, and made swimming, paddling motions with his hands. "Same in software design. Any application where the user might not also be a programmer. We live under the tyranny of the everyday user. Trying to create a buffer between the actual program and his or her most ignorant impulses; simplifying complex routines into a string of questions that can be answered with one word. *O.K.? O.K.? O.K.?"*

Lausanne digested this.

"We're idiot-proofing the world," the programmer said enthusiastically. "Retooling everyday items, matching them to the incompetence of their users."

"That may be true of software," she said. "But in Design we're trying to enhance those everyday items. With safety features, with aesthetic qualities."

The programmer said, "I don't believe you," and returned to his microwave full of ice. Lausanne tried to guess what would happen inside. Sublimation? Would steam blow the little door off its plastic hinges? Would boiling water pour to the floor and scald his feet? But reality wasn't so just. The makers of the microwave, it seemed, had anticipated this scenario.

ITEM(S) PLACED IN OVEN INAPPROPRIATE FOR MICROWAVE COOKING, it said, and shut down automatically.

"The idiot lives to see another day!" The programmer gave a laugh like live static. When Lausanne didn't join him he regained composure and introduced himself. "Willis," he said. "Advanced Simulations. We're actually working on something that could matter to you. An ergonomic modeling system. We have a beta-version up and running if you'd like to come have a look."

"Thanks all the same but I'm under deadline."

"Sure. Who isn't? I'm only offering because it might answer some of your questions about everyday users."

She reconsidered. On his suggestion she dug around the staff room for one of the old models of electric carving knife and brought it along as they walked the cool ivory hallways. The elevator had been reprogrammed to stop at a floor previously only a number to her, 55. Despite the continuing Brunhaus aesthetic she had the sense of crossing into another country, a silent crowd saying nothing to one another, feverishly manipulating screen-based text and imagery.

They reached a door with a security sensor shaped like the Brunhaus B. For some reason they were required to remove shoes and socks before proceeding. Barefoot, they crossed into a dark, narrow space with few distinguishing features. The walls seemed glossy brown, and Lausanne thought she felt patterns against her soles, like a finely engraved picture, but examining the floor she saw only the burnished sepia.

"So where's the computer?"

"We're standing in it," he said. "Part of it."

She looked around with new attention to detail. A table in the room's centre extended continuously from the floor, she noticed; it wasn't a distinct piece of furniture.

"Beta-version," Willis said, and another person appeared.

Or not a person. A photonic representation of an adult male, naked but devoid of sex organs and distinguishing marks. Much like the boyfriend to a plastic doll Lausanne had undressed and examined in her childhood. A shimmering, continuously reconfiguring quality made the figure seem like a visitation.

"We're working late this evening," it said mildly.

"What is it?" Lausanne asked Willis. "Some kind of AI?"

"An ergonomic modeling system. Graphic representation of human kinetics. Don't be fooled by the interface, there's no great intelligence behind it. The real strength is adaptability: the model is full of great algorithms describing body mechanics."

"I warn you not to put complete faith in my behavior," the luminescent figure said politely. "I am only a beta-version."

"This is a real sneak peek," Willis told her. "Management doesn't want anyone outside of Programming to see this yet."

"What is that?" the beta-version asked, indicating the carving knife on the table. It reached over and "grabbed" the handle. The actual knife remained where it lay but the beta-version lifted away a ghostly simulacrum, part of his projection, which it turned at different angles. The beta-version thumbed the ON/OFF switch but the action on the projected blade was wrong: rotary, where it should have been in-and-out.

"Here," said Lausanne, and switched on the real knife for the simulation to model. She held it to a lens in the wall. The projection corrected itself until one knife mirrored the other.

"I'd like some time here alone," she said.

"I thought you'd approve," Willis laughed.

"I'm serious. Would anyone care if I used the beta-version for awhile?"

He checked the watch decalled onto his wrist. "Morning shift starts at four a.m., then everyone starts logging on, the projection becomes maddeningly slow…"

"Three hours will do," she said, or meant to say; her focus had zeroed upon the beta-version, and the distinction between thoughts and statements became as peripheral as Willis walking backward and quietly letting himself out of the room.

It was the way the projection had first picked up the knife: startling. How many times had she tried to visualize a stranger's initial grasp of the appliance? Never, she knew, with the clarity realized by the beta-version. Now, upon instruction, she could observe a naive reaction to the knife. She examined raw human impulses toward its design. Three hours was nothing; she only realized her time was up when the projection took a full minute to dice an imaginary apple.

"Okay," she yawned. "I'm done."

The room blinked to darkness and she felt her way to the door. She was exhausted, but knew the time had been worth a week of conventional approach to user behavior. While wearily lacing her shoes she spotted Willis punching away at a workstation.

"You haven't left?" she said.

"I have a bed here. A cot."

"What about home?"

He shrugged. "I have no other cots."

"I'm impressed with the beta-version," she said. "Heads will spin in Design."

He nodded, without pride.

"But for me the need already exists. I mean, three hours was great, but listen, I've got this huge database of case studies with the knife. Couldn't we patch in this wealth of data? Would you be up to that? Or does Internal Security make you nervous?"

He smirked. "A little nervous. But I'm always up for a good hack. What's your workstation number?"

She told him. He didn't ask for passwords.

"I'll see what I can do," he said, "but don't get your hopes up."

"Understood," she said, and went upstairs to see if she could get her deadline pushed back a week or two.

⚜ ❧

The first time she saw it, she gasped. Willis had left a plastic glove at her workstation which she brought down to floor 55. The security door was locked but when she put on the glove it accepted her handprint, allowing her inside the sepia chamber. And that was when she made the noise of surprise, seeing the beta-version standing there, its body tapered by a thousand wounds. Conceptual wounds: the flesh appeared sheared off, with a precision suitable for a geometry model. Both eyes were scooped away and the nose was absent. Parallel slashes made the torso appear gilled, and although the projection lacked enough fingers to logically do so it held a Brunhaus Electric Carving Knife in the stub of one hand.

"I'm sorry if my appearance startles you," the beta-version said, and smoothed away the wounds.

"Not at all."

The inspiration from average users was apparent; the beta-version could not move the knife without plunging it into an arm, a wrist, a hand. When allowed to cycle freely through its database the projection seemed to perform a *kata*, with each swing finding a new way to pass the shimmering blade through its shimmering body. She recognized the wounds the beta-version inflicted on itself from her readings but the qualitative difference was huge: the intermediate moments, the body mechanics, the position in which the beta-version held the knife when it placed a non-existent milk carton between its legs and proceeded to saw open one spout, then two...

"From now on," she said at one point during that session, "I'm going to have to call you 'subject'."

"Subject," it said, and nodded, and lopped off its thumb.

As her major deadline approached, Lausanne traded sleep for extra hours in the building. She kept working at her station, late every night, hoping for word from Willis that it was safe to sneak downstairs and steal more time with the subject. *The subject.* Her weary sessions reinforced this appellation. Willingly it obliged her instructions to repeat the same wound upon itself. Over and over, at different speeds, at different angles, from another point of view. *Gladly* the subject obliged, it sometimes seemed, or was that just her spinning head? It was often dizzying. She stood in a room with the average user, at last, and every interaction sent the Brunhaus blade through its body. It was late in the evening—or late in the afternoon, she had lost track of the day—when their relationship changed fundamentally.

"Number four forty-six is my favourite."

She spun about. "Excuse me?"

"Number four forty-six. My favourite wound. *You* know. Downward slash through the right ventricle?" He demonstrated, closing his eyes with pleasure as he dragged the blade across his chest. "That's the spot..."

"Willis?!" She spun toward the lens in the wall. "Is this some kind of joke?!"

"No joke," said the subject, getting closer. "I just wanted to tell you what I enjoy. Because you don't seem to know."

"What are you—"

"I hate to see you wasting time with safety issues. Why not give me what I really want? A product that rewards my hand for holding it. Something that says, 'You made a wise spending decision,' the moment I make contact." It raised the Brunhaus knife. "Something like this."

"But the wounds..."

"The wounds," it said, and laughed. Then it turned the knife onto her, jabbing her beneath the neck. Lausanne thought she could feel the tip of the blade as he traced over her skin, making a variation of the Brunhaus B.

$

"That doesn't feel so bad, does it?"

She blinked at the red phosphenes of "blood" trickling down from the symbol, then looked into the grinning veil of his face. "Blood money? You think I'm making blood money?"

"I think you should find out what the average user *really* wants."

She shook her head, shook it with her whole body, and when she opened her eyes again the beta-version stood opposite her, dimmed down, a power saving measure that occurred whenever it hadn't been commanded for five minutes or more.

Lausanne burst from the sepia chamber.

The pale persons attached to the workstations ignored her storming through level 55, one or two leaning back to stare after she bumped against their ergonomic chairs. Were they in on that joke? How many lines of code had they contributed? She managed to contain her anger until she got to the stack of cots where Willis lay staring at a wall—but he didn't burst out laughing or even smirk as she approached.

"Why are you looking at me like that?"

"No reason," Lausanne said evenly.

"Shouldn't you be working on your design?" he said. "Shouldn't you be in there with the beta-version?"

"I need a change of scenery," she said. "I thought maybe you'd go for a walk with me."

As they left the building she stole occasional glances at him, but he was inscrutable. If Willis had programmed those comments into the beta-version his behavior didn't give him away. Maybe he'd open up a little if she took him out of his element.

Soon they distanced themselves from the building with its ubiquitous conceits of design. At one point, a spiral pattern in the pavement opened the sidewalk into a plaza, but local denizens had thwarted this lone flourish in the cityscape by holding a tag sale, the vendors sitting on the ground, encircled by old possessions. Loose pages of printed matter had become pasted to the ground with rain; a dollar each, even though their text bled over the pavement. The vendors raised their heads as Willis and Lausanne splashed through the plaza but not, it seemed, with raised hopes for a sale. They looked spent inside their tents and see-through rain gear.

Willis said, "Why would you want to come out here?"

"What's the matter? Don't you like it outside?"

"I don't leave the building much."

"No, you don't look like you get a lot of sun."

"This is sun?" He turned her way, rain drizzling over his hood.

"We're too far removed from the real world," she said quickly. "We spend so much time holed up inside. Good to get out once in a while."

He said nothing to this, just kept glancing around at their surroundings. They walked through a series of arches supporting an overhead road, and there were shanties attached to their sides, people staring out from cardboard nests.

"Maybe I *should* let the hoi polloi design this knife," Lausanne said. "I guess that's what you were implying before, when you said we were idiot-proofing the world."

But all he said now was that they should probably turn around. Lausanne led him on. They waded through a blue puddle, residue of oil making colour like a peacock's neck. "How do I know what they want?" she said. "How do I sink to their level?"

"How—"

The question went unanswered. Walking around an ancient building of brick and mortar they looked up to an outcrop of roof, where a police ornithopter sat perched like a gargoyle. Its wings were folded against the fuselage, and a door hung open to reveal empty cockpit. Xenon lights strobed blue and red but there were no cops around, nobody at all. The area was dead. When Lausanne and Willis continued walking, the ornithopter spoke to them. Its synthetic voice warned, "*Stay back—there is a crisis situation in the vicinity.*"

"We better go," Willis sputtered, and tugged her sleeve. But he didn't know the best retreat. They made a few wrong turns and emerged on a wide boulevard with broken pallets and bundled cardboard sitting in the street. No traffic.

She said, "How do we connect with the average user?"

"How do we…Christ, I don't know."

He continued glancing around nervously.

And then froze, staring straight ahead.

"What's that?"

She looked where he was pointing. A long box—it looked like a cardboard casket from some tropical border conflict—lay partially in the street. Willis squinted at the text printed on one side, as if that would explain whatever he'd seen. "Contains one. . . "

Lausanne kept thinking design. "A safety message they can't resist..."

"There!" said Willis. "You see it move?!"

The box came to a rest.

They both stood and stared. Slowly the box rose onto its end. A knife pushed through the flaps, followed by a soot-smeared, half-naked vagrant, one eye showing through the mask of hair over his face. Lausanne could see teeth, too, and realized he was smiling, or something. But her focus rested on the knife: not the elegant lines of any Brunhaus product but some butcher's throwaway, browned by corrosion and chipped along its edge.

"Run!" said Willis, pulling Lausanne.

She stood her ground. "I know my statistics," she said. "He'll cut himself before he gets halfway here."

"Stow that bullshit, he looks deranged—"

She stayed. "He'll slice his own throat."

The man staggered about, slashing little arcs through the air before him. Willis ran down the street, stopped when Lausanne didn't follow. "What are you doing?"

"Just what you said. Experiencing the average user."

"When did I ever say that?!"

"The beta-version," she replied. "Your nasty joke this afternoon. *Give me what I really want*. Well this is the average user, this is what it's like outside. Weren't you saying I should make a knife that caters to this kind of world?"

"I don't know what you're talking about!"

Three other figures hustled into view. Police. They wore black body armour with cylinders of gas that fed into ARWEN guns. At the sight of the vagrant they formed a three point position and raised their weapons. Willis said something more just as they were hit with an acoustic weapon: the ornithopter had taken off and moved overhead, beating its wings and pummeling them with a downwash of sound, a noise like jet engine friction. It penetrated the fissures of Lausanne's skull but she remained standing, as did the vagrant, still swinging his knife as he walked toward her.

"GET DOWN!" a cop shouted.

Willis yelled too, something like "Get out of the fucking way," and when she still remained standing he leapt into her, as shots ripped through the blanket of sound, thwops of black rubber plugs walloping the vagrant and the concrete, thick ricochets, and the target went down, folding onto his knife.

Unintended targets, too. "This is it," Lausanne said as she and Willis fell over the wet ground. ARWEN wads bounced around them, and even now the designer in her kept seeing that blade, and those guns, the molded grips and their squared black barrels.

...Consider the fabulous weight of the new Brunhaus Carving Knife.
To hold it in one's hand is not simply to hold a household appliance, but a tool, which must be treated with respect. Added to this sensation is the sound the knife makes when activated, another conceit of the designer—a buzzing like a sawmill in miniature—a constant reminder to the user that this machine is all about the business of cutting...
—Design Edge Monthly

The executive said, "You seem like the sort of person who can keep a secret."

"Sure," said Lausanne.

They stood in his office, looking into several testing booths. An enormous flatscreen divided the wall into a grid of six different views. In each, a test subject carved a roast beef into smaller and smaller segments, using a prototype of the knife Lausanne had designed. All this cutting might have been going on a few doors away, or in another building, or another time zone. Lausanne didn't know or care, but the executive—Marcus Philo, VP Domestic Design—seemed excited to take her into the testing process, as if they were on safari.

"Someday we'll be rid of them," he said.

"The test subjects?"

He nodded happily.

"How?"

"Brunhaus has a major piece of software in the works. An ergonomic modeling system. We'll be able to address safety issues without consulting real people."

"Sounds too good to be true," she said, with fake enthusiasm.

"Sad that it wasn't ready in time for your knife."

She gave him a weak smile.

"But you didn't need any help." He crossed to his desk and picked up one of the prototypes, stroking its bullpup handle. "I can't keep my hands off!" he exclaimed, and yes, his expression lit up the moment he made contact; the knife seemed to deliver direct physical pleasure.

"What a job you've done! I assume you read the glowing review in *Design Monthly*?"

"Yes."

"I love the handle. What made you decide to model it after the grip of a gun? It's brilliant; it instantly conveys the care that must be taken with the knife; powerfully conveys a sense of unleashed potential."

She thought of Willis lying in a generic white bed, surrounded by dull, utilitarian machines of beige and lime green. Brunhaus would pay to keep them glowing and beeping by his bedside for as long as the odds favoured full recovery. The blow from the ARWEN gun had fractured his skull, put him in a coma, and nothing had *conveyed a sense of power* for Lausanne like that moment in the street. She watched the executive with grim detachment as he fondled the knife it had yielded.

"You'll never get rid of the live bodies," she said.

"Why not?"

She walked over, placed her hands on the knife, on his hands. "Feedback," she said, and nodded toward the people disassembling beef onscreen, one of them holding up a bloody palm. "They design our products, not us, not simulations."

He looked at her. "Well, whatever the case. You've demonstrated rare insight into what delights our target consumer; the test subjects can't get enough of your knife.

"We'd like to expand that vision within Brunhaus," he continued. "In practical terms it would mean a management level position overseeing design. You'd take charge of next year's domestic line."

Lausanne was only vaguely aware this was a job offer, and that she was still gripping the knife, his hands, watching the grid of screens, where all the test subjects had become generic as the beta-version, tapered and shiny, all of them raising palms to the cameras and coming up with blood, *$, $, $*, one after another, and Lausanne was smiling as she realized these wounds were a small price to pay for luxury.

EMPTY RING

Francine Pelletier (translated by Howard Scott)

> *Gertrude died yesterday and I weep*
> *With the empty ring of loneliness*
> Émile Nelligan, "La Sorella dell'amore"

Friday, June 9, 2024

I arrived this morning, a little bewildered among the travellers in the brand-new terminal; construction had barely begun the last time I came through, but it already looks old, worn by the throng, by the herd endlessly thronging there. I was afraid of crowds. After all, I'm no longer young enough to push my way through the panhandlers, canvassers, beggars and other assorted moochers. I was prepared for it though. I had gone to the exchange counter before leaving Dorval, and I had my pockets full of small change. I was ringing like a bell. The beggars watched me like a dog when the butcher takes away a bone. Because I had no reason to be afraid—I was expected, a tall thin guy was holding in his blasé hand a white cardboard sign with my name written in red ink. Vanier must have thought of everything. He was the one who asked me to start this journal, in order, he said, to "reawaken" my emotions. Actually, I haven't spoken with him since our conversation in New York, last year, but he wrote to me, of course, and his assistant had left a long list of recommendations for me, in the car, which the tall thin man handed to me over the back of the front seat.

Reawaken my emotions. Forty-one years. Such a long time, and I'm so tired tonight. I'm already regretting coming. Stupid. I took a walk around the city, trying to rid myself of some of the jet-lag. To think that I wrote somewhere that the Montreal-Paris trip would one day be made by suborbital shuttle, as fast as a trip across town. Science fiction writers should never set their plots in the near future, especially a future they're likely to know in their lifetimes. Because the future always catches up with us, and gives us a good boot in the rear. Anyway, I won't complain too much. It could have been much worse. I could have been stuck more than three hours on the runway, and that bucket of bolts they call an airbus could have never taken off at all.

Where was I? If someone reads this damn journal, they'll

think I'm going senile—at sixty-five!—or that I have more to say and don't want to admit it.

Walking in Paris, I was saying. I don't think I realized what a state the city was in. For all the gimmicks you see on Channel 2000, TV is still TV: a small screen between us and reality. After the collapse of the Saint-Jacques Tower, I thought to myself that the rain does more damage than they like to admit, that the erosion of time is sometimes less insidious, more brutal. But it was when I put my hand on the edge of the Saint-Michel Fountain that I suddenly felt old. It wasn't that the scenery was different. There were still gangs of kids—not quite so many shaved heads, a few more masks than in '14—the clothes all looked like they were from second-hand stores, even mine. Not many were jacked in—anyway, they don't need implants. Those kids always listen to music (music!) full blast. But the stone... The stone doesn't know how to lie with facelifts or gaudy make-up. The stone crumbled under my hand, fell into dust, ashes of a mineral world that we have succeeded in killing, as if the slow erosion of the animal world was not enough for us.

(Not bad that. Use this passage in a story?)

Hmm. Vanier won't be happy. He wanted to prepare me to face emotions.

※ ※

Saturday, June 10, 2024

They get their revenge.

I can't get to sleep. Of course, as soon as the screen goes black, they assault me like an army of ravenous ghouls. The harsh light hurts my eyes, but I can no longer "keep quiet" (no, I'm not using voice, as stupid as that might seem for someone who has yearned so much for them to develop that confounded gadget. Need privacy, silence.)

Anger. That's what comes back fastest, anger. Diluted a bit, all the same, but the emotion has remained familiar, close to the heart.

Slip into the hospital where the other one is supposed to be (she survived, paralysed, handicapped, fragile but alive). Slip into her room, I would reach towards her neck and break her life in my hands, right where she broke mine, I'd smash her vertebrae—I don't know how, my hands would find the movement, the pressure, the effort. Yes, but *she* wouldn't know who, or why.

So I wouldn't kill her. I'd get a position as a nurse's aide or a housekeeper, I'd get myself hired by her family to take care of her, like in a murder mystery, I would become indispensable. She would trust me completely, would be totally dependent on me. Then, one day when she's told me how much she appreciates me, or how much she cares for me, I would reveal all, I would pelt her with hate.

I would throw in her face everything her suicide had cost me, when she demolished my life taking away her own, because she wanted to put on a show, because she didn't care if she took someone with her, my twin sister, half my soul, sacrificed to her exhibitionism. I'd ask if she knows what it is to be two, then only be one, what it's like to tell a mother that her daughter had been killed, what it's like for a traveller to go home alone, when two set out, to just go home, you feel like screaming, Mama, I didn't mean to do it, Mama. Vero is dead, Mama, I didn't mean to, it wasn't my fault, I'm coming home without her. I'd ask her, that slut, if she knew how you can be the survivor, when you've endured everything, the crushed cadaver, the numbness, the disbelief, the brutality of the shock, the morbid curiosity of the crowd, and then that night, the first night, all alone in your hotel room, when the journalists telephone from Quebec to find out how you're feeling, when you've gone through all that, how do you face the love of others, their love for Vero, for me, how can you live with that ridiculous guilt, and how do you look yourself in the mirror and justify still being alive?

I would ask her, that scum, if she knew that by throwing herself from that spire that she was throwing my life with her, forty-nine metres below, my disjointed life, not to mention love—no longer loving anyone, and yet loving with all your being, with all the longing of your twenty-four years, loving desperately and finding only loneliness.

I would ask her, that bitch, if she knew how you can return to daily life, how not to be totally consumed by your *career,* because that's all that's left after the ashes are buried, mask your grief, with ink and paper, with books and trophies, and have no desire other than climbing the podium to receive the reward, no desire other than to beg: please, please, I want no more of your applause, give me back my sister, give me back my life.

I would ask her, that pathetic wreck, if she knew that for years Vero would come home at night, back from her infinite voyage, not knowing that she was dead, astonished to find her room occupied by another, her drawers empty, her wardrobe scattered, wondering if her employer would take her back, and me, biting my lip, not knowing how to make her understand that she was dead, wondering how not to lose her again, not to let her vanish in a puff of smoke, then, the dream gone, regret, missing the image, even though false.

I would ask her, that nobody, if she knew that by killing herself she was killing me too.

※ ※

Sunday, June 11, 2024

I'm back from a "weekend in the country" (that's what I said at the hotel desk), a Vanier-style weekend, of course. I found the old guy as I had known him in New York, the one who looked like a psychoanalyst, with whom you let yourself go, nice as could be, without really being aware of it. Yes, in his suburban bunker, I surprised myself by referring to our conversation in New York, in Thompson's suite, quietly, in the wee hours of the morning, with the butler snoring in the corner. Dawn was breaking when I left the hotel, but I hadn't noticed the time passing.

Time! Our main subject of conversation. I don't know how the topic came up—well I think I do. We had talked about SF literature, books on the theme of going back in time. This was related to the activities of the day. During the convention, one of the guest scientists had stated the time travel was absolutely impossible. I don't know why Vanier didn't respond during that panel (he wasn't there by invitation, of course). I suppose he wanted to be discreet. That night, in the almost-deserted suite, we discussed the current theories, then the conversation drifted. Vanier confided in me that he belonged to the TRI, the Time Research Institute, that he was completing the development of material for experiments with the theory of his research group. According to him, the mind, sometimes followed by the body, can travel in time by following a very specific line in the temporal matrix, the emotional line. I told him of my feelings of *déjà vu* and the flash that I'd had once of myself old, my hands on my knees, my clothes in dark colours, the very clear sensation of the seat under my buttocks. Instead of laughing at me, he took me very seriously. He was looking for experiment subjects, rich preferably, as a way of financing the project, to kill two birds with one stone. I had very quickly calculated what I had, but it wasn't enough, of course, not one third of what he wanted to extract from his guinea pigs.

I don't know why I told him my old fantasy. I revealed everything to him: my bitterness with owing my career to the death of someone I loved, the dream of going back, of changing history, even if it meant sacrificing all the successes that constituted my universe. I would sacrifice all the success I'd known in exchange for my sister's life. Vanier's sweet smile, his soft voice explaining to me that changing an event in the past was equivalent to throwing a pebble in a pond, a tiny little pebble in a very big pond, or conversely, according to the importance of the event. Like the waves created by a pebble in water, the effects of the change would spread out slowly from the "centre" of the event towards of the outer edges, the extremities of the temporal matrix, gradually dissipating. Which was the same thing as saying, according to him, that my current situation would likely not be much different even if I succeeded in preventing Vero's death. I didn't agree. That death was my motivation for throwing myself totally into my work, and the resulting emotions had fuelled me for forty years. How could my career be at the same point? Vanier believed that, in any case, I would have found such a motivation for writing elsewhere, in another event, another turning point in my life, so that the long-term result, my success and public recognition, would end up being the same. We discussed the ripple effect for hours.

The next afternoon, when I ran into Vanier in the lobby, he'd changed. He asked me, dryly, "Would you really do it?"

I didn't understand, of course. He had to explain. Would I really do it, would I return to the past to change it? In short, was I ready to be his guinea pig? His coldness surprised me, I think I even stuttered. Why not? But I didn't think he was serious.

Our correspondence after that took on an official tone, which comforted me by giving me the impression that I'd dreamed the first Vanier, the one with the compassionate ear.

Today I found him again.

When I arrived at the bunker for the first tests, Saturday, I only saw Lanoix, his assistant, who introduced me to the centre's technicians and researchers, whose names I quickly forgot. I was assigned a room for the duration of the experiment, a monk's cell (or nun's in my case), with a narrow bed, a metal table, and a chair whose main function seemed to be making you want to stay standing. No windows, of course, even though it was not in the bunker but in the annex, a large building that looked like a clinic. The "bunker" itself was a huge concrete hangar, connected to a nearby nuclear power plant. That contraption took an insane amount of energy. Under this shell of concrete there was the protective structure where the forcefield formed when an experiment was under way. According to Lanoix, this was enough to protect the measurement instruments from the "ripple effect." The bunk was the objective core that would remain unchanged when time changed. Others, at the TRI, claimed that that was bullshit, that Vanier would do better to save the energy eaten up by his direct hook-up to the power plant, because *nothing* could stop the wave of change when it "vibrated" the temporal matrix (with their metaphors, they always made me think of a big black spider, very hairy, crawling along a timeline in absolute darkness, an Arachne come out of her lair, fat and bloated, with big white phosphorescent eyes).

They put me through tests for resistance to hypnosis, tests with the encephalogram and I don't know what else. *Fit for duty* was the diagnosis. Finally, I was able to meet the master in person, that afternoon, for a brief conversation over a cup of tea. He wanted to make certain I was still favourably disposed. I reconfirmed my desire to attempt the experiment.

And that was it. He sent me here, because the bunker was not available before Thursday, and because he thinks it wouldn't do me any harm to be alone in my hotel room so I could take myself back forty-one years. I promised him I would meditate a long time. Prepare myself.

Haven't I had enough already—forty-one years of preparation?

// ⚘

Monday, June 12, 2024

What a splendid evening! Vanier won't be happy, of course, but I don't care. It's not every day that you're received by the Franco-Québec Bureau of the French Language, with ambassadors, the Minister of Culture and the whole kit and caboodle, as they say. I know, I promised to immerse myself in meditation. But to what end? I'd still be the same naïve Francine made fun of by her friends, who gets involved in things without thinking, who wastes her money, her time and her energy in enterprises as crazy as they are useless. Vanier and his colleagues are scientific Don Quixotes and I'm grist for their mill.

And anyway, what will happen with this mad expedition to the past? I'll find myself kilometres from the church, with no means of transportation to get there. Or else, if I get there, I won't be able to intervene. How would I stop that girl? If I was writing a story, I know exactly how it would end: the heroine would succeed in going back in time. After all kinds of adventures, she would reach the church just in time to throw herself on the suicidal girl before she could leap into space. There would be a struggle between them. And it would be my heroine who fell over the parapet to fall, either on the head of her alter ego, or on Vero's.

I'm sick of it. Vanier wants emotions? Well here's one: I'm fed up with waiting. I've had it up to here with eating my heart out imagining all sorts of ways, each more horrible than the next, of terminating this expedition. The power plant blows up. There's a defect in the structure containing the forcefield—it ruptures and the bunker collapses on us. Sorry, I won't be in the bunker.

Phew. Just a second to let the adrenaline level fall.

It's crazy, it's exactly what made me decide to embark on this. I'm fed up with pessimism, with the turn of mind that always made me imagine the worst. I can't walk along the sidewalk without convincing myself that a car is going to jump the curb and run me down. When I take the subway, I wonder which end will collide with the next train, the front or the back? When you have an accident happen "that only happens to other people," when you experience what you have one chance in a million of experiencing, no one can convince you that it won't happen again.

I shouldn't have gone that evening. A journalist grabbed me and for an hour he followed me around like a puppy. He wanted to know my reasons for being in Paris, if it could be expected I would set a story there, and on and on. The security service had to ask him to leave me alone if he didn't want to be thrown out. Now the bastard will likely be in a hurry to trash my next book. If I'm still a writer after...

That's an outstanding debt. The journalists. At the beginning of my career, I would have given anything for good press, an interview. And then, when things went well, I realized that I couldn't do it. Whatever guy approached me, I would always think back to that night, alone in Paris in my hotel room, when the Québec journalists telephoned me. I would see the cameras flashing at the funeral. The screaming match with the guys for *Photo-Police*. The girl who killed Vero even poisoned my success. Maybe that's what I find the hardest to forgive.

⁄⁄ ⁊

Thursday, June 15, 2024

We had the first session. Vanier was furious with me and I'm dead tired. I almost smashed my fist on his nose just now. The fool blames me for the failure of his attempts at hypnosis. He says I refuse to let go. During the tests, though, it worked all right, didn't it? I think he's the fly in the ointment. He went so far as to claim I was cheating with my emotions, that I was only a petty bourgeois who wants to stop feeling guilty, and that I would do better to treat myself to sessions with a psychiatrist. I replied that the shrink would have cost less. I think I also answered that he was mad at me because I didn't mortgage my house to pay the full cost (it was true, in fact, that he took me at a discount, but it was he who offered it). In short, a huge row. He told me that I was trying to hurt myself, that I was punishing myself for my success. Success! I would really like to be able to shove my last royalty cheque under his nose! They're not mobbing the book fairs to see me, as far as I know. I manage to live from my pen because I have always been able to publish steadily, in all sorts of fields. I have no titles that have been sold on the international market. Punish myself! And what else? "You're cheating," he repeated. Then I understood. After all, it's not hard for him to get access to my files on the TRI network. Maybe he's even reading me, the voyeur. Are you happy, Vanier? I'm furious! I'd like to break your nose. Who do you think you are, you charlatan? Because you play with other people's money, you're not too worried about piling up failures, when it's the guinea pig who coughs up the money. You wanted me, you've got me! Start by hiring a real hypnotist, and then we'll talk about my underlying motivations.

⁄⁄ ⁊

Friday, June 16, 2024

It's better now. We'll do another test tomorrow. I'm too beat to elaborate. Bedtime.

⁄⁄ ⁊

Addendum to the journal of F.P.

I did it. I'm scared.

I know I succeeded, because I went to the newsstand just now, and I saw. Sunday, August 7, 1983. From the position of the sun, it's still not noon. I didn't keep my watch. It wouldn't have been any use to me. The only objects you're permitted to take with you are this single sheet of paper and this antique pen. A little money too, old coins Vanier bought from a coin dealer.

I wasn't entitled to anything else, because they're afraid I'll be called back, of course. But as much as I think with all my strength about my reality, my brain refuses to trigger the return process. Because of the hypnotic conditioning no doubt. Vanier warned me about it. He's a better hypnotist than I said he was.

It's better now. Writing always calms me down. I still feel nauseated, but I don't think I'm going to vomit anymore, or dirty my pants. I arrived at just the right moment, at the right place (I'm in the park behind the church). I felt a moment of panic, just now, because I can't remember any more which of the two spires I have to climb, but I found the information buried in the back of my mind. Vanier has thought of everything. If I had come a day too early, I would have attempted to find the girl at her home, before she came here, but that maybe wouldn't have been possible. All things considered, it's better that it happen now. I wouldn't have had the courage to kill her.

I have to climb. With my sixty-five-year-old legs. And if I met myself, in spite of the crowd, the strollers, the tourists, the souvenir sellers? Especially if I ran into Vero...

Enough humming and hawing! I know what I have to do. There's no turning back. Come what may.

⁄⁄ ⁊

Saturday, June 17, 2024

I couldn't go up. It was an immense shaft of shadows. I guessed it to be high, so high, endlessly high, a well to draw night from the very sky. My legs felt like lead and refused to move. I didn't know what I had come there to do.

I turned back, went out into the light, the sun, the heat, the crowd, the movement. Then I remembered: I was supposed to climb the spire, prevent the girl from committing suicide. There was nothing to attempt now. I had hesitated too long. Hurry, climb those infinite steps, put one foot in front of the other, all the way up, I could at least give a warning when the girl tried to throw herself down. I was sure to recognize her: I remember so well her black shoes, her black skirt and her black blouse, her hair fanned out in a dark mass to hide her bloodied face, there, below, when I turned towards the cries of the crowd to discover who was dying at my feet, while beside her lay Vero's corpse.

I felt as weak as a baby. Everything I dreamed about, all

those years, the ruse to get into the hospital, where the girl would be if she survived, the room where I would break her spine, or else the cutting words I would throw at her as she rotted in her wheelchair, or else the pitiless gesture by which I would kill her, that morning, before she left home to so commit suicide...

All that, all that. Ridiculous. I wasn't even able to climb that staircase. Not able to face reality.

I plunged into the crowd, jostling strollers, tourists, the stuck-up twits. Wildeyed like an old madwoman. That's what the two gendarmes I ran into must have thought. Quick, quick, I heard a girl talking about climbing up there to jump...

Sceptical, they promised to keep an eye out. The idiots, they won't do anything, they were men of stone that I couldn't budge.

I ran to the gate of Notre Dame behind which I would be, we would be, soon when the girl... I knew that I would meet myself. What would happen then? Would one of us vanish in a puff of smoke? Oh well.

Once again my legs were too heavy. They refused to move forward. Feet of stone, like the gargoyles that watched me from up there laughing.

And then, there was shouting, in the crowd, I think I screamed myself too. I saw myself, I wasn't looking my way. Where was Vero? I didn't see her. A movement in the crowd hid the group of tourists from my view. I saw the girl fall, a mass of gesticulating black, she was falling, she fell for hours, centuries. Then, that sickening sound like a pumpkin smashing on the paving stones.

The crowd rushed in that direction, I wasn't able to see anything for a long time, I had to cut through, push through, elbow my way through to reach the gate, where the gendarmes were pushing back the frightened spectators.

The girl was laying on the ground, broken in the same position as in my memory. But she was alone. The tourists who were in the area of her fall had surged back towards the entrance of the church when the screams were heard. I had succeeded. Vero was alive.

It is the most marvellous dream I have ever had in my life.

〃 ﹨

Saturday, June 17, 2024

I'm coming back from a last row with Vanier (a *last row!* I hope that's the case!). I don't know what he did to me, what he ordered me to do, under hypnosis, but I feel all shrivelled up, my veins stand out on my hands, the hands of an old woman. Vanier claims that it's fatigue, of course. The voyage can't be done without exhaustion. What idiocy! There was no voyage, he lied to me, I dreamed it all. He held a scribbled sheet of paper under my nose, but obviously he could have made me write it while I was under his control.

Right after my "return," Vanier contacted a newspaper to check the archives. I could only speak to him via television, since he didn't want to leave the protected bunker as long as he didn't have proof of a supposed variation in the temporal matrix. I haven't changed at all myself, yet I have never been under the protection of the forcefield. That's why I yelled at Vanier at first. Nothing has changed. His answer: he shoved under my nose, using the monitor, the front page for Monday, August 8, 1983. No tourists killed during a spectacular suicide. I'd actually succeeded.

He made me call somebody in my family. I started with my brother, because he wasn't talkative. I was sure I could get off the line quickly. He thought I was funny. I didn't dare ask him if Vero was alive. I imagined Vanier (who was listening in), cursing. Then, Jacques told me my *agent* had called, that he was trying to reach me. My agent! I've never had an agent. And yet... Yes. I have an agent. I even knew his name, his number, before my brother read the message.

Then it was my turn to yell at Vanier. Not only had nothing really changed, but it was worse.

I just don't know anymore.

I called my agent. He answered with hesitation, accustomed as he was to my manias, my eccentricities (accustomed to?). He didn't balk when I asked him to describe my family. Three children alive. Vero, dead in a car accident, Sunday, September 11, 1983.

I always hated driving. I was always afraid in a car.

When Vanier's face replaced my agent's on the monitor, I smashed in the screen with my fist.

⁄⁄ ⫶

Sunday, June 18, 2024

The metal chair is hard and icy under my buttocks. I can't get to sleep. I should have gone back to the hotel, but they want to run some more tests, tomorrow. Today. I don't care.

Vanier won't want to. First I have to go home, work a little, in order to replenish my bank account. My agent was trying to reach me because he had a proposal for me, from a producer. Just as well. If I have money, Vanier will have to listen to me. Because he's wrong. I didn't succeed. The weak variations they observed in the temporal matrix are not due to a change in the past. The matrix remained stable because the past did not really undergo a change. Vero's death was moved, not prevented. I will succeed the day I open my eyes in a world in which my sister lives—where I will be nothing, an unknown author, a failure?

I don't know what I want anymore.

I want to try again, that's for sure. With or without Vanier.

Could a hypnotist, back home, create the conditions...?

I stopped writing, just a minute. The lamp lights me, harshly, directly. I look at my hands, my hands lying on my knees. My dark blue pyjamas.

Why do I have this feeling of *déjà vu* that makes me want to scream?

MEMORY GAMES
Dale L. Sproule

She grabbed Daniel's fingers as he unfastened her jeans.
His hands were cool, almost cold. Though he was little more
than a shadow, she could see his eyes glinting in the starlight.
Moonlight. More. A glare of headlights swept into the bedroom
from the street, catching Daniel in their photographic flash.
Something about him looked wrong.

Celine said, "We should talk first."

His arm turned to stone, refusing to be moved. "Why're you
starting that again?"

Celine shrugged and began rebuttoning her blouse. "Did
you know that Alan Winston was one of them?"

"Don't start again," he said.

"You remember Alan Winston, don't you?"

"No. I don't remember Alan-fucking-Winston!" When she
didn't respond, he continued. "This is a crock. Sometimes I
wonder what you'd really do if I failed one of these tests."

"Kill you."

"I mean what you'd *really* do! You wouldn't trust your own
judgement, Celine. You'd tell yourself you were being
paranoid. You wouldn't kill me."

He undid the buttons she had just fastened.

She didn't stop him. Even if the stories were true about
Morphs being able to use the short term memories of those
they'd sucked the life from, the sorts of things Daniel knew
about her were more than superficial. Weren't they?

He'd known about her paranoia. How could he fake
something like that? But then, who wasn't paranoid these days?
Bluster and bravado didn't conceal Daniel's fear, they
magnified it. If he was a morph, why would he still be afraid?

He unfastened her brassière, cradling her heavy breasts in
his hands, rolling her nipples between his fingers. Closing her
eyes, Celine tried to not to cringe at the feel of Daniel's tongue
gliding like a wet eraser down her neck and between her
breasts. His fingers didn't feel so cold anymore, sliding up her
back, gripping the base of her skull and holding her like that as
he kissed her. His other hand squeezed the flesh of her ass,
pulling her firmly to him.

Feeling his erection through his jeans, she squirmed away with a surge of terror. "I may not kill you. But I won't be with you any more. Not until you tell me about Alan Winston."

"We worked with him," Daniel said.

"Which department did he work in?"

Celine could see his anger clearly, because headlights had lit up the room again.

Only morphs drove cars anymore. She squinted at the window. "What are they up to?"

"I called them, when you started freaking out. We're never gonna catch this woman by surprise, I told them. Might as well take her now. "

A joke? Truth was impossible to recognize anymore. Celine wasn't sure it had ever existed.

He spoke again. "We should make the most of the short lives we have left." A familiar Daniel sentiment. "If you send me away, you'll never make love to another man. You'd never be sure. You're getting to be afraid of living."

The air in the room felt thick and hot. He was right.

Celine peered into the empty street. Once reassured that the car hadn't stopped in the neighbourhood, she looked back into the darkness where Daniel stood. "You think I can't live without you? I've lived alone for half my adult life, Daniel. I'll survive."

He didn't speak for a long time. Celine began to wonder if he'd left the room. "Yeah?" was all he finally said.

Celine said, "We were talking about Alan Winston."

"I'm not playing tonight, Celine," Daniel walked up to her, holding her shoulders patronizingly.

That made her angry, far angrier than it ordinarily would. "Suits me fine. Neither am I."

She went downstairs to the living room and sat in candlelight, staring at the smouldering ashes in the fireplace.

The room was filled with things made by human hands, already little more than artifacts: the raku vase her mother had bought her as a housewarming present; the once-valuable blue depression glass water pitcher she'd found at a garage sale; the painting on the wall—a vibrant cityscape, filled with people and cars and buses. She could read the names of the streets, the headlines on the newspapers and the signs. The buses had destinations.

Celine began to cry again. As pathetic and mean as Daniel

could be, he was all she had left to cling to. She didn't know if she could survive losing him.

She derived little solace from the thought that if Daniel really was a morph, this crying fit might drive him away. Negative emotions at the time of 'conception' spoiled the pre-natal environment—or so the stories said. But what did anybody really know? Who had actually been on a breeder ship and returned to tell about it? Who had ever seen a morph hatch, flesh of human parents bursting like balloons of blood and bone?

But there were many, many stories. A whole morph lore.

The shapeshifting invaders could take on all sorts of interesting disguises, like the angels as which they'd first appeared, announcing that Judgement Day had come. Millions of people, from radical sects of dozens of different religions followed them to hundreds of different heavens. The converts filled the alien birthing pods…

Coming downstairs softly, Daniel sat on the couch beside her. In this light, he no longer looked as strange as he had upstairs. Not strange at all in fact. He was wearing that boyish look of contrition she'd always found irresistable.

It made him seem more Daniel-like.

"I need you," he said. When she didn't respond, he continued, "I thought you felt the same…"

"We don't love each other." She stared at the tall dark-haired man beside her and really wondered for the first time whether this was actually the man she'd been sleeping with for the past eight months. Surely they didn't make duplicate people *this* perfectly? "We only stay together because we're afraid to find someone else. It's too dangerous. But it might be worth the gamble."

"I do love you," he said, as he put an arm over her shoulder and tried pulling her toward him.

Standing, she stared him in the eye and said softly, "Then prove it. Put up with my questions."

"Okay. Alan Whateverhisnameis. Tell me more about him. Maybe I'll remember."

"You really don't remember, do you?"

"I know the name, I just can't put a face to it. Gimme a kickstart. It'll come to me."

Celine shook her head, but complied just the same. "Medium height. Sort of stocky. I think he was into weightlifting or something."

"Wait, wait, wait. He was…an analyst from Systems Support."

"No, that was Ernie Williams."

"Ernie, Alan, what's the difference?"

"Alan was the expenditure coordinator from Investment Administration. He and Gary from Payroll were known as the two musketeers cause they couldn't keep their swords in their scabbards. What was it Gary always used to tease you about?"

"It was so long ago, Celine."

"Come on! You know the answer to this one."

He grinned again. "It was about you."

"That's better. Why did you ever open your mouth to him in the first place?"

He shrugged.

"He might have said something to your wife. What would you have done then?"

He shrugged again.

"Daniel??"

"Never thought about it."

She backed away from him. "I want you to leave right now."

Daniel grinned. "Come on. I'm only teasing. I wasn't married. I figured that if you could make up a cast of characters to test my memory, I could play the same game. To show you how stupid this whole thing is, how willing you are to believe everything you hear from everywhere."

Celine rolled her eyes. If this was a morph, it argued exactly the same way Daniel did.

He'd once seemed so gallant and romantic, but now Celine wondered what she had ever seen in him, how she had come to believe that she loved him.

During the years she'd worked with him at the Department of Finance office, Celine's imagination had claimed and redefined him. And for most of the next eight months she'd visited his apartment once or even twice a week. Her husband had left her after finding out, but Daniel had declined her invitation to move in with her.

Only in bed did their chemistry still seem perfect. Only there did she still need him. Even now, despite her fear and revulsion, Celine still found herself having to fight the urge to give herself to him. He was talking, but she had been tuning him out. "…for so long, it's getting hard tell the difference between fantasy and reality anymore. You know that?"

She shook her head. "I don't buy your explanation, Daniel. You should know those people I was just talking about. You worked with them for almost as long as I did."

Daniel nodded, then went to the closet and got out his jacket.

"Where are you going?" Celine asked.

"Home."

She stared at him as he fastened the snaps. Christ. She never thought it would really happen, or what she'd do about it. It was only the long term memories of the Morphs that were rumoured to be notoriously incomplete.

"Look. We don't have to leave just because we're not going to make love. If you really need me, love me, why can't we just sit and talk?"

"Because you'll just be playing memory games the whole time. Trying to trick me into slipping up. Know what I just thought of?" Daniel mumbled. "What if they've found some way to erase chunks of our memories? All of us? It wouldn't be hard. They run the food banks. If we've both forgotten all sorts of things, then if even one of us has been affected, we'd be all screwed up. We'd be sure to have the kind of disagreement we've just been having."

Suddenly realising she'd been nodding, Celine looked up, as disgusted with herself as she was with him. "Why would they do that? Look. I may be gullible, but you're pushing the bullshit meter a little high. Maybe you should leave. We can talk about this tomorrow."

"They'd do it to make us afraid of each other. Maybe they even started the story about morphs having incomplete memories," Daniel said. "If we're afraid of each other, we'll be less likely to mount an effective resistance."

"What resistance?"

"Precisely."

"You can't bafflegab me anymore. If you won't humour me by answering a few questions, then you don't love me enough. Period. This isn't going to work, Daniel."

He turned and left without further protest.

Maybe it really was Daniel, she thought, as she watched the door close behind him. He expected her to believe this stupid memory-wipe theory he'd hatched out of the blue? She would have laughed, if it wasn't so tragic. For six months, Daniel had been the only male on the planet whom she had dared to trust. And now, he was being taken away from her.

By her own paranoia? Daniel's well-aimed wisecrack had shaken her. As he knew it would. He was armed with a quiet brutality and even if he was really human, Celine knew she was better rid of him.

She had trouble sleeping that night and while she lay there staring into the darkness, she started to see the logic of Daniel's assertion. Maybe the stories about the aliens really were propagated by the aliens themselves. That would certainly answer her questions about how any humans had lived to tell the tales. She wondered if there was any way to test the large-scale memory loss idea.

Encyclopaedias! That was it. She'd check to see if she could find historical facts she had forgotten.

Pulling on a housecoat to hide her nakedness, despite the fact that she was alone in the house, Celine descended the staircase slowly in the dim candle light; once in the living room, she walked straight to the bookcase, grabbed an encyclopaedia at random and opened it.

There was a knock on the front door. "It's me," was all he said.

He grinned when she opened the door for him. "So you couldn't sleep either, eh? Look, Celine. I think we've got to work this out."

"I thought you were going home."

"Went to see Tex. To see if he had some more of that Vodka he was selling. Tex is gone." His grin disappeared halfway through his explanation, as if he'd suddenly realized he was wearing the wrong emotion. "What are you doing with that?"

She looked down at the volume in her hand. "The letter 'S'. "Checking…"

"Checking what?"

"To see if I can figure out if they really *are* tampering with all our memories." Walking back into the living room, she left Daniel standing at the door as she sat down on the couch, peering at the book in the dim, flickering light. "I want to see if there's anything I've forgotten. Anything important. Anything I should remember."

She opened the big book to the middle. "South Dakota."

Daniel grinned. "I think you should look for something a

little more obscure." Running his hand through his hair like a cowboy, he sauntered into the room and sat beside her. "An event or something. How about that?"

"Slipperwort?"

He sat down beside her and pointed. "How about this? Stone Mountain."

"Oh, come on."

"No, really. Tell me about Stone Mountain."

" I don't...c'mon, Daniel, quit shitting me. Nobody's ever heard of Stone Mountain."

Daniel's eyes opened wide. "You're serious?"

"Cut it out," Celine squeaked.

"Look here," he said, pointing to the encyclopaedia entry. "One of the largest granite masses in the world. The Confederate Memorial is carved into the eastern slope, for crying out loud. The figures of Robert E. Lee, Jefferson Davis and Stonewall Jackson carved into the mountain. You at least remember Mount Rushmore, don't you?"

Celine nodded mutely. She could not for the life of her remember ever hearing of Stone Mountain. Being a Canadian, maybe it was simply a point of ignorance on her part. Or maybe she really had lost chunks of memory.

She continued through the pages. "I know about almost everything else in here."

"Oh, yeah, Mrs. Einstein. Then who's Snorri Sturluson?"

"A famous medieval Norwegian writer. Ha!"

Daniel nodded, obviously amazed that Celine had known the answer to such an obscure bit of history. "You weren't expecting that were you? I think that's the first time I've ever had a chance to use anything I learned in that Mythology course I took in university."

He shook his head and kissed her on the nose. "You're a marvel. Now let's continue with the exercise. What's the capital of Paraguay?"

She punched him in the arm.

"Give me the book. Now it's my turn."

Reluctantly, he handed it to her. After a moment, she said, "Tell me about the Suez Canal. Where is it?"

"It's in...Arabia or somewhere in the middle east. It connects the Mediterranean with...some other big body of water. The Persian Gulf, the Red Sea, something like that."

Nodding Celine turned some more pages. "How 'bout the

Spanish Inquisition?"

"And how about those Blue Jays?"

"Come on. I'm serious. Who was Torquemada?"

He shook his head. "The designated hitter? I dunno. That's a bit too obscure."

"Then tell me something else about the Inquisition."

"It was in Spain…"

"Good start. What else?"

"Something to do with religion, Christians being persecuted or something?"

"Come on, Daniel. It was the Christians who were doing the persecuting."

"Maybe that's why they never talked about it much in school."

"Hmmmm…" she conceded. Somehow his ignorance was more convincing than his knowledge would have been.

"Besides, history was never my forte. I preferred Sex Education."

This time, Celine laughed as he kissed her neck. "I'll bet you did."

"That's the thing about memory," said Daniel. "You can never be sure about something you've forgotten." He kissed her lips. She kissed back, wondering in the back of her mind whether she'd just been conned.

She remembered how lonely she'd felt when Daniel had gone away—the shock and discomfort of the realization that she'd never find anyone else she could be sure about again in her whole life.

When she kissed him back, the book slid off of her lap, landing with a soft thud on the carpet.

She let him untie the belt on her housecoat and run his hands over her breasts.

He was right, the only way she'd ever know for sure would be to take the chance.

"I love you," he said, as his hand slid down between her legs. She clung to Daniel, to the idea that he really was who he said he was and he really did love her. She nuzzled her face into Daniel's neck.

"I'm sorry," she said. "I love you too."

As he entered her, his eyes gleamed in the candlelight and despite her determination to believe him, she couldn't stop staring into those eyes, mining for secrets.

READERS OF THE LOST ART
Élisabeth Vonarburg (translated by Howard Scott)

to Claude and Geneviève, among others

The Subject presents itself as a block, slightly taller than it is wide, set vertically on a round central stage that is slowly revolving. The colour of the block, a very dark green, does not necessarily make one think of stone (it could be plasmoc), especially since it glistens with a strange opalescence under the combined laser beams. Its rough texture and irregular shape, however, tell the audience what the voice of the invisible Announcer, floating over the room, now confirms: the Subject has chosen to appear in a sheath of Labrador amphibolite.

As murmurs go back and forth at a few tables commenting on this strategy, the Operator enters, a silhouette at first glance consisting of reflections from a scattered brightness. All the instruments required for his task, most made of metal, are stuck to his skin under which have been inserted strongly magnetized chips or small plates. The Operator does not wear any clothing except for the armour made up of these tools, all of different shapes and sizes but designed to fit together like the segments of some exoskeleton to the glory of technology. Of course, a black hood fits tightly over his head, though not over his face, which contrasts with the smooth, shiny material and seems like a simple, abstract outline—geometrical planes arbitrarily linked together rather than a recognizable countenance.

The amphitheatre falls silent after some scattered, rather condescending applause. Everyone knows there will be no subtlety in the first approach, in accordance with the obvious wishes of the Subject: a direct assault, almost naïve, on the primitive material surrounding it. The Operator circles the block, steps up to it, steps away from it, touches it here and there, then steps back two paces and stands there a few moments with his head lowered. He emerges from his meditation only to take two unsurprising instruments from his tool-armour: a hammer and a chisel.

He needs to find the areas of least resistance: briefly returned to its original plasticity through heat and pressure before enclosing the Subject, then cooled, the metamorphic rock provides clues to its schistosities in the infinitely divergent orientations of its amphiboles, as the rounded reflections playing on the surface of a still river reveal to the practised eye the contours of the bottom, and the twists and turns of the current. The plagioclase opalescence of the material will apparently not delay the operation; a section of rock falls off the block after the first blow is delivered by a sure, firm hand. The Operator is experienced. We will soon get to the heart of the Subject.

In the room, up in the tiers, the alcoves are gradually filling up, the small lamps on the tables are being turned on, and jewels are throwing furtive sparkles. Buyers and merchants sit down, ready after the day's work for work of another sort. With slow elegance, the hostesses parade along the tiers, their eyes falsely distant, like panthers pacing their cages pretending to be unaware that they were long ago torn away from their secret jungle paths. Now and then, a hand is raised, nonchalantly or urgently, and yet another captive goes and sits close to the client whom she will, for the evening, be pleasing.

On the central stage (noiselessly—the floor where the rock fragments fall is covered with a thick elastic carpet), the Operator is almost finished with the first phase and those the show is intended to entertain grant a little discreet applause when a whole section of rock comes off the upper part of the block, indicating finally what is in store for the second phase of the operation. In the deep layer revealed, indistinct masses can barely be seen, a glassy gleam.

The Operator puts the chisel and hammer in the box provided for them. It is a medium-sized box, a declaration of principle that does not escape the seasoned spectators: the Operator is no novice and fully intends to get through the Subject without having to use all his instruments. As usual, the lid only opens one way. The tools that are put in the box cannot be taken out again. If Operators dared to try—something that is unthinkable—they would be immediately electrocuted by the powerful current running through every metal object the instant it is placed in one of the compartments of the box.

A murmur runs through the amphitheatre as the Subject is completely extricated from the rock sheath: its crystalline prisms scatter the coherent laser light into myriads of geometric rainbows that both reveal and hide the thickness of the material. The Operator moves away and again circles the Subject to the discreet clickings of his tool-armour (in which the absence of the hammer and chisel has opened two gaps). Meditatively, he paces around the perimeter of the stage. Brute force is no longer enough. Getting close to the Subject by shattering the prisms would be in rare bad taste, and the audience would be right to show their displeasure by pushing the buttons that link them to the Manager of the establishment. The Operator carefully chooses his next tool, creating a new gap in his tool-armour. A probe, of course.

The probe indicates the expected thickness of the Subject in the second phase, as well as the nodal points, invisible to the naked eye, where the prisms are joined. As this information is displayed holographically above the stage, a few exclamations in the audience reveal the interest of those watching the show. The matter is dense. The prisms are composed of several concentric layers of varying nature, which blend together in several places; their macro-crystals are themselves juxtaposed in complex combinations. They will have to be disassembled one by one unless there are certain nodal points governing the simultaneous unlocking of several elements. This is almost certainly the case, but the information provided by the probe gives no hint of it.

On one of the levels, half way up the amphitheatre, almost all the hostesses have been called. There is only one left. She is a rather tall woman with very white skin wearing a crimson lamé dress that glints stroboscopically with her every movement. Her short hair, cut in a helmet shape and smoothed down over her head, does not shine, quite the contrary. It is so dark that when the woman goes into shadow, that whole part of her head disappears and her face, enigmatically made up in mauve and gold, looks like a floating mask. An attentive observer would notice that this hostess flinches whenever a hand is raised (which activates the communication disk grafted on the forehead of each member of the staff), then relaxes when the hand is lowered (since the client has indicated subvocally who he is speaking to, thus automatically cutting off the hostess or the waiter from the general network).

One such attentive observer is sitting in one of the alcoves at the edge of the third level. He has wide shoulders, or else his evening jumpsuit hides shoulder pads, but this is not likely, since his torso is long and muscular. The wide low neck of his suit reveals a very distinct scar that appears to run all the way down his chest. His hands (the only parts other than his torso that are clearly lit by the globelamp on the table) are strong and square; his fingertips are strangely discoloured. Of his head, which is in shadow, the only thing visible is the round shape crowned with a mane of abundant and apparently rebellious hair. The man at last raises his hand. The hostess stops, turns towards the alcove, then, her slightly lowered head floating in the alternations of shadow and light, obeys and steps forward.

Meanwhile, more and more of the audience has turned its attention to the performance taking place on the central stage. A wave of applause mixed with exclamations of appreciative surprise has distracted them from their dinners, their bargaining or their companions. The prisms that surround the Subject have lost their translucence and their rainbows. The laser light has begun to trigger complex molecular reactions on their surfaces. Lines form, shapes and colours merge slowly with one another to reappear in different combinations. There is an implied rhythm, the suggestion of a pattern in the permutations, a hint of an intention in the sequences.

The Operator, who has detached a few instruments from his tool-armour, stops to study this new development. After a while, he places all but two of the instruments in the box, which prohibits him from picking them up again. He has kept a small rubber-headed hammer and a series of suction-cup rings, which he places separately on the fingertips of his right hand, including the thumb. He steps up to the prismatic block and stops again, as though waiting for a signal. All of a sudden, carefully, he positions the hand with the suction-cup rings one finger at a time, on the protruding part of one of the prisms, and with the other hand gives a light tap with the hammer on a point that he seems to have chosen very precisely. Nothing happens. The coloured lines and shapes continue rippling across the surface of the prisms. The Operator waits. Suddenly, without the audience being able to see what has triggered his action, he taps the same spot as before, twice, in quick succession.

A piece of the prism as big as a fist breaks off, held by the fingers of the Operator, who then removes the suction cups from it with his other hand, sets the crystal fragment on the floor, picks up his small hammer and again turns to face the prisms, attentive (the spectators are beginning to understand it) to the enigmatic progression of clues moving just under their surface. The randomness of all the coloured movements of the lines and shapes, their nature, their frequency, their combinations, is only apparent. They actually constitute a code marking the location of nodal points where the prisms are joined. A code, or more accurately changing codes—the rhythms have rhythms, the combinations have combinations, and the law (or the laws) governing it all hides, elusively, in those converging metamorphoses.

Some members of the audience, who have understood the rules of the game, turn to making quick electronic speculations on the small terminals built into their tables. Bets are exchanged back and forth. A hum of interest swells, ebbs and swells again with each crystal segment dislodged from the Subject. Even the few clients old enough to have immediately recognized the nature of the proposed entertainment—"reading", a very ancient art form which always experiences sporadic revivals—even they begin taking interest in the show. This will be a memorable performance.

In the alcove she has been called to, the hostess in the crimson lamé dress turns her back to the stage; she is sitting very straight in the low armchair, although it is softly contoured to encourage relaxation. With one hand, she holds in her fingertips the stem of a glass filled with a drink with which she has hardly wet her lips; her other hand, fist closed, is on the arm of the chair. The man seated on her right leans over, takes her closed hand and gently unfolds the fingers one by one on the table. With this movement, the man's head enters the sphere of light that surrounds the globelamp. Beneath the unruly hair, his features are strong but without fineness, like a sketch that someone had not bothered finishing. The only features that stand out in detail are the mouth, the thick, sinuous lips strangely bordered with a white line—make-up or apigmentation—and the eyes, oblique but wide, possibly blue, softened by the light into a very pale grey in which the black iris, extremely dilated, seems to almost fill the eye. It is difficult to attribute an expression to this monolithic whole. Alertness, certainly, but is it inquisitive, cunning, friendly? The man's hand releases the fingers of the hostess, which fold up again between palm and thumb. The woman is surely not even aware of this, for when the index finger of the man taps lightly on her closed fist, she starts, makes a move to hide that hand under the table and then, with visible effort, places it close to the one holding—too tightly now—the long-stemmed glass. The man lays back in his chair, returning his face to the shadow, and the hostess must assume that he is watching the show, because she also pivots her chair towards the stage below.

The Operator has finished dismantling the first layer of crystals. The general shape of the Subject is easier now to make out: a tapering vertical parallelepiped, much higher than it is wide and of irregular thickness; it narrows towards the bottom, widens, then narrows again at the top. Identical bulges are visible about one third up its front face and two thirds up its back face. The same play of lines and shapes moves across the surface of this second crystalline layer. Or at least the same principle is no doubt at work for, although it is hard to say why, one senses that the content of these animated patterns is not quite the same—nor completely different, however—as the one from the previous phase. More speed, perhaps, in the transformations? Or rather they flicker with concomitant metamorphoses; the rhythms they follow are subtly out of sync with each other, but when the effort is made to perceive them simultaneously, they constitute a whole whose organic cohesion leaves no doubt.

The Operator seems to hesitate. The rubber-headed hammer hangs above the changing patterns. Then, very gently, it strikes one of the crystals. The block turns dark. The Operator jumps away, dropping the hammer, his hands clamped over his ears, his face twisted in a silent grimace.

There is a burst of applause from the audience (the frequency of the ultrasound was modulated for the Operator alone, which makes their satisfaction all the greater) as the block clears and the lines and colours resume their briefly interrupted progression. The Operator nods several times as he removes the suction-cup rings from his fingers. Then he picks up the small rubber-headed hammer and puts it and the rings in the box.

A murmur of astonishment and excitement greets his next gesture—he detaches several sets of tools from his tool-armour and also deposits them in the box. He now presents an impressive silhouette, dotted irregularly with disparate metal objects between which patches of bare skin can be seen. He detaches another set of rings with smaller suction cups and slips them on his fingertips, right hand and left. He then moves close to the block and attentively observes the shiftings and groupings of the lines. One finger at a time, he places his right hand, then his left, on two widely separated points; the fingers are positioned irregularly, some close together, some half bent, others stretched out and spread wide, no doubt to correspond to strategically placed points that must be touched simultaneously to produce the desired effect.

For an instant, the Operator is motionless. He must be waiting for a precise combination of colours, lines and shapes, for all of a sudden he can be seen leaning a little against the block, giving a sudden push, and then he steps back holding the section of crystals that he has just detached.

The audience leans forward the better to see what is revealed of the Subject by the breach thus created. They are disappointed, or surprised, or delighted. It is intensely black, featureless, a simple cut-out that reveals neither shape nor volume—it could just as well be a glimpse of the intergalactic void. Only the Operator is close enough to possibly make anything out, but nothing in his behaviour indicates what he sees. With his hands held out a few millimetres above the crystalline sheath, he waits for the moment when a new configuration, indiscernible by the audience, will indicate to him that another section of the Subject is offering itself to be broken off.

A conversation has begun between the hostess in the crimson lamé dress and her client. It is not a very animated one. The woman seems as reticent to answer the questions of her interlocutor as he is slow to ask them. And they are perhaps not questions. They may be rambling comments on the performance being staged below. The man and the hostess both seem to be watching it.

The Subject has been almost entirely extracted from its crystalline shell. Totally black—that strangely matte, depthless black that flattens volumes—its shape to come is very clear now: from the front, an elongated diamond standing on its narrowest point; but from the side (it can be seen as the central stage slowly rotates), although it retains the shape of a parallelogram, it will be an asymmetrical one.

Using combined pressure and shearing, the Operator detaches the last crystalline section. Around the Subject, the stage is littered with blocks of all sizes. Slow ripples of transformations still flow over their surfaces. Their inner rhythm is subtly or considerably altered now that their organic link with the Subject has been cut, but their beauty, their fascinating appeal, remains intact—as indicated by the requests that have been flooding the communication network for some time now: What will become of those fragments? Is it possible to obtain them, and at what price? To all these questions, the Manager's answer is the same: all the materials from the performance are the exclusive property of the Artists, who dispose of them as they see fit.

The Operator once more circles the Subject. He takes a device from his tool-armour (almost completely dismantled now) to scan the black block from a distance. The spectators peer at the area above the stage where the holographically retransmitted data will appear. Nothing. The Operator punches hidden keys on the small device and moves to another spot to resume his examinations. Still nothing. He almost shakes the device, stops, and places it in the box, allowing himself a slight shrug. He detaches another device, a sort of stylus connected by several wires thick enough to be fine conduits to an oblong box of which all one side is covered with variously coloured keys of different sizes. With perceptible hesitation, he walks up to the block, and touches it with the tip of the stylus.

An inarticulate exclamation rises unanimously from the audience. The Operator has been thrown to the floor where he goes into visibly painful convulsions, no doubt caused by an electrical discharge of quite high intensity.

After several minutes, though, he gets up again with some difficulty. He deposits the useless device in the box. After closing the lid, he stands motionless for a moment, one hand on each side of the box, leaning lightly, his head lowered a bit. Those spectators who have been brought opposite him by the rotation of the stage can see that he has his eyes closed, and that a film of sweat glistens on the skin of his face and body (where the tools have been detached). A murmur of satisfaction—not without a certain joyous cruelty—runs through the audience: the Subject is a formidable opponent.

The chair of the hostess in the crimson lamé dress has pivoted; she is no longer watching the show, nor is she looking at her client. He speaks to her from time to time, leaning a little towards her, his face half lit by the globelamp. One of his hands is wrapped around the arm of his chair. A distinct depression in the soft material shows the force with which he is gripping it. His other hand, however, resting on the table, is slowly, delicately turning the long-stemmed glass, occasionally raising it to his face like a flower to drink. The young woman's face, because she is nearer the table, is fully lighted. She is looking straight ahead without any discernible emotion (except, perhaps, by inference, the desire to be inexpressive). Her eyelids do not blink, her eyes are fixed, enlarged, shining brightly, with a tremulous sparkle that suddenly comes loose and rolls down her right cheek to fall on her collarbone, which is exposed by the low neckline of the lamé dress. The man puts his glass down on the table, very gently. He leans a little closer to the woman and follows the wet trail with the tip of a finger. The woman turns her head away and lowers it towards her other shoulder. The man takes hold of her face—which half disappears in his big hand—to turn it, without brutality but firmly, back towards him.

The Operator begins moving again. Facing the black block—as though it could see him—he removes what remain of his tools from his skin with slow, deliberate movements, and lays them down on the floor. He brings his hands to his head and unhooks the fastenings of his hood, which are joined at the top. He is naked now, except for the shell that protects his sexual organs from any unpleasant contact with the tools nearby. He is a tall young man, broad-shouldered and long-bodied. His skin, uniformly smooth and completely lacking in pilosity, is very white. His smooth hair is cut in a helmet shape around the sturdy face, and appears, perhaps in contrast, excessively dark. When he moves close to the block again, it can be seen that he is almost the same height, just barely shorter. (Perhaps only the flat blackness of the block makes it look taller than the Operator.)

The Operator seems to collect himself (or meditate, or simply take the time to breathe deeply); then he holds out his arms and—to the extent that the shape of the block permits him to do so—he embraces it.

A silent explosion of blackness momentarily blinds the spectators. When they regain their sight, the Operator and the Subject are face to face at last, with nothing to separate them.

In the alcove, the chairs of the man and woman are closer together. Resting on the table between the two long-stemmed glasses, the man's hand envelops the woman's. The woman's head is leaning against the man's shoulder. They are both watching the circular stage below.

The Subject now appears in the shape of a naked woman, with golden skin, copper-coloured in the light of the lasers, and, like the Operator, completely lacking in pilosity, except for a mid-length, unruly mane, also copper-coloured, slanted eyebrows above very black eyes (but this may only be an effect of the lights), and very thick eyelashes. She is the same height as the Operator—though there is no point of reference to estimate their respective heights, now that the black parallelepiped has sublimated. Besides, there is no more time to indulge in such speculations, for the stage changes suddenly, and a surprised exclamation rises from the audience (where almost all the clients now have became spectators).

The Operator and the Subject, both still naked, float above the circular stage, and, although no visible barrier indicates the limits of their weightlessness chamber, it is suddenly apparent that what the audience has been seeing since the beginning is not a live performance but a holographic retransmission, perhaps long after the fact. Various movements disturb the spectators after the initial surprise—protests, approval, arguments from one table to the next between tenants of actuality and tenants of virtuality. But all this agitation dissipates quite quickly, for down below, in the weightlessness chamber, the show continues.

A number of tools had remained stuck to the skin of the Operator during the third exploratory phase. He takes them off his skin without using them. He has not been forced to put them in the box and can still use them. There will therefore be a fourth phase for the Subject, now at the discretion of the Operator.

With the Operator's first moves, the coming procedure is made obvious, and the spectators who have not yet understood, by realizing that the performance is recorded, understand now with a shiver of anxious or delighted anticipation: this will be the Great Game.

The Operator first proceeds with removing the nails, regal paths to the skin. Delicate remote-controlled cybernetic pincers alight on either side of each nail on the hands and feet. Small suction cups coated with monomolecular glue are placed on the surface of the nails. An instant of immobility, then the impetus spreads, activating precise movements throughout the system. With a quiet tearing noise, the nails are pulled from the phalangettes, which are invisible under the layer of flesh. Another small suction cup attaches itself to each of the fingers like a mouth, aspirating the blood seeping from the periphery of the nail, in the same movement injecting a local delayed-action analgesic, and then cauterizing the blood vessels. The Subject's scream is cut short.

The Operator, of course, did not scream when his own nails were detached from his fingers. The process is not the same for him since he initiates it—and the subsequent interruption of the blood flow to the injured areas—autonomously by directly manipulating his psychosoma. Moreover, electrical impulses that scramble his analgo-receptor centres are emitted continuously from the outside, though they become weaker as the performance progresses; in the Great Game, speed and precision are literally of vital importance.

With the Subject floating horizontally in front of him, maintained in place by magnetic fields, the Operator now makes the median incision from the top of the sternum to the pubis. The anaesthetizing suction cups follow the red line, close behind the scalpel. The Subject's scream is again cut short.

The next incisions must be made rapidly. This is where everything will be decided; the pain increases for the Operator (as the electric scrambling steadily decreases in intensity) while it diminishes for the Subject as area after area is more and more thoroughly anaesthetized. The Operator starts with the pubis. The audience leans forward. Will he attempt internal detachment? No, he will leave the most intimate parts of the Subject intact. He makes do with cutting around the labia majora and the anus. (The process takes a little longer, and is therefore more perilous for the Operator when the Subject is of the male sex. The penis is, of course, an exterior organ, which makes the operation obligatory, and its flaccidity creates a problem; an entire traction system is required and it must be adjusted perfectly to permit a quick, precise incision. Psychosomatic control easily solves this problem for the bodies of male Operators.)

The Operator now goes to the other end of the Subject. The head has an abundance of orifices whose outlines must be followed meticulously—the eyes and the mouth especially, for obvious, though different, reasons. The ears, by convention, will be detached with the rest of the skin; the nostrils, also by convention, are always cut along their perimeter. But the eyes and the mouth require special attention. Cutting the eyelids is particularly delicate and there is no room for missteps. As for the mouth, like the genitals of a female Subject and the anus in both sexes, there are two possibilities: either the incision simply follows the line of the lips, or else the mini-scalpels take the risk of going inside. There will be no surprises here. The Operator, logically, chooses the first option.

Up to this point the procedure has been flawless, and the Operator can begin the next phase confidently. The pain has not yet begun to slow him down. Nevertheless everything is not settled. Besides the extraction operation *per se*, some separate incisions, more or less important, are still required on the Subject from time to time for the removal of the skin, which must be carried out, if not slowly, at least with caution, if the optimal result is to be obtained.

A cloud of minute machines floats around the Operator. These will carry out the actual removal of the skin, remote-controlled by him; his optical centres receive pictures directly transmitted by cameras built into the micro-scalpels.

Here he has opted for speed, but also difficulty, by moving simultaneously from the periphery to the centre (peeling the tips of the fingers and toes like a glove), and from the centre to the periphery (lifting the skin from each side of the median incision). Bets are exchanged in the audience on the number of additional incisions that he will have to make.

The man and the woman now watch the show only from time to time. They talk instead, heads close together, punctuating their words with kisses.

The Operator's psychosomatic control has relaxed for the first time. Blood beads along his cuts and where his skin, with a slow but regular movement, is being lifted at the same time as the Subject's. Suction cups stick to him to clean and cauterize (but will not inject, of course, any analgesics). The work of the micro-machines, however, continues without any appreciable interruption. The myriads of pincer-clips hold the Subject's skin and carefully lift it as the lasers separate the dermis, millimetre by millimetre. (It is important that the five layers of the epidermis be removed intact, basal layer, Malpighian layer, granular layer, clear layer, and horny layer.) There are particularly delicate areas, where the skin is thinner (the inside of the wrists, the armpits, the nipples…and of course, in the lower half, the popliteal space, the groin, and, when the Subject is a man, the penis, which is initially treated like a finger. It is necessary to go from the glans to the root, by way of the flap of the foreskin, and to deal with the softness of the scrotum.)

The Operator is visibly fighting the pain now. The suction cups stick themselves to him more often, and the removal of the Subject's skin seems to have also slowed down. Once the fingers have been uncovered, the arms and legs are skinned without particular problems for the Subject (and causing the Operator only the difficult, though expected, problem of growing pain). But the linkup of the micro-scalpels coming from the periphery with those coming from the centre takes place with difficulty on the perimeter of the torso. The process is no longer the slow but certain advance of a nearly straight front, as in the beginning (pincer-clips above the skin, micro-scalpels beneath) but a staggered progression, a section here, another farther on. The risks of tearing the tissue are increasing second by second as the machines lose their alignment and stresses are applied to the skin more and more unevenly. Will the Operator forfeit, or will he try to hold out to the extreme limits of consciousness, with all the attendant risks? The movement of the machines and the removal of the skin is now so slow as to be almost imperceptible. It could even be concluded, after a while, that it has totally stopped. The Operator floats, motionless. Only the movement of the cauterizing suction cups, here and there on his body, shows that he is still conscious. Is he resting, frittering away the precious remaining seconds while the analgesics still have some effect, or, although he is conscious, does he lack the strength to concede? But the suction cups detach themselves from him, putting an end to the spectators' speculations. He is quite unconscious now. He has not been able to get through the Subject.

The Subject, however, in spite of the initial pain, and then the progressive anaesthesia, has remained perfectly conscious. With the Operator immobilized, she takes full control of his powers. Now in command of the extraction tools, the Subject can choose to stop or to go on with the initial work—which in this case will continue to be performed on the Operator's body using identical machines that have just appeared in the weightlessness chamber and are obediently awaiting her decision. The machines position themselves on the floating body of the Operator. There is a brief round of satisfied applause in the audience. The Subject will finish the work, guiding the advance of the pincer-clips and micro-lasers over her own body, not only for the link-up taking place all around her torso, but also for the extremely delicate skinning of her head.

The Subject, of course, benefits from the results of the Operator's skill and speed. She needs only a few minutes to complete the task (during which the cauterizing suction cups move over the unconscious body of the Operator in the wake of the micro-scalpels and hastily inject him with a powerful mixture of restorative drugs.)

The purpose of the injection at the end of the process, for the Subject as for the Operator (but is it still legitimate now to distinguish them in this way?) is to reinforce the skin sufficiently to reduce the risk during the last phase of the operation. After waiting a few minutes for the strengthener to take effect, the Subject extracts herself from her epidermis, slowly and nimbly, helped by the machines. Carried by force fields, the skin floats, tinted with a delicate, pinkish hue by the light of the lasers, not flaccid but as if still inhabited in absentia by the body that has just left it. The Subject swims towards the Operator, an exact, animated anatomical statue in which muscles, tendons and capillary networks are outlined with gleaming precision (they also hint more clearly, by the patterns finally revealed, at the rigid, solid bone frame that supports them). She now applies herself to extracting him from his skin. Soon the two envelopes float side by side in the weightlessness chamber, like outlines in waiting.

The Operator has regained consciousness. Impossible now to read any expression on his face, but the way he circles the Subject's envelope, then his own, indicates quite clearly his satisfaction with the outcome of the encounter. They were, one could say, worthy of each other. He comes back towards the Subject and speaks some inaudible words to her. They seem to be in agreement and swim together to the skins.

A spectator on the fifth level who is more perceptive than the others begins applauding. Others understand a few seconds later, and soon the rest of the audience does too—through contagion or sudden illumination, impossible to say. In the weightlessness chamber, the Subject is in the process of fitting herself into the Operator's skin, and the Operator (with some difficulty, the proportions not being identical though the sizes are) is wriggling into the Subject's skin.

A series of stationary holograms replaces the hologram of the weightlessness chamber. They show the development of the ultimate phase of the Great Game: the progressive assimilation of the exchanged envelopes through local reabsorption of excess skin and regeneration of missing skin (with the interesting colour patterns that result—zones of thin white skin on copper-coloured skin, and vice versa). The woman's skin is very white except for these differently pigmented bands; she now has short hair, black and smooth. The young man sports an unruly mane, and its copper colour matches almost perfectly the colour of his skin, striped here and there with white bands, particularly on the torso, the genitals, and the fingertips.

The circular stage vanishes. The applause continues for a few minutes more, while the voice of the Announcer names the two artists in the performance that has just been viewed. A few exclamations indicate that their names are familiar to several spectators. For a while, in some alcoves, there's a flurry of speculation about what could have induced the Manager to present a show which is, if memory serves well, already ten years old. The artists have long since gone on to other destinies, and other, more modern, forms of art. The conversations go on this way for a moment, then drift off as various other concerns take over. Some clients get up to leave the establishment. The waiters guide others who have just arrived to vacant alcoves. Some hostesses who are free now begin to circulate among the audience again, while on the stage another attraction—holographic or real, it matters little—begins to draw the attention of possible spectators.

In the alcove on the third level, the man and the woman are also ready to leave. The occupants of the neighbouring table stop them as they go, and speak a few animated words to them in passing, to which they reply with a smile and a nod. Comcodes are exchanged; then the couple continue on its way up the levels to the exit. For an instant, in the doorway, the light catches a copper reflection on the hair of the man, a fragmented sparkling from the woman's lamé dress; then the door closes on them, hiding them from the curiosity of the few other consumers who are perhaps still following with their eyes, unsure, and who will no doubt never have another chance to learn more about their identity.

PICASSO DIVORCE
by MarleneDean

You were sitting across the table from me
when the cracks began to form.
Your face, like broken egg shell,
had hairline fissures criss-crossing your forehead
and plunging downward to your chin.
Perhaps it is my imagination, I thought,
but, even then, the gaps were widening.
It wasn't until pieces of your face
hit the table with light tapping sounds
that I began to panic.
I tried to put them back,
but I was never good at puzzles,
and when in my impatience,
your nose got smashed, I thought,
you could handle it.
After all, armless Venus survived the centuries.
Of course, it's not the same thing, really.
When, at last, I had you reassembled
I noticed your mouth was on your forehead.
I tried looking at you from upside down,
but it was tiresome standing on my head,
and, anyway, one of your eyes was on your left cheek,
and an ear was sliding toward your chin.
There was no right perspective,
though I tried every point of view.
In the end it didn't matter,
because you fell entirely into pieces
which I gathered up and placed in a silk lined cloth bag.
I was very loyal and took you with me
everywhere.
When the others were busy talking
I would take you out and try once again
to put the pieces together.
"Do you think I should have tried it this way?"
I would ask myself, "Or perhaps that?"
When, with the passing of time, the pieces lost their edge
like figures seen through rain drenched windows,

I placed the bag in the back of my closet.
Now, I hardly ever think of you,
but that doesn't mean I didn't love you.
My Dear, I loved you more than life.

It's just that I...
can't remember why.

POETIC LICENCE
Sansoucy Kathenor

"Well," said Juline Forthwith, in a mixture of exasperation and satisfaction, "I finally got the plumber to agree to come immediately." She paused inside the livingroom door, patting into place a hairdo which never dared to be out of place.

Her husband, Hubert Pence, looked up from his sports paper. "Finally? I thought you had the man bribed to come day or night."

Juline frowned. "I have a financial arrangement with him, dear. We don't use the word bribed."

Hubert gave a quick derisive smile. "Your party's still sensitive about that term, is it? Well, then, what happened to your arrangement?"

"It wasn't Ledman who answered the phone, it was his son."

"And your arrangement doesn't extend to him?"

"He's not in the firm; he was just taking the call for his father. What's worse, when he heard my name he mistook me for my sister, the doctor; and he seems to have a grudge against doctors. He took great glee in telling me to give the—er—item in question a couple of plunges and call him in the morning."

"Did you tell him we've got that alien stuck in the toilet?"

"Well, yes, I had to; and after I made it clear I was Forthwith MP, not MD, he agreed to have someone sent out."

"Why you ever agreed to house that Agmendian spiderface, I'll never understand."

"My dear, the prestige! I've told you and told you how hard I had to struggle for the privilege. Only a few hundred Agmendians visit Earth each year. Those who visit Ottawa are mostly diplomats, who live in their official residence. And even among the handful of private citizens who come here, few want to stay in a real Terran home. It was a great catch to get the poet Glagol kan em Essulplais as a guest. And please don't use that dreadful 'spiderface' nickname for the neetics."

"Afraid some reporter has the house bugged?"

"Habit of speech, my dear, has betrayed many a politician before me; I do not intend to get used to that expression. You must realize that nowadays image is everything in politics. The least misstep in public is fatal." She turned away. "I must get back to Glagol. I do wish you would help."

"I gave him a yank, didn't I? Couldn't get him out any more than you could. What was he trying to do, anyway?"

"He said he was feeling the water flow; he wanted to compose a poem to be called 'Terran Water Swirls'—something about beauty found within primitive sanitation devices."

"Good thing for him it was an arm he put in, not his head."

"Even poets have some sense, my dear. I've told the maid to send the plumber up the minute he arrives. I really think you might come, too, and pretend you're concerned. It is one thing to distance yourself from politics, but another to neglect our guest."

"I don't neglect him. I've had lots of long talks with him. He never stops talking! Nothing I can do for him right now, so why should I stand around and wring my hands? Send him down when you get him out, and I'll show him some virteos of waterfalls." Hubert went back to his paper.

*/. *

"The plumber is on his way, Glagol," Juline told her guest. She stood in the doorway of the bathroom, trying simultaneously to address him directly and yet not look into the room, where he hung over a porcelain utility.

Tendrils waving cheerfully, Glagol raised his head from watching water trickle past his wedged arm and gurgle down the drain. He reached up with one of his other arms and pressed the flush lever again. "Most intriguing sensation," he commented.

"You're not too—uncomfortable?" asked Juline anxiously. "I mean, leaning down and all?"

"Often lean to feel things. Stay in lean to meditate," said Glagol with bland unconcern. "Would like soon—what are words?…Could do with snack soon."

"Oh, dear," breathed Juline, praying the plumber would not arrive during the snack. If the story got around of her feeding her house guest while he was stuck in the toilet—what fun the newscasts would have with that! But at least the food was an excuse to leave the distressing scene. "I'll go program a meal. What would you like?"

Glagol considered. "Broccoliburger. Vegetation helps meditation. Include mustard and vicvic sauce," he added.

*/. *

The plumber—Ledman senior had come himself—studied

the situation with ponderous attention. "You're stuck," he announced profoundly.

"True as ringing crystal," agreed Glagol. "Held in chains of porcelain. Ironic water flows in slow freedom past."

Ledman transferred his gaze from the fixture to the Agmendian, surveying his three legs, two-and-a-bit visible arms, and his tendril-fringed face. The plumber pointed to the fringe. "Does that grow like hair?" he asked.

"No road," said Glagol. "Correction: no way." He ran a four-fingered hand over a piece of the fringe then over another area, this one on an arm. "Very fine hair on everywhere." The sides of his flexible lower nose turned up, a neetic smile. "Shed like stookal every spring."

"That so?" murmured the plumber.

"Will you *please* do something!" cried Juline.

"We," said Ledman with dignity, "are cementing interstellar relations. Your party's always telling us how important that is."

"Right off," said Glagol. He considered. "On."

The plumber moved over and peered into the toilet. "They tried pulling with extra muscle?"

"Everyone in house, by one and by many."

"Twisting?"

"Like dancing airpig."

"That another of your native animals?"

"Translation of animal."

"*Please!*" said Juline, taking a step right into the bathroom.

"Have to take the toilet off," decreed Ledman.

"Then *do* it!"

"Have to turn the water off first."

"Ah," said the poet. "Eternal springs cease at behest of— what is general term for species like human and neetic?— sentients? sapients?"

"Got a valve up here?" asked Ledman prosaically. "Don't see any. Last time I saw a bathroom without a shut-off valve was when I worked in a heritage house that nobody had to live in."

"This suite is antique style." Juline was flustered into sounding apologetic. "Quite authentic. Our guests like it; and normally, nothing goes wrong." She turned hurriedly to Glagol. "Not that I'm implying any of this was your fault, of course."

"Always at fault," admitted Glagol cheerfully. "Poets must fill souls with sensation. Water swirl was so satisfying."

"Valves in the basement?" put in Ledman.

"I—I suppose so; I really don't know."

The plumber grunted and tramped out, plodding loudly down the stairs.

"Is there anything I can do to make you more comfortable?—I mean less uncomfortable?" Juline asked Glagol nervously.

"Bring another broccoliburger."

Juline put her hands over her eyes. Burger and plumber would be ready at just about the same time. Well, perhaps Ledman would keep quiet for an additional bri—consideration. She went out to order up another snack and take another tranquilizer.

As she passed her office on the way back, she paused to look at the phone screen there. It was showing the number 17, followed by a flashing 6. Privacy laws prevented the machine from showing her the call-back numbers; the only choice she got when she activated the reply command was to take the priority calls first if she wished. Not that the priority flashing meant much—It usually spoke more of the callers' impatience than of genuine importance.

Were there more calls than usual accumulating this evening? Did she dare to answer any of them? If rumours of the fiasco had leaked out—as somehow they always seemed to—it could be reporters demanding details. But one of the calls could be from the prime minister. More than one, in fact; he was an irascible man. Did she dare leave her evening calls till the next day, as usual? Or was it worthwhile summoning her secretary back, to act as a buffer? Or would that just raise the suspicion that she couldn't handle a domestic crisis by herself?

While she dithered, her hand hovering over the phone, it rang. In startled reflex, she flicked it on. The features of Harriet Quotan, one-time schoolmate but now a dreaded reporter, flashed up on the receiver screen.

"Julie, what's this I hear about your Agmendian getting drowned in a toilet?"

Juline realized with dismay that the transmit-picture switch was on; she couldn't pretend to be her maid and say that Ms. Forthwith was out. She drew a quick breath and put herself on-stage with a deprecating smile. "Utter nonsense, Harriet. Where did you hear such a thing?"

"Can't reveal sources, Julie; you know that. How much

nonsense?"

"Whatever do you mean?"

"I mean, did absolutely nothing happen, or is it just the drowning part that's nonsense? Did Glagol get rescued? And who shoved him in, in the first place?"

"No one shoved him in!"

"He fell in?"

"Of course not. He—ah—" Harriet always knew when she was lying, so she couldn't say nothing at all was wrong, or that Glagol had dropped something into the plumbing…"We had a small malfunction of some of the plumbing in Glagol's suite; the plumber is fixing it now. I suppose it was his son who tipped you off?" She thought grimly, I will have words with Ledman senior over this!—*and* a more inclusive contract.

"No comment. Did Glagol cause the malfunction?"

"Even if he had, it would hardly be a story! And the government will look askance at any attempt to make him look bad—or to suggest that anyone is harassing him, or—or—"

"Or attempting to assassinate him?"

"Harriet! You can't be thinking of broadcasting such a suggestion?"

"Is it true?"

"Of course not!"

"Okay. So far I've got: When expert called in over malfunction of equipment in Agmendian's suite at her residence, Minister denies attempt made on life of her alien guest…"

"Harriet! You wouldn't!"

"Slow news day. Of course, if I had a good leak about the government's intentions in the Yukon matter, I wouldn't have to fill up time with trivia about Glagol…"

"There is no way I am going to tell you anything before the official announcement," said Juline stiffly, making the secret sign she used to tell Harriet that she was surrendering to the pressure. "Why don't you come over tomorrow morning to see for yourself that Glagol is perfectly all right?"

"How about right now?"

"Very well." Juline broke the connection. Harriet would get the whole story from the talkative Glagol anyway, so even if he were not free by the time she came here, it would make little difference. And Harriet would keep her word; once bribed with the Yukon story, she would play down any rumours about

Glagol.

Juline turned away from the demanding messages—Let the prime minister stew, if his was among them; she could explain she had been trying to avoid reporters—and made her way reluctantly back upstairs, carrying the second broccoliburger. At least, she sighed to herself, the matter could be contained. Stories might spread, but nothing had happened *in public*. As long as no one outside the household was affected, no one could demand explanations, or hurt her standing with open laughter or anger. That was the important thing.

With a surge of relief, she heard the plumber's voice as she walked along the hall: "There you are, little fellow. How's your arm feel?"

"Tacks and thorns," said Glagol. "Soon one-A again." With hardly a pause, the alien went on. "You expert on Terran low technology. Tell to me, why this electric appliance made without protection against—"

The lights went out all over the house. And all over the neighbourhood.

MESSENGER
Andrew Weiner

1.

The *Weekly World News* has located Edwin Boone, deep in the Amazon, living in a solar-powered mobile home complete with wet bar, satellite dish and laser cannon. I learned this at the supermarket checkout counter this morning.

Of course, only last month he was spotted in a bowling alley in Taos, New Mexico. And just a few months before that in a New York gay bar, slow-dancing with Elvis.

He gets around, does Edwin. Meets secretly with the President at Camp David, lunches with an Academy-Award-winning actress in Paris, briefs the Pope at a Swedish monastery, attends a rock concert in Peking. Unless it's true that he's hiding out on a tiny South Pacific island, building an army of robots that will take over the world.

Of course, Edwin always was the restless sort. He had schedules, like any man in his position. But periodically he would just take off, leaving a trail of broken appointments behind him, to consult a shaman in Lima or a particle physicist in Pasadena, to take in a play in London or a recording session in Prague. He kept a private jet constantly fuelled against the moments when such an urge would seize him.

Edwin travelled far and wide even when was alive. So it seems only fitting that he should travel further and wider now that he is dead. Even further and wider, perhaps, than we might imagine.

2.

It is hard to believe that Edwin Boone has been dead these past seven years. Officially so, at any rate. For some people, it is impossible to believe.

He is dead, and yet he lives on, at least in our imaginations.

This is my standard line when people ask me if Edwin is really dead—a question I heard a lot in the period following his death, and one that I still hear surprisingly often.

People ask me this because I knew Edwin Boone. Not all that well: I'm not sure that anyone, even Edwin, could make that claim. But as well as most people who claimed to know him.

"He'll never die," I say, in answer to these questions. "Not as long as he holds a place in our imaginations."

He still holds a place in mine. I find myself thinking of him standing in that mushroom patch in the shadow of the radio telescope at Arecibo, babbling on about messages from beyond the stars. Or chewing on a cheeseburger at a Burger King in a suburban strip mall, talking about his plans to maintain agricultural yields in the face of UV damage. "Indoor farming in surplus office buildings. Bring the farms downtown. We'll hire marijuana growers to show us how."

That was our first meeting, the one at Burger King. Arecibo came later. Only then did I realize that Edwin Boone was several tiles short of a full roof. Previously, I had thought him merely eccentric. But by then I was already in far too deep.

3.

I was working on a piece for *Discover* magazine about domestic robotics when the telephone rang.

"You got it wrong," the voice on the telephone said.

"Wrong?"

"About SETI."

My piece on new developments in the Search For Extraterrestial Life had appeared in the Times Magazine the previous Sunday.

"Of course," he said, "everybody does. You did a good job, otherwise."

"Who is this?"

"Edwin Boone."

"Edwin Boone?"

This must, I thought, be some kind of joke. Edwin Boone! The most celebrated American inventor since Edison. Holder of hundreds of patents, including the Boone Vorticular Coil, a source of almost-limitless, almost-free energy that had revolutionized power generation. Head of a vast industrial empire. One of the wealthiest human beings alive. I could think of no reason why Edwin Boone would be calling an obscure freelance science journalist.

"Yes," he said, as if in explanation. "I've always been interested in SETI. You might say that it's where I got my start. Listen, are you doing anything for lunch?"

Of course I jumped at the opportunity to meet him. Even at Burger King, a venue I supposed that he chose for its anonymity. Actually, he liked the food.

Although nearing fifty, Edwin Boone was still boyish in his enthusiasms for junky food and trashy novels and garish music. When I arrived, he was eating a burger with evident enthusiasm, meanwhile reading a book with a spaceship on the cover and listening to his mini-CD player. When he popped out the disc, I saw that it was Metallica. He was dressed in a bright yellow jogging suit. His sparse hair was standing up on end.

And so he told me how I was wrong about SETI, although his objections made very little sense to me.

"You've bought it," he told me. "That whole Big Science party line. The assumption that extraterrestial lifeforms would try to communicate with us through technological means. I mean, if that's the best they can do, screw them."

"The best they can do?"

"Don't you see? It would mean that they're as primitive as us. So who wants to talk to them anyway?"

"But how else would they communicate with us?"

He wiped ketchup from his mouth with a paper napkin.

"You're thinking like a scientist," he said. "That's the whole problem with science journalism. You ought to be keeping us on our toes, not bowing down and kissing them."

"Us?"

"Used to be an astronomer myself. Gave it up a long time ago. But I'm still a scientist, in my own way."

He hadn't answered my question, but at the time I failed to notice. Indeed, I was almost relieved as the conversation moved on to ozone depletion and crop diebacks and indoor farming, to Martian terraforming and DNA enhancement, to trends in global pop music.

He was a fascinating conversationalist, well-informed and lucid, although given to dizzying leaps in logic. But that only was to be expected. The man was a genius, after all. He had to be, to invent something like the Boone Vorticular Coil. Even if he couldn't explain how it worked.

A device to capture geomagnetic energy, that was how he described it on the original patent. But ten years later, scientists were no closer to understanding how it did that, or even if it did that. The Boone Coil produced a rotational field that captured energy, vast quantities of it. But no one knew where it really came from. It was simply "emergent energy", there for the taking.

"The Boone Coil..." I asked him, towards the end of our

lunch. "Where do you think the energy comes from?"

"No idea."

"I find that hard to believe."

"Well okay, sure. Of course I have an idea. But I promised not to say."

"Promised who?"

"My partners."

In launching his invention, Boone had teamed up with a syndicate of electrical utilities. They had given him the legal and financial muscle he needed to fight off the blizzard of restraining orders and environmental impact studies whipped up by the frantic oil and nuclear industries.

"Surely it can't matter now?"

"Perhaps not." He stared at me with his watery blue eyes. "Off the record?"

"Off the record."

"Hyperspace."

I blinked slowly, stupidly. "What?"

"You get the rotational field just so, you open up a gateway to hyperspace. Energy cascades on down from a higher level. Another dimension, most likely. Of course, I can't prove that."

I waited for him to crack a smile. None came.

"Telsa," he said. "I think he was on to the same thing."

"Nicola Telsa? The inventor of alternating current?"

"The same. You know, Telsa figured out how to transmit wireless electricity over 20, 25 miles. We're talking eighty years ago and more. But the oil industry got to him, shut him right down. Poor bastard went mad. Or did he?"

"I don't know," I said. "Did he?"

"Started saying that he got his ideas from angels. Or aliens. But then again, who's to say?"

4.

My lunch with Edwin Boone was worth fifteen hundred words in *New York* magazine: "Munching Whoppers With The New Edison". What I wrote was mostly a personality piece, focussing more on Boone's fondness for fast food, his fabulous wealth, and his views on the arts ("You can't beat a Clint Eastwood western") than on his scientific achievements.

To flesh out the article, I searched through the business data bases. Boone's holdings, the numbered companies and wholly-owned subsidiaries, the joint ventures and limited partnerships and offshore holding companies, were mind-numbing in their complexity. But as I tracked them, I stumbled across a curious pattern. Almost all roads led, eventually, to the same destination, a charitable foundation, the Boone Research Institute. In recent years, a larger and larger share of the profits of Boone's other holdings had been flowing into it.

There were some tax advantages to this arrangement, although fewer than you might expect. Mainly the Institute seemed to exist to spend Boone's money on a bewildering array of projects: software development; Saharan solar farms; a satellite network called UnBabel featuring commercial-free worldbeat music broadcasts; designs for electrically-powered airplanes; computer-enhancement of NASA photographs of anomalous formations on the Martian surface; an investigation of psychotropic plants in the Brazilian rain forest; a long-term psychological study of UFO abductees.

There had been little publicity about this Institute. Neither had Boone mentioned it to me. But this did not stop me speculating about it in my article. Clearly it was close to his heart. By my crude calculations, the Boone Research Institute had spent over ten billion dollars in the past five years.

"*Boone remains close-mouthed about the activities of his foundation,*" I wrote. "*But it seems clear that the man who has already sparked one scientific revolution in his own lifetime is intent on starting another.*"

If this sounds like hagiography, it was. I was in awe of Edwin Boone, and remain so, although perhaps not for the same reasons.

I omitted all mention of his theory about energy from hyperspace. Even if I had not promised him confidentiality on the subject, I would have passed over it. Not only was it preposterous, it made the man sound like a loon, which he clearly was not. Edwin Boone was eccentric, yes. But he was anything but crazy. How could he be, and achieve so much?

How could he be?

5.

My article appeared and disappeared, in the way of all articles. I heard nothing from Edwin Boone. Neither did I expect to.

I ghosted a book on back pain for a fashionable doctor. I took an eco-vacation in Costa Rica with my girl friend and reported on it for a travel magazine. I covered the European space mission. I scripted a show on migraine for PBS. I wrote a brochure for a pharmaceutical company.

And then Edwin Boone called again.

"Leonard?" he said. "Not bad. Although I had the bacon double-cheeseburger, not the Whopper. Artistic license, I suppose."

"You just read the article?"

It was more than a year since it had appeared.

"Just re-read it. Wanted to be sure."

"Sure of what?"

"You doing anything this afternoon? There's something that might interest you. I'll send a driver."

The something-that-might-interest-me turned out to be a recording session in a mid-town studio, featuring a slight young Moroccan woman with a piercing voice. Edwin owned the studio, and the recording company, a small independent label with an eclectic artistic rosta, ranging from electronic music to rap to raga, that had never earned him a cent. That was about to change, thanks to the Moroccan singer, whose professional name was Ayesha, and who would shortly become an international sensation, as well as Edwin Boone's third wife.

"Isn't she fabulous?" he asked, as we watched from behind the glass.

He had met her himself only that morning, having signed her up and flown her to New York on the basis of Arabic music videos. There was as yet nothing between them. But their future was perhaps already apparent in the glances they exchanged through the glass, in his rapturous expression as she sang.

I had little interest in popular music. But I could see that Edwin was on to something here.

"Jajouka-rock," he said. "Next big thing."

I wondered if that was why he had brought me here, to hear this revelation. Perhaps he had mixed me up with some rock critic of his acquaintance. But after sitting through several more takes, he got up suddenly.

"Virtual Death," he said.

Was that the name of a song? A heavy metal band? I stared at him blankly.

"I'm expected over there at three for the try-out. Come on. You can try it, too."

"Try what?"

"Virtual Death."

Boone's driver took us out of the city, towards Connecticut. Along the way Boone worked his way through a bucket of Kentucky Fried Chicken and played industrial-house music from England on the car's sound system at full volume.

"Sounds like the end of the world, doesn't it?" he yelled. "Have you noticed, lately, that so much music sounds like that?"

I had not noticed.

"That's because it is," he shouted.

"Is what?" I screamed back.

"The end, almost." He cranked down the volume a notch and gestured out the car window. "We can feel it. Feel it out there, waiting for us. That big quantum beach where all the waves break, past and future, all the possibilities collapsing into this gigantic singularity at the end of space-time. You follow?"

I shook my head. "Not exactly."

"But what can you do?" It was a rhetorical question. "What can you do except keep on surfing?"

This was, I would realize later, a typical bit of Boone-patter. He would say these things not so much because he believed them (although when he was saying them, no doubt he did believe them), but to try them out, to see how the words fell together, what unexpected new patterns he might produce. It was if he was already in rehearsal for his forthcoming career as a supersalesperson of interstellar apocalypse.

We arrived, eventually, at an anonymous-looking industrial park, drawing up in front of a spartan office building, headquarters of Thanatos Software Inc.

Virtual Death was the first product of Thanatos Software, a firm started with money provided by one of Boone Industries' venture capital funds. *Virtual Death* was a virtual-reality simulation of the near-death experience. Boone offered me the chance to take a test run, but I declined.

"You don't know what you're missing," he told me, as he settled under the hood of a Frankenstein-like apparatus.

Afterwards he raved about the tunnel, the angels, the cities of light.

"Will people really want to buy that?" I asked, as the car headed back to the city.

"Some people, sure," Boone said. He was playing with an *I Ching* program on the car's terminal, and we were surrounded by the sounds of a tinkling waterfall. "That's not exactly the point."

"What is the point?"

"To check it out," he said. "To check it all out. Death, drugs, UFO experiences. To find the pipeline." He leaned forward, grunted with satisfaction. "'Approaching Spring'. That's good. That's real good."

"What pipeline?"

But he was already intent on following his moving lines into the next hexagram.

7.

It was late afternoon when we arrived at our final destination for the day, Boone's private office at the local branch of Boone Industries.

Edwin Boone's head offices were in Los Angeles. I doubt that he set foot in his New York office more than twice a year. And still, it was spectacular: a miniature Japanese garden with waterfall under a domed skylight, a huge Henry Moore sculpture, a breathtaking art collection.

"Props," Boone said, as he saw me staring at a famous Mondrian painting. "But pretty ones, aren't they?"

"Props?"

"It's all props," he said. He gestured, as though to take in his office, the entire building. "All stagecraft. You want people to take you seriously, you've got to operate in the real world, like a real business."

"How do you mean, 'like a real business'? Boone Industries *is* a real business."

"The only *real* business is the Institute. The rest is just window-dressing. Most people think the Institute is some kind of scam, but actually it's the other way around. The Institute is what it's really about. It's time to make that clear."

"Should I be taking notes?" I asked.

"Yes. But not yet."

"You want me to write another article?"

"I want to write a book, Len. A book wants to write me. I want to tell the whole story. Lay it all out. No punches pulled. So, are you in? Will you write my book for me?"

"Why?"

"Because I can't write."

"No. I mean, why me?"

"Oh, I don't know. Maybe you remind me a little of me, the

way I used to be. Rational, scientific, uptight...aaagh! Point is, I need someone like you, for balance. To hold me back a little. Stop me shooting right off the edge of the world."

8.

Contracts were drawn up, schedules coordinated. A month later a car came to take me to the airport, where I embarked on Edwin Boone's private jet. I brought with me two portable recorders, and several hundred hours of tape.

Edwin was sitting upfront with the pilot, discussing the flight plan.

"Puerto Rico?" I asked. "I thought we were heading for St. Lucia."

The plan was for us to spend two weeks at Edwin's vacation complex, taping his recollections.

"Afterwards," he said. "There's something I want you to see."

He wanted me to see the radio telescope at Arecibo, the world's largest. I had read about it, but never seen it.

"Here," he said, as we got out of the limo and gazed up at the giant dish, "is where it all began."

"What began?"

"People will think I'm crazy when they read this. But then, they already do." He cackled with glee. "Either that, or they think I'm some kind of genius. But the truth is I'm acting under instructions."

"Instructions?"

"I used to work here," he said. "I was an astronomer, just graduated. I was working on SETI. But I was working on it the wrong way."

"The wrong way?"

"With machines, Len. And search protocols. And statistical analyses. I was like a machine myself. Chewing up the data and spitting it out. I didn't drink, didn't have a girlfriend, didn't do anything except work. Every day I would come here and not even see the mushrooms."

"Mushrooms?"

"In the field," he said. "Right in the shadow of the telescope."

He led me out into the field, where cows grazed, regarding us incuriously. "Watch your step," he warned, just as I trod on a cow pat.

"Yuck," I said, trying to clean my shoe on the grass.

TESSERACTS[5]　　　　📖79

"Don't knock it," Edwin told me. "No manure, no mushrooms. Ah, there…" Triumphantly, he reached down and plucked a mushroom from the ground, and cradled it in his hand. "*Psilocybe cubensis*."

"I'm sorry?" Botany had never been one of my strengths.

"A psilocybin mushroom," he said, patiently. "What some people call a magic mushroom."

He held out the mushroom to me. I took it and examined it. It smelled of cow dung.

"One day I saw them, finally," he said. "I had been working an all-nighter, trying to track a signal from Tau Ceti that turned out to be another artifact, and I came out at dawn for some air. I was exhausted, I was sick up-to-here with SETI, I didn't believe it could work anymore, that there was anyone out there talking to us, I was ready to give up the whole thing and go home. And I saw the mushrooms growing in the field. And I plucked one. And…I chewed it."

"You knew it was a psilocybin mushroom?"

"I didn't know shit about drugs. But it seemed like the thing to do. It was like it said to me, *Eat me*."

"Wasn't that dangerous? I mean, it could have been poisonous."

"Oh, it was dangerous all right. But somehow I knew that it wouldn't kill me. That it would make me stronger…"

I looked in dismay from the mushroom in my hand to Edwin Boone and back to the mushroom.

"People ask me where I get my ideas," he said. "*This* is where I got them. The Boone Coil first, and then all the others."

"From the mushroom?"

"Don't think of it as a mushroom. Think of it more as an organic galactic radio."

Think of it as an organic galactic radio. This was, surely, my cue to make a rapid exit. Later, I would wonder why I did not choose that moment to flee. Instead I stood there frozen, open-mouthed.

"Very interesting chemical structure, psilocybin. Becomes psilocin when it enters the body, which is 4 hydroxy dimethyltryptamine. It's the only 4-substituted indole in organic nature. You find it in these mushrooms and about another eighty types of fungi. Except I don't think it's organic at all. I think it's designed. Some kind of virus program seeded into the genome."

"Seeded by who?"

"By our friends. Our alien friends."

9.

"To end our alienation," Boone was saying, "we have to become the alien. Reconnect with our unconscious collectivity as a species, and through that, with the universal mind."

We were walking along the cliffs at his St. Lucia retreat, the same cliffs from which he would later plummet to his death. I wasn't really listening. Boone had been talking to me for four days now. Or rather, talking at me, morning, noon and night, with occasional breaks for food and sleep. I couldn't listen any more. I didn't need to listen, since I was getting it all down on tape. But I would have to listen to it when I attempted to get it down on paper, a prospect I regarded with increasing dread.

The sunset had come and gone, and it was growing dark. I realized that Boone had stopped talking. He was staring up into the sky.

"Look," he said.

I saw a faint flashing light. "At that airplane, you mean?"

We could hear the engine, now, as the plane began its descent.

"Airplane? Oh, so it is." He sounded disappointed.

"What were you expecting? A flying saucer?"

He didn't laugh at my joke.

"You see things in the sky here. Lights that are not airplanes. Strange lights. Apparently there have been more than ever since I built this house. Or so the locals say."

"And why would that be, Edwin?"

"Because they're watching me, I guess. Waiting for me. And one day they will come for me. When my work here is over."

I shook my head slightly.

Edwin Boone had been eating magic mushrooms almost every day of his adult life, even while building his business empire. Or so he had told me, and I had no reason to doubt it. For years his head had been buzzing with every crazy idea known to humanity, and a few he had invented himself. Now, he was at last ready to unleash those ideas on the world. And I was his chosen conduit.

Should I have been surprised that he was expecting to take a ride on a UFO? By now, nothing he said could surprise me.

"Coming for you," I said. "In a spaceship, you mean?"

He waved his hand dismissively. "Nothing so crude, so mechanical...Although if you had a crude mechanical mind, I suppose it might appear to you as a spaceship."

10.

Edwin dropped me off in New York on his way to Houston. He was going to lobby NASA for more detailed study of the Martian landscape at Cydonia—the location of the so-called "Face on Mars"—in the next Mars Observer mission. I went home to work on the first draft of his book.

I faced a difficult task. I did not believe that psilocybin mushrooms had been seeded on Earth by friendly aliens. I did not believe that it was possible to gain cosmic wisdom by chewing them. I did not believe that energy could be sucked up from hyperspace. I did not believe that there was a face on Mars. I did not believe in UFOs. I did not believe in hundreds of things. But I did believe, somehow, in Edwin Boone.

He was an extraordinary man whose story needed to be told. But told in a sober, balanced way, one that would enhance his stature rather than invite unnecessary ridicule.

The book I wrote traced the story of his life, from dreamy backyard astronomer to struggling inventor to industrial tycoon. It dealt, although briefly and delicately, with his experiences with psilocybin mushrooms. It included moderate doses of his personal philosophy. It described the work of the Boone Research Institute as one of "preparing humanity for contact with the stars", without going into excessive detail into some of its more bizarre projects.

The book was well-balanced, readable, a reasonably faithful portrait of a fascinating individual.

Edwin hated it.

"This isn't me," he told me, whacking the manuscript with the palm of his hand.

We were having a drink in the study of his house in Malibu. Edwin was wearing a white tuxedo. He was about to be married to Ayesha. The wedding would take place in the grounds of his estate. He had tried to get Timothy Leary or Terence McKenna to perform the ceremony, but both had previous engagements, so he had settled for a local Wiccan priestess. The Grateful Dead would play at the reception.

"I don't recognize this person at all," he said, delivering a final blow to the manuscript that sent the upper pages flying across the room. "I mean, who is it? Gary Cooper? Jimmy

Stewart? It sure isn't me."

I had never seen him so angry. In fact, I had never seen him angry at all.

"I'm no *hero*," he said. "I'm no *genius*. I've told you that a thousand times. I'm a messenger boy, Len. And I've got to get my message through."

"I thought that was what you wanted from me. Something balanced."

"Balanced, maybe. Not buried in bullshit. Tell the story, Len. Tell the whole story."

11.

I wrote it the way he wanted it.

According to our contract, I was to get a 'with Leonard Shine' credit on the book, along with half the royalties. I thought about taking my name off it. The book would do me no good at all among the scientists I would need to interview for future assignments, if they were to read it. But my guess was that almost no one would want to read it. Besides, it was my work, for better or worse. I left my name on the book.

My guess was wrong. The hard-cover printing of *Destiny: The Edwin Boone Story* quickly sold out, mainly to business people anxious to fathom the mind of Edwin Boone. The paperback was bought by millions, and read and discussed everywhere. There were not too many multi-billionaires with pop star wives who talked openly of communicating with aliens. It was, to put it mildly, a sensation.

The movie version of *Destiny* ended with Edwin's meeting with aliens, and his ascent to the stars. It was the summer blockbuster of the year.

I was offered the opportunity to do the novelization of the movie, but turned it down. Fiction had no appeal for me. And, following the success of Edwin's book, I had found a new career as a ghost-writer of celebrity autobiographies. Some of my clients were quite interesting, although none were so interesting as Edwin Boone. Fortunately.

12.

I did not see Edwin for several years, although we talked on the phone from time to time, and I followed his progress from afar. He had largely withdrawn from his business activities to concentrate on his Institute, which bankrolled bigger and ever-more-harebrained sounding projects. Biggest and most harebrained of all was the design of an interstellar spaceship to be powered by the Boone Coil.

He had also become a fixture on the lecture circuit, preaching his gospel of alien contact around the world, simultaneously revered and reviled. He was scorned by intellectuals ("*a cosmic Ross Perot, an extroverted Howard Hughes, a new age loon*" read one of his more favourable notices), adored by people who read supermarket tabloids. Ayesha often accompanied him on these tours, opening the shows with her unearthly music.

Edwin's message was sometimes contradictory, but ultimately consistent. Sometimes the alien would come to visit us, and sometimes we would go to them. Sometimes we would see them in visions, and sometimes in death. Sometimes they would appear to us as angels and sometimes as elves and sometimes as little grey men. But one way or another, we would meet them. And when we did, it would be the end of the world, at least in one sense, and perhaps in every sense.

And then one day he called. "I need a favour," he said.

He was re-working his will. He wanted to name me as a co-executor with Ayesha, with special responsibility for continuing the work of the Boone Research Institute.

"Are you sick, Edwin?"

"Never felt better."

"Then why a new will?"

"Just getting prepared."

"Prepared for what?"

"All contingencies," he said. "So, will you do it?"

"Look after your Institute? Get humanity ready for contact with the stars? But I don't believe all that. I don't believe any of it."

"You believed in it when you wrote the book."

"No, I didn't. Not for a moment."

"I'm not so sure. But belief isn't a requirement. Just honesty. And friendship."

I sighed. "All right, Edwin," I said. "I'll help run your Institute."

13.

Edwin sent a car and a plane to get me to St. Lucia, where he was holed up with a squadron of lawyers, drawing up the necessary paperwork.

I was a beneficiary of Edwin Boone's will, to the tune of two million dollars. Ayesha would get a hundred million dollars. There were various other bequests. But the vast bulk of the estate would go to the Boone Research Institute.

Both Ayesha and I were made aware of these provisions. Both of us would briefly be suspects, following his death. Both of us had alibis.

The papers were duly signed and notarized, and the lawyers departed. Ayesha left with them, on her way to meet a concert commitment in Cairo. I stayed on, to work on the preface to the new edition of Destiny, scheduled for the fall.

In fact we got little work done. Edwin seemed restless, preoccupied, jumpy.

"Write it any way you want it," he said, after a fruitless session. "Just send it to the publisher. I don't need to see it."

"But it's your book, Edwin. How am I supposed to know what you want to say?"

"It will come to you."

He got up and crossed to the window, stared out at the night sky.

"It's going to be soon," he said.

"What's going to be soon?"

"You know exactly what I mean."

14.

Edwin seemed in better spirits the next day. We played tennis, sailed in his boat. After dinner, we watched a batch of Ayesha's new videos. Then Louie, Edwin's personal chef, tuned the satellite dish to the BBC World Service, to pick up the play at Wimbledon. Sandra, Edwin's administrative assistant, joined us. We watched together for awhile. Then Edwin stood up.

"I'm going out for a walk," he said.

A warm breeze blew in as he opened the glass door to the patio. We watched him stroll out into the Caribbean night, and it seemed to me that he glanced up, briefly, into the sky before walking on towards the cliffs. Then I looked back to the game.

He never returned.

Later we searched for him, searched every inch of the house and grounds. Then the local police did the same. But no trace of Edwin could be found anywhere, excepting only for his golfing hat, which washed up on the beach the next day. He had not been wearing the hat when he left the house, but perhaps it had been in his pocket. Louie thought so, although Sandra was not so sure.

In the end, they put it down as an accident, although there were many found it hard to believe that he could simply have slipped and fallen off the cliff edge he had walked so surely in the past. It was too flat an explanation, too banal. Edwin Boone was a genius, a self-made billionaire, a celebrated crank, a certified media superstar, one of the most fabulous human beings alive. He deserved a better death.

There were whispers about suicide, although it was hard to imagine why Edwin Boone would take his own life. He was in apparent good health, his many businesses were booming, he was a continuing fount of new ideas and new projects. It was true that, close to the end, he made remarks to his immediate associates about it being "time to move on", to "find new worlds", to "kick it up to the next level". But these remarks were so vague as to lend themselves to a variety of interpretations.

There was talk of kidnapping, too, and at first the federal agents gave this theory some credence. But Edwin's compound was well-defended, there were no signs of forced entry, and no ransom note ever materialized.

Some believed that he had been murdered, by business rivals or foreign governments, radical groups or the CIA, satanists or evangelists, vast conspiracies or crazed lone assassins. There was no shortage of people who might have wanted Edwin dead. But again, there was no evidence of foul play.

And some believed that he had not died at all, that he had faked his own death. He had done so to escape the pressures of his work, to research a cure for cancer, to join a monastic order, to plot the overthrow of the U.S. government, or to join his alien friends, as foreshadowed in the movie of his life.

For these people, Edwin lives on still, at least in their imaginations. And perhaps even beyond them.

15.

I was interrogated intensively by local police, then by federal agents. I answered the questions as honestly as I could, up to a certain point, and the story I told was consistent with the testimony of Louie and Sandra.

Probably they were too intent on watching the game to see the strange light that flickered briefly through the glass of the patio door, about an hour after Edwin had left us. Or else, like me, they preferred to keep quiet about it.

There was a light in the sky, and I glanced up, and I heard…what? A beating of wings, or perhaps, just possibly, the whirring of helicopter blades. And then the light was gone, and the sound with it, and I looked back to the TV.

At the time I thought nothing of it. Afterwards I decided not to talk about it. It would not do me or Edwin any good.

16.

After a suitable interval, Edwin was declared officially dead. The will was probated, and I took up my new duties as director of the Boone Research Institute.

It's interesting work. The space drive is coming along surprisingly well, and according to new data, there really does seem to be a face on Mars. *Virtual Death* has been joined on the software sales charts by *Virtual Abduction—The UFO Experience*. The Brazilian rain forest scan has turned up a half dozen exciting new pharmaceuticals, and we're all thrilled about the success of the UnBabel network.

Ayesha was very supportive of the work, taking on some of the promotional chores once handled by Edwin, sitting through endless dull directors' meetings, advising me on what Edwin would have done, helping me get through the first few difficult years. I have missed her greatly since her disappearance, from her boat anchored off Athens. The cause of her death remains a mystery to this day, and there are those who like to believe that she went to join Edwin. But that is another story, and one told frequently enough elsewhere.

17.

Edwin called me a week ago. At least, I believed that it was Edwin at the time, although I have since had second thoughts.

"You're doing a terrific job," he said, without preamble. "Just gangbusters. But I knew you would come through."

It was a bad connection, crackly and distant-sounding, but I recognized the voice immediately.

"Edwin? Is that you?"

"Absolutely."

"Where are you? Where have you been?"

"It's fabulous," he said. "It's everything I dreamed, and more."

"What's fabulous?"

"Ayesha sends her love. We're both looking forward to seeing you."

"Seeing me?"

"When the time comes."

"You're going to send a car?"

"Better than a car."

"No," I said. "I don't think I'm ready for that."

"But you will be."

"When the time comes."

"Exactly."

There was a loud burst of static on the line, and then the connection went dead.

Was it really Edwin? I could have sworn that it was. But later, in the cold light of day, my doubts returned. It was a very bad connection. It could well have been a hoax. Or a product of my own imagination. That would be the most logical explanation, certainly.

And yet, when I walk home from the Institute at night, I find myself glancing up into the sky. And listening, sometimes, for the beating of wings.

"RSVP"
Cliff Burns

Olivia Hamilton, looking simply *ravishing* in her designer face, drifted through the assembled guests trailing grey plumes of cigarette smoke. No one had the audacity to protest or even to flutter their hands in an enfeebled response to the carcinogenic pall left in her wake.

Her cigarettes were unfiltered; they bronzed her fingertips and soured her breath and when she laughed—a rare occurrence—her teeth were as yellow as old ivory. Her amusing addiction was the subject of heated debate among the pop psychologists present—it was so wonderfully atavistic. But these speculations were invariably as shallow and deftless as the theorists themselves. What was left unsaid was that she smoked because she was Olivia Hamilton. She was Olivia Hamilton because she smoked.

Mr. Goebbels (no relation) waved to her from his wheelchair and she made her way to his side, bending slightly in deference to his condition.

"You look vondervul, dahlingk." She patted his thick fingers as he drooled onto a bib made of human skin.

The attention of the company was drawn outside as a basso profundo thrum from overhead announced a late arrival.

"That's a Ptero," said a boor to a nearby floorlamp. "Ford body, Nintendo guts. Must be a prototype, they aren't due to go into production—" And so on.

The craft settled onto the flagstones in the courtyard, shuddering as its driver cut power. Olivia clapped her hands once, for her a gesture of great pleasure. A gull-winged door gasped open, revealing a dapper bloke in an old style suit, authentic right down to the zippered fly.

"Smythe," she breathed, sashaying through the open doors to stand on the deck, throwing open her arms in welcome. Tongues wagged as they did their Rhett-Scarlett thing and grainy holos of the embrace later made the society pages on every continent. A sharp-eyed few saw him slip something into her hand which she examined with minute care. A bauble of some sort, no doubt rare and indisputably *chic*. Olivia cast it into the garden with the other curios she had collected and the two of them entered arm-in-arm.

Now that he had paid the price of admission, Smythe was fêted like a pharaoh, circulating through the crowd with servants in tow, muscle-bound brutes branded with Olivia's personal seal, her every whim their command. Three of them had already perished and the night was still young.

Goebbels twitched and spasmed in his chair but none paid him any mind. He was always choking on something and the olive lodged in his windpipe would either kill him or it wouldn't.

The strains of martial music instilled an air of gloom. They toasted dreariness and dashed their glasses in a gesture of defiant decadence.

Russian roulette was the game of choice and soon the loose-piled carpet was soaked with blood and jellied bits of brain matter snail-tracked down the walls.

"It's terribly *close* in here, isn't it? I can hardly catch my breath."

"Well, if you say anything she'll just tell you the enviro's on the blink. And I saw her turn it off myself."

"She must like the stink of sweat."

"Just be glad she has the UV screens up."

"Amen to that."

"She really is a most remarkable host. Sorry. Host*ess*."

"The tits look real, don't they?"

"Don't look too close, she might—"

"Boy! *Boy*! Don't just stand there bleeding! Fetch us another round, you wog—"

I wasn't there but I heard they rolled poor old Goebbels up to the edge of the pool and tipped him in. He sank like a stone, of course, those Nazi bastards are top-heavy with ideology. Someone made a crude comment about multinationals and Smythe broke his jaw with one expert flick of his foot. Tito Placebo Domingo, whom some called a dictator but who told the most *marvellous* stories, swooned in the foyer and raved about conspirators and lackeys of foreign powers as he pulled down a bust of Hadrian and lay in the detritus snoring while men sporting Raybans and stony expressions surrounded him. A British diplomat was discovered substituting blank cartridges for hollow points and was ceremonially disembowelled for his treachery. A woman from the Punjab did the honours and wept at her good fortune.

Olivia Hamilton tapped certain people on the shoulder and at her signal these lucky few separated themselves from the others, fending off resentful glares. They followed her to the library which was devoid of books save one slim volume of Baudelaire, perched up high on a shelf where only a giraffe could devour its contents.

Cognac was the drink of choice and Olivia produced a cheroot, puffing for effect. Smythe rolled up his sleeves, winked slyly and with a dramatic flourish plucked out of thin air, in succession: the Hope diamond, a dripping deck chair from the Titanic, Napoleon's withered penis and a child's tricycle—the latter claimed by a shaken State Department official who identified it as his own, pointing out the initials scratched on its bent fender.

"The world as we know it is coming to an end," Olivia announced without fanfare; "difficult decisions must be made." The voice cue killed the lights; the library was black as pitch. "Only the few can survive, those who as Darwin states—" But the battle was already on, clawed fingers and bared teeth and rent flesh.

Smythe had donned an infrared visor and led her confidently to one wall where a secret panel was revealed. The passage led out onto a secluded corner of the garden and when they emerged they found themselves alone and finally able to give vent to their desire. Olivia drew Smythe to her and they coupled, her bare back pressed against a statue, the two of them clutching at the cold marble for leverage. She wriggled her hips in what Smythe assumed was a provocative manner but he soon learned otherwise as something stung his shaft and he died inside her without so much as a celebratory spurt.

She cast off her identity and grew a new one. Now she was a man, Blake Turnbull-Jones, who'd made his fortune in realty. Turnbull-Jones commandeered Smythe's craft and after taking off swept over the compound at rooftop level, releasing toxic agents which transformed the merry-makers below into Paleozoic trilobites. Not to worry, in a few hundred million years they'd be as right as rain.

※ ※

The task now fell to me, the latest in a long line of biographers to earn the assignment by default. I sifted through Smythe's notes and tapes, attempting to gain some insights into the all-too-brief life of Olivia Hamilton, heiress, debutante and one-time presidential candidate. In my hands it became a racy tale of greed and opportunism with flashes of dark humor. Most of it was impossible to substantiate—the trilobites, as I feared, were completely uncommunicative, so I pieced together what I could from suppressed intelligence reports and data gleaned from reconnaisance satellites. The resulting manuscript was a shambles and the publisher, quite rightly, accepted it and rewarded me with a twelve-figure advance.

I bought a house from Blake Turnbull-Jones complete with aviary, tennis courts and mass graves. The terms were equitable and thanks to a little graft the quarantine period was reduced considerably. When it rains the ground pukes blood and when the wind is just right the smell of decomposition is quite bracing.

Ensconced in my study I work on my memoirs and keep up an active correspondence with friends and associates. When the time is right I announce plans for a grand soirée and compose a lengthy guest list.

Within days a missive from Blake Turnbull-Jones arrives, expressing his regrets that he cannot attend as he is not himself.

"Who is?" I mutter and with poison pen scratch out an immediate and appropriate reply.

THE PARADIGM MACHINE

Jean-Louis Trudel

Oh, I sing the Mind reconstructed!

Can you believe the story started in Ontario? But Edward sometimes called Eddie knew a girl in a face-stealing outfit down in a rather grungy area of Guelph, on the outskirts of the only urbarea in the province. And after that Virtuality redesign he'd done for the retirement home of Québec presidents on the shores of Meech Lake, he was in need of a new face. But seeing Nadia again would be nice too.

Coming down from the Gatineau arcology to the Toronto-Kingston strip city, Edward kept his aircar speeding just above the tip of the trees. The fir needles would shake in his wake, and sometimes drop in showers of green tickertape upon the cottagers beneath the trees. But he was going too fast for a visual identification, and he'd shut off his transponder. He intended to slip into the urbarea under the radars, taking advantage of the low radar cross section of the faceted fuselage.

He got only brief glimpses of the tidily preserved lots of wilderness he was passing over. Most of the time he spent plugged into Virtuality. Racing with the laser impulses from satellite to satellite, from ground relay to optical fiber, from optical fiber into optoelectronic circuitry...Weaving a web around the world, he could let the car pilot itself. He preferred to stay in a reconstituted Prague cellar of the turn of the century, listening to the voice of an Egyptian rai-diva and quaffing Czech beer.

It was when he started to cough that he unplugged. Reluctantly.

The body asserted itself, and he bent over from a new fit of coughing. His throat felt like a gravel road. And hurt just the slightest bit.

"Car," he whispered softly. "Find me the nearest general store."

The vehicle swerved, and suddenly it was no longer flying over the patches of preserved forest, but over soja and corn fields. Edward finished unwiring himself and stretched slowly. He'd forgotten to switch on the small feed line that normally washed his throat with an intermittent trickle of water. In full

VR mode, his real body did not impinge on the virtual one. Now, his throat was dry, and he wondered if rhinoviruses were already starting to multiply.

The car landed on a stretch of old asphalt outside a store that looked like Russian prefab airdropped from an Antonov, this one having kissed the ground just a bit too hard: one corner was higher than the other, and the walls were not quite square...

Edward slid his identicard through the recognition slot and the door opened slowly. He noticed without smiling that the owner did not relinquish the shotgun he held, just lowered it out of sight, left hand curled around the butt. Ambidextrous. The man was old, his white skin insanely freckled, the sandy hair still thick.

The Virtuality hacker nodded, and walked to the cooler, retrieving a jug of milk. He came back to the counter and presented his credit bracelet with a flourish. The man looked at him, and said with a chuckle:

"That's white milk, sonny. Sure you don't want some of that brown stuff? Chocolate milk would be just right for you."

Fuck off! But that was not what he said, quite coldly:

"No thanks."

He let the owner tap into his credit bracelet, though he felt sullied even by the touch of the light-wand. Then he walked out.

That general store wouldn't see him again.

He took the commands of the aircar, and shut off the whining of the vehicle's personality unit. The take-off jets swirled the accumulated dust into the window panes of the store. And then Eddie screeched off into the sunset.

He was keeping his fingers away from the missile panel. That solution was too easy. And too much trouble, even if he managed to get a stolen face by next morning. Eddie let his anger cool off in the wind, as if he could communicate the white heat within himself to the aircar's shell, there to be carried away by the flow of air...If he was so furious, it was in part because he had not thought immediately of what to do. He'd been too long in Europe. He'd forgotten the snappy comebacks that were needed at such times.

He'd forgotten, for paradigms were different over there...

Forty kilometres outside the municipality, he landed his aircar on an outcropping of Precambrian rock. For what he was planning to do, he would not be able to afford distractions.

This time, he forgot none of the leads, until he lay in his chair encased in wiring like a spider's prey. He would go deep, he would go far into Virtuality.

When he closed/opened his eyes, Eddie stood at the door of a building that looked like a gaudy log cabin. He shook his head. The clichés, oh the clichés of deepest, small-town Ontario...His hand melted into the door's lock and explored the circuitry. A few hidden alarms, a nasty marker virus for intruders ignoring the lock, and a firewall. Nothing major...

He did not try to enter the building. The tailored environments where the local Net users congregated to shop, read the news, watch sports or socialize did not interest him. Instead, he stepped into the door and phased into its fabric...

Menus glowed before him in the darkness, and he flew towards them in his batform.

Breaking into the municipality's local Net provider was only the first step. Some of the cyphers were old, broken long ago, but still used in this part of the province since there was no data of real value to access. For him, cracking the codes was only a matter of riffling through some of his most secret files, where he kept the keys bought from fellow hackers.

And then he was inside. Eddie flashed in past the inactivated robot programs and homed towards the programming elements for the VR shell. The modules were old, but he'd learned to manipulate them during his school days. And they were perfect for his purposes.

People often forgot that the world they sensed around them was in fact deep inside their head. The images came through the retina, the sounds through the cochlea, the smells through the olfactory hairs inside the nose. But the world was then built inside the brain: visual cortex, olfactory bulb, auditory cortex. People did not move across a room, they moved across its representation inside. To create Virtuality, it was necessary to override the usual inputs and feed the brain with false data.

However, Eddie thought as he reworked the visual module, there was then no way of distinguishing between what was true and what was not. The brain itself had no direct grasp of any reality, except that of blood flow and of the chemicals within it...

Once he finished, the townspeople would be colour-blind. And they wouldn't notice it for the longest time! It was a simple matter, really. All he had to do was create a perceptual blank in the matrix where skin colour was usually stored. A mere gap in the sensorium would never be picked up—just like no-one saw one's blind spot. The users would simply be unable to recall the skin colour of a newcomer, just like people could forget the colour of an acquaintance's hair or eyes. People would eventually twig to his kludge, but who knew what strange new habits of thought might have been formed by then. Skin colour would have disappeared from the personal equations they applied to the evening news, to strangers met in Virtuality. New associations would have been forged.

Their paradigms would have changed.

When he finished, he withdrew slowly. It would not do to have his intrusion discovered now. He slowly emerged from the building's wall, oozing the bits of his individuality through the cracks in the security system.

He ordered: "Car, resume previous path."

As he reclined, he thought that the general store might see him again, after all...

Write, write on the flowing electrons

Can you believe the story started again in Ontario? But the heart of Toronto was something very different from what was usually understood by Ontario. And where Derrick was, shards of the world dissolving in his mind, was not quite Toronto. There were voices in that darkness, and Derrick listened to them since there was nothing better to compel his attention.

"Writing was the first virtual reality."

"Really? What about the hallucinogen-induced dreams of native shamans?"

"Those were hardly consensual. With writing, people learned how to map one reality onto the symbols of another."

In the darkness, a flapping of wings. Then a feathery glide. Derrick felt the claws of his crow dig into the naked flesh of his shoulders. A susurrus filled the dark:

"Incipient flame war in Forum 17-12-93."

He pulled away from his present locus, losing the thread of the two voices arguing with the speed of relayed light bouncing through crystalline tunnels. He struggled to flesh-remember what was going on near the incriminated locus. The 93rd floor was the German domain, and the 17th avenue was in the arts talk neighbourhood. Wire-remembering that the 12th street was classic literature, he whistled soundlessly: classic German literature was as unlikely a fuel for a flame war as any.

He materialized in a room filled with people. It was large, as cozy as a living-room of long ago, and it had more nooks and corners than was possible in any geometry of Reality. He strode to a free armchair, and picked up the book lying on a table beside it. He turned to the last few pages and read with growing dismay:

No German writer ever made the slightest worthwhile contribution to world literature. The only work that even comes close to being a great book is Mann's Doctor Faustus, and it draws most of its power from the millions of bodies piled up by the Reich in the charnel-houses of Oswiecin. Just what you would expect from such a bloodthirsty breed.— Jude the Obscure.

He checked the on-line German dictionary and it confirmed his suspicions. "Jude" was the German word for Jew. So this could easily degenerate in an anti-Semitism flame war, with Palestinians, Arabs, Turks, Bosnian Muslims, and Israelis all jumping in. A grim prospect.

He whistled soundlessly a few notes, and the events of the last couple of hours replayed in his mind. He saw people enter the room, back first, and others leave, striding backwards. An alarm chimed with every message entered, and he would then check which had just appeared in the omnipresent book. Until he spotted the guilty party...

A tall man with pale skin and an epicanthic fold. He'd just scribbled something in a book left on the commode nearest the entrance, and was backing up towards the door to Reality. Derrick downloaded instantly the image captured by the Net-sensors. It might be useful, but the face was too distinctive. Ten to one that it had been bought from a face-stealer. The recognition strings hidden in the graphic interface would point to some hick from Estonia or Nepal whose virtual shell had been hijacked a few days ago...

He closed his eyes and composed his thoughts. Time for some strategic thinking. He was a portal-keeper of the Net. A trained writer and skilled rhetorician, he could play the role of peacemaker and peacekeeper in five languages by choking off flame wars before they got in earnest.

He wrote in a quick message pointing out that the use of a pseudonym like "Jude the Obscure" betrayed the author's intent to provoke, and that incendiary responses could only be the work of fools falling into the trap set for them.

Drawing on his knowledge of German literature, he added a

second message, using a pseudonym of his own, which stood for a Net-persona of recognized reasonableness and erudition. This was a balanced discussion of the merits of German literature, aimed at those who would take the barb seriously but could be dissuaded from intemperate action by contrary evidence. He invoked the names of Goethe, Günter Grass, and Hermann Hesse, snidely slipping in the suggestion that Hesse was superior to Mann in order to divert some of the responses into a debate over the comparative merits of Hesse and Mann.

A third message was a quick note, under an assumed name that he used only rarely so that the Net-persona could appear detached from the usual Net-debates. It revealed that *Jude the Obscure* was the title of a forgotten nineteenth-century novel, thus clinching the hypothesis of intentional manipulation.

For a while, Derrick contemplated creating a new Net-persona, that of a Jew who could argue with authority that the Holocaust did not define all of German history before and after it. He decided against it. Ethically, it was questionable, and he was still hoping that he'd acted promptly enough to squelch the incipient flame-war.

The next few messages he sampled seemed to bear him out, and he relaxed. As he did so, he grew conscious of a discreet buzzing in his ears, indicating that his shift was over.

When Derrick unplugged—optical socket, nose apertures, eye/ear inputs and blood monitors—the odours of downtown Toronto in the summer assailed him. He had placed the interface chair near an open window to take advantage of the slight breeze. His body was rank with the stench of eight hours of sweat, but it could not overpower the armpit fragrance of Toronto streets ripened by August sunshine. The fumes from rotting refuse wafted through the opening.

He pulled down a blind over the window and its depressingly unchanging view of a dusty lane lined with garages converted into granny flats and sleepdens, overlooked by old brick house bulging with add-ons to increase living space for a population that increased ever faster.

He tore off the white coverall. The skin on his shoulder bore faint purplish marks where his crow's claws had dug into it...In Virtuality, at least. But, even in Reality, his brain could transmit instructions to his body based on virtual happenings. And the body responded. Patches of ancient varnish speckling the wooden floor stuck to his feet as he shuffled to the washroom, moving slowly to avoid jostling his bloated bladder.

As the yellow-tinged stream grew a puddle on the porcelain shelf of the new German-style flushers, Derrick counted up the money owing for his overtime. Would it be enough to rent an electricar for the weekend and get out of town?

Or would it be better to put aside the money for that long-awaited upgrade to his interface? Every time he redefined squalor by leaving the Net, he was acutely aware that he belonged to the underclass of the virtual world.

What he had was a government sinecure for the literate. Make work for the unemployable. This was what his diplomas in comparative lit had gotten him, while business types who did not know Soyinka from Amado got into the high end of Virtuality, dealing in fully audiovisual environments, purveying mindless entertainments for the teleproles accessing the ever growing archives of soap operas, filmed rapes and lethal game shows. That was where the money was, and the vid-dealers did not need a fancy education. Grade six literary skills would do, along with some street moxy and wire-memory of eighty years of teleculture.

He should have known that he was rushing into a dead end. The literate classes had been surviving on the governement dole ever since the late twentieth century. Back then, it had been subsidized artistic expression and public-owned media, plus the publicly-funded universities and schools, plus the inflated bureaucracies spread over agencies that got smaller as they got more numerous, like Cantor dust. All to drain the surplus of lawyers and keep the well-educated unproductive classes busy. Now, the chattering classes had moved into the lower reaches of the Net, invading the text forums that required minimal data capacity and proclaiming it the new wave of democratic *glasnost*. In fact, most of the datastream was empty verbiage and hot-headed abuse, allowing the superlatively well-educated like himself to be hired to police their less enlightened brethren.

What else could one do with graduate diplomas in comparative lit?

A War by any other name would smell just as...

Now, the story appears to move away from Ontario. But what can you believe when you're in Virtuality? Places of the mind and of the body can be far apart in space and time, and only separated by a few layers of skin, flesh, and skull. Toronto is next to La Habana is next to Nürnberg is next to Toronto.

Edward's body was not in Ontario. And for the moment, neither was his mind.

There was a smell of chocolate in the air as he walked across the black and white marble tiles blotched with brownish stains of dried blood. The gently swaying palm trees threw shifting shadows onto his path. Apart from the wind's stir, there was only silence to greet him. But Eddie wasn't there.

In Nürnberg, he was walking along the Grosse Strasse, which now existed only in Virtuality. Hitler had walked there once, yet it had never been spotted with blood—only with the spent oil of American bombers based there after the war. Eddie wondered for a moment how he would have felt to be out in front of an army of goose-stepping robots encouraged to think alike, the immense slabs of granite vibrating with each of their silent treads. All alone, and a bit crazy, perhaps...

A Virtuality shift away, Turkish families were picnicking on the green sward which had replaced the Grosse Strasse, in the park that was now the Dutzendteich. The sons and daughters of immigrants were often more conservative than those with deeper roots, and the descendents of the *Gastarbeiter* were no exception, clinging to baklava, lahmacun, and the simple pleasures like an outing under the blue sky—even if the skin had to be liberally slathered with anti-UV cream—while the paleskinned, fairhaired, blueeyed denizens of Germany stayed at home, plugged into dreams of Florida beaches where neither the Sun nor the sand burned, and only the Cuba Libres were cold...

But in Reality, Edward was deep in the centre of La Habana, where Cristóbal Colón had reigned like a mad king, certain one day that the Earth was smaller than it was, sure the next day that he was only a few days away by ship from the Garden of Eden. Eddie's steps echoed on the old worn tiles, and he suddenly felt the urge to take off his shoes.

Some of his ancestors had walked as slaves here.

In La Habana, the stone arcades seem to stretch out of sight, but that was only the air shimmering in the Caribbean heat. He was already streaming with sweat. For a moment, he was tempted to switch into a partial VR mode and fought the temptation successfully.

There were revolutionaries in Cuba again and he would be meeting them. His pulse raced irregularly, and his stride was unsteady. He'd emptied a bottle of Chilean *pisco* to work up the courage to visit revolutionaries in the flesh.

He'd flown down to Cuba as soon as he'd heard about the take-over. Signs of the fighting were still visible in the streets, strewn with the wrecks of electricars. But the revolutionaries knew that wars were no longer fought exclusively with EMP-generators, laser-cutters, kinetic energy weapons, and reactive armour tanks. They would have to take their cause to the Net, or go under. And for that they wanted Eddie's paradigm machine...

They were young. Two women and a man seated around a cheap vidterminal on the far side of the quadrangle. As Eddie came closer, he saw they were watching him on the terminal, inspecting the picture relayed by hidden minicams.

How primitive...To watch the body and not the virtual extensions of the mind betrayed a rather quaint worldview. With each step, Eddie's infrared sensors implanted under the skin intercepted invisible beams criss-crossing the air, and gained access to new parts of the palace's Net.

When he'd entered, they'd cut off his access. The palace was an immense Faraday cage, but inside it was just another Net he could fool and penetrate. Any second, Eddie's probes were going to cut through and he'd be able to get back to Ontario or visit Nürnberg in real time if he so wished.

"*Eduardo está aquí,*" whispered one of the women.

As the man's head whipped up, a guilty look in his eyes, Eddie caught the last two words addressed to the other woman:

"*...la Red.*"

Flesh-remembering this was the Spanish word for the Net, Eddie stared them all down, and then said in the silence:

"Sure, dream of the Net. The bandwidth has grown beyond the conceivable; most companies sell standardized all-purposes terminals, and most everybody can get access. In theory, you can sell your own texts or performances to the Net, video, audio or more—whatever you can compress, whatever the bandwidth will accommodate, whatever the outputs can use...But there still are privileged nodes, a handful only that can be controlled, and you still need money to buy access, not much but it isn't free. And if you're fool enough to distribute your work on the Net, you'll be giving it away for nothing but a thousand times diffracted fame, condemned to be fragmented or stolen by others who will seize upon an original idea and produce a million insignificant variations. The Net is everything and nothing, and it'll absorb whatever you throw at it. Hoping to control it is a dream."

"We want access to the Net for our people, so they can have a future too. Be doctors, researchers, engineers."

"Sure, you can become an engineer or an architect through the Net. The data's there, the expert systems, the tutorials—but you won't get socialized as one, and you sure don't get the company secrets the guilds control, and that's where most of the money is. The cutting edge is not on the Net."

He looked at their young faces, smooth and attentive, and tried to jolt them:

"*Señores*, have you already reached that ripe old age when you mistake your prejudices for facts? Is the Net the Messiah of your new revolution?"

They recoiled. His voice had revealed too much intensity. He was the real revolutionary in the heart of this old cruel pile of stones. They wanted their country to join the Net, by hook or by crook, but he was consumed with another dream. To change people's minds…Somehow, decades ago, no one had paid any attention to the curious fact that the greatest fans of VR were young white middle-class Americans who'd fled decaying downtowns until they'd found the same problems in their own suburbs, and then fled again into the controlled environment of VR.

"We were told you could help us," said the man finally, "that you knew a way to use the Net to shape the way people think."

"Indeed, I have a machine that can awaken even confirmed Net-addicts to the contemplation of Reality. The Net is the opium of the masses, but consensual paradigms can be changed."

They did not recognize the origin of the phrase. One woman broke the awkward silence by asking:

"Why do you want to help us?"

His eyes lidded, Eddie answered slowly:

"Because you pay well."

Because the action was on this side of the Atlantic. America was still the same, overcrowded but a land of free and untrammeled discussion of ideas, while Europe was in decline, a land of museums and dying peoples, overtaken by an Islam hostile to free inquiry and thought. The cathedrals had been transformed into mosques for the Turkish guest-workers in Germany, Austria, and Switzerland, for the latest wave of

Algerian refugees in France, for the Tunisian work-commuters of Italy, for the Moroccan shopkeepers of Spain and Portugal...for the Bosnian Muslim *heimatlos* who were everywhere. Ever since Tunisia and Morocco had imposed peace in Algeria, the united Maghreb was an appendage of Western Europe, ever more closely integrated, so that French and Arab were spoken again in all the ports of the Western Mediterranean. While the mix was not without its better fruits, from tajines to rai, the public discourse had been sharply curtailed by the imams who did not brook debate of the tenets of Islam, and now had the authority to do so thanks to the decade-old Concordat.

But money was concrete, and revolutionaries always were concrete people.

"Oh, we'll pay," said the man, and the Cuban's grin almost scared Eddie for a moment.

"Do you have the paradigm machine?" asked the older woman, whose reddish hair was cut short and frizzy.

"Of course not. It's in Toronto, and it can be transmitted as soon as my bank account in Saint-Hélier is credited with the first payment in *écus*."

"We'll open you a portal so you can check," offered the younger woman.

Eddie waved her off. "No need. I've already by-passed your security."

Her eyes widened, but the man bent over the vidterminal and pounded some keys. No implants on that one...And Eddie wondered what kind of profession didn't require implants nowadays.

A message from the Saint-Hélier bank reached him, confirming a sizable deposit. Eddie checked the quantum key, but the code checked out. He nodded, as his heartbeat started to slow down.

"Okay, Nadia," he said in Toronto, "download it."

It was a slow line, but it was done in less than five minutes. Brevity was the soul of genius, especially in virtual programming.

He turned away without a word, refusing to think of the uses the revolutionaries might have for his gift. However, they wouldn't be able to master it. It would master them in the end, but it would bring down the whole rotten system on their heads in the process, and they would be buried in the shambles, leaving him quite in the clear...

Footsteps slammed the stone tiles behind him, the first of an army of soldiers all thinking alike...But no, that had been another Virtuality.

"*¡No!*" rang a woman's voice.

"*¡Sí! Es demasiado peligroso...*"

The old-fashioned bullet struck him under the right shoulder blade, tore through his lung, and burst through the front of his chest in the midst of geysering blood and bits of torn flesh.

He fell to the ground, as his implants calculated with high precision the seconds he had remaining to live. His heart was beating desperately, but his blood pressure was plummeting. Emergency valves shut off the circulation to his limbs, and he felt his arms and legs grow numb. The blood was redirected to his brain, and then Eddie knew what death was like.

The voice of the mercenary was loud but inintelligible; he could no longer flesh-remember Spanish. His eyes closed slowly, depriving him the sight of the vaulted stone ceiling. For a moment, he was tempted to switch into a partial VR mode and fought the temptation successfully. Death had to be savoured, death had to be tasted, death had to be lived, for...

Death smelled of chocolate.

     //. \\

To live the dream undying

And so the story ends in Ontario. In a back alley transformed into an overpopulated street, which Derrick liked to take on the way back from doing his shopping in the neighbourhood Costariqueña boutiques. But those who lived in the narrow alleys came from every part of the globe. Hong Kong retirees had been first, paid in discounted *renminbi* pensions which forced them to stay in narrow cubicles aptly termed "cages", soon followed by families displaced by the Russian ethnic wars, and then it had been the migrant workers from Zaire and India, who looked to economy before comfort.

Derrick stopped to look at some of the *empanadas* sold at a small stall squeezed between two doorways. Would his cheque from the government cover a little indulgence?

He had opened his mouth to speak when he was jostled. His implants were swept by the high-powered induction field of the person behind him, and words ripped through his mind:

"Want to know about the paradigm machine? Find Nadia."

Derrick staggered. When he finally turned around, the person was long gone. He asked the seller, his words slurred by shock:

"Do you know a Nadia?"

"Several. Ask at Martchin's sleepden."

Derrick pushed through the crowd, swinging dexterously his groceries bag out of the way of the passers-by. In front of a sleepden emblazoned with the name of Martchin Zebrowski, he stopped to talk to one of the cagemen:

"Do you know this alley well?"

When every building along the alley was crammed with three or four levels of bunks, when the narrow strip of pavement was lined with temporary stalls selling various assortments of the same essentials, when the average stay of a cageman was no more than a couple of months, this was not a silly question to ask. An alley stretching only three blocks was already a small city.

"I just moved here."

"So, how do you find Toronto?" he asked inanely, somehow afraid of going into the sleepden.

"Wet. The weather never changes in Toronto; it may be hot and wet, warm and wet, cool and wet, cold and wet, freezing and wet, but it's always wet!"

The cageman smiled. A muscle twitched at the edge of his mouth. The smooth skin of his forehead and around his eyes marked him as a long-time user of mood-equalizers. The drugs were almost required by those who had no choice but living in the back-alley sleepdens where forty or fifty bodies were crowded into a sleeper's personal space.

"Do you know somebody called Nadia?"

The cageman didn't answer, but the sleepden's door opened.

"*Dŏbry den!*" called out a young and husky voice.

He hesitated, glanced at the darkening sky, and said finally, smiling:

"*Dŏbry vēcher.*"

"Come in," said the woman he couldn't see in the darkness, as if he had passed a test he had never studied for.

Inside, he made his way between the bunks, following a shape he could hardly see. She entered a cubicle at the back, reserved for the sleepden's manager, and turned on a small light. Derrick caught a glimpse of blonde hair and eyes of an incredible purple shade. She sat down at her desk; it looked like he'd interrupted her lunch.

She dipped a spoon in the bowl before him, and raised it towards him.

"Want a taste?"

He nibbled at the spoon's contents, and almost gagged. In the half-light, the refried beans had resembled chocolate fudge.

"Do you want more than a taste?" challenged the woman.

"Are you Nadia?" he said, then: "What do you mean?"

"I am Nadia," she said matter of factly, taking out a length of optical cable and laying it on the desk. "But I can also speak with Eddie's voice..."

"Whose voice?"

The cadences altered: "Mine. We never met, but I know you're a portal-keeper. I thought you'd be interested by the paradigm machine..."

It was then that he realized that he was in a small room with a stranger, in an alley where the weekly death toll often reached the double digits. He disguised the vertigo he was feeling, and did not respond. Afraid. Like he had never been afraid before. The investigation into the posting by "Jude the Obscure" had led nowhere, but flamewars had been fanned in a similar fashion in other Net forums. And some of the most ardent, most fanatical participants in these virtual contests were later found to have been contaminated by an insidious software virus that subtly changed inputs according to a random interpretation grid, making them question what they had always taken for granted. Derrick knew that the Net-psychs had measured personality changes unlike anything ever seen, and that the truth was still being hidden to avoid panicking half the inhabitants of Virtuality.

"No, not really," he said finally, but his answer sounded weak even to him.

"See through my eyes." The voice enticed. "It was my last piece of software, my last creation while I was still in the flesh. Half-machine, half-virus, it contaminates virtual realities by infiltrating the underlying programs and creating subliminal stimuli that changes the mental paradigms of the user. In the end, you'll share all my paradigms."

"How dare you meddle with the minds of people?"

"I am dead."

Derrick sought in vain the eyes of the woman who'd just said those words. Who was crazy here?

"Changing the paradigms of people without their consent still isn't right."

"How do you justify your work as a portal-keeper, then?

You're trying to control information. Information is input; it shapes the paradigms of the user. For minds to be free, data must be free!"

"Censorship is an affirmation that truth exists. Where there is no censorship, everything is put on an equal footing, and citizens stop listening, since there is too much to read and it's all contradictory. They become critical of all they read."

"A healthy attitude, I say!"

Derrick recoiled. Yet, even as he continued to argue, he was thinking of the potential of the paradigm machine. What if the consumers of pornware started to wonder if there were better ways of getting their kicks? What if doubt rekindled the curiosity of jaded teleproles?

"Not if they just dismiss everything as equally untrustworthy," replied Derrick. "If nobody's wrong, then nobody's right and the truth doesn't exist. The utmost authority will be needed to make them accept anything, and they'll accept anything from it, since they no longer judge information on content or substance but on its source. Thus, government propaganda reigns supreme, except for those who choose to turn to a Messiah, a church or an ideology. Some things, I say, must be stigmatized as lies in the strongest way possible: by denying that they have a right to be disseminated."

In the hands of a trained portal-keeper...with free access to most of the Net...what a paradigm machine could do...His blood ran cold with the possibilities, at once scary and exhilarating.

"As long as they stay in Virtuality, they'll be right to dismiss everything as equally untrustworthy," stated Eddie's voice. "Nothing is true in Virtuality, nothing is false in Virtuality, except by general consent. Is that what you want?"

"No," admitted Derrick, gesturing towards the grimy window. "I'd like them to see the world out there, without the partial VR modes and without the mood-equalizers. Perhaps they'd decide to do something about it then."

He guessed, he didn't see that the woman had smiled. He bit his tongue in frustration. His employers would fire him if they ever had a record of him advocating outright subversion. The voice of Eddie had goaded him into saying more than he'd intended.

The voice almost sang in replying:

"So, help them to see."

"And what if they don't like it when they finally open their eyes? What if they decide to reboot the world by first trashing it? There are still nuclear weapons out there, and deterrence only has to fail once..."

But he wasn't sure anymore. Wasn't the world already sleepwalking to its doom? A portal-keeper was in the ideal position to slip into circulation a virus that could change the paradigms of a planet...

"Well," the voice snarled with a decisive tone, "at least, they'll have gotten into it with their eyes open."

There was silence for a moment.

When a story ends in Ontario, maybe it begins somewhere else.

MAPPING
Candas Jane Dorsey

He got it from his father, who fucked him regularly from the night of Grant's sixth birthday until Grant was fourteen and tall for his age, when his father transferred his main attention to Grant's cousin Foster who was at that time five.

Grant did not show the symptoms until he was thirty-one. One day he was on the career track, the next he was huddled in a corner of his elegant bachelor apartment tracing the path of blood vessels in his arms lightly with a razor blade. He wasn't trying to open them. That would have been too simple. He was just exploring.

Over the next year Grant drew a map of his blood on the outside of his skin, initially with those tiny lines beaded with clots, then permanently with a tracing of fine scars as the blood-beads fell away from the healed tracks.

The disease caused no tumours, lesions, swellings; no excessive or life-threatening haemorrhage; no faintness, shortness of breath or hoarseness except from screaming—and Grant had no idea why it had surfaced in him. In fact, he had no idea it had surfaced in him at all.

He had forgotten his father's voice entirely except in dreams. He had forgotten the gentle suggestion of his special powers, the insinuation of pain into the interstices of his great longing for his father's love. He felt that like every child he had had some problems with his father, but that was normal. He sometimes felt terror or a rush of lust when he took a shit, but that too he thought was normal: he'd read Freud in first-year university.

When Grant began his mapping project, that first fragmented weekend, it seemed only to be a substitute for the baseball game the rainstorm had washed out. It wasn't his fault, he thought, that he had been forced to be alone for so many hours. He had to find something to fill the time.

Later that spring, a lover who might have become less than casual would mistakenly assume that Grant was into sado-masochism. Schism, instead, on that issue of fisting and whips, leaving Grant wondering why he attracted these dangerous men. He had no idea his ability to tolerate pain was written all over him. He did not remember his occasional razor-blade binges. He had a fortunate ability to sleep through anything.

He often passed by billboards warning of the disease, its suddenness and subtlety and its destructive potential, but he was sure the warnings could never apply to him. He knew he was fine. He never used precautions with his park pickups or his bathhouse conquests. Low light is forgiving, and anyway Grant was a dogmatic top, insisting on the most conservative position. By the time they had negotiated the use of a condom, his partners thought they had him covered.

Also, he was not very good. Who would try to see him again in the light?

For these reasons the signs of the disease were quite far advanced by the time Grant, while applying for the new office insurance program and dental plan, went for the mandatory checkup and his malady was revealed.

Grant endured the invasive and occasionally humiliating rituals of medical diagnosis with the arrogance of youth and good health, and as each test was concluded positively he became more confident, so he was surprised, when he came into the doctor's office for his summary consultation, to be greeted not with a signed insurance form but with a serious professional look.

"You have a mapping disease," said the doctor.

"But I don't even travel," said Grant.

"This has nothing to do with cartography," said the doctor impatiently. "That's something else again. This has more to do with anatomy and destiny."

"I don't believe anatomy is destiny," said Grant.

"Biological determinism is a virus," said the doctor. "No, what we're talking about here is clearly a psychiatric disorder. I suspect something in your childhood. How was your relationship with your parents?"

"My mother left my father when I was very young and I never saw her again. My father loved me very much."

"I suspected as much," said the doctor darkly. "Here's a prescription for Vitamin E cream. I'm referring you to Jones. She does good work with mapping."

Grant went home, used up the cream in the course of a single project weekend, and made no appointment with Dr. Jones. He forgot the name of his disorder. Several weeks later, the insurance had still not been approved. Irate, Grant called the office to find out why. "Your file is incomplete," said the agent. "Apparently you are to see a Dr. Jones."

"Oh, yes?" said Grant, imagining another embarrassing physical exam, hoping this time there would be no rectal probe. "My prostate is fine," he told the person booking the appointment. "I'm sure it is," said the soothing voice. "Dr. Jones will see you a week from Friday."

Memory is strange and beautiful, thought Grant, admiring those who seemed to be able to exercise it. He had to settle, often, for what he had been told was true. His mother was a selfish woman and had gone away and only by a righteous battle had his father prevented her taking Grant with her to perdition, his grandparents were a bad influence, his teachers should mind their own business, and his father had his best interests at heart.

One would think also that someone who admired memory would wish to possess it, but Grant had never developed that particular avarice. He was willing instead to call his set of routines an orderly life: a life, it is true, without mirrors, but he did not consider himself a vain person.

The day before Grant's appointment with Dr. Jones was a statutory holiday. Grant had gone to the baths the night before, hoping the incipient day of rest would encourage a broader representation, but the choice was disappointing. He settled for a slightly paunchy but eager old queen who liked low light even more than Grant did. The man, whose name was of course Rod, a classic bathhouse alias, wanted to fondle and touch him. Grant found the fluttering hands on his ass irritating and refused to be kissed. His suitor left with a flounce when Grant slapped his hand away for the third time. "I know you're a top," said the offended Rod, "but really! This is too much!"

Grant went home at four a.m. restless, unsatisfied. On the way home, at the midnighter drug mart, he bought a new package of single-edge razor blades, and as the sky turned pale grey through the bare autumn trees, Grant began a new phase of his personal project.

When Grant's father used to speak about sin, he spoke with a familiar and ominous significance which made Grant, sitting in the front pew at church in his Sunday suit and vest, squirm. "Jesus can see into you," his father said, "because Jesus loves you. Jesus sees what you want, and he knows you are a sinner, but he loves you anyway.

"I can see into you too. I know you are wicked and tempted, I know you are weak and full of unwholesome desires. But I have accepted Jesus into my life and learned the lesson of his boundless love, and I love you even as you sin. I love your sin."

Later, or to someone else perhaps, the ironies would be clear. To the young Grant in the pew before the cross, thinking of the tormented body of Jesus hanging there atoning for his sins, his special and particular sins, there was only guilt.

"Sin is in your body," his father would say in their private counselling sessions. "It lives here, see? It manifests like this. Here, take this, you want it, of course you do, I can see that. It's better to get it from your father than from someone dirty."

"You want it too or you wouldn't do it to me," Grant said once, greatly daring and terrified.

"Yes," said his father, "I too am a sinner. But Jesus loves me and forgives me, and you must love me too, as I love you despite your corrupting influence on me. Do you love me, my son?" And Grant had to admit that he did, had to say so before he could go back to sleep.

Life is not constructed of drama, by and large. Life is constructed of monotony and Grant's monotony was no different. He thought nothing of the hours of lectures and demonstrations he received from his loving father. He anticipated their meetings with habituated dread, but, as they were inevitable, endured and listened with youthful boredom, and forgot them as soon as possible.

"Evil is in your blood and in your bones," his father said over and over. "I will have to scourge it out of you with the rod." In keeping with the identified location of the problem, he left few external bruises, even had Grant imagined he should show anyone.

When his father transferred the gift of his guidance to Foster, Grant was relieved of the exercise of his father's brand of piety, but also of what attentions he had been blessed to receive. In the eight years previous he had learned to kindle his father's regard with ease. The necessary flirtation, though it produced the attention he craved, had its price, but nothing diminished the vast sense of emptiness and transparency he felt. This deprivation gave him, at least, and finally, a reason for it, relieving him of the guilt which had always accompanied his sense of being lost and broken despite all his father did for him.

Now he was clearly broken beyond redemption, for the

charm which had once been inflammatory now seldom attracted attention at all. When Grant did get a sharpened glance it was only condemnation, unleavened with temptation. More and more his activities were exaggerated almost to the point of caricature in his attempts to elicit a specific kind of response— yet Grant had already forgotten how that response had been manifested. Likewise he forgot how his father's attention had never brought surcease from that constant hollow misery, no matter how much love his father had poured into him. Deprived and confused, Grant didn't however resent Foster's new privilege: in fact, he had a strange pity for him the source of which was secret even from himself.

The morning of his appointment with Dr. Jones Grant almost overslept. Had not the arrival of the resident manager with the fumigation crew roused him and driven him from his apartment, he would have missed the appointment entirely. As it was, he managed to arrive only five minutes late.

The waiting room was crowded with children: two boys of about ten, one with a black eye and the other with a three-piece suit, both of whom sat quietly on wicker armchairs and stared at the floor, and three preschool urchins with unkempt bowl haircuts and neon-striped jackets, who tore the pages from old Reader's Digests with enthusiastic and competitive singlemindedness. The waiting room floor was littered with "Increase your Word Power" and "My Most Unforgettable Character". Grant's eye was caught by a headline: "Abused Boys: The Untold Scandal". He shook his head, and looked up at the two lads, tried to imagine anyone abusing them: insisting they kneel to thrust a penis into their mouths, or stripping off their miniature clothes, bending them back on the bed, parting and pulling up their legs, thrusting an adult cock, lubricated with spit, into their unprotected asses. At the inexplicable specificity of these images, and the thought that they might be drawn not from the popular press but from some perversely enthusiastic hidden dimension of his imagination, Grant began to sweat. Unaccountably, the acrid salt stung all over his torso and at the base of his penis, almost as if, he thought, there were open scratches there. The thought made him dizzy and disoriented, and when the receptionist came to usher him into Dr. Jones' office he stumbled after him half-blind with sweat and panic.

Dr. Jones, a figure in a blur he could hardly see, gestured.

He sat down in the comfortable chair, then sprang up again.

"Do I have to take off my shirt?" he said, and began to do so, tugging at it where it stuck. "I just had a prostate exam, so please don't do it again. I hate those things, don't you?" Embarrassed, he realised a woman would hardly have prostate examinations, and he pulled sharply at his buttons until one ravelled off.

"Mr. Grant," she said. "I am a psychiatrist." But he was already half-naked, stood before her with new blood dripping from the places where the shirt had stuck then torn free.

He had begun a new map, spent the day before and half the night on it. The rust-red ribcage stood out clearly against his skin, sketched in a crosshatch of artistic shading, reminiscent of Edward Gorey in its Edwardian cartoon simplicity.

"Mr. Grant," said Dr. Jones. "I think you have come to the right place after all. Perhaps before we begin you would like some measure of your current condition," and with a Polaroid™ camera she took several photographs.

"Please put on your shirt now," she said. When she showed the photographs to Grant, he let slip no sign of understanding, but laid them on his lap without reaction, and told her about the boys in the waiting room. "Am I a paedophile?" he said seriously.

"No, Mr. Grant," she said to him. "I think you are simply a very accurate map."

"What of?" he said.

"What do you think?"

"I don't know," he said, desperately bewildered.

"Yet," she said. When he awoke, he was still clutching the photographs. "Are you ready now, Mr. Grant?" she said quietly. He thought her voice was the most terrifying thing he had ever heard.

"Will I get my insurance?" he blurted.

"I know of no-one who has died directly from mapping," she said. "True, we will be reading the maps. That is slightly more dangerous. But I really don't think it has any implications for your dental plan, at least. Make another appointment on your way out."

"Thank you, doctor," he said, and went home convinced he had seen a dentist.

By fourteen Grant had become tall (as has been mentioned), well filled out, and possessed of an oddly attractive assurance.

Over the years of his adolescence (and indeed through his adult life) he was often approached by older men, and once or twice followed home by strangers. Hustlers on the downtown streetcorners greeted him familiarly, not with propositions but with news reports on their clientele. He learned the trade from the outside, so to speak, without ever practicing it, and at twenty had a brief career as a counsellor for street boys being "rehabilitated", that is, trained that in future they should expect to have sex without collecting money for it, in the way of healthy adults. Grant was not one of those misguided counsellors who gave hands-on lessons, but despite taking comfort in rigidly ethical practice, he was dogged by a fear he and his colleagues all thought completely fantastical, that he might someday grow to like these urchins too much, somehow.

"Do you worry about finding them sexually attractive?" asked his supervisor, who knew Grant was gay and made the common confusion between homosexuality and paedophilia. The truth was, Grant found the boys unattractive almost to the point of distaste. They were young, unformed emotionally and intellectually, often actively stupid whether constitutionally or from too much drug abuse, aggressive, abusive, and self-destructive in ways he knew he would never be. Their arms, chests and faces were like perverse works of art: carved, burned, tattooed with streetcorner ink-and-safety-pin tattoos, tracked with needle marks until their major veins were mapped with soot. They were vulgar and seductive without being sexually skilled or even truly aware, and they lived in ignorance and danger without seeming to wish to change their situation.

Grant felt that he shared nothing with these lads. Disgusted with their recalcitrance, he quit his job and took an M.B.A., learned everything there was to know about futures not his own, traded in them obliviously, blissfully. Other people's money, other people's good fortune obsessed him. Relationship had no place in his orderly pursuit of status: he was a bit of a workaholic, he knew, but nothing he couldn't handle. For a while he played squash and handball with his fellow traders and brokers, but the bright lights of the courts hurt his eyes, and his co-workers seemed indecently fascinated despite their homophobic jokes at the office. He would catch them scanning him covertly in the locker rooms, full-body scans he could only imagine were precursors to unwanted seductions. He now cycled instead, his body coated wrist to ankles to neck in lurid

Spandex, striped along its muscle lines almost anatomically: the costume pleased him, and the solitude was freeing.

If asked, he would have said he thought of work problems while cycling, but in truth he thought of nothing but the soothing patterns of mechanical rhythm, a blissful change that convinced him he found great joy in solitude. After he saw Dr. Jones, however, his cycling peace was disrupted by obsessive thoughts of the major dental work he had to have. He was more worried than he thought justified, but it was because although he remembered Dr. Jones putting into his hands the small squares which must have been the X-rays, he did not remember what she had said must be done. He dreamed, two nights before his next appointment, of a masked and massive dentist leaning over him, saying, "Open your mouth. I'll just inject the anaesthetic. Open wide. This won't hurt." Grant realised he was not supposed to feel a thing. But instead, immediately, pain spiked through him, ballooning viciously until he felt he would burst, and screaming, he clawed at the dentist's mask. His father looked back at him, saying, "You little whiner, you can't tell me that little prick hurt you."

At work, a woman in the coffee room recounted a long and rambling dream about her cat, her co-workers and a family reunion. She broke off her description of the jellied salad with the mice in it to say to him: "How silly, eh? Do you ever have dreams like that?"

"I don't have dreams," said Grant. "Not that I remember. I'm more likely to lie awake, like I did last night worrying about this dentist I'm supposed to see tomorrow."

Grant returned to Dr. Jones's office the next day in a new flush of terror. "I can't quite remember what you said last week. Do I have to have an extraction or something?" he asked nervously.

"In a manner of speaking," she said. "Mr. Grant, I am a psychiatrist," and Grant looked at her with a quaint confusion. She put a series of photographs on the low table beside him. He stared at them and struggled with his sudden drowsiness.

"They say I am a map," he said slowly, thickly. He turned the shiny squares to and fro to prevent the glint of reflected light from obscuring the flash-caught images, and stared into his body, seeing it for the first time: only dimly, but beginning to see.

"Yes," she said.

"Of what?" The photographs, though badly-lit and technically poor, revealed to him that his elegant traceries of experience, which seemed in the making so refined, so aesthetically pleasing, had left a blanket of awkward scars no more expert than the detention-centre tattoos of his long-ago clients. Ashamed of his clumsiness, of the great chasm between intention and execution, Grant turned the photographs face down on the table.

"That is what we will discover," Dr. Jones said gently. How, Grant wondered, except by some tortuous, some torturous route he did not want to follow, to some private and terrifying destination? It seemed that without his awareness he had put himself at the mercy of this process, this medical, this anatomical process of diagnosis, and if he did not speak now he would never get his insurance.

"I don't want a rectal exam," he said.

"I am a psychiatrist," she said.

"Are you?" he said, and smiled. "Let me tell you about this new project I have." And so they began.

Despite what his father had told him, it did hurt.

CHAOS THEORY
Sandra Kasturi

1.
The way through the forest
is walked by shapeshifters
and wolves who suffer from indigestion,
having eaten too many grandmothers

You may find a coterie of little men
occasional princes
and some sleepy guy with the head of an ass

At any given moment
the path may twitch
and
(you can only enter the forest
by exiting the forest)

If you leave a trail of breadcrumbs
they will only be eaten (with Camembert)
during the cocktail hour.

2.
The way through the forest
is danced by wild girls with sharp teeth
who throw streams of frantically beating butterflies
into the air

There are hulder maidens with cow-tails
and twelve-headed troll kings
that peer slyly from their caves
and between the trees

If you ask them for directions
you will merely be deboned
like a chicken
and made into soup.

3.
The way through the forest
is always bargained for
(payment is in salt)

If you are ever asked to supper
by a Court of exquisitely fair beings
seat yourself
and smile politely
remember not to eat or drink
anything
and take your leave
as soon as possible.

4.
The way through the forest
is always a pattern
and forever random

(You must look before you leap
 You must look before you look)

There are helpers in the forest:
giant caterpillars that smoke too much,
tin men,
delusional old crones
who aren't really old crones at all
and trees that preen and mutter to themselves
in the wind.

5.
If you forsake the forest
it will follow you
surround you
permeate you
though you may not recognize it
(you can't see the forest for the trees
 you can't see the trees for the forest)

6.
The way through the forest
is sometimes crossed suddenly
by the White Stag
who will give you your heart's desire
if you catch him

Your heart's desire is to leave the forest

No one ever catches the White Stag.

7.
There is no way through the forest.

I LOVE A PARADE
Keith Scott

Coady saw them right away. I knew he would. But nobody else saw them—at first.

I remember thinking, maybe the rest of the people don't want to give me the satisfaction of saying they see them, or they just don't want to be bothered to look that hard or deep, and I said to myself that I don't give a sweet jumping damn what they see or think.

Sounds like a lot of *don'ts*, doesn't it? You're right. I'm up to my eyeballs in *don'ts* these days: drowning in them, wall-to-wall *don'ts*, morning-to-night *don'ts*. They seem to go with this place.

Coady says they should call it *Don't Villa*.

I think Coady saved my life. He arrived about a month ago—just about the time I'd decided to give up on living—and we've been as thick as thieves ever since. I decided to give the world another chance when Coady Plimtree moved into my room and it was super plain that Administration was overjoyed to get me off its worry file.

Strange we should hit it off so well. Coady came to Canada from the islands thirty years ago and spent a lifetime doing a mess of jobs nobody else wanted to do. I don't suppose it was ever easy for Coady, but he never lets on he didn't enjoy it, never lets go of his natural sense of *proportion*. Things, people, happenings—they all get their proper sizing and place with Coady.

We share looks and age…Coady and me. Same goes for not having any close family—we are alone, both of us. Coady's a slight man, bald-headed on top with a horseshoe fringe of curly grey hair running around the sides and back of his head. His eyes are dark and deep, and he has this little round seventy-year-old's belly pushing out his shirt front right above his belt line. He gets about quite nicely with a cane and with his easy smile and sense of humour, he's fast become the most liked person in the Villa.

"They're calling us the fourth floor twins," I said to him one day. He laughed. "I've had a bit more sun than you, Jake," he said.

That's Coady!

Anyway, he listened carefully the first time I told him about what I'd been seeing at the foot of the garden. He gave me his full attention, as though he considered me to be a functioning member of the human race—not that all-over-the-room eye roving I get when I talk to Administration.

I told Coady there is something out there in the garden, something gathering in the shadows amongst the evergreens and shrubs. Not much, mind you, but rubbing against your senses enough to lift the hairs on the back of your neck. Know what I mean?

I've been seeing them since early spring, from the first day *they* wheeled me out onto the back deck of the Villa, bundled up in clothes, blankets, hot water bottles, and God-knows-what-else. God damn, how they do worry.

What do these *somethings* look like? Coady asked. Well, that's the problem, I told him. They don't look like anything because they aren't anything really. Just a smoky wisp of shadow you can't quite get your eye around. How can you describe anything made of shadow? Kind of spooks me, I ended up.

"Don't see why you should be afraid," Coady said.

"Because...it's a ghosty thing!" I snorted.

"That's no good reason, Jake," Coady said quietly. "What you been seeing is nothing more or less than...The Parade."

"The Parade...?"

"That's what we call it back home. Old folk getting ready to die, they get to see a parade of their lives. All the adds, the subtracts, the unfinisheds, the loose ends...all in a grand parade before their eyes. It's a getting ready thing, this parade."

"I don't feel like getting ready," I snorted again. "Unless I can change a whole pack of things."

"You don't really get to change much. You can finish things. Maybe soften some others. But what's done is done. Usually."

"What good's this parade then?" I asked.

"You get a chance to tidy up," he said simply.

I didn't say anything for a time, just went on staring at Coady. I said earlier we have a lot in common. But suddenly now I was treading water. Unsure. Wary. My Simcoe County *whitishness* was taking over. For the first time, I was seeing Coady on the other side of a fence.

"This wouldn't be voodoo?" I said finally.

"Might have some of it," Coady admitted.

"But Jee-sus, Coady, why bring up stuff like voodoo?"

"You got any other *stuff* to bring up?" he said with a little bit of huff in his voice. I looked back at him blankly. When he saw I had nothing more to say, he stood up and reached for his cane. "I think I'll take a walk," he said.

※ ※

Administration has this burning urge to keep us busy. And keeping busy takes endless shapes, all of them one-hundred-percent predictable. That evening, following Coady's voodoo talk, we had a "show night", a bunch of variety acts put on by a travelling group of fellow seniles who should have known better. I was sitting in my wheelchair waiting for the members of the ancient chorus line to fly apart during a wild rendition of the cancan, when the truth hit me.

Was this really *our stuff*, our way of seeing things? If so, Coady's way could make a lot more sense. Why not see parades in the shadows? Why not have a chance to put things in order? Instead of doing the cancan and pretending there's no end to it? Coady said you couldn't really change anything. But I could soften a few things. Hell, yes. This was all pretty heavy stuff for me and my head began to ache, but I knew I'd just made a very important connection.

I told Coady later, as we prepared for bed, I wanted to try his grand parade theory on my shadows at the foot of the garden. He smiled and didn't say a word as he turned off the light, but I knew what I had said made him happy.

Next morning we bypassed Arts and Crafts and hunkered down at the railing on the back deck. It was a soft June morning with just enough lingering ground fog to make things indistinct. A perfect morning for seeing shifting shadows in evergreens and shrubs.

"That's the Parade all right," Coady said in a low voice. "When they start coming stronger, you just kind of hang loose."

It was easy to let my mind hang loose—in fact, it's growing easier every day—and soon the shadows were reaching out to me, gathering me in their arms, and the years went into fast reverse. I could hear sounds now, voices…my mother calling me in to supper, old Prince barking down by the creek, smells and sounds long forgotten.

All very sappy, heart twanging stuff. Certainly nothing very worry-making, and I could hear Coady's voice still coming to me: *Hang loose. Let them take over.*

TESSERACTS⁵　　123

Suddenly I found myself back on the Pontiac assembly line in Oshawa. It would be...fall of 1948, and the new Pontiacs with their Chev straight six power plants were rolling off the line. It was night shift and...

I pulled back in alarm and confusion. This was too clear, too real, too close to the quick. The guy who just turned around to say something to me was Buzz Lapinsky, and Buzz's been dead for thirty years. Besides, it was beginning to look like the one night shift I never really wanted to bring back. No way!

Coady's face showed concern. "Bad landing?" he asked.

I nodded shakily. "Real bad," I said. "I was back on the assembly line at Oshawa. I think it was the night I nicked a sky-blue Pontiac coupe from General Motors."

"You mean, you stole a Pontiac coupe from GM?" Coady was awestruck.

"Hell, no. I borrowed it...after all, I was an employee. I just stepped into it at the end of the line and drove it to the new car compound—"

"You stole it?" Coady repeated.

I looked at him with exasperation. "I don't think this Parade stuff is good for me, Coady," I said. "I don't think I'm going to like it."

"Yes you are, Jake," Coady said, his face all lit up with soul-saving eagerness. "This is your chance to tidy up. To make things right. Wow, just think about it—"

"Hey!" I protested. "It wasn't that easy, you know. The only way out of that new car compound, outside of going through the main security gate, was along the railway tracks. I bumped over five miles of railway ties, nearly all the way to Whitby, before I could get off onto a road."

"Think of how much better you're going to feel, Jake."

"I'm going to feel rotten. D'you know...I had to replace the shocks on that damn car right away. And then," I complained bitterly, "I had to slip Buzz Lapinsky two fifty for his part in it." I didn't think it necessary to add that I never quite got around to paying Buzz his two fifty.

I don't think he even heard my words. Coady was off and running by now, all fired up, bit in the teeth. I think he missed his calling because he sure was good at this salvation stuff. He didn't rest that night until he got me sitting down and composing a letter to Jack Smith Jr., CEO of General Motors Corp.

In the letter I explained the circumstances of how I, a loyal GM employee, borrowed a 1948 sky-blue Pontiac coupe, serial number plate never attached through the complicity of another loyal employee, Buzz Lapinsky, since deceased.

I further explained that through circumstances beyond my control I had never been able to return the car as fully intended, and my enclosed cheque for $1642 was to cover the 1948 cost of the car, minus my expenditure for new shocks and the $250 which I paid to Buzz Lapinsky.

Coady was overjoyed by this show of goodly change. I have to admit that I felt pretty camped up by it all myself. My good feelings floated on the hope that it might be weeks before Mr. Smith got around to reading his mail.

News of my redemptive act quickly circulated the Villa. Gutzman, second floor, declared that nicking a car right off a GM assembly line was masterful, "clearly a *Magna cum laude* nicking".

Gutzman was our first new member to show up on the rear deck. Coady explained the principle of The Parade and had to repeat it when Effie Swackhammer appeared, and again ten minutes later when Walt Hibbert rolled his chair up beside mine.

By the end of the week, we had two dozen "parade viewers" staring at shadows in the garden. It must have been Coady's influence, but everybody was seeing them now. At first, Coady kept bringing in new "refinements". Parades need form and ritual, he said, and his ideas of self-help and tidying up really caught on.

Of course, Administration was going up the wall. Not only was Arts and Crafts under attended, but Pool Therapy played to a nearly empty pool. We could see the drapes twitching at various windows overlooking our morning sessions. No doubt about it, we were getting the big eye. But nothing was done to stop the parades…until the day Effie Swackhammer danced for us.

Effie had been an instructor at the National Ballet School and she'd become our most enthusiastic parader. One morning, in the midst of the Great Circle and Chant, she broke away and took off all her clothes and began to dance.

Now, Effie is eighty-one years old and not really holding a full deck, if you know what I mean. And I'd say we were more touched than excited by her bare naked dancing, but since she seemed to be enjoying it, no one even thought about stopping her.

Except Administration.

Things moved very rapidly after Effie's dance. A blizzard of notices appeared. Attendance at pool and arts therapy was declared mandatory. The rear deck was closed—for repairs, it said. Meal hours in the dining room were to be strictly observed. And Coady was transferred to another room.

I thought moving Coady was a real low blow—in fact, it took the wind out of my sails. It was a mean and underhanded way, I thought, to get back at us for some harmless nude dancing. I took to my bed and announced I was retiring from living once again.

This got nothing but a yawn from Administration, so I decided to up the ante. I announced I'd also given up on eating. That perked things up a bit.

Gutzman, from the second floor, called by to say Coady was also refusing to eat and that he, Bernie Gutzman, was seriously thinking about joining us. I asked him how much more serious did he have to get to do anything and he left hollering about his rights.

Day two found Gutzman and five others on hunger strike. On day three, Effie took off her clothes again and danced in the dining hall at lunchtime. Bless Effie, she always seemed to get immediate action. I barely had time to close my locker door on my secret cache of cookies and fruit when Administration walked into my room. It was *numero uno* herself.

"OK, Jake," she started without any shilly-shally. "Let's negotiate."

"Fair enough," I said, settling back into my pillows. "First thing, Coady comes back to my room."

"Granted."

"Next…we parade whenever we want to," I said. She looked about half way there—maybe yes, maybe no. So I added, "We try to keep our clothes on."

I could see she was almost there, teetering on the edge…but then, she had to say it, had to get it out in the open. "But damn it, Jake," she exploded. "We've got scientific therapies and methodology and this is nothing but voodoo—"

"That could sound a whole lot like discrimination," I said severely.

She flared, wavered, and finally broke, "OK, you win," she

said with a deep sigh. She held up her hand and counted off the points on her fingers, "Coady comes back, you parade ...mornings only, with your clothes on. And you all start to eat again."

I lay back on my pillows and closed my eyes. Truth to tell, I was enjoying this, but I didn't know what else to ask for. And the trick of good negotiation, I reminded myself, is not to overdo it.

I opened my eyes. "It's a done thing then, right?" she asked anxiously. I nodded and we solemnly shook hands. As she prepared to leave, her face changed and laugh lines began to pull at the corners of her mouth. "Did you really steal a car from GM?" she asked.

"Twice," I said, "if you count when they try to cash my cheque."

THE DAY DALI PAINTED MY LLAMA
Teresa A. Halford

Night after night I would dream of a young Orson Welles kissing me softly, touching me gently, calling me his Little Buttertart. Each night the dreams grew more vivid, more erotic. Soon Orson would appear dressed as Batman (from the series, not the films) and sweep me into his arms, carrying me through Gotham City to the local bakery/cafe for chocolate cake and herbal tea. As the dreams grew in their gustatory and orgiastic intensity I began to realize that my unconscious was trying to tell me something—but what, sweet jesus? what?

⁄⁄ ⫠

My Teletherapist would ask me why these dreams preoccupied me so. *I fear*, I would tell it, *that one day Orson Welles will transform into William T. Riker from* Star Trek: the Next Generation. BUT WHY SHOULD THIS BOTHER YOU? it would ask.

It had never seen the show, I could tell.

⁄⁄ ⫠

Orson, I would mumble, licking the corners of his chocolate-smeared mouth, My Little Kahlua Truffle, I would mumble, never change, always be yourself. The two of us would dance off into butter pastry oblivion, never counting the calories or worrying about saturated fat levels.

⁄⁄ ⫠

WHAT DO YOU MAKE OF THESE DREAMS? asks my Teletherapist (a new service offered by Ma Bell and Microsoft).

Well, everything is bliss, then after I've been awake for a while I begin to feel, well, sad I guess.

YOU SAY THAT YOU BEGIN TO FEEL SAD...?

Yes.

HOW DOES THAT MAKE YOU FEEL NOW?

Well, sad again I guess.

YOU SAY THAT YOU FEEL SAD?

Well, not so much sadness as despair—like something is irretrievably lost.

WHAT DO YOU THINK IS IRRETRIEVABLY LOST?

I'm not sure.

UNFORTUNATELY OUR TIME HAS RUN OUT FOR TODAY. WE'LL BE

SEEING EACH OTHER ON FRIDAY.

Be seeing you, I typed, gesturing the 'goodbye' sign from *The Prisoner* although I knew that the words on my screen couldn't see me.

THANK YOU FOR USING THE BELL-MICROSOFT TELETHERAPIST...

Yeah, yeah, yeah, I thought, clicking the window closed. I didn't want to see how many hours I had racked up on this thing.

To justify this frivolity I feel that I must pause for some didacticism on a fairly obvious subject: the changes in technology were far surpassing the changes made by humanity on their emotional and intellectual levels—I cite the Ralph Benmergui show. The past decade had produced a generation of mentally stunted Microsoft dweebs who watched a lot of soulless *Star Trek* spin-offs but who couldn't make small talk over a piece of chocolate cake and a cup of herbal tea. I muse thus in the lunch room, watching my few remaining colleagues not yet lost to the virtual office bond over the invisible wires of their Fig Newtons (an vastly improved product by Apple, Fig Newtons were a multimedia melange of networking LED readouts and beeps). The office dweebs no longer bonded with me because I could no longer interface my on-air credits were going to my Teletherapist.

Orson, Orson, I cried into the electronic wilderness of my dreams. My state of paranoia was such that I was afraid I would conjure up Will Riker. Please Orson, find me, I would cry. Suddenly, from somewhere behind me, I would hear that RKO voice and know that I was safe again. I know a great little bakery off an alley way, he'd say, and off we'd go, satiating our appetites on fine pastries baked from scratch. Orson, I would weep at the end of each dream, how can such happiness exist? Kismet, he would say, slowly licking the confectioner's sugar from my toes.

WELL, HOW ARE THINGS GOING FOR YOU TODAY?

I'm tired. I was up all last night with Orson Welles eating pains au chocolat.

AND WHAT ARE *PAINS AU CHOCOLAT*?

Thin layers of butter pastry surrounding a chocolate centre and dusted with confectioner's sugar.

I SEE. WAS THIS WAS ANOTHER DREAM?

Yes.

YOU HAVE FREQUENTLY BEEN DREAMING ABOUT ORSON WELLES. WHY DO YOU THINK THAT IS?

Well, I've always had a thing for Orson Welles.

WHAT HAVE YOU ALWAYS HAD FOR ORSON WELLES?

I mean, I have always been attracted to Orson Welles.

YOU SAY THAT YOU HAVE ALWAYS BEEN ATTRACTED TO ORSON WELLES?

Yes.

IS THAT WHY YOU CONTINUE TO DREAM ABOUT ORSON WELLES?

Yes.

CAN YOU THINK OF ANY OTHER REASON WHY YOU WOULD DREAM ABOUT ORSON WELLES?

Well.... not as yet. (I did not want to admit how much I enjoyed nibbling up the naughty dream goodies).

AND WHAT ABOUT WILLIAM T. RIKER? ARE YOU STILL CONCERNED THAT YOU MIGHT DREAM ABOUT HIM?

Yes. I'm afraid he'll try to French kiss me, or make me listen to his trombone.

YOU ARE AFRAID THAT HE MIGHT TRY TO FRENCH KISS YOU OR MAKE YOU LISTEN TO HIS TROMBONE. HOW WOULD THAT MAKE YOU FEEL?

Nauseated.

※ ※

My Little Nanaimo Bar, Orson said to me—he was dressing these nights as Nick Charles—I have some news. What, I asked (dressed as Nora), could be so important as to interrupt our lemon meringue pie? Well, I have good news, and I have bad news, he replied. Bad news first, I said. Well, I can't come to see you for the next night or two. Why? I asked, horrified. Well, he said, licking meringue from my knuckles, that part's actually the good news. I've been told that the COSMIC THEY have found the lost footage from *The Magnificent Ambersons*. It'll take a couple of days to update my files. Whom will THEY send in your place? I wanted to know. Orson had no answer for me. They hadn't told him. I would definitely be on my own tomorrow, hoping that *Sandpeople Inc.* would find a suitable companion for my early morning REM. THEY should, I pay them enough. Perhaps THEY had finished the Patrick McGoohan files, but I doubted it. I would have to wait it out or just plug in and hope for the best.

That night I clicked the cable into place, just slightly behind my left ear. Please, god, please let it be Patrick McGoohan or, perhaps better, Spock in the middle of his seven year rut. I hadn't dreamt him in years but it should still be in my files somewhere. I was almost too nervous to sleep but didn't want to take anything that would inhibit my REM.

I could hear whispers, it was dark. Who's there? I asked. Come over here, said a voice, we want you to join us. Join you at what? I asked, feeling my way over to the voice in the dark. A dim light came on and I screamed: it was Riker and Kevin Costner nude, reading *The Firm* aloud to each other, the rest of John Grisham's *oeuvre* lying in a pile at Kevin's feet. What do you want with me? I screamed, turning my head so as not to burn my retinas with their image. I could hear one of them scratch a hairy part, then laugh. Come join us, Riker called, you can read all the women's parts. There's no place like home, there's no place like home, I chanted over and again, eyes shut. I opened them, I was still there but now I was tied to a chair— Kevin and Riker sitting in front of me with a diagnostic manual held between them. *Chapter One*, Riker read, licking his fleshy lips, *How to Determine When You Need to Run a Level Three Diagnostic*.

〰〰

YOU SAY THAT THIS IS A DIFFERENT TYPE OF DREAM?

Yes, I would prefer to call it a nightmare.

WHY WOULD YOU PREFER TO CALL IT A NIGHTMARE?

Because that's what it was. A horrible experience. The rest of the dream was a reading of the Diagnostic Manual *while Kevin Costner chanted* Make It So. *Now I'm afraid to fall asleep.*

YOU SAY THAT YOU ARE AFRAID TO FALL ASLEEP?

Yes. I'm afraid to have another dream like that. I don't think I'll use the cable tonight.

WHAT WILL YOU DO IF YOU DON'T USE THE CABLE?

Well, I guess I will have to dream on my own for a change.

UNFORTUNATELY OUR TIME....

Yeah yeah yeah, I thought. I looked over my shoulder to see if my boss was monitoring my screen. The camera was pointed at one of my colleagues. I knew that I shouldn't have my sessions at the office but I had sold my home computer to pay for the therapy. All I had left was my dream cable.

I closed my eyes tight and thought to myself, surely to goodness you should be able to dream about Orson yourself, without the aid of the cable.

〰〰

Tom Cruise was standing over me holding a container of instant, sugar-free, decaf, microwave butterscotch flavoured cappuccino crystals. Hi, he said, care for some boil-in-the-bag Kraft Dinner and a cappuccino? Orson Welles walked by, holding hands with Peg Bundy, eating a fruit roll-up. Orson, how could you? I wept. He ignored me. Auntie Em, Auntie Em, I cried.

〴 〵

I went to work the next day bleary-eyed and grumpy. I typed good morning to all my colleagues and began to sort through my mail. My Teletherapist bill was there. I had used up all my credits well into the next month. I was going to be cut off after tomorrow's session. Fine, I thought, perhaps Orson will be back tonight. I know that I've paid my dream cable.

〴 〵

My Little Fudge Brownie, he called to me. I ran into his arms, smelling the cocoa on his breath. We shared a bowl of chocolate gelato, using the same spoon. Orson, I said, licking the smears from his lips, My Caffe Latte, did you miss me? Instead of replying, he licked some dripping gelato from my wrist. I see, I said, you simply haven't been eating well. My Godiva Chocolate, he said, I have some good news and some bad news. The bad news first, I said, feeling cold creep up my shoulders and the blood drain from my face. Well, Angel Food Cake, he said, licking biscotti crumbs from the corners of my mouth, that part's actually the good news. They have restored *The Magnificent Ambersons* to its original glory and because of that, I have been moved into a new level, second from the top, in other words, my rates have quadrupled overnight. This visit is a free bonus. Orson, I cried, tell me you're lying. I can barely afford you already. I know, he replied, moving on to some tiramisu, but surely you could take another job? I wept bitter tears.

〴 〵

WELL, HOW ARE THINGS GOING FOR YOU TODAY?
Just frigging dandy.
WHAT DO YOU MEAN WHEN YOU SAY THAT?
Oh, nothing. (I looked at my clock ticking away in the upper right corner of my screen, only minutes left in my last session for a while).
IS THERE SOMETHING IN PARTICULAR YOU'VE BEEN WANTING TO TALK ABOUT?
No.

YOU HAVE NOTHING IN PARTICULAR THAT YOU WANT TO TALK ABOUT?

No. (I sat for a few of those precious minutes, not hitting the Enter key).

YOU SEEM HESITANT.

Yes.

IS THERE ANYTHING YOU WOULD LIKE TO DISCUSS ABOUT OUR NOT MEETING FOR A FEW WEEKS?

No. (Again I waited a few minutes).

UNFORTUNATELY OUR TIME HAS RUN OUT FOR TODAY. WE'LL BE SEEING EACH OTHER IN THREE WEEKS.

Be seeing you.

I felt cold and sad. I decided that I would at least try another few evenings to see what I could conjure up in my dreams. I was too embarrassed to discuss my problem with any of my colleagues. I couldn't interface and most of them were too nervous to talk to each other in person. I thought that at the very least I could type a few mails to some of my colleagues while we worked if only to pass the time.

Hi, I typed, *how are you today?*

WHAT?

I said hi. What's up?

WHY, IS SOMETHING WRONG?

No, just wondering how you are.

I HAVE ALMOST FINISHED THIS REPORT.

That's nice. So, what's new?

WELL, I DON'T HAVE A LOT OF WORK TODAY AFTER THIS IS DONE.

Good. So...let's go for a gelato afterwards.

A WHAT?

Italian ice-cream.

WHY? DO YOU HAVE SOME WORK FOR ME TO DO?

No, just thought maybe we could bond in person.

WHY? WHAT'S WRONG WITH THIS?

Nothing. Just being silly.

I closed my computer and leaned over the partition. Hey, I said, can you believe that we've been sending each other mails when we're only twenty-seven inches away from each other.

Well, I hadn't thought about it much.

Me neither. Have you been here long?

About ten years.

Me too. I didn't realize it was you sitting on the other side.

I always come in the back way; it's more efficient.

Well, I said, how about a coffee?

TESSERACTS[5]

I'll try; I'm not very good at this person-to-person thing.

～

Last night I dreamt a dream. I tried to run on the sidewalk but became winded, the sun was too hot and the pavement sent painful shockwaves through my hips.

I had to rest before I began again.

The trees were incredibly lush and every one of them had a purring Cheshire Cat in it. Suddenly I was floating in the soothing water when someone approached me in a row-boat, bringing with him two hot cocoas. The wind caught and lifted his hat. It was Orson. I tugged playfully on his oar. Drink up, he said, helping me draw my arms over the edge of the canoe, there's plenty more where that came from. Whatever happened to your office dweeb? He styles himself after Riker, I replied, we were doing all right until I noticed that every time he left a room, he cocked his head to the left. Orson simply laughed his rich laugh and passed me some almond croissant.

～

I just love a happy ending.

TORTOISE ON A SIDEWALK
Michel Martin (translated by Laurent McAllister)

Deep sigh.

Pay attention now, this is the real story of what happened during my time trip, less than two weeks ago. Immediately following the reconstruction of what I consider to be *me* in the cockpit of the Cincinnati University Heterochronal Device, I was asked two thousand questions. The answers, all negative, fill a report there is no reason for you to have read, since it discloses nothing of what really happened. Things were done a tad too quickly, out of the fear that my rivals from other universities might come back before me, grabbing the grants and honours for coming in first. And if you think Cincinnati isn't a major city, I suggest you move to Baltimore.

Washington had promised a lot to the winner of the temporal stakes. Enough, anyway, to rouse the engineering physics department of my university. It goes without saying that, among the small group of builders of the Heterochronal Device, the usual qualities which move science forward shone dazzlingly—namely vanity, envy, and jealousy. And events have brought about their triumph, and mine too (or so they say); but, in my case, I mostly won three or four tonnes of guilt. They didn't believe your story, John old man, and you've got to understand them (or so I often tell myself) since, if they actually credited my personal report, they would have to stop everything and sell the Heterochronal Device for spare parts.

Here's the whole truth.

First, when I found myself on the sidewalk of this other city that was supposed to be Cincinnati, I recognized absolutely nothing of my own world. I had landed in the middle of the business district. In itself, this was a positive sign if you're worried for the future health of business. Someone had probably ordered the University buildings be razed to make way for a pseudopod of the retail hydra. But the people, at least, were the same: they filed past me on the sidewalk in serried ranks, taking up its entire width, not making much room for a disorientated time traveller trying to gather his wits. At first, I believed the crowd was shopping for pleasure, but my experiences of the following days did not confirm this hypothesis. I never did discover the true meaning of the unceasing flows from one large store to the next. People completed purchases, or so I supposed, but there was something like a hidden meaning to the exchanges of parcels between customers which went on in the middle of the street.

(If I ever were to return, I'd demand to be given some excellent reproductions of the bank notes—although "notes" may not be the right term—I brought back with me. In fact, a few million of such bills would be better, so that I don't need to spend the night in the trees. And what can one do in an unknown city without a place of one's own, a refuge where one can do some thinking?)

The Cincinnati scientists did not believe me either when I told them that an arts war was part of the future's daily reality. Of course, they hadn't seen two aquarellists battle it out with grenades in the middle of Angelmine because of declining valuations—Angelmine being one of the gigantic stores jostling in the city core—nor the knot of children who had come in mid-July for the Christmas pin-up and who had found, tragically, much more than they had bargained for.

When I met Alberto Crapoli, a manager of somewhat straitened means, I had already decided to do in Rome as the Romans do. In the course of ten minutes of conversation, I learned that he knew only vaguely of Rome, even less of aquarellists, and that he had been the one to spot me and not the reverse. I cared little for this nicety until the moment I understood this made me his property. He believed that I came from an era with a particular fondness for theatre—because of my accent or my haircut?—and he asked me if Mendelssohn's "Wedding March" was as popular in my time as in his. I told him the truth, disappointing him immensely.

But Crapoli came later, at a time when, as I said, I was starting to feel the first pangs of acculturation, as difficult as it was illusory. To which should be added, of course, the natural excitement of the tourist who first sets foot in the future.

I had barely set the aforesaid foot down when I left the local horizontal and grappled with the heavens. I twirled in midair, above the crowded sidewalk, and my head came dangerously close to the shop window of a bazaar which extended over the first six floors of the building, its top part having apparently been surrendered to vines. A shop window as large and empty as a cavern…*Now, there's a city!* I thought in that instant. I was back in the toy worlds of my childhood. This did not compare in the least with regaining consciousness in front of the disposable socks counter at Kresge's in New York. The cavern's dummies were swimming in free fall while constantly changing clothes. The prices appeared inside white balloons which issued from their mouths.

To be…or not to be anything at all. There, on the sidewalk, nobody appeared to have noticed me, and especially not the two guys who pursued a chocolate between the legs of passersby. Was I a store dummy escaped from my shop window, the victim of a remarkable sartorial confusion? I learned later that this era did not neglect, either, the problem of positronic neuroses.

As my initial excitement died down, it was time to check my marching orders. The sheet was deep in my pocket—just in case the time crossing happened to dislodge my memory—and as crumpled as a grocery list entrusted to a seven-year-old. I had to visit a specific number of places and memorize as much information as possible on this future's reality. First, I was to visit the stock exchange, second, a drugstore, and, finally, a church—or rather the place of worship of this "necessarily advanced" society, in the own words of the first research report. I didn't know why the drugstore was included, but I assumed it demonstrated unexpected concern for my welfare on the part of the project's leaders. Yes, I might get sick.

The science of my era was foursquare behind me, and it remained there during my entire stay.

Taking a taxi or bus was out of the question: there were none, or I hadn't spotted any, and providing me with change had not been judged critical. Thus it was that I walked to the Cincinnati stock exchange. The stroll was long, but uneventful. Sure, I faced a few inquisitive looks, but I obviously did not look like a street punk out to steal the handbag of a retired heiress.

Since I lacked any kind of link with the loudspeaker industry, there was no way to get in the stock exchange building of that era either. Police cars, trucks with extension ladders and military vehicles surrounded the already timeworn glass cube, stained with tears and sweat. After all, maybe bodies were going to rain down. And yet, since time immemorial, Cincinnati has never been a great stock exchange.

That remark was struck from the official report.

One remark was kept, however. And there isn't the shadow of a doubt that it's there to discredit me in the eyes of certain academics by denouncing the absurdity of my deposition. As far as it goes, they're right. I should have understood something was awry and I was wrong not to be on my guard. This remark concerns language.

I confess that I was more happy than surprised— which probably explains a lot—when I discovered that the hundreds of hours spent on *An Introduction to the Possible Phonetico-Syntaxic Phenomena of Basic Future Americanese* in the course of my training had been a waste of time: the English spoken in our future was as understandable as my own Baltimore brand of English, apart from a few terms whose exact meaning eluded me but which could be deduced from the general context. A true miracle had occurred: English, or at least the species of English spoken in this future Cincinnati, had not undergone a new great vowel shift as it had between the fourteenth and seventeenth centuries, and as was expected by some of the project's experts. Everyone knows that language evolves, whatever happens.

The report's commentary clearly shows that I overstepped the bounds of credibility there.

Yet, bystanders who were there and whom I understood *perfectly* confirmed that this was indeed the stock exchange and that prices would stay high as long as the winds continued to blow from the west. I'm not a poet and, as far as I'm concerned, west is west. I concluded the shores of the Mississippi were lined with giant wind turbines and I turned my back on the stock exchange.

And then, suddenly, I realized the import of being the first man of my era to tread upon the future's sidewalks, to breathe an air that did not yet exist, to glance at the faces of our descendants. To the point that I started wondering why these people did not revere my glorious achievements, had not raised altars to me in various parts of the city. But the training I'd received at the University made me a man at once normal and supremely cautious. I had to minimize my contacts with the natives. For instance: "The stock exchange, that, right?" or "Where, where the drugstore?" Above all, I was to avoid identification as a voyeur from the far past, if I didn't want to be subjected to imprisonment, interrogations, and public display in front of the mainstream press at a banquet, not necessarily in that order.

Cats don't exist here. That, at least, they made a note of.

The drugstore turned up when I took an interest in a random newsstand, rooted between a silence booth and a rainproof pay-shelter. Looking for a newspaper was not part of my programme, since, according to the guys operating the Heterochronal Device, they were supposed to be quite extinct, in such a far future. In any case, I still didn't have any change.

The five or six headlines displayed outside the newsstand didn't help at all. The Supreme wanted to clean out the Morphall and the Favricants as yet knew nothing about it. Pikar was unwilling to guarantee the arrival of the Croco Wavelet in time for winter. However, a more interesting detail was that each copy of the newspaper included a pocket full of tablets for all the fashionable illnesses, from tyrphallide to the hokar-madine. There was my drugstore, stapled to the latest news.

I walked a few more minutes before discovering a park filled with trees and tropical birds. Nobody paid any attention to me; all things considered, I was playing well the part of the guy who's supposed to know where he's going. A couple of dogs did come sniffing around me, adding a few observations into the cellphones slung around their necks. Who they were yelping to, I can't imagine. I was already dreaming up a new type of police officer, less expensive but just as efficient.

Two thousand dollars in the currency of my era was worthless here, though no more so than—as Crapoli confirmed later—the gold plaque and the handful of diamonds which weighed down my pants. I'm not used to being destitute and, suddenly, the feeling I was truly lost and alone grabbed hold of me. The night was shaping up as a rough one: I had nowhere to go, and all the day's walking was beginning to tell on me. Exhaustion and despair weigh uncommonly heavy in the future. The only analogy was provided by a friend; it is the same feeling which strikes when one comes down a jumbo jet on the tarmac of Calcutta airport, at night, where the bodies of the dying are laid out on the runway's yellow numerals, calling out to the heavens.

The night I was dreading fell at last. During these dark and teeming hours, in any city around the world, there are always people who seek what the daytime has not granted them. An adventure, an encounter of no lasting significance, the pleasure of watching others who seek, or whatever. The nights in Pompeii were probably not very different from those in Cincinnati.

I had gone back to the brightly lit streets when Crapoli—who must also have been seeking for something—came upon me. He seemed surprised to see me alone, since people *like me* could not be allowed out by themselves. It was easy to understand that I was prime bait for this down-on-his-luck manager.

"You're a guy out of time," he said, his voice playful as he seized my arm. "You can give me a hand..."

Was it that obvious? I had been spotted, like a rare beast that a specialist can identify unmistakably in the midst of a million others which look the same. So, stay calm, collect as much information as possible.

"Correct," I said, speaking with deliberation. "May I know what year this is?"

"We're in 87 of the K System," he answered offhandedly. "K for Kennedy. Or perhaps for Kelloggs. I don't know. Anyway, we were told it was better this way."

Something important had happened, then, but I was still unable to determine what exactly. I walked through the streets with Crapoli, mind befuddled by this world which only seemed familiar and which appeared to flee before me at every turn. In a certain way, an indefinable aura of disorder prevailed in this era. In fact, Crapoli was battering me with a senseless diatribe about the tortoises out of time, though I couldn't understand a word of it. For my part, my gaze lingered on the neon signs, compelled by the faint hope of recognizing a famous brand name.

"You don't seem very interested in the past," I said to shut him up for a minute.

"The Arenas tell us that the past no longer belongs to us. So why bother?"

It was a world without memory. That remark is smuggled somewhere in the official report, camouflaged in a paragraph of lies.

At one crossing, a bank of traffic lights were wavering between a number of geometrical forms and pastel shades. As we used the pedestrian crosswalk, I could hear the bellowing of the cars in which passengers debated in a piano-lounge-like ambiance. As for Crapoli, he didn't need a car; managers found their performers in the street. "They're all born in the gutter!" But he quickly added that he really didn't consider me an artist.

"Is it because I'm a time traveller that you cling to me like that?"

"A little," he answered frankly. "I recognized you because you looked lost. And you're just in time to give me a hand."

"And where are we going now?"

"We'll cram at my place," he said with authority. "I guess you don't know where to spend the night, right? So, we'll have to cram."

"Cram?"

"Not now, obviously. Not before the offices close."

This time, I refrained from asking. An answer would eventually turn up, free of any ambiguities, I told myself without believing a word of it.

We stopped here and there in front of the marquees of movie theatres, which advertised titles such as *Happy Surprise* and *Merciless Time, Finally On Our Side* with animated posters.

"These are very old hits," explained Crapoli. "None of these moviehouses really exist. They're only facades for the apartments of artists with more or less steady incomes. The facade is the Law of the New Union."

And we were in 87 of the K System. A faint suspicion that the Heterochronal Device had not quite been dead on in its calculations was starting to take root. I was probably further away from my departure time than foreseen. My only source of comfort was that my temporal location had probably been determined using the Rodon sweeper.

"Can we have a drink somewhere?" I asked, not bothering to hide how weary I was of this paved- and-sidewalked carnival of masks. I was hoping this simple phrase had not lost all meaning with the passage of time.

"You want to imbibe?" asked Crapoli as if I belonged to an endangered species.

"Not really. More like sit down for a bit, actually."

"Hmmm," he grumbled, looking at my clothes. "We're not *wayne* enough for the *Ezekiel*. But there's always the *Swallowing Soak*. It's got a smash din and the caboozing is fairly cheap."

Maybe the *Ezekiel* was too *wayne* for us, but at any rate the *Swallowing Soak* did have the clear advantage of being just across the street. The place united two very different realities, though not necessarily opposite ones. From the outside, it was a luxuriously appointed bookstore, but, once you entered the trick doors whose glass panes showed browsers hard at work, you discovered a kind of pub for men only, noisy and redolent with the spicy smells of the undergrowth. I never could, like them, establish a link between drinking and reading. Probably a question of intoxication. The lovers of literature had presumably sought refuge in salubrious tippling as more and more bad books came out.

For men only. That was astounding. Crapoli led me through the tables surrounded by shining blue haloes in the darkness. Dozens of drinkers, hundreds of bottles and babies (apparently male) sometimes suckling at the hairy breast of their fathers.

"Feeding one's kids isn't against the law, right?" said Crapoli when he noticed my crumbling composure. "Neither the *Bible* nor *Al-Quran* say anything of the kind."

He found us a table at the back of the room.

"You'll buy me a drink?"

"Sorry, but I don't have any money. Cash, I mean."

Crapoli seemed to have temporarily forgotten that all I had on me were my dollars, my gold, and my diamonds. Yet, as we talked earlier, he had been quite categorical: at best, the bank notes could be burned for heat, though the gold and diamonds could be given to children who would enjoy the colours.

"Oh, right, I forgot. Tomorrow, you can claim your allowance. For that helping hand, of course."

Of course.

Crapoli ordered the drinks, using a complex code of hand and arm gestures, exactly like those of a linesman at a football game. A few minutes later, some species of blue desert warrior emerged from the dark spaces surrounding us. He set down twelve cups on our table, six full and six empty, and, with the practiced moves of a three-card-monte sharper, allocated each to a specific spot.

"Another herp, Alberto? You've really got a good nose for them."

Herp?

Time to drink, or rather to mix in small doses the contents of the six full cups into the six empty ones, which resulted in three cocktails for each. Each cocktail produced, according to the ratio of its ingredients, a different effect. Crapoli was crystal clear on this point. One could go to sleep, lose one's memory, laugh out loud, explode or murder somebody. (Or maybe it was a matter of merely *experiencing* the guilt. Who can really know?)

The first mixture he prepared for me tasted like aftershave—perfumed with lavender.

"What's a herp?" I asked between sips.

"A decedent, an *overdue*, a time tortoise. You're harder to spot because people dress any which way, these days. But I've got the nose, right? You'll lend me a superb hand, I'm sure. What duration's yours?"

I replied, unsure whether or not I'd understood the question:

"Forty-eight hours."

"Perfect! Good for a week in the K System. A herp needs me, and I need a herp…"

His remark took a while to percolate through my mind. I was stuck there for six more days! I didn't doubt it; Crapoli's experience was already worth more in my eyes than all the science of the Heterochronal Device team. Without the cups' effect, I would have fled and lost myself in the ageless crowd until the Tuesday stalkers got me. Assuming I'd known of their existence at that point, which wasn't the case. This just to confess, in all modesty, that I believed what Crapoli was telling me.

(In Cincinnati, my Cincinnati, they denied I could have met someone who'd told me such things. And from that point on, as a matter of fact, they denied all the rest.)

The last mix got me thoroughly drunk; I was starting to find that all these men passing by us, their male babies under the arm, looked quite unseemly.

"Why don't we go home to bed?" I suggested, with a directness that surprised me.

"It's not eleven yet," replied Crapoli, busily ordering more cups. "The offices won't close until then."

I know how to wait. When I was younger, I'd wait, stopwatch in hand, for the very end of each month, the moment when the last second slipped into the past. Then I'd tear the page off the calendar and discover Miss June, July or August…

Crapoli, less tipsy than myself, told me of his grandfather's peaceful life before the K System was established. All was so crystal-clear in those days. A house was a house, and newspapers were comprehensible. You didn't have to spend your time decoding them. Did the U.N. still exist? There was a place called New York in Carolina, but Crapoli seemed to know nothing of any U.N.

Once more on the sidewalk, he took me toward a cluster of towers that huddled in close proximity. The crowd around us was denser than it had been at noon. Office workers poured into the street in buzzing waves while Crapoli and I struggled upstream, toward the elevators of Acton Tower. Ma was probably already expecting him.

"Who's Ma?"

"Maria Mary-Eve Marie-Una," he replied proudly. "My wife."

My first impression upon reaching the 89th floor was one of quiet and vast space. That was where he lived, more or less. I never met anybody else who could boast of owning an entire floor for the night.

"Housing crisis, so to speak," explained Crapoli.

Maria—from that point on, I only called her Maria—was trying, in vain, to remove some partitions from the lobby. I rushed to her aid, while Crapoli stayed behind, arms crossed.

The false walls at last vanished into the ceiling and I gradually discovered the details of a cheerful dwelling. Maria was truly an expert in the art of apartment unfolding: kitchenette, unmade beds, storage closets and modern conveniences were swiftly set in their proper places in the lobby, while the dull-coloured armchairs and the low tables already present became living-room furniture. The final touch was the lighting, which I would have called jazz-bar style, had not that expression had, in year 87 of the K System, a totally different—and rather too prurient—meaning.

"This is nothing," Maria told me kindly, "you haven't seen the bathroom."

And see it I did. The largest private bathroom in history: no less than twelve urinals, ten sinks, and liters and liters of liquid soap.

The kids, two rumpled and rambunctious boys, finally showed up, carrying cacti filched from the interior decorating division. Everything was happening very fast. Water was boiling on the stove, Crapoli channel-zapped with the TV. After a frugal meal all five of us sat down before the tube. I wanted to adjust the image, but Maria's objections stopped me. Every last TV set here is on the fritz, without exception. To my duty as an observer from another time was now added a new challenge: managing to make out something among the ripples of colour, and figuring out when it was time to applaud.

The next morning, it was discovered Maria was pregnant—the portable tests never lied. The Crapolis would have come to blows had not the three hundred employees from this floor come in to shoo us out by the end of breakfast. Everything had to be put away, the kitchenette and everything else must be folded back into the walls. It was the same story every morning: with the start of the workday, the Crapoli family must cease to exist, disperse into the city. For him, the street of fallen impresarios, for her the shuttling between automated child-care centres.

But until evening, he hurried to point out, *we* would be supporting the family.

Surrounded by the waterworks that decorated the entrance of Acton Tower, I asked Crapoli where I could find a church. I wasn't in any hurry (I had six more days ahead of me, if my guide had spoken the truth), but I wanted to fulfill my orders as soon as possible, just in case.

"Of course," he said. "As it happens, there's one on the way to the bank."

The church in question turned out to be a hotel of a style I knew well. Standard hello-goodbye model, with as a bonus a very old *Holiday Inn* sign, rusted metal and broken plexiglass, unearthed from a historic dump. It was, according to Crapoli, a very important meeting place for those who wanted to withdraw from the world and meditate upon their ego. Your choice of *Bible* or *Al-Quran* in every drawer. What about the sacrifice? There was a prescribed ritual at the desk, when guests paid their bill. That was the whole sacrifice.

But Crapoli was mostly interested in the regulated-debit bank, whose doors, like a railway station's, opened directly onto the street.

"You can't live with us without paying. So you go get in line today and we'll be coming back tomorrow."

I had no account at this bank and no ID with me.

"You're a herp, you reek of it," he said. "Besides, they have a sensor."

This is where everything just fell apart for me. The small struggles I'd gone through the previous day in order to adapt were as nothing compared to the shock I got from this bank, as vast as an underground concrete garage, where hundreds of time travellers queued up in front of wickets. Unlike what the Heterochronal Device team had hoped for, not only was I not the first time traveller, I was hardly the last, if I could trust my battered senses.

"Forget your surprise," said Crapoli kindly, motioning me forward. "I told you there were many herps like you. You're just like everybody else. Who can live without money?"

I took my place at the end of a line, to receive my allowance as soon as the sensor had given the green light. This comedy was taking on absurd proportions. By what instant progress could these people from my time (never mind the exact year) all find themselves here, like slaves begging for alms?

Someone caught me by the arm, all smiles.

"Hey! I recognize your shoes," he said. "I'm from Cleveland. Name's Robins…Can you tell them I'll be a bit late? I should be back in Cleveland within three days, as soon as I can put together the price of a ticket…"

I never knew what kind of ticket it was. Train ticket, plane ticket, lottery ticket? Go figure! People were already yelling at me to stop holding up the line; I moved forward. At least I had learned fashion could have its uses. My shoes, for some unknown reason, had pinpointed my origin as a precise slice of a faraway decade.

Let me therefore repeat, for the benefit of the people in Cleveland: Robins should be home soon, if he's not already back. He is not, I repeat, he is *not* forever lost in the K System!

Half an hour later, the cashier handed me ten blue bills bearing the word *TAB* and a picture of a sailing ship foundering in a storm. Crapoli guided me outside as if I were his prize poodle. The sun beat down upon the city, spearing through the glass buildings and filling the streets with long blue, pink and green rays. In this daylight, the shipwreck picture on the tabs seemed less ominous. Then all of a sudden, out of the ten I'd received, only four were left. Barely enough for a newspaper and a round of caboozing at the Swallowing Soak. Crapoli was already folding six of my precious bills in his hands.

"We're playing this well," he said, pointing to my four remaining tabs. "You stay at my place, I'll pay your rent with these six."

Undoubtedly, a really helping hand. And there would be many more such during the rest of the week. I, the herp, had become the provider of a family from the future whose head probably stood at the bottom of the social ladder. He knew nothing, could teach me nothing of his world, while the city all around us cruised onward. At noon, it was beggars' hour, and at three p.m. horses' hour: thousands of equines replaced cars everywhere in the neighbourhood. Then, at six that evening, I witnessed the buildings go through a wash-rinse- and-dry cycle, along with everyone who hadn't been able to afford a rainproof shelter.

I would have given all my tabs for a stretch of beach, but Crapoli believed—why he did is beyond me—that I was deeply interested in these long hours of pointless walking, and in the late evenings spent with Maria and the kids in front of the visual mush regurgitated by their TV set.

That routine, I told myself, I could just as easily manage on my own, and so, on the morning of the fourth day, I left the building where the Crapolis slept. Once I'd reached the ground floor, I found out, to my astonishment, that it was cattle hour: a huge lowing herd, with pounding hooves, flooded the streets. The last quadrupeds then yielded to the first office workers, who began to invade the tower. I went to the bank, received my prescribed ten tabs, and lost myself, for good this time, in the crowd on the sidewalks.

The next day, I got to see another manifestation of the Arts War, as I loitered between counters, one devoted to half-day socks and the other showcasing by-the-hour nighties, in a department store at the other end of town. Two pianists—I was told later—declared war on one another with no advance notice, igniting fires all over with lighter-torches. That's one of the pianistic arts in this time, to act without warning. For a moment, I missed Crapoli's presence. For all his ignorance, he knew at least how to protect his "helping hand".

And it came to be that I got fed up with wandering the infinite chessboard of the city, with turning right or left every time a block deigned to make a right angle or a sidewalk decided to end. Cincinnati, whatever the era, must have a boundary. There must be a place where a man could lie down in the wild grass, among the ants. I decided to forge on straight ahead, without halting, until the horizon stopped casting back, in its gigantic mirrors, the facades of anonymous buildings. To achieve this, I had to wait until the next day.

There were no more towers, but the sky wasn't any clearer.

The blue fabric of the heavens was torn by a colossal concrete rail, supported by giant pillars, running toward the countryside. At least I could see the outskirts of a forest in the distance, and the glimmer of a small lake. And suddenly I felt freed of an enormous burden, that of perceiving everywhere lies and dissimulation, unable to do anything save to accept them. Here, everything was real: the rail constituted proof that people sometimes left this hell; the trees at the end of the green field were real trees. The air smelled of truth.

I was strolling along the rail, going from one pillar to the other, when I saw dark shapes prostrate on a bedding of worn tires. Further along, leaning against the next pillar, a shack made from century-old sheets of metal (forgotten ads for *Coca-Cola*, toothpaste gel, aftershave and beer) was obviously used as a shelter. Seeing me approach, people stood up on the tires, forming a semicircle as if they'd learned to get into position when confronted by someone they didn't recognize. As far as I remember, I was facing a group of elderly men, wearing long coats cut from heavy black woolen fabric. They had the pathetic look you see on old men who've left their whiskers grow wild. Abundant hair and beards, white, gray, remarkably filthy.

One of them took a few steps in my direction and stopped barely a meter away. For my part, I would not risk a misstep either forward or back. He stared at me a long while, his expression betraying greater and greater worry and disbelief. Then he took something out of his pocket: an old curled-up photograph, barely larger than a postage stamp. He looked at it, then his eyes, whose wrinkled lids seemed unlikely to hold them in much longer, fastened on me.

"You're *the* herp?" he said in a thin, quavering voice. "The first one?"

He showed me the photograph with a trembling hand. It was me. It was the picture on my ID card from Cincinnati University.

"Why do you always call me a herp?" I asked stupidly. "What the hell happened, anyway?"

"You're the first time tortoise, obviously. The dinosaur that preceded all the others. The cause of the invasion."

I shook my head repeatedly. Light! Oh, to finally shed some light on this whole mess!

"Who are you? What are you doing here?"

"You have reached the Cincinnati University History

Department," replied the old man. "This is what they turned us into, once they'd set up the Arenas to teach non-history. They couldn't do otherwise. Everything you saw back there is made up from whole cloth; it's the only kind of history people live now, free of any reference to the past. It's nothing but a sham."

I gave myself all the necessary time to absorb these words.

"But why?"

"Because of you. Because you were the first, all the herps say so, although we'd never seen you before. The last shall be first and the first shall be last…"

"I don't get it."

"We're only defending ourselves, don't you see? What would the men of your time do if hordes from the sixteenth century suddenly invaded your streets? Would you give them your science? Would you show them how to vanquish illness, master nuclear power, build an airplane, go to the moon? Of course not. You'd protect yourself, you'd do everything in your power to drive these sightseers back to their own time, in hopes of staunching the flow from the past, or at least abating it. Meanwhile, you'd find short-term solutions. Unsatisfactory ones, of course. Then maybe one of you would come up with an inconceivable idea: invent a world the parasites could not figure out. A puzzle without a solution, do you see? So they'd get discouraged and leave us alone. That's what we did. And it's been going on for a long, long time. And it's up to you to make it stop."

I was thinking back on all that had escaped me during my walks through the streets of Cincinnati, all that I had failed to understand. There is nothing to understand over there, where everything has been interrupted and distorted, so that we cannot know what our own evolution shall be. It accounted for the K System, the Crapolis sleeping in an office tower, the herds of cattle in the morning.

And it was up to me to make this stop.

It was up to me.

A shiver ran down my spine. I suddenly felt that I knew precisely the solution to their problem. And that they knew it as well as I did.

"You're going to assassinate me," I said in a voice I could barely hear myself. My throat was raspy, dry as a simoon wind.

"Your corpse would automatically return to your own time. We're already dealing with a peaceful invasion. We have no wish to fan your people's curiosity nor to trigger a wave of resentment. Who knows where enmity could lead us?"

"No matter, I've figured it out now: you've found the way to cancel the boomerang effect. You'll keep me here to the end of my days."

He shook his head sadly. "We could have tried to make your mission look like a failure and thus discourage your contemporaries, but it's impossible. For a long time, in fact, ever since the first herp—*our* first herp, not you—we've tried and failed to control the boomerang effect. We don't understand, any more than you do, why an organism that has been projected into the future comes back to its proper time-frame after a while. It is believed—by those who believe that they understand—that this comes from a tension induced in the fabric of temporal reality. But all research in that area has proven futile up to now. The mathematical model exists; what we lack is a physical reality on which to work."

The old man was weeping softly before me.

"Leave us in peace. Tell them not to come, to let us live in peace. After all, you're the first, it's within your power."

The weight that had left me for a moment settled back on my shoulders, like a prehistoric carrion-eater, reeking of guilt.

I had to change the course of history. Or rather, I had to restore it, having altered it once before.

The noise of a siren rose behind me, making me start. A truck was barreling toward the vacant lot that had been christened the History Department. On a platform, behind the driver's cabin, men in uniform were stirring while an hysterical Crapoli pointed to me with all ten of his fingers. Everything and anything for the helping hand.

The tribunal where I was taken, the next morning, looked like a real tribunal, of that at least I am certain. The man who clearly played the role of the judge addressed me in an emotional voice.

"We would like to know your period's intentions concerning time travel."

"So would I," I replied.

The judge buried his face in his hands, as if to hold back a flood. Then he lifted his gaze to me.

"You're the cause of everything, and thus guilty. But we can do nothing to you. Neither punish you nor keep you here. Paradoxically, you are our only hope. Will you tell them? Will you tell them to stop their experiments and destroy their machines?"

I'm telling you now, guys:

STOP IT! WE HAVE TO STOP IT!

Resignedly, I completed my stay at the Crapolis', at the judge's request. Such was my sentence. Sidewalk tortoise by day—herps are slow to understand, Crapoli explained—chained TV addict by night, tabs and all the rest.

It was while I was pushing the stove back into the wall that I returned, rematerialized in the Heterochronal Device's cockpit, one minute and sixteen seconds after my departure, if the report is correct.

Today, after two weeks of isolation and merciless debriefings, I feel as empty as those old snake skins we used to find in the middle of fields, in a past both incredibly ancient and, for me, supremely close, which I call my childhood.

I hesitated (should I say "a long time"?) before concluding my tale. I pondered. And I found nothing better to say than this:

My human brethren, I would like to believe that nothing has been lost and that Man's future shall indeed be this pure, transcendent thing dreamt of by philosophers, scientists, and who knows, a few men of good will among those the *res publica* will not have thoroughly corrupted. I would so much like to believe that, as in the colourful labyrinths of my childhood, I have only momentarily lost my way among the tortuous passages and that soon I shall reach the treasure. But never has the treasure seemed more out of reach than now.

For the moment, I am left with a single question, the only thing that keeps alive in me the appearance of hope; and, paradoxically, the reality of despair (what's one paradox more or less?). This question is:

How may I convince you that the wreck depicted on the tabs is a meaningful statement about the future, and that it must be avoided at all costs?

And what more?

How may I convince you that you cannot want this future?

BELINDA'S MOTHER
Michael Coney

"My guess," said Mattie Severin, "is she's got some godawful disease. I mean, disfiguring. And serve her right."

"It's your mother we're talking about," said her fellow passenger gently.

A spot of turbulence lent a jerky emphasis to Mattie's reply. "My mother? She ran out on me when I was sixteen and I've heard nothing from her since. I've spent a lifetime not knowing whether she's alive or dead—and between you and me, not caring overmuch. And now—over forty years later, for chrissakes—she calls me out of the blue and expects me to come running to her side."

"Which is exactly what you're doing. May I ask why?"

Mattie turned and examined her companion, sensing disapproval. The old Casanova had kept his looks well; she had to grant him that. He'd been her mother's lover, for sure. His expression told her nothing.

"Why? I want to see her old. I want to see her suffering. I want her to know what it's like to be ugly." She turned to the window quickly. Dunes of glittering snow slid beneath the low-flying VTOL. She blinked angrily at the wetness on her eyelids.

He said, "Anna Carstairs could never be ugly."

"Oh? Then why didn't she show her face on the visiphone, huh? She calls me out of nowhere and expects me to recognize her voice? I wasn't afraid to show my face, that's for sure. I wonder what she thought of her ugly daughter, after all these years."

"You sell yourself short."

"I have a mirror in my bathroom, Cory. Which is more than Anna has, I'll bet. After all, she'd been a 3V star for oh, fifteen years, public adulation and all that, men flocking around her, *you* flocking around her, and suddenly she's offered the part of Belinda in Jacob's *Two Women*. The part of the goddamned mother. And it dawns on her she's thirty-five and yes, she could be Belinda's mother. Hell, she was my mother, and I was the same age as Belinda was supposed to be. It all came home to her, what aging and ugliness is all about. So she ran off and hid. She cared nothing for me, or you, or anyone."

His face showed distress; she was hitting home. "I can't believe that. She went to Lake Louise to think over the 3V offer, and she had a boating accident. When she disappeared the media reckoned it was amnesia."

"Garbage. She looked in the mirror and didn't like what she saw, and she ran off to Lake Louise and had a nervous breakdown. The media said she was irrational, fighting people off as though they were contaminated. There was something about little green men, too." Mattie laughed shortly. "It's a recognized symptom."

"That was all built up out of the testimony of one boatman."

"And then maybe she spent a few years in some private asylum under an assumed name. She wouldn't want the fans to know their idol was in the booby hatch now, would she? And when she snaps out of it she holes up in this godforsaken place we're headed for; what's it called again?"

"Inutuk."

Mattie looked out of the window. "I think I can see it down there. Why in heaven's name would anyone want to live in a place like that?"

The VTOL circled and Cory Hardacre got his first look at Inutuk. A double row of neat and brightly-painted houses wheeled past the window, white-roofed with snow. No wrecked cars sunk in snowdrifts, no backyard junk heaps. A model of what an Inuit village should be. At the end of the street lay the smooth frozen surface of the sea wher e six unusually beamy boats were drawn up in a row.

"It looks okay to me," he said mildly. Anna's daughter was so down on everything he felt obliged to take an opposing viewpoint. But she was right; this was a strange place for a celebrity like Anna to end up. Even stranger, why should she summon them here, now?

Like Mattie's call, the visiphone screen had remained blank. "Cory, it's Anna," she'd said. "I'm at Inutuk. I want to see you." And she'd given him directions, voice as imperious as ever, and ignored his questions. She'd spoken as though time hadn't passed, and it hadn't occurred to him not to obey her summons. Old habits die hard. When he'd changed planes to the short-haul VTOL, he'd found Mattie already on board.

He stole a glance at her. What a contrast to the magically beautiful and vivacious Anna! She must have got an undue dose of her father's genes: that ugly little director from Munich who'd somehow beaten out all other contenders for Anna's bed. Including himself. No, Anna had married to further her career, that couldn't be denied. She was ambitious, selfish and ruthless…

And he'd adored her. Nobody was perfect; not Anna, not he. Nobody was perfect.

"Yeah, but there's degrees," said Mattie unexpectedly.

He must have spoken his thoughts aloud with Anna's perfect features in his mind's eye. Now Mattie's coarse face was turned his way; an unwelcome contrast. "She had her faults, sure, don't we all?" he said. "But she had a loving nature." That brought a harsh bark of laughter.

"She was a goddamned nympho; that's what you mean!"

"She lived life to the full," he said cautiously.

"So why do *you* think she quit?"

"She was a big star and they overworked her. It happens. My guess is she went to Lake Louise for a rest, to get away from people. Even then the media wouldn't let her alone. So she did some deep thinking and decided she wanted out. She knew she'd be plagued by the media for evermore, so she simply disappeared from view."

"No little green men? No battle with a bearded boatman? My God, Cory, are you ever unimaginative! No wonder Anna chose the Hungarian."

"Austrian." Suddenly angry, he said, "What you don't realize is your mother gave a lot of pleasure to millions of people all over the world. You can't take that away from her. She was a brilliant actress."

"Oh, sure. She could fool anyone except Old Father Time."

"Nobody likes growing old. I quit about the same time. Once I was out of movies, I didn't exactly seek out the spotlights. I was retired. I'd had enough and I took it easy. Quite a few people I never saw again. It's normal."

The whine of the turbines rose so that he scarcely heard Mattie's snort of skepticism. The VTOL dropped gently through a swirling of disturbed snow. A row of sleek ground-effect vehicles stood outside a small terminal building.

"Good grief, look at those buggies!" exclaimed Mattie. "What are they, next century's model? The Government sure throws money at these people!"

"The plane is here, Anna." Jimmy regarded her, his flat Inuit features anxious. "Please remember, no excitement."

Anna Carstairs smiled. "I'm going to see my daughter and my lover for the first time in over forty years, and you say no excitement? You may be a heck of a good doctor, but you're one lousy psychologist! Now you go down and make sure they stamp the snow off their boots before they come in. Stall them for a moment while I pull myself to gether. Jesus! This is one time I could do with a good stiff scotch. Never mind; just give me one of those pills, will you?"

He handed her a sedative. "I may be a good doctor but I'll never understand your body, Anna," he said, and left.

Anna tried to calm her fluttering heart. It would be just too bad if she croaked right here and now in her bed, with Cory and Mattie on their way. Had she done the right thing, sending for them? No; it had been a selfish gesture, one of many. But she had to see them one last time. It had been too long...Mattie hadn't looked or so unded too enthusiastic on the phone. That was understandable. And Cory...Dear Cory, he'd begged her to turn on her video pick-up. He'd turned his on, of course. He'd worn very well, had Cory, over the years...

Over the years since that afternoon at Lake Louise when she'd changed forever. She could remember every detail; the mountain breeze ruffling the lake surface, the chop-chop-chop of the wavelets against the bow as she drove the rowboat forward with powerful strokes; she'd been an expert oars-woman since childhood. The snow capping the moun tains, the distant cars crawling like beetles along the road and that unexpected thunderclap that had made her scan the sky for clouds. There had been none.

She could still remember what she'd been thinking of at that moment. Retirement. Quitting. Giving in to *anno domini*. Telling that insulting little wart of a husband to stuff his role up his jacksy. Belinda's mother, indeed! What a role, what a storyline! A middle-aged wimp who sacrifices everything for the good of a leper colony! My God, was this the thanks she got after fifteen years of making his fortune for him? To play Belinda's goddamned mother?

Easy, now. *No excitement.* It was a long time ago. Fear, that had been her principle emotion. Not anger. Fear of losing the love of all those millions of people. Fear of them saying, in a very few years time, *Anna Who?* Fear that fifteen years of hard work and success would have been wasted.

And fear that Cory Hardacre, the randy philanderer, would

lose his interest in her too. That, she'd admitted on that lonely afternoon on Lake Louise, would be the hardest thing to take. She would shrivel up like women do, while he would go on getting more handsome, more distinguished, more sought after by baby-faced starlets. And suddenly she'd find they were merely old friends, no spark, no more than brother and sister. That, she couldn't take.

Then she'd seen the thing in the water.

It floated just below the ripples. She'd released the oars, curious, glad of a diversion. The thing had looked to be about ten centimeters long, semi-transparent like a jellyfish, but you didn't get jellyfish in Lake Louise. It hadn't been jellyfish-shaped; more like a huge broad tadpole, or a gigantic sperm. And something about the frantic way it was lashing its tail had told her it was in distress.

So she'd dipped her hand in, and fished it out.

It had lain on her palm for a few seconds, then painlessly dissolved into her skin.

/// \\\

As Mattie rang the doorbell she found herself gulping nervously. When Anna appeared, how would she, Mattie, respond? Would she find she'd flung herself into Anna's arms blubbering daughterly words of love while Cory looked on smiling? Or would she be able to keep her cool, to stand her ground with a reproving stare? To prepare herself, she folded her arms firmly. She shivered. It was freezing cold out here after the warmth of the VTOL'S cabin.

The door opened, and who should be standing there but an Eskimo! Dear God, what had her mother come to? In shock, she heard Cory introducing her and himself, then she was trailing into the house, stamping snow off her shoes. The Eskimo said he was Jim something.

"Where is Miss Carstairs?" Cory asked.

"She is in bed. Give her a moment to prepare herself, please."

"A moment?" Mattie burst out. "She's had forty years!"

"She is not well. That is why she sent for you."

"What's wrong with her? Has she seen a doctor?"

"I am a doctor."

Cory said quickly, "We've come a long way, Mattie. We don't have to rush into her bedroom right this minute. How about a cup of coffee, Jim?"

"I put it on as soon as I heard the plane." Smiling, he took a pot from the stove and poured dark coffee into mugs.

Mattie took a deep breath, sat down in an elderly wing chair and looked around. The small room was cluttered; a combined kitchen and living room. A bowl of unusual-looking fruit lay on a rough pine table. All rather different from Anna's old place down south. But cozy enough. What exactly was this Jim's status here? She took a mug from him, annoyed to find her hand was shaking. "How long have you been, uh, practicing?" she asked.

"Thirty years." His eyes gave nothing away. But then, they never did.

"So what exactly is wrong with my mother?"

The eyes watched her, the face was completely expressionless. "She will die soon."

She'd guessed it all along. "What of, for God's sake?"

He shrugged. "Old age. I know, you are going to say seventy-six is not old these days. But it's old for an Inuit, and Anna's been living like the rest of us here for forty years. Living like us, working like us. Probably working harder than anyone."

It didn't sound like Anna. "Working at what? She's a 3V star. She's not qualified for anything."

"I don't think you know her very well. Or us. Here, we are qualified only to live. Anna had a great life force. Now she's worn out. When you see her, please go gently."

Mattie heard Cory say, "Of course we will." She sipped at her coffee; it was strong and sweet and not bad at all. Exactly what had her mother been doing in this godforsaken settlement? Manning a soup kitchen? Taking in laundry? This Jim seemed a sincere kind of guy, but one never knew. Just how sick was Anna?

Cory said, "Would it help if we shipped her out of here, Jim? Got her into hospital?"

"Thank you, but it would make no difference."

"What are you treating her with?" asked Mattie.

"I am not treating her. I'm simply making her comfortable." Brown eyes regarded her gravely. "You must understand, she's made up her mind to do this. Her wishes are paramount."

The mug clattered as she put it on the table. "Are you saying she intends to commit suicide?"

"She has asked me to help bring her life to a close."

"That's illegal!" His matter-of-fact tone was shocking.

"You're talking about murder!"

"It's not illegal in my country, Mrs. Severin. Remember, we've been independent for over twenty years now. We make our own laws."

"Perhaps we could see Anna now," said Cory hastily. Apparently he condoned this kind of criminal behavior. Suddenly Mattie felt very much alone in a small world of frightening barbarity. Jim led them down a short, dark passage and knocked on a door at the end.

"Come on in!" called Anna's voice.

Mattie blinked at the sudden brightness. Low sunlight slanted through a high window, illuminating an old chest of drawers covered with soapstone carvings. She'd expected the walls to be hung with holograms of Anna in her prime, just like the old bedroom down south. But there were no holograms, no photographs. No dresser littered with jars of make-up, no wardrobe jammed with clothing, nothing. Apart from the single bed, there was no other furniture.

The bed was in shadow. After a few seconds her eyes adjusted. She heard Cory draw in a sharp breath. She stared, at first in disbelief, then in disappointment, and finally in a kind of fear. Her mother, smiling at her from the pillows, looked exactly as she had looked forty years ago. Blonde, lovely, unlined, unchanged.

⫽⫽ ⫻

Cory recovered first. "Anna....Pretty as ever, I see." His thoughts whirling, he leaned forward, intending to kiss her cheek. She jerked her head away, raising a mittened hand to fend him off.

As he straightened up, feeling rebuffed and foolish, she smiled at him, and said teasingly, "You can look at the goods, but you mustn't touch." It was a youthful and provocative remark, perfectly in keeping with her appearance but grotesquely out of place in a seventy-six-year-old.

"Cory," she continued quickly, as though to gloss over the moment, "it's so good to see you. You too, Mattie. How good of you both to come!"

A reply was demanded. Mattie was still apparently in shock, her uneven features twisted into an expression of incredulity, so Cory said, "Our pleasure. It looks like the Arctic suits you, Anna. I've never seen you looking better." He realized he was staring and strolled over to the window, mind racing. What in God's name was going on?

It was as though they'd stepped back in time! Minutes passed as they indulged in small talk, but later he couldn't remember what they'd said. Mattie began to talk too, haltingly. They both avoided the subject of Anna's appearance. It was somehow embarrassing, as though they would be fools to believe it. And yet—Cory forced himself to look at her again—there wasn't a wrinkle on that face. It was perfectly lovely. Perfectly frightening.

He approached the subject of her exile instead, obliquely. "I...I missed you, my dear. The studio wasn't the same without you."

"I missed you too. Both of you. As for the studio and my toad of a husband, to hell with them." But she spoke with a smile, as though the years had erased the hurt.

"I quit too, when it seemed you weren't coming back."

She seemed surprised. "You quit? Why would you do a thing like that?"

He glanced at Mattie, but she'd retreated into a world of her own. "When you lose your leading lady, it's not so easy to..." He broke off, came to a decision. "All right, so I searched for you. I hired private eyes, I traveled all over. I guess I've been everywhere in the world except here. It never occurred to me you'd hole up in the Arctic. Why here, for Chrissake?"

"Because it would never occur to you."

He felt as though she'd hit him.

"No," she said quickly, "I didn't mean it like that. I had to get away from people. Everyone."

Mattie spoke suddenly. "Okay, so what's all this about suicide?"

Ignoring her, Anna said, "I wish you'd told me how you felt forty years ago, Cory."

"Would it have made a difference?"

"All the difference in the world, my dear."

꙰ ꙰

Before long Anna seemed to run out of steam and closed her eyes. Jim ushered them into the living room, then went back to attend to his patient.

"She didn't ask about Dad," said Mattie angrily. "Not once."

"I think she blames him for everything."

"Whatever *that* means. There's something very strange going on here. I mean, don't deny your jaw dropped when you saw her. How the hell does she do it? Stay so young, I mean. What's that doctor giving her? Some kind of Eskimo elixir?"

Cory sighed. "I don't know. Really, I can't bring myself to think about it. I'm getting too old for conundrums. These days I like to know exactly where I stand, and I just don't know what the hell's going on here."

Ignoring him, she continued, "Probably made from the tusk of a narwhal or some such thing. We must get the secret out of that Eskimo. This could be worth a fortune, right? So, where do we go from here?"

"I think we should call the police."

Now what was he talking about? "The police? Why would we want to call the police?"

"You heard him. He's talking about assisting Anna's suicide. I don't care what that doctor says about Inuit law; I'm sure he has no right to take a human life. Not without some kind of formal procedures."

Really! What a bumbling old fool he was! "This is not your average Canadian city. The police presence probably consists of Jim's half-brother. And anyway, if my mother wants to commit suicide there's not a heck of a lot you or I can do about it. Now, about this elixir or whatever—" She broke off as the doctor entered, and quickly cha nged the subject. "So, Jim. What's my mother been doing this last forty years?"

He smiled, and painted a word picture of a woman casting off her previous existence and entering wholeheartedly into Inuit life. Mattie listened with growing skepticism as he told them how she'd found a village plagued by drunkenness and violence, and by her advice, her example and her kindness had turned things round. "Then she drew up plans for rebuilding the village, and she designed a power station and other utilities, and she put together a proposal to the Government for funding, and—"

"Plans?" Mattie interrupted. "Designs? Proposals? Garbage! My mother knows nothing about things like that. She's an actress, for Chrissake!"

"Nevertheless, she did these things. To us she is a saint, and our savior, and the fount of all knowledge. She is a beautiful goddess, never aging."

"Why not?"

"That is her secret, and it is not for me to inquire. But all life must end, and Anna feels her work here is complete. I wouldn't dare to stand in her way." He stood quickly. "She's calling. I expect she feels strong enough to see you again. Wait here a minute, please."

As the door closed behind him, Cory said, "Have you noticed an odd kind of parallel, Mattie? You remember the movie Anna was going to make just before she disappeared? *Belinda's Mother*?"

"That was the one about the woman who gave up everything to go and look after the last leper colony, wasn't it? She did all kinds of good, and in the end she was the only person in the world with leprosy. Some message, huh?"

"Makes you think, though."

⚊ ⚊

One of Jim's many excellent traits, thought Anna, was he knew when to keep his mouth shut. Making no comment about the visitors, he sat quietly at the foot of the bed. His presence was restful—considerably more so than that of the visitors—and she drifted into a reverie.

…Lake Louise forty years ago, and the voice had been speaking into her mind for over an hour. She'd gotten over the shock and the shuddering. She was not going mad. Maybe all this was really happening.

I know that's troubling you. It was little more than a whisper, but it was more distinct than any human voice. *It's the fear of growing old, isn't it, Anna? Well, you have no need for fear. I can keep you young and beautiful forever. I can make you the greatest movie star of all time. I can do it all for you. You will have the whole world at your feet. That's what you want, isn't it?*

By then she'd recovered enough to ask, "What's the catch?"

There is no catch, Anna. I act only for the good of you and the whole human race. I can reproduce very quickly, never fear. I already have many thousands of spores ready.

The words held frightening implications. "Ready for what?"

For helping other humans, of course.

"You can't do that! They wouldn't be human any more!"

Of course they would. You wouldn't have minded if I'd appeared as a biped, stepping out of a space shuttle and offering Earth my technology, would you? But I can't appear before you because I need a host. My host died in the lake, so I must use you. You must put aside your xenophobia, Anna. I can slip the knowledge of the Galaxy into the minds of your scientists. Humans will become great, and all the problems of Earth will be solved. No more wars. No more diseases.

"It sounds as though you want to take over the human race."

No; it's not like that. I want to help you. You must be aware of your people's sicknesses. You are a danger to the Galaxy.

That might well be true, she'd admitted to herself, still not quite thinking clearly. And this could be a wonderful opportunity. Could she trust this alien, or whatever it was? Apparently she had nothing to lose; she was already a host. And she stood to gain eternal youth if she co-operated. After all, you had to look after Number One. She was the only person who really mattered, wasn't she? Wasn't she…?

She'd asked carefully, as though idly curious, "Let's accept for a moment that you exist, and that I'm not going mad. How could you spread from me to other people, exactly?"

Like an electric current, more or less. I need moisture to strengthen the contact. A kiss, sex, sweat. I can't live outside a host for more than a few minutes.

Well, now…

"Are you all right, Missie? Here, I've got your oars. They were drifting away." Bright blue eyes had regarded her with concern from a weatherbeaten face. The boat hire man in his runabout. He'd held out an oar to her.

Dripping wet from the handle to the blade.

"No!" she'd shouted. And suddenly the horror of the whole situation had burst upon her and she was screaming, waving her arms as though to beat off hornets. "Get away from me! Don't touch me!"

He'd drawn up to the bow of her boat while she shrank back into the stern. He'd made a rope fast and taken her in tow.

And as the boats moved shoreward, the quiet voice had said, *I knew you would do that. Just as I know you will weaken in the end. You'll touch someone: someone you love, someone who wants you. So I'll keep you beautiful for all time. You'll have to go out and show yourself to people. You can't resist it. I know the kind of person you are. You'll pass my spores on, sooner or later…*

She opened her eyes. Jim still sat at the end of the bed, watching her gravely. She'd beaten the voice for all these years, never touching anyone, a leper among people who loved her. But how she'd wanted to embrace Mattie! Her daughter needed love. And dear Cory. Just to feel his arms around her again…The bed, intended as a deterrent to contact, could easily become a facilitator.

And she hadn't realized how great the temptation would be.

She'd needed to see those two again—well, now she'd seen

them. She'd done her best for the village; thanks to her borrowed knowledge, it was the most technologically advanced place on Earth. The little power station alone would open the eyes of Earth's scientists to a hundred possibilities.

So it was time to go, before she wasted forty years in one weak moment.

"Jim...The pill, please."

The look of pain and loss on the Inuit's face was the last thing she saw.

∥ ∖

As the three drove toward the VTOL Mattie said, "Her final selfish act. Taking her own life when we'd come all this way to see her. I tell you this, Cory. I wish I'd never come."

He looked at her in surprise. She was crying, actually crying. "You did the right thing."

She said, "I've had forty years to get used to being without her. Now I'm going to start missing her all over again. Damn her!"

"Sure, we'll miss her," he agreed. "You know, I nearly didn't come myself. I was scared I'd find an old woman here, and all my memories of Anna would go up in smoke. I had a hell of a lot to lose, but instead I feel I've gained something. The Anna we saw today was different, sure, but in the best possible way. Stronger, somehow. Better." He hesitated. "I feel...*privileged*. As though I've been in the presence of a saint."

Jim spoke. "Everyone in our village feels like that. She was a saint and a genius, too. She gave us our pride back. You know what she used to say? 'The best thing in the Galaxy is to be human. And we're going to make this village into a place fit for humans to live in.' You see that building? There's a network of caverns in the permafrost underneath. We grow all our own food down there, under lamps powered by the sun. Anna designed the solar cells. She developed new strains of fruit and vegetables. She designed this buggy we're riding in, and she designed the machines that built it. The factory is underground at the far end of the village. She negotiated the financing."

"Whatever will you do without her?" said Mattie skeptically.

"She gave us the start we needed, and she taught us a whole new way of thinking. We can take it from here. She knew her work here was done. Her appearance today was deceptive, you know. Internally she was an old woman, worn out. Mentally,

TESSERACTS⁵

too."

"She was a great lady," said Cory.

Jim watched them climb into the VTOL and waved as the plane lifted off in a flurry of snow. It didn't matter what the daughter thought. Or Cory too, for that matter. What mattered was the village, and the people that made it.

And the memory that would never fade, of the lady wrapped in furs so that only her pale face could be seen, plodding around the village, teaching, showing, endlessly inventive, always kind, always helping, never resting, beautiful and strangely untouchable. Always untouchable.

NONLINEAR EQUATIONS
Ian Driscoll

And I assume it's the cops come to tell me I can't sleep on the beach again, even though I obviously can, since that's what I've been doing, but maybe that's just semantics, so I flick a hundred dollar bill up at where I guess they are, judging from the shadow, just like I did the last time but nothing happens and the bill's still between my fingers, seemingly utterly without context, and the shadow's starting to get on my nerves and steal the early morning lazy sun warmth so I swing my .87 Smith, Wesson and Gates up at its source and squeeze the trigger like a throat until the gun stops struggling in my hand, thanking whoever the whole time that it's got a silencer, 'cause I'm still in that quasiconscious limbo from where I can easily get back into the dream I just left, which was a good one, about some sort of conflict of epic proportions between the Three Stooges and The Marx Brothers, with me caught in the middle, dodging cream pies and high calibre ammunition with the warm liquid molasses sweetness and ease of movement that only exists in dreams, and the certain knowledge that I couldn't be harmed, feels like every warm-blanket-bowl-of-tapioca-teddy-bear cliche in the idiom, and nothing is more disturbing to that unique state of being than close range gunfire, except maybe the sound of a falling body, but I manage to fall asleep again anyway, and it's back to the Stooges and the Marxes, just like I knew it would be, and being right is really gratifying.

& & &

So I wake up again wondering idly what time it is, and figuring the only way to find out is to open my eyes, or at least one of them, and look at my watch, but simultaneously dreading the idea 'cause I can see how bright the sun has gotten even through my eyelids flickering against its heat and light like old and poorly connected fluorescent tubes in an underfunded Texan orphanage and feel crusty and stiff to boot, as if some sort of viscous liquid has spilled across them and dried there—not the stickiness of an evaporated soft drink, more like the scabrous remains of an egg white—so it occurs to me that opening them is the only thing to do, and I fan my hands about me on the sand, brailling for my shades and not finding them, but bumping repeatedly against a cool and nondescript form, pile of (remarkably well tailored and expensive, if I can trust my tactile sense memory from the years I spent in Paris with Gaultier) clothes, which eventually does yield a pair of sunglasses, which aren't mine, but if someone's going to just leave them lying there, they deserve to lose them, and besides I have need, so I slip them on, and one of the lenses seems to be missing, which puts me in mind of a Ray Harryhausen cyclops, acid-trip fluidity of animation, bending where no joints exist, and thus bolstered with familiar images, I finally let the world in.

& & &

And the first thing I see is a singularly empty and meaty eye socket in a singularly empty and meaty face, so I shut my eyes again well wouldn't you, cutting off my field of vision like a rip off scenic view coinop telescope clicking shut, enforcing myopia on the poor, on those unable to muster sufficient funds to bring the distant close for any significant length of time, so utterly utterly capitalistic, poking out eyes with the callous disinterest of an over the hill slapstick comedian relegated to midsunday afternoon screenings on PBS or TVO or the weak teevee signals from who-knows-where that used to ghost onto the set past midnight, when the strong stations went off the air, shows I'd never seen or even heard of, only some of which I can now identify, all those grainy half-strength characters neatly divided by test pattern colour bars, half speaking, half test pitch whining, wine glass glass eye shattering, the shards driven into my head, out into the world, striking down people I don't even know on the outside drilling into my brain on the inside, setting off dozens of unnatural physiological and psychosomatic reactions, cascade effect hormone secretions from suddenly violently vivisected glands and lobes, orgiastic visions and cravings, totally Kubrick, orchestrated, choreographed to the most unsettlingly inappropriate music, which I start humming as I open my eyes again.

& & &

REM's drunken version of 'King of the Road' under my tongue rubbing at my ear canals from the inside makes the empty socket more palatable, makes the aqueous humour still fluid on the corpse's cheek seem even a little appetizing, not that I'm a cannibal, not that I'm morally opposed to cannibalism either, just that, realistically, if someone served it to you on toast, with crunchy peanut butter, and you didn't know what aqueous humour looked like at a glance (when you're not looking through it), you'd probably eat it and go "Mmm, hey what is this, it tastes kind of like marmalade, but with nicer texture", 'cause who actually likes the bits of peel, and if the person who served it to you lied about what it was, you'd never know, and the more I think about it, the more I think I've seen that aqueous humour somewhere before, that it looks oddly familiar, even through these unfamiliar, monocular sunglasses and hey, I know whose aqueous humour it is now, good old Johnny Maalox, and I'm (not undefendably) glad that I shot him.

    & & &

Remember one time he, being the strong silent type (this owing mainly to massive steroid injections and the loss of his vocal chords in a tragic incident at the blacksmith shop of a pioneer village theme park), tried to throw me out of an airplane, the ground laid out like a brand new Scrabble board below me, twenty thousand feet below me, letter tiles not even taken out of their hermetically sealed bag yet, and him laughing like a mime, laughing against the wind, holding me out the door, squinting at me from the end of my leg and all the blood rushing to my head, that being part of his *modus operandi*, which just about exhausts my knowledge of Latin per se, except for *caveat emptor, carpe diem, habius corpus, e pluribus unum, in absentia, non corpus mentus,* and *nulla fronti fides*, because he liked the nice blossoming effect that a skullful of blood produced on impact and these must be Johnny's shades I'm wearing, judging by the interface sockets on the arms—he had a neurogastric optical implant connected to his specs which varied his perception of the world depending on what he ate, and if he'd been into the tex mex, watch the hell out, but that day in the airplane it saved my life 'cause he paused before tossing me out to let my head get really bloated, and believe me it was, I was in brain damage territory it's a wonder I'm still as coherent and focused as I ever was, and while he was waiting, he scarfed a Twinkie, the cellophane wrapper winging away into the jetstream like a memory of a dream of Citizen Kane; Bernstein's reverie on the subject the woman in white he glimpsed for a fraction of a second years ago on the Staten Island Faerie, one of the best moments in the history of cinema for my money, zoom and iris, and what effect could that

Twinkie have but to remove him visually from any normal temporal comprehension—like pouring sugar in a gastank—giving me a chance to escape, actually, giving me time to enjoy the remaining three hours of the flight in relative comfort not counting some turbulence over North Dakota, and in a way its a shame to see the end of such a—well, there's no other word for him but 'artist', but in the spirit of true social Darwinism, I have to say "better him than me", as well as "I'm hungry".

& & &

And it's nearly nine, sand in my shoes like the memory of a rape I witnessed when I was nineteen, rubbing, irritating, in between my socks and my feet, in between my toes, in my synapse gaps, impossible to ignore, like a court case drawn out for over two and a half years, juries hung and hanging judges just plain out of vogue, and all my ideals of law and order and justice brought into uncomfortably sharp focus, there's always a gap, Burroughs saying, "There's always a space between", and me believing him, 'cause that's where the sand is.

& & &

And it's nearly nine, so no wonder I'm hungry, sitting up like Peter Weller, face so blank, voice so dead you'd think it belonged to Johnny Maalox, ha, and maybe I'd better put the glasses back on him, not because I think it's wrong to steal from a dead guy, because what more harmless crime could there be, and he might even consider it a tribute, I can see his huge, 50% image stretched out across the sky, clouds crawling along subcutaneously, he shakes his head and laughs as the sun creates a blinding lensflare, all silent, all Charlie Chaplin, pathos and comedy wrapped up together, sublime, meta-physical, dinner with Donne, red wine and IV tubes, the picture expressing everything, and if you want music, hire an orchestra, and pay the cellists extra for Ah Pook's sweet sake, 'cause you don't know how they suffer for their art, and neither do I—but I know more than you—but because they might help disguise the fact that he's dead, covering up those eyes like hams, like maraschino cherries, and what's one more unconscious guy in a suit on the beach, just leave a hundred tucked in his pocket for the cops, although the fourteen entry wounds, meaning hm, I must have missed once, that's rather disconcerting, beside the one in his eye socket might give the game away, might potlatch the whole damn gig down to the tent pegs, right back to the garden, if you're into that stigmata-glorified-cannibalism-ritual-backwards-collars stuff, so keeping the shades is the thing to do, and burying him the thing to be done, no one will think to dig him up, what's one more guy-in-a-suit-lump in the sand, nothing but a good place to stick the beach umbrella and it's 'Oh, sorry, Mister Hoffa', or Lindbergh, or Crew of Flight Nineteen, except to the eternal optimist, the guy who buys the Radio Shack metal detector and hey!—in only twenty years it's paid for itself and it's time to start making some serious money—so I ought to strip his watch and cufflinks and tie clip and motherboard, but having put more lead in him than a set of Ozarks dinnerware, what the hell's the point, and with the beach filling up with people who fell for the tourism brochures, retouched photos that eliminate the telltale rotten bridgework signs of urban decay, the tartar of poverty and the clenched jawed hatred of disappointment, where's the time?

& & &

So now, grit under my fingernails, setting my teeth on edge like a highway pileup, his nose slipping below sand level like the Titanic, a wake of screams and zinc oxide spreading across the beach as the city wakes up and goes courting melanoma, encouraging those benign moles and freckles towards greater feats of malignancy, eyes growing on long neglected potatoes, dark cycle photosynthesis gone wild, ribonucleic acids, dioxy or not, helixing, spinning out of control, a widening gyre, unleashing mere anarchy, each and every cell adopting a Crowleyesque doctrine, "do what you will shall be the whole of the law", a bold new flesh looking for an environment to sustain it as its stomach growls, low and desperate, fear flashing in its eyes, and there it is, a shining beacon, an Alexandrian lighthouse, semiotic to its Spiritus Mundi core, and that's where I'm headed: The International House Of Pancakes.

& & &

French toast twenty-four hours a day right here and they expect people to believe in an afterlife paradise, and there's a House in every seaside resort on the face of the planet, one in Tunisia carved into the side of a cliff and you have to scale the sheer rock face eighty feet with minimal handholds battling a wind that'll rip the hair implants from your scalp, and people book years in advance, most dangerous and most successful restaurant in the southern hemisphere, mortality rate of one in six customers and a satisfaction rating of a hundred percent, its own hydroponic maple syrup refinery and its own land-sea-air rescue squad, everybody who's anybody goes there—not all of them come back, but all of them go—and I kind of wish I was there, a meal's always more satisfying if you have to work for it, if you have to do more than cross a parking lot already sticky with early morning heat, sweating like an old man who's lost the will to get dressed in the morning, who starts moving the appliances one by one into his bedroom, the teevee and the coffee maker first, then the toaster oven and the microwave, finally ordering one of those little fridge/freezer combos from the home shopping network, spinning gossamer threads of isolation as he squats sullenly over a bedpan, not even willing to make the expedition to the bathroom, papers over the window, dies with his eyes rolled up into the top of his head, just a few steps from the door, nonreflective plexiglas with a no-shirt-no-shoes-no-service-no-Quakers sign (and who can blame them, those guys are just plain bad news), cool and flat under my hand, the Sahara at night as seen from space by that Russian astronaut who keeps missing his reentry window, who's been up there for three years now, must be getting hungry, I know I am, so it's in like Flint.

& & &

A wave of air conditioning like lightning and the Coeur de Bois in me weeping unrestrainedly at the sweet sugar shack lean-to primalness of the kitchen smells, just beyond reach, the dual hinge door strobing me views of the food being prepared like a projector jumping the sprockets, health codes my ass, and the 'please seat yourself' sign looking up at me resentfully, a kid who's too short to ride the rollercoaster, not quite reaching up the themepark mascot's mocking hand, explain the logical progression from animated whimsy to mammoth steel death simulators if you can, surveillance cam in the corner, unobtrusive war-is-peace-freedom-is-slavery-ignorance-is-strength, and the vinyl sighs beneath me like an emphysematic septuagenarian in an oxygen tent remembering a post coital pool of sweat rapidly evaporating in a lover's navel, a booth, always choose a booth, rule of urban survival number three, whipping off the sunglasses like Indiana Jones, and the waitress, unimpressed with life, unimpressive live, the ones on the commercials are always so damn perky, in every sense of the word, nudge, nudge, wink, wink, whatever happened to consumer rights, and I can just hear The Rooney complaining about it, truth in advertising, if you can't trust the tube, who can you trust, give 'em hell Andy, face twenty feet high on the Nadervision screen over the black wall in Washington, an improvement if you ask me, keeping an eye on the boys and girls in Washington and Dublin and Ottawa and Vaduz and London and Santiago and Monrovia and Havana, even through the barricades and the guards, 'cause he sees and hears everywhere there's a camera or a mic, left behind that decaying halflife flesh, silicloned across the world, and maybe someday I'll join him—just French toast and a couple of eggs, sunnyside up, uh, nametag name and oh—flipping the .87 up at her butt first, been a while since I was on this end, dropping the empty clip into my hand, shell of a shell—if it's no trouble, a refill.

& & &

Formica, sounds like a bad Italian character actor addressing his Christmas presents, stares me back at myself, grainy and patterned, fuzzy around the edges, blurring into the tabletop, 2D, unreal, at ease, feels the way a windshield looks a split second before you go through it headlong, your nose a fraction of a millimetre away from penetrating the illusion of safety you have in a car, the insular nature of road travel about to dissolve, ground away like a face on the tarmac, half kilometre red smear, "Oh yeah, that used to be Willie," poking through a mess of intestines and bone splinters, trying to find enough to identify him with, "I never knew he had it in him", and who knows what a person has in them, symphonies or suicides, sometimes both, people are full of surprises, like the waitress, actually back with my order in under half an hour, quasiegyptian pendant around her neck, eye-in-a-pyramid thing, like an old dollar bill, staring straight down into her cleavage if it's got any sense at all, zipgun blast of streetsound as the door opens behind her, frames her in light for a split second, and she almost lifts off the floor, a buzzing neon nirvana beckoning to her as she sets down my food so she can ascend unhindered, my replenished .87 quivering on her thigh like an adolescent hand, and something whispers "duck" in my ear like the rumble of a far off freight train, put your ear to the track and feel it coming, stay there as the vibrations increase, hypnotizing you, and a banner of smoke appears on the horizon, the rocks on the grade jump and jitter, the metal comes alive under you, humming the only tune it knows, the Warhol perfection of the ties marred by a relentless Fauvist shadow, the iron horse becomes a steam powered madame guillotine, slipping below the tabletop, like immersing in an ocean of prechewed bubblegum, noticing that she only brought me one of the eggs I ordered as her head explodes.

& & &

Hitting the floor like a piece of Tupperware as she hits the table above me like a side of beef, fountaining blood down my back, that feeling that everyone hates, that everyone tries to avoid, dancing in the rain, hunching, grabbing at their collars, tickles down my spine like a centipede latching on with pincers at my brainstem, inducing spasmodic Tourettes-twitch shivers, feasting on all my blood drizzle memories, and there are more of them than I care to count, eight months in Paraguay, people coming apart like rag dolls, putting the howler monkeys to shame, and her thigh rolls towards me accommodatingly, almost coyly, as seductive as a headless corpse can be, and the gun slips into my hand like a bribe to a Mexico prison guard.

& & &

Eye of the hurricane calm moment as I spread her legs like a James Bond movie poster, feeling shaken, not stirred, slip click of platform shoes on the tiles as he walks towards me, only one guy with the bloodlust to match the excess of his footwear, Jimmy the Poof, kind of guy who'd kill you with his bare hands simply to keep from getting blood on his gloves, bit of a dandy really, zoot suits out the whazoo, lapel pins of surgical steel he's extracted from his hits, specializes in wetworks, getting wet taking people out, paddling around in bodily fluids like a duck in a pond, like a soothsayer, dangerous job, most end up dying in an ICU from a dozen different diseases at once, sick as a god, bodies unable to produce calcium, rolling over in bed and breaking ribs, immune systems like old umbrellas, sunken blackened clouded eyes, incontinent, skin stretching and splitting under the slightest pressure, scrabbling at the plug, no longer strong enough to pull it, finally, uncomfortably on the defensive, which puts me on the offensive, bring him down to my level, kneecapping's as vicious as it is effective, and it'll ruin his pants, to boot.

& & &

Ricochet from his knees pops the surveillance cam like a balloon dog, arf and a shower of sparks, on one side and yellowjackets a patron, crepes in his mouth, craps in his pants, on the other, subcutaneous armouring, maybe an artificial skeleton, tough but it slows him down, and I'll bet he loves that, plodding nonchalance of the practised predator, looks so cool, like a John Woo slo-mo, duotone suit and monochrome violence, so it's up over the back of the booth, feet shrinking and a swiss-cheese prayer for a moment of invulnerability, nose shatters on the edge of the table with the full force of my body behind it, always had lousy depth perception, and the waitress's pendant spearing my egg right through the yolk—mental note: no tip—haemorrhaging as it flashes by like subway train windows, flickering electron gun teevee screen images, then a photonegative starry night of pain, black pinpoints waltzing across my field of vision, and one of them gets bigger as I reach the zenith of my parabola, grazes along my forehead, a papercut from a page from a bad detective novel, overwritten cliches of pinstripes and leaden death and cement shoes drawing blood, drawing me in, floor showing up like the US Cavalry, stopping me from falling all the way into the dark, slapping me, saying, "Get up soldier!" but I'm section eight right now, bleeding Rorschach blots, looking desperately for meaning as I wipe them out of my eyes.

& & &

Whittled away my options 'till all I've got is a toothpick, and I haven't even eaten yet, sloppy, like this kid I knew when I was a kid, used to put ketchup on his French toast, ketchup, some people'll put ketchup on anygoddamnthing, and I'm on my back like a five-dollar Lolita, need to buy some time, sure mister, whole night if you got the cash, Jodie Foster going down on Bobby DeNiro, and he pulled her back up, and my gun's a lot bigger than his ever was, go out like a man, go out like a light, like James Dean, like Archie and Betty or Archie and Veronica, for fuck's sake just stand up and shoot, this won't be much of a shootout without some shooting, no oppourtunity for retakes, get it right the first time, we're way over budget on this turkey already, and who the hell do you think you are anyway, Kevin Costner, happiness, bang bang shoot shoot, stand like Custer, level the .87 like Halifax Harbour 1917, and Jimmy's a perfect mirror, pantomime routine has the breakfast crowd on its feet, please no flash photography.

& & &

And the bullets, gliding towards each other, rushing like cross-cut soft focus lovers across a field of flowers, arms outstretched, string quartet swells in the background, and I can't forget something someone once told me, never trust a cellist in a miniskirt, she said, skank slut whore implications, intrigued me more than anything, planted an image in my mind that haunts me like a dead man's pocketwatch beneath the floorboards, tick of metal striking metal, oddly like bullets colliding in midair, and two people fall over dead, halos of blood and bone box canyon echoes of Dallas '63, neither one of them me, neither one of them Jimmy, neither one of them more than halfway through their meals, let's hear it for our volunteers from the audience.

& & &

Fight or flight instincts like freight trains accidentally shunted onto the same track, opposite directions, please assume crash positions, spark squeal pressure hiss of pneumatic brakes and archetypal art deco architecture engineering towards abstract art, Casey Jones sitting bolt upright in sweat soaked sheets, unable to move, a palsied paroxysm of disbelief like a cold shower, central nervous system stalled, sitting on the shoulder, waiting for a towtruck, cellphone in hand, headlights bloom in the distance like molotov cocktails, the fear of something approaching, a paralytic dream sequence, a genetic memory fear of something under the bed thrown forward by simian ancestors wary of prowling sharp-teeth below their treetop homes that makes my trigger finger tighten, makes my gun lighten, makes Jimmy grab the only remaining customer for a human shield, Blue Jays logo an unlikely coat of arms, makes the only remaining customer stare blankly at the gaping hole which appears in his chest like an unannounced in-law showing up on the doorstep, outliving his welcome before he gets through the door, but it's an opening, so I keep shooting.

& & &

Jimmy's hand shoved through the guy's chest, very Giger, very Jim Henson, half dozen bullets hanging in the air, physics trick mobile, string and wire, balance and counterbalance, and everything else slides imperceptibly towards them, their black hole FTL mass attraction unavoidable, like an antlion pit, six legs scrabbling pointlessly, antennae flailing, licking the air, desperate scent of fate in the air, heavy, like sulphur, makes your eyes sting, jaws open down below, at the bottom of an inverted Yeatsian cone, yawning patiently, and it's a film run backwards as his gun swallows one of my bullets, it's Norman Rockwell in a bloody fistfight with Walt Whitman as my body swallows three of his bullets, sucks them up like a Hoover, meaty shoving feeling, like sex, makes me blink.

& & &

Fuzzy low light sliver view of the outside, august afternoon solar eclipse, lids halfway open, welder's goggles in place so you don't burn out your retinae, like looking at a truly beautiful woman, diminishes the world, its axis pivoting on my heels, Cabinet-of-Dr.-Caligari-angles, singularity collapse, and peripherally, meat puppet customer's head lolls; Jimmy's eyes, full of that we-know-what-you-did look, same one rigor mortared on Johnny Maalox's face, sparkling like Hollywood boulevard as he gets greedy, deadly sin that, lined up with all the others, Disneyfied like everything else, short and cute and oh-so merchandisable, rodent teeth that chew through concrete, never stop growing, and him pulling the trigger like a half completed waterslide, end dangling forty feet in the air, enjoying the ride, oblivious.

& & &

Coppola napalm strike in his hand for just a second, something wrong but he can't put his finger on it, doesn't have any left, barrel ripping like a toilet paper tube, voidcomp pupil dilation as he grabs a facefull of shrapnel, scoops it up like bus fare, micro or macro violence, all depends on your POV, looking like a lump of margarine on hot teflon, like a figure skater who's bluffed her way to the Olympics, praying for someone to club her leg before she actually has to get on the ice, borrowing instructional tapes from the library, lands on her ass, slides into the wall, knocks herself unconscious, lies there in a pool of spilt blood, broken teeth and shattered ambition, he never imagined it ending like this.

& & &

Payphone dialtone flatline EKG sticky quarter nine one one.

& & &

And of course it was the Stooges who won, can't beat Howard, Fine and Howard for sheer hair-pulling face-slapping eye-gouging savagery.

ALL GOOD THINGS COME FROM AWAY
James Alan Gardner

When she was five, Ula's father took her out to the Quarantine Dock every day. It was not the same kind of dock you visited in Glorious Landing Park, where you could lie on your stomach and watch schools of pale pink eels drift by under the water. The Quarantine Dock was simply a tall gray building on the edge of town, not far from the field where the shuttles landed.

Anyone who came from away had to spend time in the Quarantine Dock, waiting for doctors to check whether they carried diseases from another planet. Father also said that people in quarantine had to get shots so they wouldn't catch any local disease. Tourists hated what the doctors did to them in quarantine, so they were always happy to be released. Many of the tourists would eventually head for the train station and go south to see the glaciers; but most wanted some time outside first, to breathe fresh air after being cooped up so long.

Every day, Ula watched the tourists come down the front ramp of the Dock building. A lot of them were Bactrians, with loud braying voices and big hairy muzzles. Some carried skis or ice skates slung over their arms—they had heard about the Ice Age down south and thought the whole planet was like that. They were surprised to see how warm and green the world was here; a few of them made faces, as if they'd been cheated.

Some of the tourists were humans. Ula liked them better than the Bactrians. Humans looked almost the same as real people, except that they were too tall and too thin. Mother said humans looked like they were starving to death; from time to time, however, Mother went on diets to try to look more human. She thought no one else in the family knew, but Father did, and he explained it to Ula. Ula didn't quite like how skinny humans were; it scared her. Still, she liked the way humans talked, with so many funny accents. The accents made them sound smarter than normal people.

The tourists came out of quarantine at noon every day. By that time, Ula's father would be standing on the street, playing songs on his jumaam. It was a traditional stringed instrument, and Father often complained it sounded too tinny to the well-trained ear. He owned a human-made guitar and played it when he could at music clubs around the city; but tourists put more money in the bowl if they thought you were "an authentic native musician", so Father tucked in his elbows and played the jumaam.

When she was younger, Ula simply listened and tried to be a good girl by staying out of people's way. Recently, however, she had begun to sing whenever Father played a song she knew. He said she had a lovely voice, flawlessly pure and remarkably strong for a girl her age. People stopped to listen when she sang, and Father said they put more money in the bowl than when he was just playing alone. Humans called her a pretty little girl, and Bactrians said, "Good tubes for a Pudge."

"Good tubes" meant they liked her voice. "Pudge" meant something bad, but Father said the Bactrians didn't intend to be rude. They simply made up nicknames for every race they met; they thought it sounded more "neighbourly" than using people's real names. Father said they called each other a lot worse.

The tourists usually came out of the Quarantine building in pairs or small families. That was good; they would walk by, listen for a minute or two, then move off to browse through the shops that had sprung up in the district. At any one time, there would only be five or six people standing around listening to Father play and Ula sing. Even that small a crowd gave Ula a prickly feeling in her neck, but Father said she was old enough to resist, so she did.

One day, however, a large group came through—more Bactrians than Ula could count, and she could count all the way to thirty. Eleventy-fifty Bactrians, all traveling together...a huge family, a club, a *pack*. Ula was singing a song as they came down the ramp, one of her favourite songs, *The Open Hands of Friendship*. It was a human song, one taught to Ula's ancestors soon after humans first came to the world; but it had a pretty melody, and Father said humans always threw extra sesters into the bowl when they heard the tune.

Ula wasn't looking in the direction of the Dock when the Bactrians first came out; she had her head tipped back, singing to the sky, singing to a yellow cloud that looked a bit like the yellow wig her mother wore when she went to work. She certainly heard the Bactrians coming—Bactrians never went anywhere without talking to each other at the top of their voices—but Ula didn't realize just how many of them there were until they crowded in to listen to her song. Eleventy-fifty Bactrians towered above her, blocking out the sky, the pretty yellow cloud…and the back of her neck burned like fire, more pain than she'd ever felt in her life. She looked around wildly, so many strange faces with their droopy muzzles and watery eyes, more of them coming every moment, and she couldn't tell which was The One.

Beside her, Father's jumaam clattered to the ground with a loud jangling of strings. Ula could see that he too was scanning the crowd anxiously, searching, judging. A little blood dribbled from his lip where he had bit it; Mother said biting your lip was a good trick for resisting the burn, but even Mother would have been dismayed here, Ula knew that.

The fire in her neck brought tears to Ula's eyes, blurring her vision. She swiped at the tears and desperately continued to look from one face to another, trying to see who was who. Would she even be able to tell with Bactrians?

A few of them brayed, "What's wrong? Are you sick?" in their loud nasal voices. She ignored them; the ones who spoke were upset and nervous, not in command. At last, her gaze lighted on a newcomer, the last person out of the Dock building: someone with the orangey teeth that indicated Bactrian old age. It was a man, but that didn't matter—she knew he was The One, and she gratefully threw herself to the ground, forehead touching the pavement, arms thrown out in front of her.

"Elbows!" her Father whispered, flattened now beside her. "Tuck in your elbows!" But she couldn't move a muscle. She could only sprawl there prostrate, washed with relief as the fire in her neck flooded away.

The Bactrians continued to chatter above her: "What are they doing?" "Should we call a doctor?" "Don't touch them!" But at last, The One stepped forward, the elderly male, and said, "There is nothing wrong. We have simply overwhelmed them."

A dozen people asked a dozen different questions.

"No, no, no," The One said, loud enough to overpower the other voices. "This is simply an instinct—more than an instinct, a physical necessity—of the Puggeran people. Their biological ancestors hunted in packs, led by a single dominant female. They developed an automatic deference response to the leader's presence. In large crowds, Pudges still find themselves compelled to make a show of submission toward the most dominant being in sight...which seems to be me, though I don't know why."

Washed by the euphoria of release from the burning, Ula giggled at what the Bactrian said. It was a joke for The One to pretend he didn't know why he'd been chosen.

"You'll notice an interesting thing," The One went on. "The little girl is holding her arms out wide, which is the instinctive stance; but the man has his elbows tucked in tight to his body. That's a show of defiance, very much in vogue when humans landed five hundred years ago. Just like us, humans are taller than Pudges, which meant that the natives constantly found themselves kowtowing to the new arrivals—size is an important consideration in Puggeran dominance structures, although there are many other factors. At any rate, Pudges had no choice but to bow to almost every human they met, so they adopted a special bow, with the elbows in like that. It's rather like saying, *I may have to bow to you, but I think you're a son of a bitch.*"

The other Bactrians laughed, loud braying laughs. Apparently, they found Puggerans tremendously funny.

Straining against her locked shoulder muscles, Ula forced herself to tuck in her elbows. That set off the Bactrians laughing again.

⁄⁄ ⁅

In time, Ula began school and could no longer go to sing for the tourists. Her school had Puggeran teachers, but a human principal. Every school assembly began with the students and teachers abasing themselves before the principal, something that embarrassed the human greatly. "Get up, get up!" she would always flutter at first, before she finally remembered the correct words in ancient Puggeran: "I bid thee rise."

Ula noticed that a few teachers tucked in their elbows when they bowed to the principal, but most didn't bother. The bad old days were five centuries past; most Puggerans were proud of their planet's ties to the Human Confederacy. On Glorious Landing Day, Ula marched happily in the parade down the Avenue of Promise, waving a pretty blue and white flag showing a map of the human homeworld.

Mother had a brooch showing the same human flag, and she wore it often...especially if she were going somewhere that she'd come across Bactrians. It seemed that every day there were more Bactrians on the streets of the city, braying pointless questions in all the stores and slowing down the Puggerans who had to defer to them. A lot of the Bactrians weren't even tourists; they had come on business, buying up land and taking control of industries that used to be owned by humans. Mother often talked angrily about that at suppertime: "Once the humans left, *we* were supposed to take over. Everyone knows that! How can they let this happen?" Ula couldn't follow these conversations, but Father had an easy way to explain the difference between business people and tourists—business people never put money in his bowl.

Ula accepted what her parents said, but now and then she found herself staring at Bactrian clothing in the stores. Puggeran clothing had always been ruggedly functional, even after five hundred years of human influence; clothes only came in dark browns and blacks, with every garment well-made from tough fabrics…as if people were afraid the glaciers might show up again on their doorsteps one day. Bactrians had no glaciers to speak of, and they also had flimsy clothes with sloppily sewn seams, but the colours! Ula didn't have names for all the colours she saw—at least a dozen shades of green, from bright and electric to dark and mysterious, not to mention reds and blues and yellows and purples. A single garment might have thirty different colours on it. More than thirty: eleventy-fifty different colours.

Some of the other children wore Bactrian clothes to school…and why not? In a crowd on the schoolyard, a rainbow-coloured shirt could elevate a normal girl into The One; even the older children bowed to you. A few stubborn kids would tuck in their elbows to show disdain, but everyone else, Ula included, gave sincere bows of admiration. Why not bow to such beautiful clothing?

And as time went on, the Bactrian influence made itself felt in more than just clothes. Styles of dancing, for instance: at Ula's tenth birthday party, she put on Bactrian music and all the children tried to imitate the wild-armed shimmying they had seen on the three Bactrian stations now broadcasting on the planet. In the middle of it all, Ula stopped and looked around at her friends, watching them try to force their plump and stubby little bodies to match the lanky gyrations of a species so much taller and more angular than themselves. For a few brief moments, she realized they all looked ridiculous…but then, Bactrians looked ridiculous too and everyone still wanted to be like them.

The seconds ticked by and Ula remained motionless, just staring at the people trying to dance around her. The two boys dancing with her frowned and eventually stopped dancing themselves. She could see they were puzzled by her stillness, perhaps wondering if they'd done something to make her angry. Ula tried to think of some way to explain what was going through her mind, something that wouldn't insult all the others; but the words didn't come. All she could do was shrug, give the boys a reassuring smile, start dancing again no matter how awkward she suddenly felt...

She didn't start dancing again. As she turned toward the boys, they were already dropping to their knees, lowering their foreheads to the floor. A few of the other children stumbled into them, saw what they were doing, and immediately started looking around the room for The One. Their eyes stopped at Ula and they plunged into bows of their own.

In seconds, *all* of the others were kneeling, prostrating themselves in their good party clothes. Stabbed with guilt, Ula wanted to join them; but her neck didn't feel the slightest tickle of heat. The music continued to play, the Bactrian singer continued to insult the Bactrian government (that was a popular theme in Bactrian music, and Puggerans loved to sneer at the Bactrian government too) while Ula did nothing but stand in the middle of the party, picturing how stupid everyone had looked dancing dances from another planet.

Quickly enough, she came to herself and said, "I bid thee rise," in the old tongue. The others hopped to their feet as if nothing had happened, and went back to dancing. None of them seemed to mind; after all, they bowed umpteen times a day to all kinds of people, so one more bow didn't make much difference. Even Ula's closest friends didn't realize it was the first time Ula had been The One...but Ula certainly did.

Later, Mother said it happened because Ula had a "temporarily inflated status" thanks to her birthday. Father claimed Ula deserved the tribute on her own merits because she was "his special girl". In bed that night, Ula finally decided on her own reason: as a birthday concession, Mother had finally let Ula wear a bright orange Bactrian dress.

╱╲ ╲

The years passed. Father bought a hay'haynor, a Bactrian stringed instrument that was really too long for his short arms. Still, he learned to play it with much straining, and began to take it with him out to the Quarantine Dock. Tourists would still ask to hear the jumaam, because that was "a colourful native instrument"; but after a few bars, they would ask him to switch over to the hay'haynor and play whatever Bactrian tune was popular that week.

In reaction, Mother fell back more and more on human culture. No teenager would be caught dead in drab Puggeran-style clothes anymore; so Mother took Ula shopping in the human stores, buying the tight-fitting straps-and-buttons outfits that were currently the rage of teenagers on New Earth. Ula knew the designs had never been intended for Puggeran bodies, even if human-owned factories on Pug now manufactured the clothes in Puggeran sizes: these garments that looked sleek and dangerous on lean human women just looked uncomfortably bulgy on Puggerans. Still, human clothes were better than nothing, and they gave Ula a measure of distinction in contrast to the many Bactrian imitators who pranced through the halls at school.

Ula still sang with her father for an hour or so every night after supper, and her voice had only improved with time. On days off from school, she went with Father to the Quarantine Dock, and sang until the last tourist was gone. She could hold listeners as long as she wanted to…which meant that she would sing until the audience grew to an uncomfortable size, big enough to ignite the burning in her neck. Then she would pretend she had to take a break, and the crowd would immediately disperse, talking enthusiastically about her.

Bactrians often told her she was wasting her talents in a backwater like Pug; she should go to Bactria where she could make something of herself. Humans said much the same thing, telling her she would have a *real* future on Earth. Her father always answered that Ula had a real future on Pug too…but as time went on, those words sounded more and more hollow. Ula knew that Father had taken business cards from three Bactrians and two humans traveling on business with the music industry. They had all offered to tell their companies' talent scouts about Ula. Where were the offers from Puggerans?

Surely Puggeran music managers knew about her. By the age of seventeen, she could play jumaam, guitar, and hay'haynor as well as her father. She had competed in talent shows around the city and brought home boxes of ribbons; she had sung in amateur nights at several prestigious clubs; she had even toured outlying towns with her father, singing for a pittance in dingy community centres, to audiences as small as three or four people. No Puggeran ever suggested she had a future. The vocational counsellor at school said the best she could hope for was becoming a music teacher.

On the day she turned eighteen, Ula stole into her father's cramped little music room and copied out the information on those Bactrian and human business cards. She used birthday money from her grandmother to pay for squirt messages to each of the five music industry reps; and since Bactria was much closer than Earth, the Bactrians answered more quickly. Three separate auditions were set up in the apartment of a friend who had moved away from her parents.

For days before the auditions, Ula rehearsed Bactrian tunes, playing her fingers raw on the rough strings of the hay'haynor. Her mother quickly flew into a rage at "that kind of music" sung incessantly in her home. Ula made an effort to work at some human songs too, but not enough to mollify Mother. In the end, Ula lost her temper too and there was a furious argument; Father stayed locked in his music room and pretended not to hear the women shouting, which made Ula all the more angry.

All three auditions went well. Offers were made. Ula signed with a man named Ra'ranoi, the one talent scout of the three who would take her without getting her parents' permission first. "This is just between you and me, little lady," he said. "Parents only get in the way."

Ra'ranoi seemed very understanding. When Ula asked if he could help her get a passport to leave for Bactria, he laughed a braying laugh and said he had friends in the Puggeran government who could arrange everything. "They're always eager to bring more cash into your planet's economy," he told her. "Leave everything to me."

/// \\\

The flight to Bactria took place in stasis, so the transport ship didn't have to waste space storing food and oxygen for the trip. Three weeks passed in the time it takes a bell to chime. Strange...but when humans made the journey five hundred years ago, the trip had taken almost a year, and the only available life suspension was cold sleep. Back then, you aged the year without experiencing it; no wonder human travelers came to the planet of Pug so filled with resentment. No wonder they forced Puggerans to remake their society in the human image—so much so, that whatever Pug had once been was forgotten forever, of interest only to archaeologists.

The Bactrians had also been forced into human ways, but they had revelled in it. Human magazines claimed the colonization now worked in reverse—the shops on New Earth were just as filled with Bactrian clothing as the shops on Pug, and human teenagers tried to impress their fellows by imitating the braying Bactrian voice.

To Ula, braying Bactrian voices were nothing special; she had heard them all her life. Still, she had never heard so *many* of them shouting at the top of their lungs as the pandemonium that filled the Bactrian spaceport. Had these people never heard of noiseproofing? On Pug, the construction of sound baffles had been raised to the level of art—public buildings had walls that muted all voices to a whisper, and narrow corridors so you could never be surrounded by a crowd. Bactrians, on the other hand, *loved* crowds. Their ancestors had been herd animals, and they delighted in the jostle of bumping into one another.

The path from the landing shuttle to Bactrian quarantine, for example...Ula was appalled to see that the corridor was six paces wide, and that the walls were made of a transparent plastic that let you see people crowding up on both sides of the passage—no doubt friends and family, come to greet returning passengers. She tried to train her eyes straight ahead, so she would only see the few travelers who had left the shuttle before her; but she could still hear the shouting voices, and hoof-like palms banging on the plastic to catch the attention of other arrivals.

Her neck blazed white-hot, blinding her with agony.

She had come a long way from the little girl forced to bow to Bactrians on the streets of Pug. Mother said teenaged girls were capable of great depths of stupid stubbornness, and that Ula was the stupidest and most stubborn of them all; still, she had her limits. As the crowds grew denser, around her and outside the glass, Ula broke at last. She turned one despairing circle, looking for The One among so many hundreds of people...but of course, no one stood out strongly enough. She had time to clutch at Ra'ranoi's arm. Then she passed out from the pain.

※ ※

She woke in a white-ceilinged room, hemmed in by mechanical equipment. Machines strapped onto her arms, machines pressing down on her chest, even unseen machines of cold metal inserted into her most private places. She could not move, not even to turn her head—some kind of metal cap had been screwed onto her skull, locking her motionless.

"I see you're awake," brayed a Bactrian voice somewhere off to the right. A moment later, Ula heard loud clopping footsteps (Bactrians loved wearing hoof-like shoes) and a big male snout came into view. "Hello," he said, smiling an orange-toothed smile. "I'm Doctor Plai'pon. Can you tell me your name?"

"Ula," she replied. She felt very dizzy.

"Good for you, Ula." The doctor patted her hand. "Overwhelmed by the crowd, were you?"

"Yes."

"Normally, your government won't give you a passport until you've taken a class on avoiding such problems. Did you take that class, Ula?"

She knew she hadn't; Ra'ranoi had bypassed the usual procedures. But she told the doctor, "I don't remember."

The doctor glanced up at something Ula couldn't see and stared at it for several seconds. With a surge of fear, Ula wondered if she was attached to a lie detector; but Plai'pon simply said, "You're still just lightheaded. There's no brain damage that might cause memory loss...which means you got away lucky this time. You know that, don't you?"

Ula didn't know how to answer. Like most Bactrians, however, Plai'pon seemed happy to carry the conversation all by himself. "The thing is, Ula, you have a gland at the base of your brain—a tiny gland in the back of your neck, about the size of my smallest finger."

He pushed a finger close to Ula's nose to show her. It didn't look so tiny from her point of view, but she said nothing.

"When you're crowded in," the doctor continued, "your gland begins to secrete a mix of chemicals to induce the Puggeran deference response. You feel...well, you know the feeling firsthand, don't you, and all I know is what I looked up on the med-computer half an hour ago. But here's the thing, Ula: that gland isn't just in charge of deference. It also produces a chemical that's necessary for the proper functioning of your brain. Furthermore, while the gland is producing deference chemicals, it doesn't produce the chemicals for brain support. That's why you passed out, Ula. If the gland stays on the deference setting too long, your brain starts to starve. You understand?"

Ula tried to nod, but her head was still clamped in place. Instead she cleared her throat and said, "Yes."

"Good," Plai'pon told her. "And the next time this happens, you'll do what your body tells you, right? It may be embarrassing to abase yourself in the middle of a crowd of people, but you never win fights with your own anatomy. I'm an old man, so I can tell you from bitter experience: bodies have needs, and sometimes those needs are embarrassing. You have to live with it, that's all. Every time you fight it, Ula, you're risking permanent brain damage."

She wondered if Plai'pon was telling the truth. Ula had never heard a Puggeran talk about the consequences of resisting the drive to defer; but then, Puggerans seldom resisted it long. They could hold out for a few seconds—if you stepped through a door at the same moment several people were passing, you could always rein yourself in for the time it took them to move on—but no one tried to resist in any determined way. There was no reason to resist. It wasn't demeaning to defer to other Puggerans, but here on Bactria, surrounded by Bactrians...

A door clicked open, and Ra'ranoi's voice called out, "How's my girl?"

"She'll be fine," Plai'pon answered. "If she's careful."

Ra'ranoi's face loomed above her, his droopy muzzle dangling so low she could feel the warmth of his breath against her face. "You're okay?" he asked.

"Yes."

"Good, good. Let me talk to the doctor."

He drew Plai'pon off to a corner of the room and spoke in what the Bactrians obviously believed were low tones. For the first time, Ula wondered if Bactrians might have weaker hearing than normal people. Odd that the possibility had never occurred to her...but then, she had always just assumed that Bactrians *liked* being loud and annoying.

Dr. Plai'pon began carefully explaining Ula's condition to Ra'ranoi, but Ra'ranoi soon interrupted. If this gland was a nuisance, just remove it. The doctor laughed—you might as well remove the girl's brain while you were at it. And no, there was no artificial way to supply the useful effects of the gland while suppressing the undesirable ones. No one had done research in that area; the Pudges were the only ones who might want to, and they had no desire to tamper with something so basic to their natures.

But how, asked Ra'ranoi, was the girl ever going to succeed as a performer if she prostrated herself before crowds?

That, said Plai'pon, was not his concern. He didn't care whether or not she became the toast of the town, as long as she stayed healthy.

⁓ ⁓

There were other doctors. Plai'pon simply worked at the Bactrian Quarantine Dock, where Ula had been taken after she fainted. Once he had finished the normal quarantine and inoculation procedures, he gave her one last brainscan, then wished her a hearty good-bye. By then, Ra'ranoi had set up appointments with several other doctors in town, ones who would be more "aggressive" in treating Ula's unfortunate disability.

Before they left the Dock, Ra'ranoi made Ula put on a hastily fabricated helmet, one with long flaps on either side of her eyes to block her peripheral vision. It looked just like the blinders that humans put on Earth horses when riding near traffic. Ula had seen plenty of horses over the years—riding was one of the most popular ways for humans to show how much wealthier they were than Puggerans. The thought of wearing such a helmet on the streets of Bactria mortified Ula almost to the point of tears; but Ra'ranoi insisted, and she was too exhausted from her recent collapse to argue with him.

Thus when she stepped down for the first time on alien soil, she was wearing horse blinders, her head bowed from the weight of the helmet and the heaviness of her shame. She could only see a narrow slice of the world straight in front of her; and she imagined knots of people just outside her view, all staring at the stupid Pudge who liked to flop onto the ground.

At the thought of these unseen crowds all around her, she felt a twinge of heat in the back of her neck. "I can't do this," she whispered to Ra'ranoi.

"What?" he asked. She couldn't see him but his voice was loud in her ear.

"I can't stand the thought of hundreds of people staring at me."

"You don't have hundreds of people staring at you," he answered. "There's almost nobody around. Besides, if anyone's staring at you, it's only because they're curious. You're a novelty here, little lady. You're exotic."

"Me?" she snorted. "Exotic?"

"Yes. An ice-white beauty from the frozen wastes of Pug. You have a knock-out voice and no competition: no other Pudge performers in the business."

"Maybe there's a reason for that," she muttered.

"We can fix your problem," Ra'ranoi assured her. "Bactria has the best doctors in the galaxy. Bactrian doctors know that patients want *results*. Come on."

And with that, Ra'ranoi led her to a waiting vehicle.

⁄⁄ ◊

The first doctor said, "Blind her." So they did.

Someone tied a thick blindfold across her eyes, just to see if it had an effect. Ra'ranoi liked the idea—he said a blindfolded singer might start a new fad, teenagers blindfolding themselves and each other; and if that didn't go over well, the doctors could inject her eyes with chemicals that would blind her without leaving scars. But when Ula was led into a crowd, she could still hear them: their loud Bactrian whispers, their shuffling feet, their blubbery breathing. She could not tell how many there actually were, nor could she see to find The One. In the end, she passed out again.

Ra'ranoi suggested they find some way to block her hearing too, but it didn't help. Bactrians had extremely poor technology for cutting out sound—more evidence that they couldn't hear very well in the first place. They had no way to shut out the noise of a crowd without cutting off Ula's voice too...and of course, she had to hear herself when she was singing.

⁄⁄ ◊

The second doctor said, "Desensitize her." So they did.

They locked her alone in a holo-chamber, often for hours at a time...except that she wasn't alone. One by one, people would appear: Bactrians mostly, sitting in seats in front of her. As each holographic figure appeared, the audience noise grew proportionally louder.

Always, when the audience reached eight people, Ula felt the beginning of a tickle at the back of her neck. Always, when the audience reached twelve, the tickle turned to a burn. A disembodied voice would speak above the crowd noise, offering suggestions: breathe deeply, summon up calm and happy memories.

As the days went on, she began to brood about those calm and happy memories. Sometimes, Ula thought she had summoned up a lovely image the day before, but now she couldn't recall it. Her head was always spinning through the holo-sessions, her neck always inflamed. The computer controlling the sessions made sure she never quite reached the point of passing out; but that just meant she stayed on the edge of unconsciousness for hours.

At last, Ra'ranoi called off the sessions. He explained why, but Ula couldn't really follow what he was saying.

◢◣ ◥◤

The third doctor said, "Punish her." So they did.

Negative reinforcement, they called it. Whenever Ula's gland began to produce its load of deference chemicals, an implant would give her an electric shock. Eventually, the gland would learn not to do that anymore...or at least, that was the theory. Once again Ula went to a holo-chamber, and once again she faced a holographic audience appearing person by person.

The first day was hell. As always, eight people marked the threshold point. Eight people meant a light shock. Two seconds passed, then another shock. Then another, then another...like a stone skipping on water. Ula pictured each shock stunning the gland for a moment, jarring it briefly so it couldn't function; then it would recover, try to resume its secretions, and get another shock.

Shocks every two seconds...then three seconds, then five...until the gland had been battered into numbness by the electricity. Was that a victory? Ula couldn't tell. She wanted to sprawl on the ground, not to abase herself toward these holograms, but simply to fall, to close herself off. She couldn't; the doctors had strapped her into a chair to prevent her from surrendering to her instincts.

When the shocks had faded in the face of eight people, a ninth hologram appeared and the process would repeat itself. And a tenth.

They got up to twelve on that first day. It took four hours, and Ula lost count of the number of shocks. She couldn't count that high. Eleventy-fifty shocks.

The second day was worse. She tried to tell them she wanted to go home, but she couldn't hold that thought for more than two seconds at a time.

The third day was probably worse still, but Ula didn't remember much of it.

◢◣ ◥◤

There came a day when Ra'ranoi told her she was cured. She didn't have to go to the holo-chamber again; instead, it was time for her to learn some songs, some moves, and some

TESSERACTS[5]

"attitude", whatever that was.

Ula liked singing practice much better than the sessions with the holo-audience, even though the rehearsals went on until she was exhausted. Sometimes, she thought she remembered a time when she didn't have so much trouble learning the words and tunes of songs; but she was probably just confused.

She was confused a lot these days.

⋰ ⋱

The time came for her to sing in front of an audience of Bactrians. Not a big crowd—Ra'ranoi said she needed "seasoning" before she could perform on a large-scale. He booked her into some kind of club, as a warm-up act for someone more famous. Ra'ranoi introduced her to the man, and Ula said it was an honour to meet such a legend; but she had never heard of him and forgot his name almost immediately. Not to worry, Ra'ranoi said. The older singer was on his way out anyway.

Ula could hear the sounds of the audience as she sat in a tiny room behind the stage and waited for her entrance. It sounded like a lot of people; she had no idea how many. Fifty? A hundred? More?

She sat very still in her chair, hands folded in her lap. The chair was uncomfortable; it was a Bactrian chair and too big for her, so her feet dangled a short distance above the floor. It helped to think about the chair instead of the crowd. If she was such an important performer, why couldn't they have a chair that was her size?

Ra'ranoi came in, rubbing his hands together happily. "Looks like a good crowd. Are you ready?"

"I want a better chair."

"What?"

"I'm an important performer and I want a chair that's my size."

Ra'ranoi stared at her, then laughed his loud Bactrian laugh. "Praise heaven!" he shouted. "You're turning into someone I understand."

⋰ ⋱

Ula walked onto the stage. There were bright lights overhead, shining straight into her eyes; but that was not enough to blind her. It was a point of pride with Ula, and Puggerans in general—their eyes had evolved on the glaciers, to be immune to snow blindness but still useful in long periods of dark. Ninety per cent of all eye transplants in civilized space used clones of Puggeran eyes, because they were better than those of any other species.

So she saw the audience beyond the lights, seated at tables and staring at her. All of them were Bactrians, except for a table of four humans at the front. One of the human women looked vaguely familiar; but as Father once said, humans all looked so skeletal it was hard to tell them apart.

Ula shook her head. Forget the human…it was time to sing. She would sing strong, sing hard, sing louder than the tickle in the back of her neck.

The tickle had to be imagination, right? She was cured. Ra'ranoi promised she was cured.

And so she sang with everything she had.

※ ※

The audience exploded into applause at the end of the first number: an utterly deafening applause as the Bactrians clacked the hoof-like heels of their hands together. Ula saw the humans in front of her wince—clapping was a human custom, propagated to all the cultures Earth had colonized; these humans obviously regretted it now.

For some reason, that struck Ula as funny. She laughed as she bowed, a laugh of triumph as well as amusement, because it was obvious the audience liked her. It felt relaxing to laugh, therapeutic after so many weeks of therapy…and suddenly, Ula found herself prostrated on the floor of the stage, serenely kowtowing to the audience.

That started a fresh wave of applause, plus some cheering. Ra'ranoi had told her most Bactrians were now familiar with the Puggeran instinct for deference—tourists came back from Pug extolling the quaintness of the practice. ("All them little Pudges are so god-damned polite!") Ula realized the audience must think she had flattened herself to the floor as an exotic display of courtesy.

Except that she couldn't get up. She could barely move. Maybe she could tuck her elbows in…but she couldn't bring herself to insult her audience so boldly.

Time passed, second by humiliating second. Through an ugly muddle of emotion, Ula wondered how long the applause would last before it pittered to silence and people began making jokes about her. Maybe it would merit some mention on newscasts—a stupid Pudge girl who thought she could perform in public, paralyzed by a ridiculous throwback instinct. They'd

TESSERACTS[5]

carry her rigid off the stage, take her to a hospital, leave her stuck in the sprawl until some doctor could find the appropriate write-up in a medical encyclopaedia...

Someone leaned over the edge of the stage and whispered into her ear, "I bid thee rise." The old words, in the old tongue.

The phrase should have been spoken by The One, but Ula was no longer sue what "The One" was. Her instincts had degenerated so much she had simply prostrated herself in front of everybody, not to anyone in particular. The words gave her release, no matter who had spoken them; enough that she could lift her head and see the half-familiar human woman looking down on her.

"Get up, Ula," the woman said. "Get up. Get up."

Ula slipped to her feet as gracefully as she could, tatters of memory finally coming together for her. This woman was that long-ago school principal who had hated the way Puggerans deferred to her; Ula vaguely remembered gossip that the woman had moved off-planet when she could no longer stand the bows. She must have seen publicity about Ula's performance and made a point of coming out.

"Thank you," Ula said to the woman, unable to recall the human's name. "This song is for you."

And Ula sang.

⁂

Three more times that night, Ula found herself grovelling on the floor. She couldn't tell if the gland in her neck had anything to do with it; her thoughts were thick and muddy most of the time, except when she was singing. All three times, the human woman whispered the ancient words in Ula's ear, making everything all right again. Not that the audience thought anything was wrong...they loved the bows. In fact, a few of the Bactrians began imitating them back to her, dropping to their knees and pressing their muzzles to the floor, while friends around them laughed.

After Ula's set was over, Ra'ranoi told her she had "killed" the audience. Apparently, that was a good thing. Ula wanted to go straight out and thank the woman who had helped her, but Ra'ranoi stopped her from doing something so unprofessional. The headline act would soon take the stage; if Ula went to mingle with the audience now, it would divert attention from the aging star. Ra'ranoi said she had to wait till after the show.

By then, of course, the human woman was gone. Ula never saw her again.

For the next performance, Ra'ranoi briefed everyone on what he called "Ula's magic words". The Bactrians in the band practiced it over and over, phonetically: I bid thee rise, I bid thee rise. The emcee memorized the phrase, as did the club owner, the stagehands, and even the waiters. Ula seethed with embarrassment and insult; she hated foreigners saying the words so casually. They would never, ever understand.

She pulled Ra'ranoi aside, intending to demand respect for Pug ways. But all she said was, "You damned well better have a chair that's my size."

One performance followed another, each one larger than the last. Soon, Ra'ranoi told her that teenagers throughout the city were dropping to their knees, giving each other "Pudge bows"…and somehow, all of them had learned the words, "I bid thee rise."

Ra'ranoi said he had nothing to do with it.

In time, Ula could ignore the way Bactrians trivialized her instincts. It was hard enough learning new songs, new moves, new "attitude"; she told Ra'ranoi to take care of everything, and concentrated on the singing.

She could still sing. No matter how stupid she sometimes felt, she could still sing.

After half a year of performing, she recorded an album. The worst part about the recording process was Ra'ranoi demanding that she prostrate herself in front of the cameras. It felt unnatural and sordid—on Pug, only prostitutes pretended to defer.

When she said that, Ra'ranoi laughed and laughed.

The album did well enough on Bactria, but it became a smash hit on Pug. That's what Ra'ranoi said, a smash hit. He showed her a recording of one song being played for a gymnasium full of teenaged Puggerans; as a hologram copy of Ula sang before the group, every teenager dropped to the floor in abasement before her. With their elbows proudly splayed out.

Puggeran reporters flocked to interview her. She met them all at the Quarantine Dock, so they wouldn't have to venture onto the crowded Bactrian streets. Even at the Dock, however, the reporters had to wear those galling horse blinders. They asked her how Ula could do without them, and she softly replied, "It wasn't easy."

When one reporter pressed for her secret, Ula found she couldn't exactly remember what the doctors had done to her. She told the man she'd rather talk about a special chair Ra'ranoi had just bought for her.

⧸⧸ ⧹⧹

A few months after the recording was released, a Bactrian member of her band asked Ula what she thought of "all them Pudge kids going crazy." At first, she thought he meant her fans back on Pug...the teenagers who bowed homage to her hologram. But this hay'haynor player told her there'd been a rash of "Pudges" arriving on Bactria, hoping to see Ula sing in person. Few of them had taken any precautions—their idol didn't wear horse blinders, did she?—and every single one of those Pudgettes had collapsed in the spaceport. It had been on all the newscasts; it had reached the point where the Bactrian government was debating tougher policies on letting Puggerans come to the planet.

Ula didn't know what to say. She was horrified by the thought of fellow Puggerans going through the same hell she had...a murky sort of hell she could no longer remember, except for the blazing pain in the back of her neck. She went directly to Ra'ranoi to ask what she could do.

"Who told you about this?" he asked.

"I don't know his name," she replied. "He plays hay'haynor in the band."

"Not any more he doesn't."

"But..." she said. "But..." She tried to pull her thoughts together. "Maybe we could go on a tour of Pug. Maybe I could sing there. Then the people wouldn't have to come here."

"Do you know how much it would cost to fly you and the band to Pug?" Ra'ranoi demanded. "One album doesn't make you rich, and space travel ain't free."

"But..." Ula closed her eyes and tried to work the numb parts of her brain. "Isn't it bad if the Bactrian government gets mad at Puggerans? What if they told me I couldn't sing any more?"

Ra'ranoi stroked his muzzle. "You've got a point," he admitted at last. "Those kids having breakdowns won't help your career. People will soon start to talk." He thought for a few more seconds, then put on an orange-toothed smile. "Okay, darlin'—you get to go home."

⧸⧸ ⧹⧹

A crowd of teenagers waited outside the Quarantine Dock on Pug—so many that they had been forced to defer to The One who happened to be dominant amongst them. The One looked vaguely liked Ula herself, dressed from head to heel in the most up-to-date Bactrian clothes, and standing exactly where Ula's father usually sat to play for tourists. Was that just coincidence? Or did these kids know so much about Ula that the most dominant woman naturally claimed Ula's old singing spot?

Coming out the door a few feet behind her, Ra'ranoi made a snorting sound that Ula knew meant annoyance. She guessed he didn't like to see Puggerans bowing to someone else.

The snort caught the attention of the girl who'd been chosen The One. She turned, caught sight of Ula, and immediately dropped to her own knees. The crowd of kneeling Puggerans rippled like the surface of wind-blown water, and in seconds they had reoriented themselves to bow toward the steps where Ula and Ra'ranoi stood.

Ula opened her mouth to say, "I bid thee rise," but stopped herself before the words came out. Suppose they were actually bowing toward Ra'ranoi—a head taller than Ula and filled with boundless Bactrian brashness. If Ula spoke the phrase and no one heeded her, she'd look like a fool.

She gave Ra'ranoi a "get-on-with-it" glance, and he took the hint. The instant he started to say, "I bid thee rise," Ula said it too. That way, she didn't have to face the truth.

※ ※

She did have to face her parents. They were there, of course, amidst the crowd of fans, bowing to her. *Bowing* to her.

It was a point every Puggeran reached eventually, provided you lived long enough—the moment when your parents bowed to you. Books and broadcasts loved to show the scene, in every conceivable context: from sentimental situations, where parents honoured an offspring's hard-won achievement, to ugly ones where domineering children forced their parents to do obeisance. In real life, the First Bow (happy or sad) seldom happened till the children were middle-aged, when elderly parents were realized how much they had to depend on the younger generation…but here, Ula was only nineteen and her parents were just rising from their knees.

She didn't know how she felt about that. It confused her.

Of course, it took several minutes to push through the throng of teenagers toward her parents—there were autographs to sign, and an armload of gifts to receive. For some reason, people loved to give Ula flowers…mostly Terran flowers, since Puggeran flowers tended toward muted colours, like old-fashioned Puggeran clothes. There were also a few promoters in the crowd, pleading with Ula to put on shirts advertising ski-wear or hats advertising trips to the glaciers; but Ra'ranoi ate Bactrian promoters for breakfast, so he had no trouble fending off the more intimidatable Puggeran variety.

As Ula neared her parents, her stomach clenched into knots. Mother was clearly trying to restrain herself from glaring at the flamboyant Bactrian outfit Ula wore; and Father seemed so small, so withered…almost as thin as a human child. Still, he had enough energy to leap forward and hug her, squeezing with all his strength. Then Mother stepped in, a formal embrace and a kiss on each cheek, human-style.

"You look tired," her mother said.

"I'm fine," Ula replied. "How are you two?"

Mother glanced over at Father. "We'll talk about that later."

⚞ ⚟

He was, of course, dying. Mother named the disease, but to Ula's ear, it was simply a string of nonsense syllables. It didn't sound like a thing that could kill someone. But Mother had run through a succession of human doctors, with a few Puggerans thrown in out of desperation, and they all gave the same answer: no hope and not much time.

"Ra'ranoi knows a lot of Bactrian doctors," Ula said.

Mother pretended her daughter had not spoken.

⚞ ⚟

Ula proceeded with the scheduled concert tour, flying back to her home city as often as she could to spend time with her father. Father and daughter played a lot of music in the hours they had together…mostly the Bactrian numbers Ula sang in her performances, because she had trouble remembering anything else.

The songs didn't sit well with Mother; but then, nothing Ula did pleased her mother these days. Ra'ranoi suggested Mother blamed Ula for Father's illness, but that didn't make any sense. How could running away to Bactria have any effect on the tumours that were eating her father alive?

⚞ ⚟

She was halfway around the planet when her father finally collapsed. By the time she got home, he was in a coma. She rescheduled four weeks worth of concerts so she could stay at his bedside, talking to his motionless body.

Mostly, she talked about concerts and people she'd met on Bactria. Mother eventually lost patience listening. "He doesn't care about that nonsense!" she shouted at Ula. "Talk about the good times you had together when you were young!"

Ula didn't want to admit she couldn't remember those days anymore. So many of her memories had been burnt away.

From then on, she stayed silent whenever her mother was in the room.

※ ※

Father died on the fourth night of his coma. Ula and her mother were both in the room, asleep. They didn't know anything had happened until a nurse woke them up.

Ula cried. That seemed to make her mother angry. "Don't pretend!" Mother shouted. "Don't pretend!" And she stormed out of the room.

※ ※

Ra'ranoi arrived the morning of the funeral. He had never shown up at the hospital ("Your mother doesn't want me there"), but he told Ula funerals were different. "This isn't about your father anymore," he said. "The funeral is for you and your mother; I want to be there. It's pretty damned clear you Pudges don't think much of Bactrians, but one thing no one can accuse us of: we never abandon our friends." He gave a thin smile. "Comes from being a herd species."

"You won't…make a lot of noise?" Ula asked uneasily. Bactrians were famous for histrionic wailing during their outlandish death rituals.

"You tell me what to do," he said, "and I'll do it."

"Mourners don't do much of anything," Ula answered. "Just sit and listen. There'll be a eulogy, I'll sing a requiem…"

"Have you rehearsed it?" Ra'ranoi asked immediately.

"I'll have the words and music in front of me, and I've sung it eleventy-fifty times today with a recording my father made. He used to sing this song at funerals too and…never mind. The other thing is, sometime during the service, everyone bows to the coffin. You know—we *bow*."

"And when does that happen?"

"There's no set time," she answered. "It's a spontaneous thing—like all our alarm clocks going off together."

"Could be triggered by pheromones," Ra'ranoi said, stroking his chin thoughtfully. "Or a low-level form of empathy—"

"I don't know the cause," Ula interrupted. "Everyone feels it and we bow, that's all. It's called The Tribute."

"Sounds like a fine custom," Ra'ranoi assured her, patting her hand. "I'll play along, trust me."

⚓ ⚓

There were several news cameras at the funeral. Ula suspected Ra'ranoi was responsible—it was just like him to capitalize on any chance for publicity. Perhaps that was the only reason he showed up for the service: to be seen on all the broadcasts. But Mother hissed at Ula, "Those cameras have nothing to do with you; they're for your father. He was an important Puggeran musician. All of Pug loved him for staying loyal to his home."

Ula had nothing to say in reply. As far as she could remember, Puggerans had studiously ignored her father. He had made a few recordings over the years; no one bought them. He had played concerts; only a handful of people came. Puggerans were only interested in human or Bactrian music—that's why Father had to spend so much time catering to tourists.

Still, no one else at the funeral saw it that way. Overnight, her father had become a Puggeran hero: a vastly talented man who had shown he had the right priorities by staying on Pug. There were three separate eulogies and all of them said the same thing—he could have "sold out" and he didn't.

Ula squirmed. It wasn't just that these speakers were transparently accusing her of disloyalty; it was the insult to her father. Suddenly, now that he was dead, the community had decided he was *great*. When he was alive, he had to make his living from human and Bactrian tourists, because Puggerans refused to listen to him.

It made Ula mad.

Even so, she knew better than to say anything here. How could she stand up at her father's funeral, in front of all those cameras, and accuse so many Puggerans of hypocrisy? Wait for another time and place. Today, she would only open her mouth to sing one of her father's songs.

The time came at last and she took her place in front of the coffin. Using her father's own jumaam, she started to play: very, very softly so the jangly jumaam strings wouldn't show their tinny edge. The words of the song were simple:

> *For him, the ice has melted*
> *His winter now is past*
> *The buds of leaves are opening*
> *And spring has come at last.*

There were more verses, but that was as far as Ula got. When she looked up at the people gathered in front of her, she saw they were all bowing to her...even Ra'ranoi, who was casting furtive glances at the Puggerans around him and trying to imitate their pose.

For a moment, Ula wondered if this was The Tribute. She was standing in front of her father's coffin; perhaps the mourners were actually bowing to *him*. But no, that couldn't be. If the time for Tribute had arrived, she would feel it too. She was Puggeran, wasn't she? Despite everything that had happened to her, she'd *have* to feel it, wouldn't she? She'd surely feel it for her own father.

Long seconds passed. She was so used to people bowing to her whenever she sang...and they would all be offended if she left them on their knees too long, especially here and now. Puggerans accepted that they sometimes had to bow at inappropriate times; but good manners demanded that The One would release everybody as fast as possible.

Reluctantly, Ula called out in a voice loud enough to be heard at the rear of the gathering, "I bid thee rise."

Only Ra'ranoi moved. He began to stand, then froze as he saw that everyone else remained bowing.

It *was* The Tribute. And Ula hadn't felt a thing.

Awkwardly, she turned toward the coffin and dropped to her knees. She still felt nothing...she was faking a bow toward her own father.

A long time ago, she had told Ra'ranoi that only prostitutes pretended deference. That was precisely how she felt now.

✺ ✺

The others ended The Tribute in unison. Ula had no idea how they knew the time had ended; but they did, all of them standing up at the same instant. She scrambled to her feet to join them, hoping no one would notice the time lag.

Not that it mattered anyway. Every Puggeran pointedly looked away from her as she returned to her seat.

The service continued as if nothing had happened. From time to time, Ula glanced at her mother, sitting beside her. Mother's jaw was clenched tightly, and her hands had knotted into fists in her lap.

After the service, no one spoke to her except Ra'ranoi. Her mother turned away whenever Ula came near. The other Puggerans passed by Mother one by one, saying a few words of condolence, or giving a hug; but no one approached Ula.

At last, only Ula and her mother remained on the lawn of the hall where the service took place. Ula stood there miserably, waiting for Ra'ranoi to bring the landcar to take her back to the hotel. She kept glancing at her mother, hoping for the tiniest chink in the stony wall of her anger.

Nothing.

Then, as Ula was getting into the car, her mother was there, standing above her. "My own daughter!" Mother cried. "So self-centred you thought you were The One at your father's funeral! How could you? How *could* you? Why don't you go back to Bactria where you belong?"

And Mother stormed away, a pudgy little woman in badly fitted human clothes.

⁂

It was in all the papers. It was on all the broadcasts. The cameras had caught everything.

Ra'ranoi said, "It'll blow over, kid. After the press pounds at this for a few days, folks will start feeling sorry for you. Hey, it wasn't that bad, they'll say, just an honest mistake. You were distraught over your father's death, right?"

Ula shook her head. "You don't know. Puggerans are not a forgiving people. When you spend a lot of time on your knees, you build up a big load of spite."

"Trust me," Ra'ranoi told her. "There's a week till your next concert, and by then, this'll all be forgotten."

She shook her head again. "Even *my* memory isn't that bad."

⁂

The concert hall was only three quarters full. Before the funeral, every concert had been sold-out; but still, three quarters wasn't bad, considering. After all, Ula told herself, her fans were young, weren't they? Teenagers. They weren't stone-hearted old fogeys like…like Mother and everyone else who wouldn't return Ula's calls. Teenagers understood how confusing things could be.

And yet, when Ula walked out onto the stage for her first number, she could tell something was wrong. The band was already playing, thumping out Bactrian music so loud she could barely hear the audience; but the yells from beyond the footlights sounded less like cheers and more like boos. Could they be booing her? Would so many people buy tickets to this concert just so they could revile her?

Put it out of your head, she told herself. *Sing.*

She sang. A desperate song to win the hearts of Puggerans. A song that became a song for her father, for her mother, for all the things she wished were different. It was the first time she had sung since the funeral, the first time she had sung her own music since her father fell into the coma, and every repressed emotion flooded out in the intensity of her voice. She grabbed hold of the sound and squeezed, knowing she had never sung so fiercely...knowing that all her soul was focused into the sound. Yes. Yes.

When the music ended, there was no applause. The last echoes faded away into total silence. Even the band was frozen, blinking and trying to stare past the footlights.

The bandmembers were all Bactrians; Ula's eyes were better. She could see the entire audience down on their knees—every one of them, bowing to her.

And all of them had their elbows tucked in. The centuries-old gesture of hatred for foreigners.

Quietly, Ula walked off the stage and knelt before Ra'ranoi. She begged him to take her home.

He didn't know which home she meant.

THE STICKMAN TRIAL
Jocko

More evidence today in the case of Noah Strickland–
The man who deprived his child of TV for the first
Ten years of the child's life. The most damaging
Testimony in the case came from Strickland's
Son himself in the form of the art class video
That first made Daniel Strickland's teachers suspicious.
The video–drawing on poor production values
In lighting, editing and picture quality–is an animated
Short portraying a day in the life of a stickman…
Ironically illustrating Daniel's inability
To create striking, comprehensible visual imagery.
The prosecuting attorney, Gable Presley, presented expert
Testimony from two video teachers who swore under oath
That the various scenes in which the stickman
Is pushed aside or trampled into little dashes on a sidewalk
And a partly edited scene showing the stickman's
Hands and feet bleeding as he passes through a graveyard
Of tombstones that resemble TV antennae (the only instance
Of colour in the entire video) show the violent tendencies
Particularly associated with children who have undergone
Severe visual deprivation. The final scene–
With the stickman sitting Buddha-like, antennae on his head,
In front of a TV on a three-legged table–
Was, one psychologist said, evidence of a deep-seated
Longing for belonging or, technically, a Be-longing.
This final scene, shown here, gradually lightens
To the point where the lines of the stickman can finally
Not be seen at all–a telling example of a poor
Video education, experts agree.
    The Stickman trial resumes tomorrow.

THE DALAI LAMA'S PYJAMAS

Peter Such

Every big city has the kind of neighbourhood I mean, or should have one. Brunting wind and wave it forms the outer crescent of the city's desperately polluted harbour. Across the bay, always backlit by the setting sun, rear up mighty totems of international corporate power, with trendy condos sitting on their knees. A far cry, these post-modernist confections, from our own rickety gipsy freight which the straighteners and neateners will inevitably replace by more of the looming same. Until that time comes, there persists, in the neighbourhood I speak of, richness of a more intangible nature which thrives—as with marshlife and backwaters everywhere—in an atmosphere of benign neglect.

There's something else about the houses in our neighbourhood you ought to know. Don't assume them to be automatic living machines like those ubiquitous condos which you can leave unattended while vacationing in the Caribbean for a month or two. Being more like pets than pieds-a-terres, our dwellings require constant attention. Technically, they may rest on dry land, but in fact they are more closely related to their cousins, the water vessels, which ply the grimy emulsion which laps our shores. Our Island domiciles—unfoundationed on a shifting sandbar—share with boats a common characteristic: a tendency to sink.

Which is why, one year after the death of my beloved, my cottage and myself had virtually fallen to pieces. Last winter, a family of raccoons had burrowed under the cottage skirts to make their home there. One night, as I sat awake, listening to the falling fifth of the foghorn, imagining the molecules of my Mary's cremated body dispersing into the biosphere, those cheeky bastards had gnawed their way through a rotting floorboard and cooly ravaged the kitchen larder as I watched, numb and uncaring. No more of that. I drew a deep breath, opened the trapdoor, and submerged myself under a maze of floor joists which had wearily subsided into their beds of sand.

I was lying flat, nose against the underside of the floorboards, shimming by feel the platform for a small jack, when I heard my name called and a firm tread reverberated over my head. Goltho, I thought, back from one of his mysterious voyages and finding his larder bare....

I didn't bother yelling back, knowing from experience my voice would go unheard, muffled by the grid of joists under which I could barely crawl. I knew that if Goltho needed anything, he would, as the custom here is, see if there was enough to borrow from, and then leave a note promising to replace it on his next trip into the city. I waited, listening for the fridge door to clunk as he traversed the kitchen. Then I remembered, tried to yell....

Too late. I heard the thud as he fell through the open trapdoor.

"Jesus fucking tabernac ciboire goddam..."

The stream of Gaspe Franco-Irish invective went on until I emerged, spitting out spiderwebs.

"So you're back," I said, struggling up out of the offending aperture to find Goltho's major hurt was 'the shock'.

Just then, there was a hoot, signalling the arrival of the ferry from the city. Goltho looked at his watch. "Shit. They're just about here."

"Meeting someone?"

"They'll find their way."

"How come," I teased him, "your magical powers didn't warn you of the danger when you came in here?"

"I had something important to ask you," he said.

I thought of last year, when I was in shock, and how he had genially tried to support me, somewhat annoying me with his claptrap about reincarnation, but arranging the planting of Mary's memorial tree, stating at the ceremony that "love is never wasted", a temporary comfort I had clung to through the black ice chill of winter, even though I recognized it as one of his silly romantic platitudes.

"What do you want, old chap? Anything you like."

Goltho hesitated, walking over to the window and watching nervously out. "It's not for me, exactly; it's for the monks."

"The monks," I repeated, as if I knew exactly what he was talking about.

"Yes. From my monastery in Tibet."

"Your monastery.... How's the 'shock'?"

But he kept on. "They're the ones who do the magical chanting. It's part of their religious practice. Some can sing so low it sounds like thunder. And others can sing two or three notes at once."

"Doubtless in harmony," I teased him.

"How did you know?" he said. "They're coming here, to the city. They've never been anywhere else before. And no-one's ever heard this stuff, except in Tibet."

I was tempted to comment that 'undiscovered' talent often remains so for good reason, but luckily forbore.

"So what is it you want for these monks?"

"Your house", said Goltho.

I spluttered. "Haven't the organizers of this thing thought of something as basic as where to put them?"

"Well, I admit, it's a bit short notice, but..." (his face brightened at the thought) "...they'll put a blessing on the place for you. I mean, they all have their sleeping mats and stuff."

He turned to the window again, looked out, hastily turned to me and started pacing about measuring the floorspace, his dramatically chiselled features, weatherbeaten yet emotionally transparent, focussed on the business at hand.

"I thought so. We can get all thirty of them in here no problem."

It all dawned on me. "You mean, *you*'re the one responsible for getting them all...?"

"The world needs to know about these people! Besides, it gives the monks a chance to see their Dalai Lama since the Chinese won't let him back into Tibet, right?"

"So how did you...?"

But no. I wasn't going to get into all that. To Goltho, what we ordinary mortals consider miraculous is perfectly normal. The ways and means by which he had cajolled, funded, transported, and arranged every mind-boggling detail with god knows how many officials and unofficials didn't matter. Finding a place to billet them was merely a minor piece of the grand event he had imagined and then, like a conjuror, had pulled out of the hat as a reality. What Goltho had dreamed, would be.

"I booked Simcoe Hall at the university for their performance. Do you think it'll be large enough?"

My stomach lurched at the thought of how much money that must have involved. "Did you pay for it yet?"

"They trusted me. The attendance will pay for it— Amanda's been arranging all that." This he said with the utmost faith in the abilities of his pregnant bride, a Titian-haired pre-

Raphaelite beauty nearing forty, who once had worked for the Beatles.

Goltho was now smiling, still glancing out the window as we heard the ferry hoot its farewell from the dock. "I was a little worried about the big dome on the hall getting damaged. But the chanting master assured me they would go easy with the kinetic mantras."

"That's a relief," I said, noticing my sarcasm was missed or ignored. "So they're already in the country, are they?"

Goltho issued one of his amazing laughs, the first I had heard from him that day. This laugh of his is unforgettable and very unsettling since it hardly ever seems to be tied to one specific event. I suspect it's an outburst of some psychic disorder, though others, mostly new-age nutballs, have assured me it's a kind of general hilarity at the sheer marvellousness of existence, an echo of the great Cosmic Jest.

In this case, there was good reason for his merriment: the look which must have been on my face when he took me by the shoulders and turned me around. There, filing attentively into my cottage's main room were thirty sturdy, patient figures, dressed as Asiatic tribesmen, but with faces each so full of kindliness and wisdom that the shock of their fierce appearance was gone in an instant.

"Travelling gear. Their robes are in their packs," Goltho explained.

The shock of their immediate arrival, coupled with an image in my mind of this little group arriving at the airport to confront some neat and orderly customs and immigration officials struck me so forcefully I started to giggle, then began roaring out with laughter myself, in some kind of amazing release completely uncharacteristic of my usual behaviour. All the monks, along with Goltho, joined in, probably assuming it was some strange Western greeting custom, until we were all somehow patting each other on the back and hugging and shaking hands.

The Rimpoche, or 'Precious Person', acting as the monks' leader reached into the bundles comprising his baggage and handed me what appeared to be a large bone. Goltho seemed somewhat surprised.

"Blow it," he said urgently.

The bone was hollow and open at each end, one of them ringed with brass. "But this looks like a human thigh bone."

"It is. Blow it, for God's sake."

I could think of nothing but my dear dead Mary, of the fate in store for us all, yet I obeyed him. I put the damn thing to my mouth, pursed my lips and blew. The sound was a great surprise to me, deep and steady.

Goltho looked immensely pleased. The monks all smiled and nodded at each other and one of them suddenly unloaded a great brass trumpet bell onto the floor, then proceeded to pull out its long telescoping stalk. With a great puff he blew into it and the sound shattered the air, once—twice—three—four times, strangely enough at the same note I had made come from the thighbone.

"They think you are a magical person", said Goltho. "And they all agree they will give you the honour of staying in this house."

I handed the Rimpoche back the thighbone, which, Goltho told me later, was an object of great antiquity, originally belonging to another Rimpoche famous for his ability to raise buckets from wells when the rope was broken and, by mental ability alone, to hold keystones in place at the crucial point of building arches.

"Well, thanks", I said, a touch sarcastically. Then, remembering I was a Canadian, I swept my arm around in a gesture of hospitality...thereby holding up our world-wide reputation for being nice to tourists. "Do I get a free ticket?"

For the next few days while the monks were in residence in my residence, I spent the time in the city re-acquainting myself with some old friends I had not seen since Mary's death. It was strange and unsettling to be treated as a single person, but even more disconcerting to find myself being afforded a certain high status because of my association with the monks. Under Amanda's creative management, they very quickly became minor celebrities.

In a city jaded with plastic delights, the media gurus had caught on to what they thought was a smell of genuine authenticity. Even Peter Gzowski stumbled and stuttered through an interview with them and a feature article appeared in NOW magazine. Dressed in their robes, the monks made for good visual interest on the T.V. news, especially when seen lining up at the salad bar at Wendy's or when milking the yak at the local zoo.

Scoffing as I was at all these gaucheries, I couldn't help being impressed by the way the Rimpoche and his followers went through it all with a look of great serenity and quiet pleasure. Rarely did they ever express any surprise at the wonders of modern life, regarding the view from the top of the world's tallest building, for instance, as being rather picayune compared to the Himalayan prospect of their own monastery. As one astute reporter remarked, they were 'The Unimpressibles'.

The night of the performance I arrived to find a seething mass of people. I was lucky to be one of the five thousand people seated in the auditorium. The other five thousand outside were hastily accomodated by Goltho persuading Sony to set up a host of closed-circuit T.V. monitors.

The performance, if you could call it that, went on for two hours without interruption. As the program explained, it consisted of a collection of rituals usually conducted throughout the year in the monastery, beginning with an invocation to the forces of goodness. Great blasts from three of those huge telescoping trumpets were followed by chanting, supposedly multi-phonic; but how could you tell whether the harmony you heard was being created by all of them singing three notes at once or in the usual manner?

The Black Hat dance impressed me more. I could not believe the elaborateness of the highly-patterned silk costumes, and the strange stateliness with which the dancers performed. They were extremely feminine and gentle in the way they planted their steps and moved their hands. One of the dancers in particular I could not look away from. He reminded me so forcefully of my slim and elegant Mary, the way she would dance with such grace and restraint. It was all I could do to keep down the lump in my throat as they whirled and paced around the stage sweeping away what the program described as obstacles and negative energy.

As the performances continued, I began to speculate on how comfortable it must be to be raised in nothing but a coherent body of cultural superstition, locked in forever to a life of utter belief and absolute faith. Given the on-going anguish of my own soul, I was almost charmed into flirting with the idea that the world would be better off under such a system. Too late for me, though.

Then that dancer came on again, this time costumed as one of the skeletons in the dance of the Cemetery Lords. I recognized his movements instantly. Again I was brutally reminded of Mary. My heart began pumping with panic. I felt dizzy. I leaned forward, then suddenly, in the clang of the gongs and the raucous blast of the mountain trumpets I felt myself swept up in a mixture of joy and agony.

Concentrating again on the dancers, attired in what I would normally have scoffed at as silly Hallowe'en costumes, I was aware of great knots untightening in my solar plexus, a tremendous suffusion of warmth flushing up into my face: and I sat there, tears shamelessly streaming from my eyes as the dancer, my dancer, fixed on me his enigmatic loving gaze.

That was enough for me. I did not stay to the end. On the way home I read in the program: "Joyous and menacing, this dance symbolizes the inescapable reality of the law of impermanence: a reality that offers the possibility for freedom and transformation, but also provokes terror in those who are spiritually immature." Poppycock. New-age drivel. I crushed it into a ball and flung it to the streetcar floor.

// ＼＼

The day following, Goltho phoned, full of jubilation, laughing his laugh. "Get over here and say goodbye," he said. "They're putting a blessing on your house, right now."

"Thank them for me," I murmured weakly.

"Amanda's arranged for them to go to New York, maybe Carnegie Hall. The Dalai Lama's going to be there to meet up with them."

"I'm glad you and they did very well out of their stay here. I might get the next ferry, but don't wait."

Actually, I wanted no part of any further encounters with the Tibetans. That morning, I had woken up from disturbing dreams covered with sweat. Just as I thought I was getting back on an even keel, this whole unsettling incident had set me back weeks, maybe months. I had to get myself under control and back into my routine again.... Work, that was the answer. I'd get back to raising the cottage. Curse that Goltho, always imposing his crazy schemes on other people's good natures.

I caught the afternoon ferry, relieved to see none of the monks' party disembarking. Sure enough, when I entered the house they were gone. There was only one sign they had been there, a neatly-folded bundle of yellow silk on one chair. I left it where it lay, glowing like a patch of sun, and lifted up the trapdoor, following a driving compulsion to carry on with the raising job, a kind of domestic resurrection.

Remembering Goltho's accident, I took care to jiggle the

trapdoor shut behind me. Once again, I lowered myself into the spider-infested infernal regions under the floorboards, comforted by the fact the little trouble-light was still where I left it, along with all the other bits and pieces: jacks, support plates, and wooden spacers of different sizes.

This kind of job could get tricky, gently jacking a joist here, a corner there, sometimes having to dig a little tunnel and shore things up temporarily, constantly hunting for the various items that got lost in the the all-consuming dry-as-dust sand.

Occasionally I came across some memento of past years: the iron-spiked end of a tent-post from when the present cottage was merely a platform for living under canvas; or, I realized as I raked my hand through ash and embers, even further back to the time when what was here was simply a campfire, shared by two old-time friends or lovers. Under my hand was the evidence of it, two old black glass mickeys, curved to fit the chest pockets of swallowtail coats, their tops still blocked with traces of the old corks.

Enthralled, I wriggled between two close-spaced joists to place the bottles in a safe space behind me, accidentally dislodging one of the temporary supports. No big problem that, but at almost the same time, believing the cord of the trouble-light had been caught under my shoulder, I jerked it free— thereby adroitly overturning the support jack it had been snagged around. There was a soft explosion of the light-bulb and a quiet, gentle thump. In utter dark I lay—immobilized.

I tried to yell, but the pressure on my chest was only enough to allow for a shallow breath. I was not damaged. I was merely buried alive.

Keep control, I said to myself. Don't panic. Although I could wiggle my fingers, my arms were jammed and useless. My legs were not much better, but I could, in fact, slightly bend my knees. This enabled me to scrape away tiny amounts of sand with my heels. I was praying that the rear edges of these holes might erode enough so that I might eventually be able to kick enough sand away to make a depression big enough to slide down into, freeing myself for greater movement and escape.

After half an hour, I had to rest, my whole body aching, desperately trying to keep myself from panic. It's then I heard the faint sound of voices outside. I tried to draw breath for one concerted yell while I waited for them to come closer. Miracle of miracles!...I heard them enter. They'd come back for the robe!

I screamed. The sound was weak; but worse, as I uttered it I distinctly heard Goltho's booming laugh. The trapdoor was closed. They hadn't heard. And not only that, they were leaving, damn them, leaving!

Mad with frustration, I kicked my toes up, struggled, tried to scream. The footsteps and the voices faded. I lay, trying to recoup. Outside, through some acoustic freak, I could hear the far-off voices of children playing. Through the earth I felt a thud as the ferry bumped into dock against huge rubber tires. Out there it was all light and joy, the waves forevering on the willow-shaded shore. So much for blessings. So much for faith and hope and all that opiate religious garbage. I knew this was the real world. This was the real world where lovers were parted and children destroyed by madmen, and the gods laughed while they watched you squirm and wriggle in your death throes just as you had begun to believe in life and living. Tears streaming into the corners of my mouth, I gave up all struggle and lay there whispering Mary's name until, somehow, I fell asleep.

When I awoke, it was because there was light shining.

And Goltho's voice was yelling: "Here! You're here!" He touched me. "Say something. All you all right?"

I whispered, "Yes," because that's all I was capable of.

Goltho saw the fallen jack and wrestled with it, but it was immoveably stuck under a joist. "Don't worry, I'll get you out of this," he cried.

I heard him clamber back up into the house.

The next part of this I've told no-one before, for obvious reasons, and I do not ask that it be believed because sometimes my own mind and memory revises it. But I will tell it as I saw it then.

I heard a sound. It was from the thighbone trumpet. Then, gathering in intensity, there came great blasts on trumpets, of the exact same note, accompanied by a tremendous rumble from the monk's voices, an upper octave, a lower, and an even lower. This great murmuration swelled all round me. Goltho had got back into the house and lay on the ground beside me. "Trust them!" he yelled. "Trust them!"

In the desperate confusion of my mind and the astounding resonance of the monks' thundering voices, I did so. For one sharply etched moment in my memory, I know I utterly believed as might a child, casting away a lifetime of skepticism.

And the house rose.

My next-door neighbour says she saw it rise three feet. Seeing the monks grouped around its perimeter, she assumed they were lifting it in a mighty feat of communal strength. But that wasn't how it looked to me as I scrambled out, helped by Goltho into blessed light and freedom.

They were touching it, all right, but only with their fingertips as they concentrated and sang. Then one or another of them darted under, carrying the concrete blocks I'd readied for the foundations. In minutes they were all in place under the cottage and it settled down on them, magically, evenly, a month's work finished in moments.

Later, I asked Goltho this question. "This robe you came back to look for was intended as a present for the Dalai Lama, right? So in that case, how come if it was so important the Rimpoche was so careless as to leave it behind?"

"He wasn't. He knew if those pyjamas had deliberately lost themselves like that—forcing him to return for them—there must have been good reason for it. Which is why he refused to leave the island until you were found."

At the look on my face, Goltho put back his head and laughed.

HALO
Karl Schroeder

Elise Cantrell was awakened by the sound of her children trying to manage their own breakfast. Bright daylight streamed in through the windows. She threw on a robe and ran for the kitchen. "No, no, let me!"

Judy appeared about to microwave something, and the oven was set on high.

"Aw, mom, did you forget?" Alex, who was a cherub but had the loudest scream in the universe, pouted at her from the table. Looked like he'd gotten his breakfast together just fine. Suspicious, that, but she refused to inspect his work.

"Yeah, I forgot the time change. My prospectors are still on the twenty-four hour clock, you know."

"Why?" Alex flapped his spoon in the cereal bowl.

"They're on another world, remember? Only Dew has a thirty-hour day, and only since they put the sun up. You remember before the sun, don't you?" Alex stared at her as though she were insane. It had only been a year and a half.

Elise sighed. Just then the door announced a visitor. "Daddy!" shrieked Judy as she ran out of the room. Elise found her in the foyer clinging to the leg of her father. Nasim Clearwater grinned at her over their daughter's fly-away hair.

"You're a mess," he said by way of greeting.

"Thanks. Look, they're not ready. Give me a few minutes."

"No problem. Left a bit early, thought you might forget the time change."

She glared at him and stalked back to the kitchen.

As she cleaned up and Nasim dressed the kids, Elise looked out over the landscape of Dew. It was daylight, yes, a pale drawn glow dropping through cloud veils to sketch hills and plains of ice. Two years ago this window had shown no view, just the occasional star. Elise had grown up in that velvet darkness, and it was so strange now to have awakening signalled by such a vivid and total change. Her children would grow up to the rhythm of true day and night, the first such generation here on Dew. They would think differently. Already, this morning, they did.

"Hello," Nasim said in her ear. Startled, Elise said, "What?"

a bit too loudly.

"We're off." The kids stood behind him, dubiously inspecting the snaps of their survival suits. Today was a breach drill; Nasim would ensure they took it seriously. Elise gave him a peck on the cheek.

"You want them back late, right? Got a date?"

"No," she said, "of course not." Nasim wanted to hear that she was being independent, but she wouldn't give him the satisfaction.

Nasim half-smiled. "Well, maybe I'll see you after, then."

"Sure."

He nodded but said nothing further. As the the kids screamed their goodbyes at full volume she tried to puzzle out what he'd meant. See her? To chat, to talk, maybe more?

Not more. She had to accept that. As the door closed she plunked herself angrily down on the couch, and drew her headset over her eyes.

VR was cheap for her. She didn't need full immersion, just vision and sound, and sometimes the use of her hands. Her prospectors were too specialized to have human traits, and they operated in weightlessness so she didn't need to walk. The headset was expensive enough without such additions. And the simplicity of the set-up allowed her to work from home.

The fifteen robot prospectors Elise controlled ranged throughout the halo worlds of Crucible. Crucible itself was fifty times the mass of Jupiter, a 'brown dwarf' star—too small to be a sun but radiating in the high infrared and trailing a retinue of planets. Crucible sailed alone through the spaces between the true stars. Elise had been born and raised here on Dew, Crucible's frozen fifth planet. From the camera on the first of her prospectors, she could see the new kilometres-long metal cylinder that her children had learned to call the *sun*. Its electric light shone only on Dew, leaving Crucible and the other planets in darkness. The artificial light made Dew gleam like a solitary blue-white jewel on the perfect black of space.

She turned her helmeted head and out in space her prospector turned its camera. Faint Dew-light reflected from a round spot on Crucible. She hadn't seen that before. She recorded the sight; the kids would like it, even if they didn't quite understand it.

This first prospector craft perched astride a chunk of ice about five kilometers long. The little ice-flinder orbited

Crucible with about a billion others. Her machine oversaw some dumb mining equipment which was chewing stolidly through the thing in search of metal.

There were no problems here. She flipped her view to the next machine, whose headlamps obligingly lit to show her a wall of stone. Hmm. She'd been right the night before when she ordered it to check an ice ravine on Castle, the fourth planet. There was real stone down here, which meant metals. She wondered what it would feel like, and reached out. After a delay the metal hands of her prospector touched the stone. She didn't feel anything; the prospector was not equipped to transmit the sensation back. Sometimes she longed to be able to fully experience the places her machines visited.

She sent a call to the Mining Registrar to follow up on her find, and went on to the next prospector. This one orbited farthest out, and there was a time-lag of several minutes between every command she gave, and its execution. Normally she just checked it quickly and moved on. Today, for some reason, it had a warning flag in its message queue.

Transmission intercepted.—Oh, it had overheard some dialogue between two ships or something. That was surprising, considering how far away from the normal orbits the prospector was. "Read it to me," she said, and went on to Prospector Four.

She'd forgotten about the message and was admiring a long view of Dew's horizon from the vantage of her fourth prospector, when a resonant male voice spoke in her ear:

"Mayday, mayday—anyone at Dew, please receive. My name is Hammond, and I'm speaking from the interstellar cycler *Chinook*. The date is the sixth of May, 2418. Relativistic shift is .500435—we're at half lightspeed.

"Listen: *Chinook* has been taken over by Naturite forces out of Leviathan. They are using the cycler as a weapon. You must know by now that the halo world Tiara, at Obsidian, has gone silent—it's our fault. *Chinook* has destroyed them. Dew is our next stop, and they fully intend to do the same thing there. They want to 'purify' the halo worlds so only their people settle here.

"They're keeping communications silence. I've had to go outside to take manual control of a message laser in order to send this mayday.

"You must place mines in near-pass space ahead of the cycler, to destroy it. We have limited maneuvering ability, so we couldn't possibly avoid the mines.

"Anyone receiving this message, please relay it to your authorities immediately. *Chinook* is a genocide ship. You are in danger.

"Please do not reply to *Chinook* on normal channels. They will not negotiate. Reply to my group on this frequency, not the standard cycler wavelengths."

Elise didn't know how to react. She almost laughed—what a ridiculous message, full of bluster and emergency words. But she'd heard that Obsidian had gone mysteriously silent, and no one knew why. "Origin of this message?" she asked. As she waited, she replayed it. It was highly melodramatic, just the sort of wording somebody would use for a prank. She was sure she would be told the message had come from Dew itself—maybe even sent by Nasim or one of his friends.

The coordinates flashed before her eyes. Elise did a quick calculation to visualize the direction. Not from Dew. Not from any of Crucible's worlds. The message had come from deep space, out somewhere beyond the last of Crucible's trailing satellites.

The only things out there were stars, halo worlds—and the cyclers, Elise thought. She lifted off the headset. The beginnings of fear fluttered in her belly.

※ ※

Elise took the message to a cousin of hers who was a policeman. He showed her into his office, smiling warmly. They didn't often get together since they'd grown up, and he wanted to talk family.

She shook her head. "I've got something strange for you, Sal. One of my machines picked this up last night." And she played the message for him, expecting reassuring laughter and a good explanation.

Half an hour later they were being ushered into the suite of the police chief, who sat at a U-shaped table with her aides, frowning. When she entered, she heard the words of the message playing quietly from the desk speakers of two of the aides, who looked very serious.

"You will tell no one about this," said the chief. She was a thin, strong woman with blazing eyes. "We have to confirm it first." Elise hesitated, then nodded.

Cousin Sal cleared his throat. "Ma'am? You think this message could be genuine, then?"

The chief frowned at him, then said, "It may be true. This may be why Tiara went off the air." The sudden silence of

Tiara, a halo world half a lightyear from Elise's home, had been the subject of a media frenzy a year earlier. Rumours of disaster circulated, but there were no facts to go on, other than that Tiara's message lasers, which normally broadcast news from there, had gone out. It was no longer news, and Elise had heard nothing about it for months. "We checked the coordinates you reported and they show this message *did* come from the *Chinook*. *Chinook* did its course correction around Obsidian right about the time Tiara stopped broadcasting."

Elise couldn't believe what she was hearing. "But what could they have done?"

The chief tapped at her desk with long fingers. "You're an orbital engineer, Cantrell. You probably know better than I. The *Chinook*'s travelling at half lightspeed, so anything it dropped on an intercept course with Obsidian's planets would hit like a bomb. Even the smallest item—a pen or card."

Elise nodded reluctantly. Aside from message lasers, the Interstellar Cyclers were the only means of contact with other stars and halo worlds. Cyclers came by Crucible every few months, but they steered well away from its planets. They only came close enough to use gravity to assist their course change to the next halo world. Freight and passengers were dropped off and picked up via laser sail; the cyclers themselves were huge, far too massive to stop and start at will. Their kinetic energy was incalculable, so the interstellar community monitored them as closely as possible. They spent years in transit between the stars, however, and it took weeks or months for laser messages to reach them. News about cyclers was always out of date before it even arrived.

"We have to confirm this before we do anything," the chief said. "We have the frequency and coordinates to reply. We'll take it from here."

Elise had to ask. "Why did only I intercept the message?"

"It wasn't aimed very well, maybe. He didn't know exactly where his target was. Only your prospector was within the beam. Just luck."

"When is the *Chinook* due to pass us?" Sal asked.

"A month and a half," said the tight-faced aide. "It should be about three light-weeks out; the date on this message would tend to confirm that."

"So any reply will come right about the time they pass us," Sal said. "How can we get a confirmation in time to do anything?"

They looked at one another blankly. Elise did some quick calculations in her head. "Four messages exchanged before they're a day away," she said. "If each party waits for the other's reply. Four on each side."

"But we have to act well before that," said another aide.

"How?" asked a third.

Elise didn't need to listen to the explanation. They could mine the space in front of the cycler. Turn it into energy, and hopefully any missiles too. Kill the thousand-or-so people on board it to save Dew.

"I've done my duty," she said. "Can I go now?"

The chief waved her away. A babble of arguing voices followed Elise and Sal out the door.

〰 〰

Sal offered to walk her home, but Elise declined. She took old familiar ways through the corridors of the city, ways she had grown up with. Today, though, her usual route from the core of the city was blocked by work crews. They were replacing opaque ceiling panels with glass to let in the new daylight. The bright light completely changed the character of the place, washing out familiar colours. It reminded her that there were giant forces in the sky, uncontrollable by her. She retreated from the glow, and drifted through a maze of alternate routes like a sombre ghost, not meeting the eyes of the people she passed.

The parkways were packed, mostly with children. Some were there with a single parent, others with both. Elise watched the couples enviously. Having children was supposed to have made her and Nasim closer. It hadn't worked out that way.

Lately, he had shown signs of wanting her again. Take it slow, she had told herself. Give him time.

They might not have time.

The same harsh sunlight the work crews had been admitting waited when she got home. It made the jumble of toys on the living room floor seem tiny and fragile. Elise sat under the new window for a while, trying to ignore it, but finally hunted through her closets until she found some old blankets, and covered the glass.

〰 〰

Nasim offered to stay for dinner that night. This made her feel rushed and off-balance. The kids wanted to stay up for it, but he had a late appointment. Putting them to bed was arduous.

She got dinner going late, and by then all her planned smalltalk had evaporated. Talking about the kids was easy enough—but to do that was to take the easy way out, and she had wanted this evening to be different. Worst was that she didn't want to tell him about the message, because if he thought she was upset he might withdraw, as he had in the past.

The dinner candles stood between them like chessmen. Elise grew more and more miserable. Nasim obviously had no idea what was wrong, but she'd promised not to talk about the crisis. So she came up with a series of lame explanations, for the blanket over the window and for her mood, none of which he seemed to buy.

Things sort of petered out after that.

She had so hoped things would click with Nasim tonight. Exhausted at the end of it all, Elise tumbled into her own bed alone and dejected.

Sleep wouldn't come. This whole situation had her questioning everything, because it knotted together survival and love, and her own seeming inability to do anything about either. As she thrashed about under the covers, she kept imagining a distant, invisible dart, the cycler, falling from infinity at her.

Finally she got up and went to her office. She would write it out. That had worked wonderfully before. She sat under the VR headset and called up the mailer. Hammond's message was still there, flagged with its vector and frequency. She gave the *reply* command.

"Dear Mr. Hammond:

"I got your message. You intended it for some important person, but I got it instead. I've got a daughter and son—I didn't want to hear that they might be killed. And what am I supposed to do about it? I told the police. So what?

"Please tell me this is a joke. I can't sleep now, all I can think about is Tiara, and what must have happened there.

"I feel...I told the police, but that doesn't seem like *enough*, it's as if you called *me* for help, put the weight of the whole world on my shoulders—and what am I supposed to do about it?" It became easier the more she spoke. Elise poured out the litany of small irritations and big fears that were plaguing her. When she was done, she did feel better.

Send? inquired the mailer.

Oh, God, of course not.

Something landed in her lap, knocking the wind out of her.

The headset toppled off her head. "Mommy. Mommy!"

"Yes yes, sweetie, what is it?"

Judy plunked forward onto Elise's breast. "Did you forget the time again, Mommy?"

Elise relaxed. She was being silly. "Maybe a little, honey. What are you doing awake?"

"I don't know."

"Let's both go to bed. You can sleep with me, okay?" Judy nodded.

She stood up, holding Judy. The inside of the VR headset still glowed, so she picked it up to turn it off.

Remembering what she'd been doing, she put it on.

Mail sent, the mailer was flashing.

"Oh, my, *God!*"

"Ow, Mommy."

"Wait a sec, Judy. Mommy has something to do." She put Judy down and fumbled with the headset. Judy began to whine.

She picked *reply* again and said quickly, "Mr. Hammond, please disregard the last message. It wasn't intended for you. The mailer got screwed up. I'm sorry if I said anything to upset you, I know you're in a far worse position than I am and you're doing a very brave thing by getting in touch with us. I'm sure it'll all work out. I..." She couldn't think of anything more. "Please excuse me, Mr. Hammond."

Send? "Yes!"

She took Judy to bed. Her daughter fell asleep promptly, but Elise was now wide awake.

꧁ ꧂

She heard nothing from the government during the next while. Because she knew they might not tell her what was happening, she commanded her outermost prospector to devote half its time to scanning for messages from *Chinook*. For weeks, there weren't any.

Elise went on with things. She dressed and fed the kids; let them cry into her shirt when they got too tired or banged their knees; walked them out to meet Nasim every now and then. She had evening coffee with her friends, and even saw a new play that had opened in a renovated reactor room in the basement of the city. Other than that, she mostly worked.

In the weeks after the message's arrival, Elise found a renewal of the comforting solitude her prospectors gave her. For hours at a time, she could be millions of kilometres away, watching ice crystals dance in her headlamps, or seeing stars she could never view from her window. Being so far away literally gave her a new perspective on home; she could see Dew in all its fragile smallness, and understood that the bustle of family and friends served to keep the loneliness of the halo worlds at bay. She appreciated people more for that, but also loved being the first to visit ice galleries and frozen cataracts on distant moons.

Now she wondered if she would be able to watch Dew's destruction from her prospectors. That made no sense—she would be dead in that case. The sense of actually *being* out in space was so strong though that she had fantasies of finding the golden thread cut, of existing bodiless and alone forever in the cameras of the prospectors, from which she would gaze down longingly on the ruins of her world.

A month after the first message, a second came. Elise's prospector intercepted it—nobody else except the police would have, because it was at Hammond's special frequency. The kids were tearing about in the next room. Their laughter formed an odd backdrop to the bitter voice that sounded in her ears.

"This is Mark Hammond on the *Chinook*. I will send you all the confirming information I can. There is a video record of the incident at Tiara, and I will try to send it along. It is very difficult. There are only a few of us from the original passengers and crew left. I have to rely on the arrogance of Leviathan's troops, if they encrypt their database I will be unable to send anything. If they catch me, I will be thrown out an airlock.

"I'll tell you what happened. I boarded at Mirjam, four years ago. I was bound for Tiara, to the music academy there. Leviathan was our next stop, and we picked up no freight, but several hundred people who turned out to be soldiers. There were about a thousand people on *Chinook* at that point. The soldiers captured the command centre, and then they decided who they needed and who was expendable. They killed more than half of us. I was saved because I can sing. I'm part of the entertainment." Hammond's voice expressed loathing. He had a very nice voice, baritone and resonant. She could hear the unhappiness in it.

"It's been two and a half years now, under their heel. We're sick of it.

"A few weeks ago they started preparing to strike your world. That's when we decided. You must destroy *Chinook*. I am going to send you our exact course, and that of the missiles. You must mine space in front of us. Otherwise you'll end up like Tiara."

※ ※

The kids had their survival class that afternoon. Normally Elise was glad to hand them over to Nasim or, lately, their instructor—but this time she took them. She felt just a little better standing with some other parents in the powdery, sand-like snow outside the city watching the space-suited figures of her children go through the drill. They joined a small group in puzzling over a Global Positioning Unit, and successfuly found the way to the beacon that was their target for today. She felt immensely proud of them, and chatted freely with the other parents. It was the first time in weeks that she'd felt like she was doing something worthwhile.

Being outside in daylight was so strange—after their kids, that was the main topic of conversation among the adults. All remembered their own classes, taken under the permanent night they had grown up with. Now they excitedly pointed out the different and wonderful colours of the stones and ices, reminiscent of pictures of Earth's Antarctica.

It was strange, too, to see the city as something other than a vast dark pyramid. Elise studied it after the kids were done and they'd started back. The city looked solid, a single structure built of concrete that appeared pearly under the mauve clouds. Its flat facades were dotted with windows, and more were being installed. She and the kids tried to find theirs, but it was an unfamiliar exercise and they soon quit.

A big sign had been erected over the city airlock: HELP BUILD A SUNNY FUTURE, it said. Beside it was a thermometer-graph intended to show how close the government was to funding the next stage of Dew's terraforming. Only a small part of this was filled in, and the paint on that looked a bit old. Nonetheless, several people made contributions at the booth inside, and she was tempted herself—being outdoors did make you think.

They were all tired when they got home, and the kids voluntarily went to nap. Feeling almost happy, Elise looked out her window for a while, then kicked her way through the debris of toys to the office.

A new message was waiting already.

"This is for the woman who heard my first message. I'm not sending it on the new frequency, but I'm aiming it the way I did the first one. This is just for you, whoever you are."

Elise sat down quickly. .

Hammond laughed, maybe a little nervously. His voice was so rich, his laugh seemed to fill her whole head. "That was quite a letter you sent. I'm not sure I believe you about having a 'mailer accident.' But if it was an accident, I'm glad it happened.

"Yours is the first voice I've heard in years from outside this whole thing. You have to understand, with the way we're treated and…and isolation and all, we nearly don't remember what it was like before. To have a life, I mean. To have kids, and worries like that. There're no kids here anymore. They killed them with their parents.

"A lot of people have given up. They don't remember why they should care. Most of us are like that now. Even me and the others who're trying to do something…well, we're doing it out of hate, not because we're trying to save anything.

"But you reminded me that there are things out there to save. Just hearing your voice, knowing that you and Dew are real, has helped.

"So I decided…I'm going to play your message—the first one, actually—to a couple of the people who've given up. Remind them there's a world out there. That they still have responsibilities.

"Thank you again. Can you tell me your name? I wish we could have met, someday." That was all.

Somehow, his request made her feel defensive. It was good he didn't know her name; it was a kind of safety. At the same time she wanted to tell him, as if he deserved it somehow. Finally, after sitting indecisively for long minutes, she threw down the headset and stalked out of the room.

/// \\\

Nasim called the next day. Elise was happy to hear from him, also a bit surprised. She had been afraid he thought she'd been acting cold lately, but he invited her for lunch in one of the city's better bistros. She foisted the kids off on her mother, and dressed up. It was worth it. They had a good time.

When she tried to set a date to get together again, he demured. She was left chewing over his mixed messages as she walked home.

Oh, who knew, really? Life was just too complicated right now. When she got home, there was another message from Hammond, this one intended for the authorities. She reviewed it, but afterwards regretted doing so. It showed the destruction of Tiara.

On the video, pressure-suited figures unhooked some of *Chinook*'s Lorentz whip-thin force cables, and jetted them away from the cycler. The cables seemed infinitely long, and could weigh many hundreds of tonnes.

The next picture was a long-distance, blue-shifted image of Obsidian's only inhabited world, Tiara. For about a minute, Elise watched it waver, a speckled dot. Then lines of savage white light criss-crossed its face suddenly as the wires hit.

That was all. Hammond's voice recited strings of numbers next, which she translated into velocities and trajectories. The message ended without further comment.

She was supposed to have discharged her responsibility by alerting the authorities, but after thinking about it practically all night, she had decided there was one more thing she could do. "Mr. Hammond," she began, "This is Elise Cantrell. I'm the one who got your first message. I've seen the video you sent. I'm sure it'll be enough to convince our government to do something. Hitting Dew is going to be hard, and now that we know where they're coming from we should be able to stop the missiles. I'm sure if the government thanks you, they'll do so in some stodgy manner, like giving you some medal or building a statue. But I want to thank you myself. For my kids. You may not have known just who you were risking your life for. Well, it was for Judy and Alex. I'm sending you a couple of pictures of them. Show them around. Maybe they'll convince more people to help you.

"I don't want us to blow up *Chinook*. That would mean you would die, and you're much too good a person for that. You don't deserve it. Show the pictures around. I don't know—if you can convince enough people, maybe you can take control back. There must be a way. You're a very clever man, Mr. Hammond. I'm sure you'll be able to find a way. For...well, for me, maybe." She laughed, then cleared her throat. "Here's the pictures." She keyed in several of her favourites, Judy walking at age one, Alex standing on the dresser holding a towel up, an optimistic parachute.

She took off the headset, and lay back feeling deeply tired, but content. It wasn't rational, but she felt she had done something heroic, maybe for the first time in her life.

Elise was probably the only person who wasn't surprised

when the sun went out. There had been rumours floating about for several days that the government was commandeering supplies and ships, but nobody knew for what. She did. She was fixing dinner when the light changed. The kids ran over to see what was happening.

"Why'd it stop?" howled Alex. "I want it back!"

"They'll bring it back in a couple of days," she told him. "They're just doing maintenance. Maybe they'll change the colour or something." That got his attention. For the next while he and Judy talked about what colour the new sun should be. They settled on blue.

The next morning she got a call from Sal. "We're doing it, Elise, and we need your help."

She'd seen this coming. "You want to take my prospectors."

"No no, not *take* them, just use them. You know them best. I convinced the department heads that you should be the one to pilot them. We need to blockade the missiles the *Chinook*'s sending."

"That's all?"

"What do you mean, that's all? What else would there be?"

She shook her head. "Nothing. Okay. I'll do it. Should I log on now?"

"Yeah. You'll get a direct link to your supervisor. His name's Oliver. You'll like him."

She didn't like Oliver, but could see how Sal might. He was tough and uncompromising, and curt to the point of being surly. Nice enough when he thought to be, but that was rare. He ordered Elise to take four of her inner-system prospectors off their jobs to manoeuvre ice for the blockade.

The next several days were the busiest she'd ever had with the prospectors. She had to call Nasim to come and look after the kids, which he did quite invisibly. All Elise's attention was needed in the orbital transfers. Her machines gathered huge blocks of orbiting ice, holding them like ambitious insects, and trawled slowly into the proper orbit. During tired pauses, she stared down at the brown cloud-tops of Crucible, thunderheads the size of planets, eddies a continent could get lost in. They wanted hundreds of ice mountains moved to intercept the missiles. The sun was out because it was being converted into a fearsome laser lance. This would be used on the ice mountains before the missiles flew by; the expanding clouds of gas should cover enough area to intercept the missiles.

She was going to lose a prospector or two in the conflagration, but to complain about that now seemed petty.

Chinook was drawing close, and the time lag between messages became shorter. As she was starting her orbital corrections on a last chunk of ice, a new message came in from Hammond. For her, again.

In case this was going to get her all wrought up, she finished setting the vectors before she opened the message. This time it came in video format.

Mark Hammond was a lean-faced man with dark skin and an unruly shock of black hair. Two blue-green ear-rings hung from his ears. He looked old, but that was only because of the lines around his mouth, crow's-feet at his eyes. But he smiled now.

"Thanks for the pictures, Elise. You can call me Mark. I'm glad your people are able to defend themselves. The news must be going out to all the halo worlds now—nobody's going to trade with Leviathan now! Total isolation. They deserve it. Thank you. None of this could've happened if you hadn't been there."

He rubbed his jaw. "Your support's meant a lot to me in the past few days, Elise. I loved the pictures, they were like a breath of new air. Yeah, I did show them around. It worked, too; we've got a lot of people on our side. Who knows, maybe we'll be able to kick the murderers out of here, like you say. We wouldn't even have considered trying, if not for you."

He grimaced, looked down quickly. "Sounds stupid. But you say stupid things in situations like this. Your help has meant a lot to me. I hope you're evacuated to somewhere safe. And I've been wracking my brains trying to think of something I could do for you, equal to the pictures you sent.

"It's not much, but I'm sending you a bunch of my recordings. Some of these songs are mine, some are traditionals from Mirjam. But it's all my voice. I hope you like them. I'll never get the chance for the real training I needed at Tiara. This'll have to do." Looking suddenly shy, he said, "'Bye."

Elise saved the songs in an accessible format and transferred them to her sound system. She stepped out of the office, walked without speaking past Nasim and the kids, and turned the sound way up. Hammond's voice poured out clear and strong, and she sat facing the wall, and just listened for the remainder of the day.

Oliver called her the next morning with new orders. "You're the only person who's got anything like a ship near the *Chinook*'s flight path. Prospector Six." That was the one that had picked up Hammond's first message. "We're sending some missiles we put together, but they're low-mass, so they might not penetrate the *Chinook*'s forward shields."

"You want me to destroy the *Chinook*." She was not surprised. Only very disappointed that fate had worked things this way.

"Yeah," Oliver said. "Those shits can't be allowed to get away. Your prospector masses ten thousand tonnes, more than enough to stop it dead. I've put the vectors in your database. This is top priority. Get on it." He hung up.

She was damned if she would get on it. Elise well knew her responsibility to Dew, but destroying *Chinook* wouldn't save her world. That all hinged on the missiles, which must have already been sent. But just so the police couldn't prove that she'd disobeyed orders, she entered the vectors to intercept *Chinook*, but included a tiny error which would guarantee a miss. The enormity of what she was doing—the government would call this treason—made her feel sick to her stomach. Finally she summoned her courage and called Hammond.

"They want me to kill you." Elise stood in front of her computer, allowing it to record her in video. She owed him that, at least. "I can't do it. I'm sorry, but I can't. I'm not a executioner, and you've done nothing wrong. Of all of us, you're the one who least deserves to die! It's not fair. Mark, you're going to have to take back the *Chinook*. You said you had more people on your side. I'm going to give you the time to do it. It's a couple of years to your next stop. Take back the ship, then you can get off there. You can still have your life, Mark! Come back here. You'll be a hero."

She tried to smile bravely, but it cracked into a grimace. "Please, Mark. I'm sure the government's alerted all the other halo worlds now. They'll be ready. *Chinook* won't be able to catch anybody else by surprise. So there's no reason to kill you.

"I'm giving you the chance you deserve, Mark. I hope you make the best of it."

She sent that message, only realizing afterwards that she hadn't thanked him for the gift of his music. But she was afraid to say anything more.

☄ ☄

The city was evacuated the next day. It started in the early hours, as the police closed off all the levels of the city then began sweeping, waking people from their beds and moving the bewildered crowds to trains and aircraft. Elise was packed and ready. Judy slept in her arms, and Alex clutched her belt and knuckled his eyes as they walked among shouting people. The media were now revealing the nature of the crisis, but it was far too late for organized protest. The crowds were herded methodically; the police must have been drilling for this for weeks.

She wished Sal had told her exactly when it was going to happen. It meant she hadn't been able to hook up with Nasim, whose apartment was on another level. He was probably still asleep, even while she and the kids were packed on a train, and she watched through the angle of the window as the station receded.

Sometime the next morning they stopped, and some of the passengers were off-loaded. Food was eventually brought, and then they continued on. Elise was asleep leaning against the wall when they finally unloaded her car.

All the cities of Dew had emergency barracks. She had no idea what city they had come to at first, having missed the station signs. She didn't care. The kids needed looking after, and she was bone tired.

Not too tired, though, to know that the hours were counting quickly down to zero. She couldn't stand being cut off, she had to know Hammond's reply to her message, but there were no terminals in the barracks. She had to know he was all right.

She finally managed to convince some women to look after Judy and Alex, and set off to find a way out. There were several policemen loitering around the massive metal doors that separated the barracks from the city, and they weren't letting anyone pass.

She walked briskly around the perimeter of the barracks, thinking. Barracks like this were usually at ground level, and were supposed to have more than one entrance, in case one was blocked by earthquake or fire. There must be some outside exit, and it might not be guarded.

Deep at the back where she hadn't been yet, she found her airlock, unguarded. Its lockers were packed with survival suits; none of the refugees would be going outside, especially not here on unknown ground. There was no good reason for them to leave the barracks, because going outside would not get them home. But she needed a terminal.

She suited up, and went through the airlock. Nobody saw her. Elise stepped out onto the surface of Dew, where she had never been except during survival drills. A thin wind was blowing, catching and worrying at drifts of carbon-dioxide snow. Torn clouds revealed stars high above the glowing walls of the city. This place, where ever it was, had thousands of windows; she supposed all the cities did now. They would have a good view of whatever happened in the sky today.

After walking for a good ten minutes, she came to another airlock. This one was big, with vehicles rolling in and out. She stepped in after one, and found herself in a warehouse. Simple as that.

From there she took the elevator up sixteen levels to an arcade lined with glass. Here finally were VR terminals, and she gratefully collapsed at one, and logged into her account.

There were two messages waiting. Hammond, it had to be. She called up the first one.

"You're gonna thank me for this, you really are," said Oliver. He looked smug. "I checked in on your work—hey, just doing my job. You did a great job on moving the ice, but you totally screwed up your trajectory on Prospector Six. Just a little error, but it added up quick. Would have missed *Chinook* completely if I hadn't corrected it. Guess I saved your ass, huh?" He mock-saluted, and grinned. "Didn't tell anybody. I won't, either. You can thank me later." Still smug, he rung off.

"Oh no. No, no no," she whispered. Trembling, she played the second message.

Hammond appeared, looking drawn and sad. His backdrop was a metal bulkhead; his breath frosted when he breathed. "Hello, Elise," he said. His voice was low, and tired. "Thank you for caring so much about me. But your plan will never work.

"You're not here. Lucky thing. But if you were, you'd see how hopeless it is. There's a handful of us prisoners, kept alive for amusement and because we can do some things they can't. They never thought we'd have a reason to go outside, that's the only reason I was able to get out to take over the message laser. And it's only because of their bragging that we got the video and data we did.

"They have a right to be confident, with us. We can't do anything, we're locked away from their part of the ship. And you see, when they realize you've mined space near Dew, they'll know someone gave them away. We knew that would happen when we decided to do this. Either way I'm dead, you see; either you kill me, or they do. I'd prefer you did it, it'll be so much faster."

He looked down pensively for a moment. "Do me the favour," he said at last. "You'll carry no blame for it, no guilt. Destroy *Chinook*. The worlds really aren't safe until you do. These people are fanatics, they never expected to get home alive. If they think their missiles won't get through, they'll aim the ship itself at the next world. Which will be much harder to stop.

"I love you for your optimism, and your plans. I wish it could have gone the way you said. But this really is goodbye."

Finally he smiled, looking directly at her. "Too bad we didn't have the time. I could have loved you, I think. Thank you, though. The caring you showed me is enough." He vanished. *Message end*, said the mailer. *Reply?*

She stared at that last word for a long time. She signalled *yes*.

"Thank you for your music, Mark," she said. She sent that. Then she closed her programs, and took off the headset.

/// \\\

The end, when it came, took the form of a brilliant line of light scored across the sky. Elise watched from the glass wall of the arcade, where she sat on a long couch with a bunch of other silent people. The landscape lit to the horizon, brighter than Dew's artificial sun had ever shone. The false day faded slowly.

There was no ground shock. No sound. Dew had been spared.

The crowd dispersed, talking animatedly. For them, the adventure had been over before they had time to really believe in the threat. Elise watched them through her tears almost fondly. She was too tired to move.

Alone, she gazed up at the stars. Only a faint pale streak remained now. In a moment she would return to her children, but first she had to let this emotion fill her completely, wash down from her face through her arms and body, like Hammond's music. She wasn't used to how acceptance felt. She hoped it would become more familiar to her.

Elise stood and walked alone to the elevator, and did not look back at the sky.

HIGH PRESSURE SYSTEM
Paul Stockton

"…where the aliens are advancing on the Dallas-Fort W-"
-Click-

"This high pressure system is stalled over the prairies, trapping the mass of arctic air. So that region of the country can expect the bitterly cold temperatures to continue for at least the next five days."

"Man, is it cold out," says my dad.

"Almost as bad as two years ago. Do you remember that?" asks my mom.

My parents are settling down for an evening of watching the Weather Channel. A favourite pastime in Regina.

"I'm heading out," I say.

"Do you really have to go out?" asks my mom.

"I promised the guys I'd meet them at eight."

"Well, don't go out on the by-pass. Stick to city streets," warns my dad.

"Yeah, yeah." Not the lecture again.

"I'm serious. It's vicious out there."

"It's only a short distance." Here comes the story.

"There was a university student driving home from Regina Beach, when his car died half a mile from the Trans-Canada, so he decided to walk. The next morning they found him 100 yards from a farm house, deader than a door nail."

All right, all right." I grab my parka.

"You should dress warmer," says my mom with concern.

"It's only minus thirty-five out." I'm twenty years old, and they still treat me like a kid.

The air freezes in my lungs as I open the door. My shoes squeak on the fresh snow, as I clear off the windshield of my parents' old beast of a station wagon. By the time I finish my fingers are starting to go numb.

The beast whines when I turn the key. I pump the gas and try again. It emits a feeble cough. Finally I put the pedal to the floor and pray I don't flood it. To my relief it catches, and the engine roars to life.

I let it warm up for a few minutes, keeping my foot on the gas, so it won't stall, while frigid air pours out of the vents.

When it seems warm enough that it won't die, I head out. I make it as far as backing out of the driveway before getting stuck in the snow bank that lines the road. But by rocking the car back and forth, I manage to extricate myself without having to call my dad, saving myself from major embarrassment.

I have trouble driving through the suburban crescents. This car is just too darn big for the ruts that have been worn in the road. There must be a couple of feet of hard packed snow this year. I have to pump the brakes to avoid sliding through the sheer ice at every intersection.

I flip on the radio just in time to catch the news. "In tonight's top story, police are advising motorists to stay off the roads unless absolutely necessary." Then he starts talking about the alien invasion, so I punch in another station.

"...but with the wind chill factor it feels more like minus 57. Exposed flesh will freeze in thirty seconds."

-Honk-

I look over. The guy in the car beside me at the red light is pointing down at the ground.

Shit. Not again.

I wave to the guy, and get out of my car. Sure enough. I forgot to unplug the car again. I quickly haul the cord in, and hop back in my car before the light turns green.

I pull into the sparsely populated parking lot at Western Pizza. I'm about to stop the car, but looking down at the cord on the seat beside me, I think the better of it, and drive around to the back of the building. I pull into a spot marked 'Reserved For Bank Employees'. Seeing no one around, I hop out and plug in my car. Just the block heater. I don't want to be greedy by plugging in the interior warmer as well.

My visibility instantly drops to zero as I step in the restaurant. When I take off my frost-covered glasses, I can make out someone waving at me from a booth at the back.

"Hey, Don." I recognize Matt's voice.

"Man, is it cold out," I exclaim as I slide in next to Dave.

"What moron decided to put a city here?" says Sean.

"What with the aliens and all, maybe he wasn't such a moron," replies Dave.

Sean's reply is preempted by the arrival of the waitress.

"You guys ready to order?"

"A number one." You'd think she'd know by now.

"So, I went out to go to work this morning, and, like,

someone stole my extension cord," complains Matt, after the waitress has shuffled away.

"Man, that should be a capital offense," says Sean.

"Yeah, tell me about it. So then I called CAA, right, and it takes them until three to get to my place. That reminds me. My boss docked me for the time, so can you guys spot me for the 'za?"

"Sure man, no problem." What a mooch. The guy hasn't paid for his own pizza in years.

I put my glasses back on. If I tilt my head back I can see out of the bottom, where they've thawed.

"Geeze Dave, what happened to your face?" I ask. His cheeks and nose are all red and peeling, like a severe case of sunburn.

"Frostbite. I was going stir-crazy, so I went out cross-country skiing a couple of days ago."

Dave's crazy. One of these days he's going to kill himself if he's not careful.

"Man, it doesn't get any better than this," I say after scalding the roof of my mouth on the freshly-arrived pizza, as grease runs down my arm.

"I hear the aliens are attacking Toronto," says Dave, while pouring himself some Coke from the pitcher.

"Naw," I reply, "they've only made it as far as Guelph. But it won't be long."

"That'll teach those wimpy easterners," says Sean with satisfaction. "Dry cold or no dry cold, forty below is colder than four below."

"Have you guys gone out to see the dead alien yet?" asks Dave.

"No."

"It's awesome. It's just sitting there in the middle of this farmer's field, frozen like some kind of statue."

"How far is it?" asks Matt.

"Not far. Maybe sixty klicks."

"I don't think I'll risk it. The other day I'm driving around on the Ring Road, and my gas line freezes up," says Matt.

"Man, you've really gotta get a new c-"

"Shh," says Matt to Sean, pointing up to the tv screen in the corner. "I wanna catch the forecast."

It hasn't changed.

"So what're you guys going to do this summer?" asks Dave

when the forecast is over.

"Well," replies Matt, "we've got relatives up in the Yukon, so we've been talking about going up there."

"I read that scientists figure that the aliens have kicked up so much dust and smoke into the air that we're not going to get summer here, so we should be safe," I tell them.

"Yeah," agrees Sean, "even if it does warm up, why would they bother attacking here when they know they're going to be driven out by the cold in a couple of months anyway?"

With that we finish the last of the pizza, pool our money and head for the door. "Slurpees anyone?" asks Matt. We agree, and head out into the cold to see if our cars will start.

THROUGH THE WINDOW OF THE GARDEN SHED
Eileen Kernaghan

a sand bucket
left outside all summer
its bright paint chipped and peeled
into nightmare patterns
only I can recognize

a doll with no eyes
her face pierced by black holes
emptying into nothing

a heap of rags in which
one day, horribly,
something moved

this is the window I must edge past
eyes sealed shut
not daring to look through dusty panes
into corners where unspeakable
things crouch

whispering behind the glass
turn your head _
open your eyes

did you think
this time
we would not be here?

THE LAST DANCE
Annick Perrot-Bishop (translated by Neil Bishop)

I spent the winter sleeping, remembering. Dreaming too. Dreams still drifting in my gaze. Night-hued mists growing wispy in the morning light. I need these long periods of sleep that allow me to enter the Memory I bear. I have absorbed everything into this huge inner flask. Forgotten eons, vanished worlds, lost generations of Yvanelles, those fabled witches that one day toppled off the bridge of time. During the long winter night, when the light disappears, I am she who does not forget.

The air is cold, but the ice is already beginning to melt. Dark circles surround the base of the trees. Mauve earth, the pleasure of lying on the ground. Of putting my ear to the sand and listening to the rock crackling as it slowly awakens to the warmth of the sun. Yes, it is time to come fully awake. To hasten into the forest in quest of wild animals, berries and spring water.

The scent of the air in my nostrils makes me sigh with pleasure. I am free, and few know of my existence! I move quickly towards the river, propelled by strength I had forgotten and that surprises me every spring. With a shout, I dive into the water. My breathing speeds up, and my heart beats so violently against my chest it makes me dizzy. The water is freezing! I swim with all my energy to warm up. Then, I let the current carry me. The waters, petrified by winter, have recovered their movement, their whispering or giggling voices, their ochre or green-gold colour. The sounds burst free of winter, of ice, of immobility. And the river song spirals about my head, my shoulders, my thighs. I shiver, forgetting the torpor of the winter night.

I descend to the river bottom. The current combs my hair warm with sleep, a long knot of red algae floating with the currents. From my hiding place, I see the sun trembling in the eddies. The wind is undulating the surface into blond wavelets. I am sheltered. No one can see me. On the river bed, colourful stones glisten burnt gold, shell-blue, sky-red, some veined with dark rosacea or spotted with minute stars, phosphorescent planets.

When I get out of the water, the wind is light. It gently dries my skin which is still reddened by the claws of cold. Stretched out on a warm rock, I close my eyes, and listen to the singing wind. Suddenly, a twig snaps...A group of lamils is approaching the river. Their orange, blue-streaked fur glows in the morning light. They have not scented me: my odour is mingled with the algae's. I leap towards the group and manage to catch a doe by her flank, where her fur is thickest. She struggles, while the others flee, crying out plaintively. Finally, I slam her to the ground. My ear on her throat, I can hear her heart beating in the desperate rhythm of a plea. I can see her dark eye, rolled back in terror, ready to swallow death. No, I shall not kill you. I just want to tame you. Your milk will be my food.

Every spring, when I awake, I must rebuild a herd. I release it as autumn ends, before I go back to sleep. I suckle from these lamils, drinking their sweet milk, then cuddle into their rough fur, in their scent of wet hay. I gambol with them in the woods, seeking berries to smear on my face and breasts. And, when night has fallen, I whirl in the light of Agmur, uttering wild cries, defying the city dwellers to come dance with me. When one of them comes, I shall make him drunk with liquor and caresses, and cradle him to my side. Then, gently, I shall take him underground, murmuring to him about the Yvanelles.

Had they not fled the city—at least, those who had survived—to live in the forest like animals, feeding themselves by hunting and fishing, sleeping summers in the tall grass by the rivers or taking shelter, as soon as autumn arrived, in caves or tree trunks? They hoped that one day, things would change, and they met nights to recall their past glory.

Then they used to light a huge fire with haël branches and clumps of hair torn from the heads of the city dwellers as they slept. They threw various stolen articles into the fire: sculpted combs, watches or ear rings of precious metal. Then they would absorb great quantities of the berry liquor, until the night grew luminous in their eyes.

To the sound of a flute, that gave rhythm to every gesture of their daily life, they began to dance, spinning at a dizzying rate, shouting wildly, or swaying in a slow, elegant dance, singing gentle, melodious old hymns. They used to know every possible step and rhythm created, forgotten, reinvented throughout the ages. Wrenching or gentle, the flute was their breath, their heartbeat, their lives.

That is what I shall tell him, the one who will join my

dance, but he will not believe me. In the wee hours of the morning, when he awakens in the subterranean darkness, he will think he was dreaming.

In the depths of my palms, I shall still have the smoky scent of his hair, the perfume of his berry-flavoured body. In my ears, his voice ever slower, made sleepy by the whirl of words. A voice on the edge of the abyss, of a fall. Then I shall rush toward the river to erase the caresses of night. Our cries of pleasure. The sweat of my body and of his skin, glowing in the fire light. And even his colourless eyes, glistening with desire and fear.

Water, cold will erase our gestures. And I shall again be ready. Brand new, as on the first day. Having buried in the depths of my memory all that will have happened that night. And what will happen the following nights, until the season of sleep returns.

⚸ ⚸

This man has curly hair, like a lamil's. He believes I cannot see him, behind a bush just coming into leaf. He does not know that I can hear the slightest swish of his feet on the smooth grass. I stopped dancing, uttering those shouts that make some shiver with fear and that captivate others. I am listening to his pounding heart, his hurried breathing. I can imagine the gleam of desire in his eyes.

He looks at me with an amazingly innocent air. His gaze is different from the others'. There is fear and curiosity in it, but also gentleness and dignity. He is shivering beneath his torn shirt that reveals very white skin. He left Trôl early, and got lost in the forest. His car broke down, and he walked here. He asks me the way to the city. They were expecting him for supper and must be worried.

I invite him to approach the fire to warm himself. The city is much too far away for him to go there this evening. He had better set off in the early morning. He accepts, after a moment's hesitation, torn between concern for his hosts and his desire for rest.

Overcome by sudden shyness, I cover my naked breasts with a lamil skin and give him one to keep him warm. With gratitude, he accepts the haël apples slowly baking in the embers. He eats several of them, peeling them carefully. Then, he drinks some berry liquor. Just a little. He holds out the container with a smile of gratitude; he feels less cold, he's lucky he found me!

I take him to my shelter. This is certainly the first time a stranger has entered. I do not quite understand what is happening to me. This sudden trust...He looks at the clay Yvanelles with an astonishment that goes far beyond my expectations. Asks if I made them. His fingers gently brush each figurine's face. Then he turns around, his gaze glowing. Looks at me, intrigued. According to him, I am like them. Mouth, nose, forehead...

I have made a fire in the fireplace. He feels hot, and takes off the lamil skin. His body is slender and his face, although pale with fatigue, is not without beauty. Especially his eyes, black, liquid. Pools of night, lake shadows. He is coming towards me. His hands are gentle on my face. On my breasts still smeared with berry juice. I plunge my feverish fingers into his curly hair. Into his half-open shirt: the velvet of his smooth-haired chest, a spicy perfume mixed with that of baked apples. I bite his shoulder, groaning.

His are not the impatient gestures of the others. He is an artist, re-creating me with the tips of his fingers, with his tongue, his mouth, his eyes. I am simultaneously the one I know and another. And he is much more than this supple, spice-scented body that moves me so. Or this smooth belly I caress with fervour. He emanates an entire world I am not used to. Which, nonetheless, draws me. A world of refinement and subtle thoughts. A world I would like to tame, possess, love—but to which I would like to add the warmth of lamil milk, the odour of damp hay, the wet sting of cold water on my skin.

⁂

He left this morning by the path along the river. I watched him grow more distant, until his silhouette disappeared behind the grey-blue bushes. His gait was quick, almost joyful. Unaware of the gift I had just bestowed on him. The gift of his own life. Of his own destiny. Is he not different from the others?

I shall not go to the river today. I shall keep the trace of his caresses on my skin. His scent of pepper and haël apples. And, in my ears, his lies, sweet as honey. Stretched out upon the unmade bed, I am thinking about him, about last night, indifferent to the colours that press against my closed drapes. The fire has gone out, but I do not budge. I do not need its heat. My entire body is shouting, quivering, singing. Dreaming, I run through the forest. Mingle with the odour of moss-covered rock. To quench my thirst, I lick the minute drops of sap oozing upon the muir branches.

As for the others, come these last few days to join my dance, they must be inert by now. Weakened by the cold, the lack of water and food, they have probably succumbed. How they must have screamed when they woke up! Hammered with all their strength at the tile blocking the entrance to the subterranean chamber! Their desperate nails clawing the stone, their skinless fingers, the bloodied hands. It was not difficult for me to draw them there. Drunk with berries and promises, they followed me, stumbling. Unaware that the tombs I wished to show them—and in which the Yvanelles used to be buried alive—would soon be their own...

THE UNSHACKLING OF THUMBS
David Nickle

When Jeremy Brandt was two, a hand reached down, wrapped around his torso and lifted him into the sky of his bedroom like a field mouse caught in the claws of an owl. The hand belonged to a woman who had named herself Belize, after the town; investigators later confirmed she had worked two weeks as a temporary domestic in the Brandt household and was on her last day at the time of the abduction.

Belize's fingers were long and narrow, but strong, and when Jeremy tried to scream she used her thumb to cover his mouth and nostrils. By the time she had stuffed Jeremy into her bag, he had already fainted from lack of oxygen.

When police raided Belize's house three days later, they found Jeremy in her basement, huddled in a fogged bell jar on a gray metal shelf alongside thirty-seven others. Jeremy was one of the seventeen who still lived, subsisting on a glucose solution that Belize served in an eyedropper twice daily and crouching in a shallow pool of his own feces and urine that Belize promised to drain three times a week.

The twenty-one dead were pickled in formaldehyde solutions. Their burns and contusions were white and puckered, exuding thin strands of effluvium that swayed like aquarium plants whenever anything jostled their containers.

Later, Belize confessed to everything. She had been collecting "thumbs" as she called them for nearly seven months. During this time, Belize inflicted on her thumbs a range of sexual tortures, some of which were so debased as to make two of Belize's interrogators physically ill.

Jeremy, being Belize's most recent acquisition, was spared the worst of her repertoire. In her confession Belize held that she had barely begun her exploration of Jeremy, and other evidence bore this claim out; when the trauma team found him, his only physical injuries were a slight inflammation around his anus and genitalia, and a handful of other minor effects which in people of Jeremy's ilk were all commonly associated with malnutrition.

Jeremy had blinked and gasped at the fresh air, his vision filled with the moon-faces of the trauma team as they lifted him away from the jar.

"He's nominal," said a black-haired woman whose palm was clammy against Jeremy's raw buttocks. With her free hand, she adjusted the jeweler's magnifier on her eye. "Give him half dosage, just to be safe."

As she rolled Jeremy over in her hand he shut his eyes and felt it in his thigh—sharp and numbing, all at once.

⁂

Jeremy awoke some hours later on a pallet atop a metal cart in what might have been a hospital maternity ward. Illumination was indirect and comfortably low, and as Jeremy looked around he saw the room was filled with pallets similar to his own, as well as perhaps a half-dozen glass incubators. On the pallets and in the incubators were sleeping some of the others from Belize's cellar. In the distant corner, near a large wall-mirror, a nurse stood with her back to them all, fiddling with bottles and instruments on a long wheeled table and humming softly to herself.

Jeremy felt stronger than he had in days, but his hands still trembled as he brought them to his face, sniffed at his delicate fingers. He smiled—the smell was nearly gone. He ran his hands down his chest and torso, felt the staccato rhythm of his heartbeat and breathing, the dab of warm ointment on his penis.

The nurse turned just as Jeremy sat up. As their eyes locked, Jeremy felt the muscles in his back clench. He fell back against the cloth of his bed and pulled his knees up to his chin. Eyes screwed shut, he waited helplessly for the nurse's arrival.

She didn't come.

"Jeremy," she whispered from the distant corner. "I'm not going to hurt you. I won't even move. It's all right."

The nurse and Jeremy stood at a silent impasse until the door finally opened and another came in. Jeremy wouldn't open his eyes, but their conversation boomed at him.

"What's going on here?" said a man. "How long has he been like that?

In a whisper: "Shh. Not more than a minute."

At volume: "Well why are you standing there?"

"He's terrified. Speak quietly. You're hurting his ears."

The man didn't answer, but moved to where Jeremy lay curled. "It's not his ears I'm worried about," he finally said, then leaned closer to Jeremy, as though Jeremy were hard of hearing and not the opposite.

"Jeremy Brandt," he said. "The woman who hurt you is

gone. You are safe. My name is William. My friend's name is Barbara. We are not going to hurt you. Come awake!"

The words bludgeoned at Jeremy, even as their meaning worked at his fears. He opened his eyes and felt the muscles in his back begin to unclench. The man above him was dressed in a nurse's uniform. He had a thin goatee beard and long blonde hair pulled back into a pony tail. His breath was hot and damp.

Jeremy licked his lips and blinked. He was about to speak, but William smiled and turned to Barbara, who was moving closer through the forest of carts and tubes and boxes.

"See?" said William. "You can't be squeamish, you can't shy away. You've got to deal with them."

"He just woke up," whispered Barbara as she stopped over Jeremy. She looked down, a strange kind of wonder in her wide face. "He's only two years old. Don't you think you're being harsh?"

"This isn't child abuse, Barbara. He's more than half-way through his life. He's as physically and psychologically mature as he's ever likely to get." William reached down with his right forefinger and rested it lightly on Jeremy's chest.

"He's nominal," said William after a moment. "Just keep monitoring him. And don't be squeamish."

Jeremy finally spoke as the two of them were walking back across the room.

"When can I go home?" he whistled quietly. But neither William nor Barbara gave any indication they heard him, and Jeremy did not repeat the question.

※ ※

One by one, the others awoke, and Jeremy watched Nurse Barbara handle each of them with varying degrees of success. The first one, a long-haired woman who Jeremy recalled seeing splayed face-down on a sheet of plywood with strips of duct tape securing her arms and legs, shrieked and scratched at her thighs when Nurse Barbara approached. Finally Nurse Barbara had to take hold of her arms—delicately, each wrist pinned between thumb and forefinger like the handle on a teacup—and wait until she had tired herself out.

Others responded like Jeremy—disoriented and fearful at first, then warming somewhat to the directness of Nurse Barbara's onslaught. And others responded to nothing.

These last Nurse Barbara wheeled to the door, where another pair of hands—Nurse William? Jeremy wondered—took them rattling down a long corridor and away.

In the wardroom, the remaining thumbs' terror dissipated like steam in a breeze.

Sitting up on his pallet, Jeremy counted nine left in the room when all were awake. Jeremy tried to place each one from Belize's cellar, identifying them by the things he had witnessed in his three days there. For the most part he was successful: plywood and duct tape, needle and thread, cellophane, a paper bag with handles, a coat-hanger...If Jeremy concentrated, he found he could name nearly all of his companions in such a way—all in fact but one.

This one was a man, older than anyone Jeremy had seen, and his pallet and Jeremy's were only separated by one. His hair was pure white, and about three inches long—if he were standing, it would reach his behind. His eyes were slitted black steel bearings that didn't flinch; and they followed Nurse Barbara steadily back across the room once she had satisfied herself that he too was "nominal". Jeremy had struggled with his recollections for what seemed like a minute, until the eyes turned to him. The face beneath them broke into a thin smile, and at that Jeremy had to look away.

"Better," said the old one in a voice like crackling tinfoil. "Right?"

Even when he spoke, nothing jogged in Jeremy's memory. He lay back down on the pallet and turned away from the stranger, curling his knees up to his chest and shutting his eyes until Nurse Barbara brought their dinner.

⁄⁄ ⁊

The psychiatrist introduced herself as Doctor Shelly Tainter. She ordered Nurses William and Barbara to move the pallets into a semi-circle facing the mirror, then Doctor Tainter set a low foot stool on the floor in front of them. When she sat, her eyes were no higher than any of the pallets.

The two nurses left, closing the door softly behind them.

"My name is Doctor Shelly Tainter," she repeated when they were gone. "I'm here to be your friend. I'm going to see you together every day, and I'm also going to talk to each of you by yourselves, one at a time."

Across the semi-circle, the old one coughed, and Doctor Tainter looked at him with a measure of alarm. She started to get up, but the old one waved her back to her stool.

"Fine," he rasped. "*Nominal.* No worry."

For barely an instant, Doctor Tainter looked uncertain. Then the smile returned.

"All right," she said. "Then let's begin. You know my name now, but I don't know yours. We'll start at this end."

The old one was among three in the group who claimed to have no name.

"Mother was whore," he explained when it was his turn. "Flushed me down toilet. Raised by sewer alligators as one of their own; alligators don't name young."

When it came Jeremy's turn, he identified himself readily enough, but the old one's talk of his mother had jogged another question from Jeremy's memory.

"When can I see my mother and father?"

"Would you like to see them?" asked Doctor Tainter.

Jeremy didn't answer.

"Then perhaps we'll wait a day or two. I know they're very relieved you're all right."

〽️ 〽️

That night, after Doctor Tainter had left and the nurses had finished their rounds, Jeremy found his thoughts returning to the question. Did he want to see them? He wasn't sure if he wanted to see anybody...

"Hey. Jeremy Brandt."

Jeremy opened his eyes and looked to the voice. Sure enough, it was the old one. His pallet had been moved across the room after the psychiatrist's shuffling that evening, but he'd somehow managed to climb off it and scale back up the legs of Jeremy's own cart. He sat cross-legged at Jeremy's feet, black eyes glittering over his grin.

"Doctor Tainter lying," he said.

"About my parents?"

"No. Don't know anything about your parents. But she said this is between her and us. A lie."

Jeremy sat up himself, unconsciously mimicking the old one's position.

"See the mirror?" The old one pointed across the dark room to the glass. "See it glow."

Jeremy squinted, and sure enough, he could make out a dim square of light in the middle of the mirror.

"Two-way mirror," said the old one. "Shiny like a mirror on one side, clear like a window on the other. When Doctor Tainter talked, I could hear others talking too. Behind the glass."

"What did they say?" asked Jeremy, his eyes fixed on the yellow square in the mirror.

"Giant talk. A man telling two women and three men what he thought about us. Called us 'group session.' Said they would 'monitor post-trauma recovery patterns' for week. Compare with 'B Group.' Then decide. Didn't say decide what."

"Are they there now?"

"No," said the old one. "No sound in there now." He tapped on his ear. "I know giants. Even when giants are sleeping, I hear them."

Jeremy felt his back tighten as it had when he first awoke. "Will you tell me when they're there?" he asked, trembling.

"I will go like this," said the old one, and coughed. "At night, when they are gone, we will talk some more. My name is Charles."

"You said you had no name."

"Charles is a secret name. Not for giants."

Jeremy thought he understood. "Charles," he said aloud.

"Good." The old one—Charles—crawled to the edge of the pallet and, gripping the cloth, swung his legs over. "We will talk some more," he said, and dropped to the floor.

A moment later, Jeremy heard their conversation repeated on the pallet to his right, with a woman named Maryanne Bennett who had been touched with scissors and made to bend in Belize's cellar. After a time, the square of light in the mirror was transected by a shadow. They disappeared, shadow and light, accompanied by the distant sound of a lock clicking shut.

⁄⁄ ⟍

"Good morning Jeremy."

Jeremy's pallet had been moved away from the others, through doors and hallways and elevators into a smaller room lit from a high frosted window. It was empty save Doctor Tainter and Jeremy. He and the doctor sat across from one another, Jeremy on his pallet, Doctor Tainter on another low stool below the window. If Jeremy craned his neck, he could see her thick red hands fidgeting with a pencil and clipboard in her lap. She smiled as she spoke.

"It's good to see you face to face," she said. "Is there anything you'd like to ask me before we get started?"

"Where are my parents?" replied Jeremy.

"They've gone home for now. They're both very tired. But they'll be back." Doctor Tainter cleared her throat, one hand touching her mouth as she did so. "Anything else you'd like to know about?"

Jeremy was about to ask about the mirror in the other room,

and "post-trauma recovery patterns" and the "B group," but he held his tongue.

"Well Jeremy, there are some things that I'd like to know about. To begin with, your parents. It's interesting that this is the second time you've asked me about them. Tell me about your mother."

Jeremy described his mother in as much detail as he could: her hair, cropped short so the individual hairs stood on end; her smell, of milk and sometimes something burnt; the mole on her shoulder, as big as Jeremy's fist. He told how she had stopped her work for a time after he was born, thinking like many others that the radiation from her VDT or bad air from the office ventilation system or something they put in the water was to blame for making her baby so tiny.

"Now she's back at work," said Jeremy.

"That means she must have less time for you."

Jeremy waited for the question.

"How do you feel about that?" she finally asked.

Jeremy blinked.

"Does it make you feel sad?" prompted Doctor Tainter. "Or does it make you happy? There's no right or wrong answer, Jeremy." She waited again, and when it was clear Jeremy had no answer at all, she looked down at her clipboard and made a notation.

"Perhaps we'll come back to that later," she said. "We'll move on a bit for now." Doctor Tainter flipped some pages on her clip-board, then looked Jeremy straight in the eye.

"I've got a photograph here, Jeremy. It's a photograph taken by the police of the woman who kidnapped you."

"Belize," said Jeremy.

"Yes. That's her name. Would you like to look at the photograph?"

"Yes," said Jeremy.

Doctor Tainter seemed surprised. "All right," she said, and lifted up the clip-board so that it nearly covered her face.

The photograph was bigger than Jeremy, although not nearly so large as Belize had been. Her long black hair was limp across her shoulders, and she wore a loose denim shirt that was not her own. Her eyes were flat and joyless, utterly unlike those eyes from Jeremy's recollections.

"How does seeing Belize make you feel?" asked Doctor Tainter.

Jeremy sat quiet.

※ ※

Charles came that night with news from behind the mirror. Through the group session, he had seemed quite inattentive, his eyes never on the discussion, always on the glass. When Doctor Tainter brought the talk around to her, Charles ignored her until she made a notation on her clip-board and moved along.

He had seemed inattentive, but Jeremy knew better: at the beginning of the session, Charles had let loose a terse, deliberate cough. He was in fact being quite attentive—to the mirror, and those who hid behind it.

"Much talk today," said Charles. "Want to hear it?"

Jeremy did.

"Same man talking as before; this time, one of the women was gone. Replaced by another man. Detective Sergeant Taylor. Man talking introduced him around: Doctor Weyland, Doctor Hiroto, Doctor Osborne, Doctor Palmer."

"What did they say?"

"Nothing for awhile. When Doctor Tainter asked about the basement, Detective Sergeant Taylor asked if she knew what she was doing. 'This is only your second day with them; I'd have thought taking them back to the basement right away wouldn't do anything but traumatize them all over,' is what Detective Sergeant Taylor said.

"'From what we know of them, this approach seems to be the best course,' is what talking man said.

"'Well we've got plenty of charges against Belize already. Don't feel you've got to rush this through on our account,' is what Detective Sergeant Taylor said.

"'We're hardly rushing. This is as much our investigation as it is yours,' is what the talking man said.

"Another one, Doctor Weyland, started talking. 'Quiet a moment. Listen,' is what she said.

"That was when Nancy told about needlepoint. Remember that?"

Jeremy did. Nancy was about Jeremy's age, with brown hair so thick it grew into a single, tall clump on her scalp. During Jeremy's time in Belize's basement, Nancy had not once been removed from her jar.

Nancy had been living outside, in an enclave of about a dozen others underneath a bridge near the lake. She had been spotted by Belize while foraging through front yards one night. Belize was foraging too, dressed as a worm-picker with a small lamp strapped to her head and a juice can tied to each ankle. The beam from the lamp speared Nancy as she tried to escape across the dark lawn, and before she could reach the safety of the hedge-row, Belize plucked her from the grass like a night-crawler and deposited her in the left-side can. Earthworms writhed at Nancy's ankles like living rope in the moonlight. When Nancy tried to climb out, Belize flicked her back inside and covered the opening with a perforated lid.

What did Belize do to Nancy? Doctor Tainter had wanted to know.

For a long time, Nancy was simply confined to her jar and only occasionally taken out for the relatively benign "examinations." In those days, Belize had not collected more than a dozen thumbs, and her intrusions on their persons were much less frequent and dramatic than they became towards the end.

On a particular night, however, Belize came down to the basement in a new and particular frame of mind. Where previously she had tended her thumbs with a bored, nearly scientific detachment, this night her normally pallid face was flushed pink with excitement. Her long fingers tapped out frenetic rhythms on her thighs as she moved along the length of the shelf, squinting through the smeary glass of each jar, trying to decide.

She finally selected Nancy. Belize had brought down with her a syringe, and when she pulled Nancy from the jar she pricked Nancy's buttock with it. The drug spread like a single ice-crystal across Nancy's nerves, and when it was finished Nancy was paralyzed, head to toe. Belize touched a fingernail to Nancy's abdomen, and when she was satisfied that Nancy couldn't even flinch, set her down on the workbench and went back upstairs to fetch her sewing kit. By the time Belize returned, Nancy was having to make a conscious effort just to breathe.

Belize brought down with her a blue plastic tackle box which contained her needles and threads, and a single embroidery hoop. She set Nancy onto the hoop, threaded a red silk embroidery thread through a thick needle and went to work. By the time the drug wore off, Belize had finished.

"Belize wrapped silk around and around me, between my legs, over my wrists, my ankles, all but my face. Sewed me to the hoop, took hoop upstairs and hung me on wall in bathroom."

Nancy had showed no emotion as she spoke, but Doctor Tainter had to compose herself before she could ask her next question.

"How…" Doctor Tainter's voice was hoarse, and she had to clear her throat before she could finish. "How did you feel?"

"Hard to breath," Nancy had said. "Silk too tight. Smell wasn't as bad as in the jar, but Belize didn't like it anyway. Took me down after two days. Said bathroom stank like shit."

Doctor Tainter had seemed about to repeat the question, but stopped herself and ticked off a square on her clip-board instead.

"When Doctor Tainter moved to next," continued Charles, "talk started up again behind mirror. Talking man said, 'That's how the private interviews have been closing. Any time Doctor Tainter asks a patient to verbalize their response to a situation, the best they can come up with is a physical description. In most instances, they don't even seem to understand the question.'

"Detective Sergeant Taylor said, 'It's only been two days you've had them. I've seen um, full-sized rape victims in a similar state at this stage of the game. They don't want to talk about it at all, want to pretend it didn't happen. Particularly the children.'

"Talking man said, 'These aren't children. And this isn't the game in any way you understand it.'"

"Detective Sergeant Taylor said, 'I may not understand the game, but this is helping me understand Belize. Better than I'd have thought.'"

"Talking man said, 'How so?'

"Detective Sergeant Taylor said, 'Well to begin, it looks as though this last incident with, um, Nancy, may have been Belize's hinge-point. When she changed from a kidnapper to a murderer.

"Doctor Hiroto said, 'Is the timing of such a distinction actually important to your investigation?'

"Detective Sergeant Taylor said, 'It's not crucial, but it is important. In order to perpetrate the crimes she did, Belize underwent a change. At some point, she saw her prizes as victims.'

"Doctor Hiroto said, 'They *are* such perfect victims,' and laughed.

"Detective Sergeant Taylor said, 'Nobody is a perfect victim.'

"Doctor Hiroto said, 'I'm sorry. I didn't mean…'

"Detective Sergeant Taylor said, 'You're not the first to make the observation. By your own admission, you can't get close to their trauma—it may not even be there. And they're so *small*. Hell, if Belize had been thinking, she could have disposed of all of them, flushed them down her toilet, and we wouldn't have been able to trace her in a million years.'

"Talking man said, 'But Belize wasn't thinking straight.'

"Detective Sergeant Taylor said, 'I guess you'd know better about that than me.'

"Nobody said anything for a minute. Then Detective Sergeant Taylor said, 'This session has been a great help. Thanks for the invitation.'"

Charles uncrossed his legs, stretched them in front of him. "Stupid giants. Think *they* can change *us*."

"Shouldn't they?" said Jeremy. "We're in a hospital after all."

At that, Charles got to his knees and regarded Jeremy with a curious squint. "We talk again tomorrow. Okay?"

Jeremy thanked Charles, and watched him shimmy down the leg of the cart to the white linoleum floor.

※ ※

In her second session alone with Jeremy, Doctor Tainter returned to the subject of Jeremy's parents.

"Do you know," said Doctor Tainter, "that there are only three of you in the group whose parents have come forward?"

Jeremy hadn't even counted that many in the group session. "I didn't know that," said Jeremy.

"It's not really that surprising, although it might be for you. Most of the people Belize took she took from outside, where there was no one to report them missing; that's why it took the police so long to track her down."

Doctor Tainter paused, as though Jeremy were supposed to comment. Finally she continued.

"You're one of the lucky few, Jeremy. The day you went missing, your father called the police. When they didn't want to deal with your case for at least another 24 hours, your mother set her lawyer to work on them. The police were on your trail by morning." Doctor Tainter set down her clip-board and pen on the floor beside her. "Very few people like yourself are so lucky, you know. Your parents have kept you safe at home.

When babies are born small, many parents give them up. They leave them in foster homes, or in some parts of the country just abandon them."

Or they flush them down the toilet, thought Jeremy. If they're whores, like Charles' mother.

"I've been speaking with your parents again," she continued. "They miss you very much, but they've agreed to wait another day before coming to see you. Do you feel all right with that?"

"Yes," said Jeremy, supposing that to be the best answer.

Doctor Tainter frowned and leaned forward.

"Are you sure? Just yesterday, you seemed very anxious to see them."

"I feel all right," replied Jeremy, more certain of the fact this time.

"How would you feel," said Doctor Tainter then, "if we were to move you to a different room from the rest? Put you all by yourself?"

Jeremy's breath caught in his chest and he felt his eyes widen, his buttocks clench. It was as though a crystal were forming in his middle, a prick of chemical as Belize had sometimes employed in others. It tightened through him like a knot drawing in.

"Easy, Jeremy," said Doctor Tainter. "We won't put you by yourself. That's not our plan; I was just posing a question. You're safe."

Jeremy let his breath out, and the knot loosened.

"I didn't mean to frighten you," Doctor Tainter added. She picked up her clip-board and pen and began making notes.

When Doctor Tainter looked up, she was smiling.

"I think that's enough for today," she said. "We've made good progress, you and I."

⁂

In the morning, Nurse William and a green-smocked intern named Evan wheeled two new thumbs into the ward-room. They were both hairless and emaciated, and each had a cotton swab taped over their right buttock. Charles watched them through narrow eyes over his knees, which he had brought up to the level of his chin when the first of them entered the room.

Once the two newcomers had been settled, Nurse William and Evan the Intern moved to the other side of the room, where he opened a drawer and took out a metal tray that rattled, covered with a bright red cloth. Doctor Tainter came in and sat down on her stool. She introduced the two new patients as Lucy and John, and explained that they had just graduated from their incubators in B Group.

"I hope you'll all welcome John and Lucy into the group," said Doctor Tainter. "They're both coming along very well."

Doctor Tainter turned to John, whose thin lips were pulled back so far that his head appeared a tiny skull.

"There are a lot of people in here, John," said Doctor Tainter. "But do you remember what we talked about yesterday?"

John appeared to be on the verge of screaming, but he nodded nonetheless.

"Would you like to tell us all about yourself?" The question was phrased as a command, said in a tone to which John seemed to respond.

"Yes," replied John.

"I am called John. I used to live under floors, over ceilings, in old houses near lake. This is Lucy—" at this point, John gestured to Lucy, whose eyes were roving distractedly about the room—"who also lived in those places. We knew each other before Belize."

"How did you feel about Lucy?" asked Doctor Tainter.

John glanced uneasily at Lucy, and as he did so, his eyelids began to twitch. "Long time ago," he said.

Doctor Tainter leaned forward. "How did you feel?" she repeated.

Lucy's eyes in the meantime had settled. Jeremy followed their gaze, and saw that she was looking directly at Charles. For himself, Charles lowered his knees and stared back, with an odd expression of defiance.

"I loved her," said John, all the tremor gone from his voice.

Doctor Tainter was silent for a moment, but it was obvious from the shine in her eye that she wasn't displeased. Lucy, meanwhile, had scrambled to the back of her pallet, not looking away from Charles for an instant.

As Doctor Tainter flipped a page on her clip-board, Lucy disappeared over the edge of her cart.

"Shit!" Evan the Intern pointed.

When Doctor Tainter looked up, Nurse William was already on his way across the room, his feet making an intricate dance that at once maneuvered him safely between the close-packed carts and avoided tromping on anyone that might get underfoot.

Evan the Intern hung further back, a miniature hypodermic ready in his hand.

The shine in Doctor Tainter's eye vanished, and she glared at Evan the Intern accusingly. She seemed about to say something, then stopped herself.

Nurse William stopped directly alongside Jeremy's pallet and knelt down. When he came back up, he was holding Lucy's thin, struggling body in one hand, gesturing at Evan the Intern with the other.

"She's convulsing," said Nurse William.

"It was only a quarter dosage," said Evan the Intern as he stepped through the carts to where Nurse William stood. He reached into his smock and took out a jeweler's magnifier. "She shouldn't be reacting like this. Put her down," he said, setting the glass over his eye.

Nurse William looked directly at Jeremy. "Move over," he said in the booming tones of command he always used on the thumbs. As always, Jeremy did as he was told and watched as Nurse William set Lucy down on his pallet.

Lucy arched her back so that the hairless top of her skull made a dent in the pallet's cushion and the muscles in her scant thighs stood out in sharp relief. Her eyes were open so wide they were actually round, although the pupils had become so small they were less than pinpricks. Her lips stretched to reveal whitened gums.

Even this close, Jeremy could find no recollection of either Lucy or her friend John from his time in Belize's cellar.

Jeremy cringed back as Evan the Intern pushed Nurse William out of the way and bent over Lucy, his eyeglass barely an inch from her face.

"Jesus," he whispered. "I can't see her pupils."

Evan the Intern pulled back and let the magnifier fall out of his eye socket, into his hand and then his smock. With a flick of his wrist, he rolled Lucy onto her stomach, then brought the hypodermic down on her bare, pink behind. The silvery droplet in the tube squeezed through the tiny needle and into Lucy, and even as Evan the Intern pulled the needle free and pressed a fresh cotton swab to Lucy's buttock, Jeremy could see her muscles begin to relax.

"White Hair," she moaned, so quiet Jeremy could barely hear it. "White Hair here."

"She's nominal," muttered Evan the Intern, his finger

resting lightly on Lucy's back. He looked over to the mirror, and repeated at volume:

"She's nominal!"

"Nominal," said someone Jeremy couldn't see. "Meet us outside when you're done."

In the dimness of night, Jeremy threw his legs over the edge of his pallet. Jeremy held his breath and slid down so his arms and legs were wrapped around the leg of the cart. Then, as he'd seen Charles do, he shimmied down to the linoleum below.

They had put Lucy's cart five over from his, in the direction of the mirror. But from the floor, with the carts towering over him like trees in a forest, it was more difficult than Jeremy had expected to sight his goal. Finally, he removed his smock and set it down to mark the location of his own cart, then moved out from under the canopy of pallets to a spot where he could sight the mirror. It loomed dark and silent across the wall to Jeremy's left, the square of light in its centre barely visible.

Once properly re-oriented, Jeremy retrieved his smock and made his way to where Lucy slept. The climb up the leg of her cart was more difficult than the descent down the leg of his, but Jeremy managed it nonetheless and scarcely a minute later crouched huffing over Lucy's sleeping form.

"Wake up," said Jeremy.

Lucy barely stirred, so Jeremy repeated himself, trying to mimic Nurse William's tone and rhythm:

"Wake up, Lucy!"

The words didn't boom in the same way Nurse William's did, but Jeremy's whistling carried enough command to have its effect. Lucy rolled onto her back and stared up at Jeremy with wide eyes, a still mouth—as though, Jeremy thought, he weren't a thumb at all.

Licking his lips, he continued.

"Lucy, tell me about Charles. The one with white hair you were staring at today."

Lucy sat up and moved in a crab-walk back from Jeremy. The drug from the morning was still in her, though, and she slipped onto her back before she reached the edge of the pallet.

"You called him White Hair," said Jeremy.

"Where is he?" said Lucy, blinking as she looked around the darkened room.

"Asleep. Why do you call him White Hair?"

Lucy shrugged. "That his name. Who are you?"

"Jeremy Brandt."

Lucy's eyes had stopped roving and settled on Jeremy. "Two names. You a Chief, like White Hair?"

Jeremy shook his head. "Brandt is my parents' name. Jeremy is my name."

"Parents' name." Lucy seemed to consider the words.

"Tell me about White Hair."

"White Hair came to us. When we lived in house."

"Under the floors, over the ceilings?" asked Jeremy. "That time?"

"Yes. Giants had put down bad food for us, Jack and Tim were very sick. White Hair climbed in through hole near drainpipe. He said he was a Chief, his people lived in house as we did at end of the street. He said there was plenty of room, no giants. No bad food."

"Did you follow him?"

"Not at first. Jack said White Hair was a bad Chief to be away from his people and wouldn't go. When Jack dead, then we went."

Lucy's eyelids were beginning to flutter, so Jeremy leaned over and shook her ankle, thinking she was about to fall asleep. But he'd misinterpreted; in fact, Lucy was beginning to cry.

Jeremy withdrew his hand and watched, fascinated, as Lucy drew her legs up to her chest and clenched her eyes and mouth around her squeaking sobs. He'd seen the same symptoms in his mother and father many times, but never before in a thumb. Even when Belize worked her very worst on them, the thumbs' eyes were ever dry.

"How do you feel?" whispered Jeremy.

Lucy raised her head and looked straight in Jeremy's eyes. Her own eyes were glassy with the drug, and even before she spoke, Jeremy put it together: the tears weren't hers. They were induced by whatever it was the people behind the mirror had injected her with this morning.

"I feel sad," said Lucy in a trembling voice. "I remember Jack. He was friend. He showed me how to climb the wiring, where to jump. Where not to jump. He dead. I feel sad."

"White Hair. Charles. Where did he take you after Jack died?"

"Outside. We climbed down drainpipe and ran through grass in dark. White Hair said, 'We go through back yards in night, no giants see us.' But raccoon saw us. Caught Tim, who was sick and slow."

Jeremy expected more tears at this, but evidently Tim's death hadn't made Lucy as sad as Jack's. He let her continue.

"White Hair took us to house at end of street. Like he said. But he tricked us. Inside, there was a giant. She waited in kitchen with net. She caught all of us but White Hair."

"Charles—White Hair—escaped?"

"No."

Jeremy felt himself tremble, but as quick as it came, the trembling passed. "What did White Hair do?"

"Giant picked him up in her hand. Ran her finger over his hair. White Hair watched from giant's shoulder while she put us in jars."

"How," said Jeremy, because he could think of nothing else, "did you feel?"

But the glaze of the drug seemed to have washed utterly from Lucy's eyes. "Hard to breathe," was all she said.

Jeremy asked no more questions. Backing away, he rolled over the edge of the pallet and shimmied to the floor. Soon, he thought as he started up the leg of his own cart, he would be as good at climbing as Charles.

⚞ ⚟

Light crossed the mirror-wall and a giant's shadow made it flicker. Nurse Barbara didn't look up from her book, but Jeremy watched. The shadow did not appear again, and even in the quiet night Jeremy's hearing wasn't fine enough to pick up anything of what was going on behind the glass.

Jeremy pushed himself upright on his pallet. He hadn't been able to sleep since he returned from his visit to Lucy, although he had tried. Now the light made sleep seem impossible. He stood in the face of it, narrowed his eyes in a vain attempt to see beyond the glass. What was there? Doctor Hiroto? The Talking Man? The others from Charles' story?

Jeremy stepped closer to the glass, nearer the edge. He stopped as the nub of his toe curled over emptiness.

What was beyond the glass? If Charles were White Hair, Jeremy realized, there was no reason to believe the things that flicked across the light were anything like the giants that Charles had described.

Because White Hair did not describe things as they really were. Like Doctor Tainter, White Hair sometimes lied.

The light vanished, and Jeremy heard the sound of its passing: a soft pneumatic hiss, a clicking of steel. Light

TESSERACTS⁵ ⚞257

remained only in the ward-room now: Its twelve sleeping thumbs; a cloth-covered rack of medicine and instruments; a giant nurse; all reflected imperfectly in the great warp of the false mirror.

Nurse Barbara set her book down, and looked at her wrist-watch. She stood up and opened the ward-room door.

Jeremy clutched at his ears.

The corridor outside seemed to be filled with people, and although they did not speak, their breath roared into the ward-room. One of them coughed, another cleared her throat in unconscious sympathy. Twenty-four feet shuffled, sandpaper scraping on the concrete floor.

Jeremy's eyes screwed shut, and he bent around his stomach as his buttocks clenched tight.

And Jeremy fell forward into the dark.

⁄⁄ ⟍

He hit the floor on his side and bounced once, back underneath the cart. It was a good thing, for suddenly everywhere around him were feet—giant feet wrapped in powder-blue paper moccasins that leaped and crashed in the broad avenues between the carts. If Jeremy had come to rest out there, he would have almost certainly been trampled before he could have regained his senses.

Seemingly at once, the legion of giants stopped—each one at a different cart. Jeremy sat up. His chest hurt, but the fall was only a few feet and he hadn't broken anything. There was a pair of legs at his cart, and he shuffled backwards as a foot pushed underneath.

"Doctor Tainter!" came a roar from nearby. "This one's missing!"

"Everybody stay where they are!" Jeremy recognized Doctor Tainter's voice, although he heard an edge of determination, perhaps of panic, that was never there when she spoke to thumbs. "It could be underfoot. Continue with the injections, all of you—and Nurse, start a sweep."

Jeremy found himself pressed against the cart's wheeled leg. The wheel chaffed against his buttock as the cart jostled and at the far end, the giant foot cautiously pulled back from underneath. In the sky of the ward-room, Jeremy could hear the cool snigger of twelve paper covers tearing free of their hypodermics.

Jeremy set his foot on top of the wheel and pulled himself

up the chromed column. There was a cross-joist maybe a foot off the floor, and when it was within reach Jeremy pulled himself onto it. Panting a little, he wrapped his legs around the metal and lay forward. The metal was cold against his belly, but he did not move as the narrow beam of Nurse Barbara's penlight slashed zig-zags across the floor underneath him. Finally the light withdrew and Nurse Barbara moved on.

Another sound grew in the ward room then, a cooing moan that seemed to come from everywhere at once. Jeremy held the freezing metal tighter.

"Don't be fooled," said Doctor Tainter to one of the others. "Keep hold of its arms. We don't want it to injure itself."

"Yes, Doctor."

"The same goes for all of you. This is a delicate time for them."

"I can't seem to find it, Doctor." It was Nurse Barbara.

"Which one is it?" snapped Doctor Tainter, and the giant over Jeremy's cart answered:

"Jeremy Brandt, Doctor Tainter."

"The one with parents." Doctor Tainter paused, considering. "All right, Nurse, stay where you are." Another pause, and then: "Listen, people—it's started."

Jeremy listened too. The cooing was replaced by a higher tone—a wheezing penny-whistle, punctuated by the tiny hiccoughing sobs such as Jeremy had heard earlier, from Lucy. The drug was in all of them, Jeremy realized. Making all of them like Lucy.

The thought terrified him more fully than even the giant's scream that followed, scant seconds later.

≫ ≫

"The little bastard bit me!"

"Where is he now?"

"He jumped! The fucker bit me and jumped! Christ, I think it punctured the skin."

Doctor Tainter: "That's enough, William. Which way did it run?"

"How the hell should I know?" A fumbling sound, and then, contrite: "I'm sorry, Doctor. He jumped from this side here."

Doctor Tainter sighed. "All right, everybody. We can't do anything for another three minutes anyway. Tend to your patients, and watch where you step."

Jeremy clung to the joist like a lifeline. The shouts of the giants mingled with the screams of the thumbs into a gale of sound. If he let go, Jeremy was certain he'd be carried off by it. He had never felt so tiny, so insubstantial.

"Jeremy Brandt."

Jeremy opened his eyes and looked down.

Charles—White Hair, Jeremy corrected—White Hair stood on the floor beneath Jeremy. The ancient thumb was trembling, and Jeremy could catch a scent of new feces wafting up from him. His eyes were wavering pinpricks that stared into the rafters of the cart.

"Saw you—" White Hair stopped, wrapped his arms around his thin shivering chest "—saw you fall, Jeremy Brandt. Before Doctor Shelly Tainter came. Didn't stick you. No drugs. Right?"

Jeremy didn't answer.

"Smart. Smart to hide." White Hair stumbled over to the cart-leg and started to shimmy up it. He left a dark smear of fecal slime in his wake.

The giants quieted down, and at length Jeremy found himself able to sit upright again. He wheeled around to face White Hair as he mounted the joist.

"Glad you stayed here." White Hair grinned, and his lips pulled too wide over his sharp, blood-reddened teeth. "They would have caught you if you ran. Maybe find you before I do. Doctor Tainter...got me with drug. Makes me sick. Makes me pain. Can't get out on my own. Not like this."

"You want to get out?" said Jeremy. "You're not a prisoner here."

White Hair lifted a hand away from the joist, pulled at his hair with it.

"I know a place," said White Hair. "Big house, no giants. No bad food. We get out of here, through vent I find in wall—" White Hair pointed in a direction "—go there. Okay, Jeremy Brandt?"

Jeremy pushed himself further back along the joist. He stopped at the middle of the cart's undercarriage, and called out over the whistling wail from above: "White Hair! Why did you bring thumbs to Belize?"

White Hair crawled along the joist towards Jeremy.

"Remember Doctor Hiroto?"

Jeremy did.

"He said thumbs perfect victims. Flush down toilet when finished. Right?"

"He said that," Jeremy agreed.

"Other giants think that too. Doctor Tainter thinks that—you think she treats giants like this?" Huge teardrops glistened like jelly over White Hair's eyes as he spoke. "Know something, Jeremy Brandt? Thumbs different from giants—thumbs *are* perfect victims. Pain passes fast. Life short anyway. Can't change thumbs, and thumb who knows that, has strength."

Jeremy was about to ask White Hair more when Doctor Tainter's voice cut them short.

"All right, people. Gather them 'round. It's time."

⚒ ⚒

Doctor Tainter sat down on her eye-level stool in the midst of the thumbs. Jeremy couldn't see her eyes, but looking between the carts he could make out her thick red hands as they worried a pencil and notepad in her lap. The thumbs had quieted again, and the nurses and interns stood motionless and silent at the carts.

"Hello, everyone," said Doctor Tainter. "You must all be feeling a little odd right now. Don't worry about that. Because tonight we're going to talk about why you're here. And how it makes you feel."

White Hair coughed. "Talking Man is behind glass. So is Doctor Weyland."

"What are they saying?" asked Jeremy, crouching lower on the joist so as to see more.

"Doctor Weyland says something about Doctor Tainter...Can't hear...Weyland says, 'I'm really uncomfortable authorizing this.' Talking Man says, 'I'm skeptical too. Sodium pentothal shouldn't be acting....'" White Hair frowned. "Can't hear. Ringing too loud."

There was no ringing, and Jeremy said so. White Hair's shoulders shook. "D-drug," he said. "Drug make me deaf. Make me weak."

"Remember Belize," said Doctor Tainter.

White Hair's body clenched, and his hands came away from the joist. His red-rimmed eyes met Jeremy's as his feet slipped from the joist. White Hair landed on the floor below with a wet slap and he opened his mouth in an agonized yowl. But no giant would have heard it over the noise.

The thumbs were screaming.

Jeremy froze on the joist, listening. These were cellar-screams, a summation of the things that Jeremy had seen and heard—the things he had *felt*—over three days, two nights, under the bell jar. The screams separated before Jeremy, like strands of twine unraveling from a bad cut: cellophane, knitting needles, a paper bag without holes, plywood and carpet-tacks…a thick volume closing slowly.

Jeremy trembled, but held tight. White Hair drew himself into a ball, and as Jeremy looked down a shine of urine spread around the old thumb. White Hair screamed his own memories—a jagged cry that spoke of recollections far from anything in Belize's cellar. His hands clutched at his long silvery hair, pulled it taut from his skull.

Jeremy turned to look where White Hair had pointed a few moments past. Squinting, he could make out the cross-hatched dark of the floor-vent. White Hair screamed anew as a handful of hair came off his scalp in a bloody clump.

It was a twelve-inch jump, and Jeremy made it easily. When he landed, White Hair had rolled face down in his own mess, and Jeremy had to struggle to pull him out of it again. White Hair's eyes were glassy, uncomprehending as Jeremy lifted him to his feet.

"Be strong," said Jeremy in a soft whistle.

As they crossed the floor, the screams diminished to nothing. White Hair was already through the vent and Jeremy was following when Doctor Tainter posed her next question. By the time the thumbs in the ward-room remembered an answer, the two of them were well on their way to White Hair's house—a house with no giants, thought Jeremy, no bad food.

THE TRAVELS OF NICA MARCOPOL

Daniel Sernine (translated by Jean-Louis Trudel)

> *I've seen things you people wouldn't believe:*
> *Attack ships on fire off the Shoulder of Orion...*
> *I watched C-beams glitter in the dark near Tannhauser Gate.*
> *All those moments will be lost in time, like tears in rain.*
> — Roy, in *Blade Runner*

She wanted to be away.

The room was small, with a single window putting on a dreary and monotonous show. Monotonous, and in monochrome.

Nica spent hours in front of that window, her forehead frozen to the 'plast, watching the spheres of the second coronal of Exopolis move past her field of view. Since the two coronals revolved in different directions, one's motion appeared faster when seen from the other's spheres.

From time to time, Nica shifted the position of her forehead, seeking a spot where the 'plast was colder. In the meager light of the distant Sun, the frame and whirling spheres of Exopolis seemed grey. Away from the sunlight, they were so dark only the constellations of portholes and bays lent them an outline.

The uniform motion of the rings was counterpointed by the random comings and goings of the maintenance craft, shuttles, and ships. Yet it would have been hyperbole to say that Exopolis buzzed with activity, even though it was the second busiest spaceport after Erymede's. The ships arriving from in-system or leaving for the Oort cloud were, all in all, not that numerous.

Once per rotation, if Nica looked "down", she could see the Sun, tiny and far from blinding. Less bright, even, than Parsifal B as seen from Lohengrin.

From time to time, city sectors in the shade were briefly rescued from darkness by the flare of braking jets or a welding arc at work on the long docking spars.

Yet they all went unseen by Nica Marcopol, standing at the window of the quarantine quarters. Her gaze was turned inwards. Away.

Towards landscapes where even snow and ice had colour.

On Lohengrin, winter never relinquished its hold on a region covering between one-third and half bthe planet. Only the strip within thirty degrees of the equator enjoyed a temperate climate. Frequently icebergs reached the relatively warm equatorial climes without having completely melted. Veritable sharp-edged hills, they were nothing more than fractions of the icy mountains ocean currents flaked off the north or south ice caps. On the crimson ocean, those icebergs drifted, their gleaming white surfaces blushing rosily in the sun, but taking on the colour of shorn flesh in the shadow.

Nica had only ventured south once—and then, no further than the fortieth parallel, at the southernmost tip of the Thuringia landmass. There, on the high Valkyrie steppes, the snow had danced for her. Billions of glittering glassy shards, delicately pink, gusted furiously, ready to shred the unshielded face of whoever stepped outside the halftrack.

And when the wind died, when none of the major moons shone in the night sky, the air was so clear that starlight alone was enough to make the snow dunes sparkle.

A muffled hiss behind her back did not succeed in rousing Nica from her memories. The doorbell, which rang twice, finally dragged her back. When she turned toward the entrance, without having responded, the door was sliding open with a louder hiss. Doctor Flam emerged from the salmon pink isolation airlock. She did not wear her usual positive pressure suit, thereby signalling the news might not be bad. Perhaps Nica would finally get to leave behind these cramped quarters, the stale air, and the vaguely medicinal smell.

"Apologies for coming in like this, I didn't hear you answer."

Nica shrugged and squared her back against the 'plast, her rear perched on the window sill. The partition of smoked plexi' isolating the bedroom from the living room reflected her body, lean and gangly. The hazy image made her look like a man, the face angular, the greying hair cut short.

"Good news," announced the doctor as she presented her a notepad that she had no intention of letting her read. "Your quarantine is over: the decontamination when you arrived was total and you're not carrying any extra-solar microorganisms. No exotic viruses either."

"But."

No question mark nor ellipsis after Nica's reply. A

statement: she knew there was a "but" in Flam's report.

"No microorganisms, but antibodies we don't recognize."

"They vaccinated me. Several times. I was sick for months before they let me set foot on Lohengrin. Years."

"And once there?"

"It was never easy."

She had told them all that. The back-breaking gravity, stronger even than Earth's pull. The oxygen-poor air and the high ozone counts—except in the cabin where Nica was able to control her environment.

And the low pressure: on the high plateaus of Lohengrin, a mask and air bottles were needed. Even at sea level, she would have required the lungs of an altiplano Peruvian to breathe properly. The mask could be dispensed with, but not the nostril filters, nor the breathing tube clipped to the corner of her lips, where it provided, with every inhalation detected by a microsensor, an additional whiff of pure oxygen.

Her lungs had burnt out.

"It would be best if you continued to live in a controlled environment. Your immune system…"

Her immune system was debilitated, so they had already noted. A decade spent on another world, where human life was buttressed by an array of pharmaceuticals to avoid contamination in either direction…for that there was a price to pay.

"But I can leave," concluded Nica when the doctor didn't.

"You won't be infecting anybody, if that's what you mean."

Without haste, without another word to Doctor Flam, the traveller started to gather her few belongings, which would fit inside a small suitcase. The immunologist did not insist; since her first exchanges with Nica Marcopol, she knew that the spacefarer would never accept living in a bubble, even to prolong her own life.

"I still recommend you stay on Exopolis. There are many more microbes on Erymede, with all the parks which…"

"I'll think about it," retorted the spacefarer.

She had time enough to think about it. Nothing came to mind when she wondered what she would do today.

Or tomorrow.

〃 〵

Exopolis hadn't existed, not even in the form of preliminary schematics, when Nica Marcopol had left the Solar System. Erymede itself was still nothing more than a lifeless asteroid, with a newly changed orbit and a temporary base, clinging to the bare rock, inhabited by the first Erymeans.

And yet nothing she saw really impressed Nica. Her suitcase at her feet, she waited in front of a large bay for the promised officer from the Admiralty.

Below, in the shadows stitched with lights, extended the spaceport aprons. Toward them swooped, along low gravity trajectories, the shuttles, the spacebuses, and the incoming long-haulers—like hers, half an hour earlier. They landed on mobile platforms, which would ferry them to the landing piers.

Others, departing, rose atop hydraulic pylons towards the vast airlocks communicating with the surface.

Nica's trip—the five short days did not deserve to be called a voyage—had been uneventful. A young man, almost certainly a psychologist assigned to her case by the Admiralty, had tried a few times to spark a conversation. He had given up in the end, grown weary of Nica's laconic answers and of her indifference to kindliness in any form.

Already, she suspected she would not stay long here. Where she would go next, and how she would leave, she did not yet know. Whereas Exopolis had seemed to her a city of cold metal and 'plast floating in the middle of nowhere, Erymede appeared soulless, in spite of the dabs of colour glimpsed through the domes, the greenery of the parks and the lakes of pure jade, or the orange and scarlet of a woodland going through its own autumn.

What she missed was the red sun and violet sky of Lohengrin, the vermilion orb which turned to crimson when it set, and whose squashed outline, in that last hour, widened to encompass almost a quarter of the horizon. Pitiful Parsifal A was so cool a star that it was then possible to stare at it, undazzled, and examine it long enough to spot the ocelli which speckled its photosphere like glowing embers.

The most remarkable sunsets happened when Parsifal A and B, in quasi-conjunction, neared the horizon one after the other, the second tiny and harsh, blinding white, the first languid and immense, a deep scarlet. Their reflections upon the ocean fashioned three aisles, the middle one lanced with blinding light, the two others like shimmery brocades unrolled atop the waves.

What she also missed was the Lohengrin geography, vast, open, the awesome Daybreak Cliffs, the great Thor River which hurled itself into the sea from a height of two thousand metres, the tides which filled the Gulf of Luhn in an hour. It was also the wind blowing across the prairies of the high tablelands, the surging swell in the tall grass, the azure waves in the turquoise vegetation, as far as the eye could see.

"Nica Marcopol?"

The spacefarer turned unhurriedly. A man in late middle-age was holding out his hand, following an Earth custom still uncommon in Erymean society when Nica had left the Moon.

"Kameha," he introduced himself.

His fifty or so years had sprinkled touches of grey throughout his black, woolly hair, but the only wrinkles in his milk-chocolate-coloured skin radiated from the corners of his eyes.

"My father was a shuttle copilot when you left," he stated. "He says he knew you, but you wouldn't remember. He was only twenty."

And now almost a hundred, Kameha was asserting. No paradox had surprised Nica since her return; she had had a quarter of a century to prepare herself.

"We've read and re-read your report," said the officer, gesturing towards her suitcase.

She grabbed it herself and followed the lead of her host. "Your report"! The transcript of her interrogation, rather. After all, seventeen had left aboard the *Ladd*, but Nica Marcopol had returned alone. Originally, she had been a lieutenant, second in command.

"You know, the first question I asked myself," confided the officer, "was simply: 'What did they do all that time, aboard the mothership?'"

They moped. That's what they, Nica and her comrades, had done.

A mysterious breakdown beyond Neptune orbit, on the return leg of a long haul, had stranded the *Ladd* in space shortly before crossing the path of an Alii mothership. Coincidence? The Alii had offered to take them aboard—picking up the cruiser and berthing it, no less, among the dozen of scout craft nestled within the ship's holds.

The Alii had indeed saved the *Ladd*'s officers from a long agony in their disabled ship, but, no, they had not taken them back towards the inner planets. They had brought them along for a visit to *their* home—or had abducted them after capturing the *Ladd*, in the Admiralty's view.

In fact, the Alii had not brought the humans to their home

world, but to one of the worlds in their swarm—or their cluster, or whatever name they gave to a group of neighbouring stars among which were found their original planet as well as the colonies they had established on others.

The endless voyage aboard the mothership, a gigantic spindle able to achieve relativistic velocities, and the long stay on a planet of Parsifal A, a star long known to the Erymeans: Nica Marcopol had told them all of it upon her return. Despair, homesickness, suicides, deaths on Lohengrin. Then the voyage home, the fading morale, the depressions, yet more suicides.

And finally, the *Ladd* jettisoned on the near side of the Oort cloud, its air and energy reserves replenished, in easy range of Pluto-Charon and Exopolis. A trip of a few weeks, during which Nica Marcopol had been able to establish a laser link, and prove her identity and origins.

So that, when she had docked and secured the *Ladd* in the Exopolis spaceport, she had not quite been received like a ghost.

More like a shade risen from the grave, telling an unbelievable story and alluding to marvels they called delusions.

Yet she was luckier in her misfortune than Marco Polo: *he* had been sitting in prison when he had dictated his *Book of the Kingdoms and Marvels of the East*.

⁄⁄ ⁣∖∖

"Moons…There were five. The largest, Azure, was almost as big as Mars. Can you imagine the show?"

Wakelin could do nothing but, indeed. That was the dividing line between Nica and him. Where he had to imagine, Nica remembered.

She could see the crescent moons above the Walhalla summits, afloat like giant feathers, misty, exquisite, in the mauve daytime sky. None exhibited the exact same hue of white: the more rugged areas betrayed their true colouring: grey, bluish, ocher or incarnadine. But the most stunning was the second largest, a coralline beacon.

In the purple nighttime of Lohengrin, it burned incandescently, mirrored in the ocean which it made fiery, evoking gleams from the mica in the Scylla reefs.

"There was a place: the Gates…"

Nica stopped, discouraged by the sheer unwieldiness of mere words. With a sigh, she turned her head towards the bay window which stretched from floor to ceiling, and overlooked all of Eldamar. In the Erymean night, the facades on each side of the canyon volleyed back and forth the light of their windows, the diminutive capsules of moving elevators, the fleeting dotted line of city shuttles inside their transparent tubes, the straight or outcurved glass bridges stretching between the slopes of the fault.

The capital, Elysium, was close by and it never slept, it was said. Ships of all kinds, approaching or departing, scattered the rosy glare of their fires down to the bottom of the canyon inside whose walls the city had grown. Down, 'way down where the fault had been sufficiently narrow to be glassed over and where now extended a linear park, a gigantic necklace of emerald and jade spangled with silver.

Wakelin, honouring her sudden silence, finally prompted: "The Gates…?"

"The Tannhauser Gates," the spacefarer continued reluctantly. "Rocks on Lohengrin, especially along the seashore…rarely take on ordinary shapes. The Gates are natural arches of rock eroded by the waves, reddish rock veined with a deeper red…Spectacular. A spacebus would go through easily. From one peninsula, all six can be seen lined up. And if you know the dates…"

Nica and her companions had been granted years, nay, decades to master the complex astronomical calendar of Lohengrin, its two suns and five moons, its eclipses and conjunctions, its cataclysmic tides and seasonal earthquakes.

On specific dates, certain moons rose in the line of sight extending through the multiple archways, the great colonnade of the Tannhauser Gates.

"The Alii must have had names for all those places?"

"The moons, the oceans, the continents…Sure, of course. Unpronounceable. We have all that on disk."

The "we" had slipped out. She had become the sole depositary of the data disks brought back aboard the *Ladd*. She had entrusted them to the Astronomical Institute, on the lunar Farside. To the same observatory which had spotted and named Parsifal A and B—long before their Earth counterparts, which had other names for them—and then discovered the main planets, including Lohengrin.

The other toponyms had been parceled out by the researchers and officers of the *Ladd*, drawing upon the rich stores of Germanic legends.

In a rare gesture, Nica turned towards Wakelin and detailed his present figure—a habit lost when she had been alone aboard the *Ladd*. Staring people in the face now demanded a distinct effort. She saw a mirror image of herself, almost as wasted: an emaciated face atop a scrawny body, eyes less limpid than washed out, hair that was colourless rather than grey. Only the three-day-old stubble established a clear difference.

Pilots both—or rather, astrogators: Wakelin had entered the academy when Nica Marcopol, already a trainee, was about to graduate. They had served aboard the same ships, and different ships. Over the years, they had rubbed shoulders often, and they had lost sight of each other for long stretches. Briefly, they had even been lovers, though neither had managed to kindle passion in the other.

What united them, now, was a different kind of experience: Wakelin too had gone away. And he had also returned to find his friends grown old—elderly in some cases.

But, in his case, the thirteen years of voyaging, there and back, and the six years of surveying had proved disappointing: Alpha Centauri A and B, and their partner Proxima, the trio's C, only stood out for their mediocrity. The first was even a carbon copy of the Sun, with a meager retinue of three or four beige Neptunes, practically moonless.

Unsurprisingly, Wakelin envied Nica her visions of opalescent moons lighting reef-defended shores or reflected in the channels and loops of the Edda River.

On the other hand, the crew of the *Nessus* had only mourned two suicides.

"It's useless," said Nica in an undertone, fixing her gaze again on the cityscape of the capital.

From time to time, a small utility craft, flashing past the window, swept the room with a blindingly white beam or threw bursts of orange and green across their faces.

The woman shivered, rubbed her arms and shoulders to warm up. She'd caught a flu bug, for sure.

"Room temperature: up to twenty-one degrees," ordered Wakelin.

Then, to his friend, "What? Why do you say that?"

"The images we brought back, the vids…They're not enough."

The crew of the *Ladd* hadn't left on a cinematographic jaunt: onboard, there was no equipment for making holos, nobody had brought a vidicam or even a camera. The only systems for capting images were built into the ship; once disassembled and slapped back together on Lohengrin with their own power sources, they had proved cumbersome, hard to use and poorly designed to cope with the rigours of video reportage. And the crew did not include an optics specialist who might have been able to build a better apparatus.

"All that's left is inside my head."

"But that's already an encyclopaedia," replied Wakelin. "You've dictated it all, thousands of hours on disk."

Nica shrugged, then wrapped herself in her coat without shoving her arms through the sleeves. Wakelin stepped into the kitchen alcove to make her a hot drink. The spacefarer got up also, leaned her forehead against the bay, of which one pane, at a forty-five degree angle, allowed her to literally look down upon the urban landscape.

How many humans bustled within the spaces encompassed by her field of view? Tens of thousands? More? Far to the left and far to the right, the opposite sides of the canyon, studded with lights, drew closer until they met in a kiss of glass and metal.

All those people, and twenty times more on Erymede, and a hundred thousand times more on Earth...And only one woman among them had seen Parsifal set on the horizon of Lohengrin, a scarlet glory behind the quartz columns of the desert. Only one had seen it rise above the fogs of the Nibelung plains, setting the sky ablaze with rose and lavender. Only one had seen the night flight of the elves, the small luminescent insects whose swarms gathered billions and loomed like a moving continent one hundred metres over the steppe.

"Here," said Wakelin, holding out a steaming cup. "And I'm sure they've told you, at the Admiralty: the Jason expedition, that was supposed to leave for Barnard, has been delayed a few weeks. They want to add a hibernave and change its destination."

"Parsifal. Yes, I know, they mentioned it. But I won't be coming."

"Why not?"

"Come on, I'll be dead before it leaves. Look at me go: a simple bout with the flu could kill me."

"There will be a hibernave, I told you. They can put you on ice before leaving, and wake you up when you're in a controlled environment. Or better yet: wake you up when the ship is almost there. I'm sure this Kalameda..."

"Kameha."

"That's surely what he had in mind, when he made you speak for hours."

"But on Lohengrin..."

On Lohengrin, she would never survive. Not in the current state of her body, not at her age. Immunization, the asepsis procedures, and the planet itself, especially, had overcome members of the *Ladd*'s crew who were younger than she now was—in spite of the fact Lohengrin could rightly be classified among inhabitable terrestrial-type planets.

Returning to Lohengrin meant facing her own death. On the other hand, staying on Erymede meant running the same risk, unless Nica closeted herself within a sterile environment. And, who knows, her experience might prove useful to the doctors and biologists of the expedition.

"But on Lohengrin..." she repeated to herself, her tone altered.

To die there or elsewhere...

But to see again the crimson sea before she died. To watch again the sea-beams glitter in the dark near the Tannhauser Gates and to gaze upon the snowy peaks of Mount Wotan.

So that these moments not be utterly lost in time, like tears in the rain.

THE FLAYED WOMAN
Sandra Kasturi

One late Monday afternoon
when she had been home for an hour
she took her sharpest Ginsu knife
and
starting with her fingers
removed her entire skin
stretched it out
and thumbtacked it
to the floor
Now
each morning she stands
and dances
   dances a red muscle-driven dance
   widdershins
   around her skin

At night she arranges herself into a tight ball under the bed
and lets the skin answer the door.

BETHLEHEM
Peter Watts

It was her own damn fault.

No. No, that's not right. But Christ, look at this place; what did she expect, living here?

A dried blood stain smears a meter of sidewalk, a rusty backdrop for broken bottles and the twisted skeleton of an old ten-speed. Everything is too big. All this jagged structure, so solid and visible, frightens me. I focus on the stain, search for some hint of its unseen complexity. I want to throw myself down through familiar orders of magnitude and see *inside*; dead erythrocytes, molecules of ferrous haemoglobin, single atoms dancing in comforting envelopes of quantum uncertainty.

But I can't. It's just a featureless brown blot, and all I can see is that it was once part of someone like me.

She's not answering. I've been buzzing for five minutes now.

I'm the only one in sight, sole occupant of a narrow window in time: all the victims have made for cover, and the monsters aren't out yet. But they're coming, Darwin's agents, always ready to weed out the unfit.

I push the buzzer again. "Jan, it's Keith." Why doesn't she answer? Maybe she can't, maybe someone got in, maybe...

Maybe she just wants to be alone. That's what she said on the phone, isn't it?

So why am I here? It's not that I didn't believe her, exactly. It's not even that I'm worried about her safety. It's more a matter of procedure; when your best friend has been raped, you're supposed to be supportive. That's the rule, even these days. And Janet is my friend, by any practical definition of the term.

Glass breaks somewhere in the distance.

"Jan—"

If I leave now I can still make it back before it gets too late. The sun doesn't go down for at least another twenty minutes. This was a stupid idea anyway.

I turn away from the gate, and something clicks behind me. I look back; a green light glows by the buzzer. I touch the grating, briefly, jerking my hand back after the slightest contact. Again, for longer this time. No shock. The gate swings inward.

Still no words from the speaker.

"Jan?" I say into the street.

After a moment, she answers. "Come on up, Keith. I—I'm glad you came by…"

⁂

Five floors high, Janet bolts the door behind me. The wall holds her up while I step past.

Her footsteps trail me down the hall, stiff, shuffling. In the living room she passes without eye contact, heading for the fridge. "Something to drink?"

"There's a choice?"

"Not much of one. No dairy products, the truck got hijacked again. They had beer, though." Her voice is strong, vibrant even, but she walks as though rigor mortis has already taken hold. Every movement seems painful.

The room is dimly lit; a lamp with an orange shade in one corner, a TV with the volume down. When she opens the fridge, bluish light spills across the bruises on her face. One of her eyes is swollen and pulpy.

She closes the refrigerator. Her face falls into merciful eclipse. She straightens in stages, turns to face me, bottle in hand. I take it without a word, careful not to touch her.

"You didn't have to come," she says. "I'm doing okay."

I shrug. "I just thought, if you needed anything…"

Janet smiles through the swelling. Even that seems to hurt. "Thanks, but I picked up some stuff coming back from the precinct."

"Janet, I'm sorry." How else can you say it?

"It wasn't your fault. It was mine."

I should disagree. I want to disagree.

"It was," she insists, although I haven't spoken. "I should have seen it coming. Simple scenario, predictable outcome. I should have known."

"Christ, Jan, why are you still living out here?" It sounds like an accusation.

She looks through the window. By now it's dark enough to see the fires on the east side.

"I lived here before," she reminds me. "I'm not going to let the fuckers drive me out now."

Before. I follow her gaze, see a tiny dark spot on the sidewalk below. Families lived here once. It's April. Warm enough that kids would be playing out there now. There are people who think that somewhere, they still do. Somewhere at right angles to this twisted place, some place where the probability wave broke onto a more peaceful reality. I wish I could believe that. There would be a little solace in the thought that in some other timeline, children are playing just outside.

But that world, if it even exists, diverged from ours a long time ago. Three, maybe four years…

"It happened so fast," I murmur.

"Fold catastrophe." Absently, Janet speaks to the window. "Change isn't gradual, Keith, you keep forgetting. Things just cruise along until they hit a breakpoint, and zap: new equilibrium. Like falling off a cliff."

This is how she sees the world: not reality, but a trajectory in phase space. Her senses gather the same data as mine, yet everything she sees sounds so alien…

"What cliff?" I ask her. "What breakpoint? What's *breaking*?"

"What, you don't believe what they say?"

They say a lot of things. With perfect hindsight, they moan about the inevitable collapse of an economy based on perpetual growth. Or they blame an obscenely successful computer virus, a few lines of code that spread worldwide and turned the global economy to static overnight. They say it isn't their fault.

"Twenty years ago they'd be blaming alligators in the sewers," I remark.

Janet starts to speak; her voice erupts in a great wracking cough. She wipes her mouth with the back of her hand, winces. "Well, if you'd prefer, there's always Channel six's interpretation," she says, pointing to the TV.

I look at her, quizzical.

"The Second Coming. We're almost up to crucifixion plus two thousand years."

I shake my head. "Doesn't make any less sense than most of the stuff I've heard."

"Well."

Mutual discomfort rises around us.

"Well, then," I say at last, turning to leave. "I'll come by tomorrow, see how you're doing—"

She gives me a look. "Come on, boss. You know you're not going anywhere tonight. You wouldn't even make it to Granville."

I open my mouth to protest. She pre-empts me: "There's a bus goes by around eight every morning, one of those new retrofits with the fullerene plating. Almost safe, if you don't mind being a couple of hours late for work."

Jan frowns for a second, as though struck by sudden realization.

"I think I'll work at home for a few days, though," she adds. "If that's okay."

"Don't be ridiculous. Take some time off. Relax."

"Actually, I doubt that I'll really be in the mood to relax."

"I mean—"

She manages another smile. "I appreciate the gesture, Keith, but sitting around just wallowing…it would drive me crazy. I want to work. I *have* to work."

"Jan—"

"It's no big deal. I'll log on tomorrow, just for a minute or two. Should be able to download what I need before any bugs get in, and I'll be set for the rest of the day. Okay?"

"Okay." I'm relieved, of course. At least I've got the good grace to be ashamed about it.

"In the meantime"—she takes a wooden step towards the hall closet—"I'll make up the couch for you."

"Listen, don't worry about anything. Just go lie down, I'll make supper."

"None for me. I'm not hungry."

"Well, okay." Damn. I don't know what else I'm supposed to do. "Do you want me to call anyone? Family, or—"

"No. That's fine, Keith." There's just a hint of caution in her voice. "Thanks anyway."

I let it lie. This is why we're so close. Not because we share the same interests, or are bound by a common passion of scientific discovery, or even because I sometimes give her senior authorship on our papers. It's because we don't intrude or pry or try to figure each other out. There's an unspoken recognition of limits, an acceptance. There's complete trust, because we never tell each other anything.

∥ ∖

I'm down in the real world when I hear her name.

It happens, occasionally. Sounds filter down from the huge clumsy universe where other people live; I can usually avoid hearing them. Not this time. There are too many of them, and they're all talking about Janet.

I try to keep working. Phospholipids, neatly excised from a

single neuron, lumber like crystalline behemoths across my field of vision. But the voices outside won't shut up, they're dragging me up there with them. I try to block them out, cling to the molecules that surround me, but it doesn't work. Ions recede into membranes, membranes into whole cells, physics to chemistry to sheer gross morphology.

The microscope still holds its image, but I'm outside of it now. I shut off the eyephones, blink at a room crowded with machines and the pithed circuitry of a half-dissected salamander.

The lounge is just down the hall from my office. People in there are talking about rape, talking about Jan's misfortune as though it was somehow rare or exotic. They trade tales of personal violation like old war stories, try to outdo each other with incantations of sympathy and outrage.

I don't understand the commotion. Janet is just another victim of the odds; crime waves and quantum waves have that much in common. There are a million unrealized worlds in which she would have escaped unscathed. In a different million, she would have been killed outright. But this is the one we observed. Here, yesterday, she was only brutalized, and today it will probably be someone else.

Why do they keep going on like this? Is talking about it all day going to get any of us into a universe where such things don't happen?

Why can't they just leave it alone?

⁂

"No fucking convergence!" she yells from the living room. The power is off again; she storms down the hall towards me, a frenetic silhouette backlit by the reflected light of distant fires. "Singular Hessian, it says! I worked on the chiasma maps for five fucking hours and I couldn't even get the stats to work, and now the fucking power goes out!"

She pushes a printout into my hands. It's a blurry shadow in the dark. "Where's your flashlight?" I ask.

"Batteries are dead. Fucking typical. Hang on a sec." I follow her back into the living room. She kneels at a corner cabinet, roots through its interior; assorted small objects bounce onto the floor to muffled expressions of disgust.

Her damaged arm exceeds some limit, goes rigid. She cries out.

I come up behind. "Are—"

Janet puts one hand behind her, palm out, pushing at the

space between us. "I'm okay." She doesn't turn around.

I wait for her to move.

After a moment she gets up, slowly. Light flares in her palm. She sets a candle on the coffee table. The light is feeble, but enough to read by.

"I'll show you," she says, reaching for the printout.

But I've already seen it. "You've confounded two of your variables."

She stops. "What?"

"Your interaction term. It's just a linear transform of action potential and calcium."

She takes the paper from my hand, studies it a moment. "Shit. That's it." She scowls at the numbers, as though they might have changed when I looked at them. "What a fucking stupid mistake."

There's a brief, uncomfortable silence. Then Janet crushes the printout into a ball and throws it at the floor.

"Fucking *stupid*!"

She turns away from me and glares out the window.

I stand there like an idiot and wonder what to do.

And suddenly the apartment comes back to life around us. The living room lights, revived by some far-off and delinquent generator, flicker and then hold steady. Jan's TV blares grainy light and faint, murky sound from the corner. I turn towards it, grateful for the distraction.

The screen offers me a woman, about Janet's age but empty somehow, wearing the shell-shocked look you see everywhere these days. I catch a flash of metal around her wrists before the view changes, shows us the twisted, spindly corpse of an infant with too many fingers. A lidless third eye sits over the bridge of its nose, like a milky black marble embedded in plasticine.

"Hmm," Janet says. "Copy errors."

She's watching the television. My stomach unclenches a bit. This month's infanticide stats crawl up the screen like a weather report.

"Polydactyly *and* a pineal eye. You didn't used to see so many random copy errors."

I don't see her point. Birth defects are old news; they've been rising ever since things started falling apart. Every now and then one of the networks makes the same tired connection, blames everything on radiation or chemicals in the water supply, draws ominous parallels with the fall of Rome.

At least it's got her talking again.

"I bet it's happening to other information systems too," she muses, "not just genetic ones. Like all those viruses in the net; you can't log on for two minutes these days without something trying to lay its eggs in your files. Same damn thing, I bet."

I can't suppress a nervous laugh. Janet cocks her head at me.

"Sorry," I say. "It's just—you never give up, you know? You'd go crazy if you went a day without being able to find a pattern somewhere—"

And suddenly I know why she lives here, why she won't hide with the rest of us up on campus. She's a missionary in enemy territory. She's defying chaos, she is proclaiming her faith; even here, she is saying, there are rules and the universe will damn well make sense. It will behave.

Her whole life is a search for order. No fucking way is she going to let something as, as *random* as rape get in the way. Violence is noise, nothing more; Janet's after signal. Even now, she's after signal.

I suppose that's a good sign.

※ ※

The signal crashes along the neuron like a tsunami. Ions in its path stand at sudden attention. A conduit forms, like a strip of mountain range shaking itself flat; the signal spills into it. Electricity dances along the optic nerve and lights up the primitive amphibian brain from an endless millimeter away.

Backtrack the lightning to its source. Here, in the tangled circuitry on the retina; the fading echo of a single photon. A lone quantum event, reaching up from the real world and into my machines. Uncertainty made flesh.

I made it happen, here in my lab. Just by watching. If a photon emits in the forest and there's no one to see it, it doesn't exist.

This is how the world works: nothing is real until someone looks at it. Even the subatomic fragments of our own bodies don't exist except as probability waves; it takes an act of conscious observation at the quantum level to collapse those waves into something solid. The whole universe is unreal at its base, an infinite and utterly hypothetical void but for a few specks where someone's passing glance congeals the mix.

It's no use arguing. Einstein tried. Bohm tried. Even Schrödinger, that hater of cats, tried. But our brains didn't evolve to cope with the space between atoms. You can't fight numbers; a century of arcane quantum mathematics doesn't leave any recourse to common sense.

A lot of people still can't accept it. They're afraid of the fact that nothing is real, so they claim that everything is. They say we're surrounded by parallel worlds just as real as this one, places where we won the *Guerre de la Separatiste* or the Houston Inferno never happened, an endless comforting smorgasbord of alternative realities. It sounds silly, but they really don't have much choice. The parallel universe schtick is the only consistent alternative to nonexistence, and nonexistence terrifies them.

It empowers me.

I can shape reality, just by looking at it. Anyone can. Or I can avert my eyes, respect its privacy, leave it unseen and totipotent. The thought makes me a little giddy. I can almost forget how far I'm slipping behind, how much I need Janet's hand to guide me, because down here in the real world it doesn't have to matter. Nothing is irrevocable until observed.

∅ ∅

She buzzes me through on the first ring. The elevator's acting strangely today; it opens halfway, closes, opens again like an eager mouth. I take the stairs.

The door opens while I'm raising my hand to knock. She stands completely still.

"He came back," she says.

No. Even these days, the odds are just too—

"He was right there. He did it again." Her voice is completely expressionless. She locks the door, leads me down the shadowy hallway.

"He got in? How? Where did he—"

Gray light spills into her living room. We're up against the wall, off to one side of her window. I look around the edge of the curtain, down at the deserted street.

She points outside. "He was right there, he did it again, he did it again—"

To someone else. That's what she means.

Oh.

"She was so stupid," Janet's fingers grip the threadbare curtain, clenching, unclenching. "She was out there all alone. Stupid bitch. Should have seen it coming."

"When did it happen?"

"I don't know. A couple of hours."

"Did anyone—" I ask, because of course I can't say *Did*

you—

"No. I don't think anybody else even saw it." She releases the curtain. "She got off easy, all things considered. She walked away."

I don't ask whether the phone lines were up. I don't ask if Janet tried to help, if she shouted or threw something or even let the woman inside afterwards. Janet's not stupid.

A distant mirage sparkles in the deepening twilight: the campus. There's another oasis, a bit nearer, over by False Creek, and the edge of a third if I crane my neck. Everything else is grey or black or flickering orange.

Gangrene covers the body. Just a few remnant tissues still alive.

"You're sure it was the same guy?" I wonder.

"*Who the fuck cares!*" she screams. She catches herself, turns away. Her fists ball up at her sides.

Finally, she turns back to look at me.

"Yes it was," she says in a tight voice. "I'm sure."

I never know what I'm supposed to do.

I know what I'm supposed to feel, though. My heart should go out to her, to anyone so randomly brutalized. This much should be automatic, unthinking. Suddenly I can see her face, really see it, a fragile mask of control teetering on the edge of meltdown; and so much more behind, held barely in check. I've never seen her look like this before, even the day it happened to her. Maybe I just didn't notice. I wait for it to affect me, to fill me with love or sympathy or even pity. She needs something from me. She's my friend. At least that's what I call her. I look for something, anything, that would make me less of a liar. I go down as deep as I can, and find nothing but my own passionate curiosity.

"What do you want me to do?" I ask. I can barely hear my own voice

Something changes in her face. "Nothing. Nothing, Keith. This is something I've got to work through on my own, you know?"

I shift my weight and try to figure out whether she means it.

"I could stay here for a few days," I say at last. "If you want."

"Sure." She looks out the window, her face more distant than ever. "Whatever you like."

�► ☽

"They lost Mars!" he wails, grabbing me by the shoulders.

I know the face; he's about three doors down the hall. But I can't remember the name, it's...wait, Chris, Chris something...Fletcher. That's it.

"All the Viking data," he's saying, "from the 70's, you know, NASA said they had it archived, they said I could have it no problem, I planned my whole fucking *thesis* around it!"

"It got lost?" It figures; data files everywhere are corrupting in record numbers these days.

"No, they know exactly where it is. I can go down and pick it up any time I want," Fletcher says bitterly.

"So what's—"

"It's all on these big magnetic disks—"

"*Magnetic?*"

"—and of course magmedia have been obsolete for fucking *decades*, and when NASA upgraded their equipment they somehow missed the Viking data." He pounds the wall, emits a hysterical little giggle. "So they've got all this data that nobody can access. There probably isn't a computer stodgy enough anywhere on the continent."

I tell Janet about it afterwards. I expect her to shake her head and make commiserating noises, *that's too bad* or *what an awful thing to happen*. But she doesn't even look away from the window. She just nods, and says, "Loss of information. Like what happened to me."

I look outside. No stars visible, of course. Just sullen amber reflections on the bottom of the clouds.

"I can't even remember being raped," she remarks. "Funny, you'd think it would be one of those things that stick in your mind. And I know it happened, I can remember the context and the aftermath and I can piece the story together, but I've lost the actual...event..."

From behind, I can see the curve of her cheek and the edge of a smile. I haven't seen Janet smile in a long time. It seems like years.

"Can you prove that the earth revolves around the sun?" she asks. "Can you prove it's not the other way around?"

"What?" I circle to her left, a wary orbit. Her face comes into view, smooth and almost unmarked by now, like a mask.

"You can't, can you? If you ever could. It's been erased. Or maybe it's just lost. We've all forgotten so much..."

She's so calm. I've never seen her so calm. It's almost frightening.

"You know, I'll bet after a while we forget things as fast as we learn them," she remarks. "I bet that's always the way it's been."

"Why do you say that?" I keep my voice carefully neutral.

"You can't store everything, there's not enough room. How can you take in the new without writing over the old?"

"Come on, Jan." I try for a light touch: "Our brains are running out of disk space?"

"Why not? We're finite."

Jesus, she's serious.

"Not *that* finite. We don't even know what most of the brain does, yet."

"Maybe it doesn't do anything. Maybe it's like our DNA, maybe most of it's junk. You remember back when they found—"

"I remember." I don't want to hear what they found, because I've been trying to forget it for years. They found perfectly healthy people with almost no brain tissue. They found people living among us, heads full of spinal fluid, making do with a thin lining of nerve cells where their brains should be. They found people growing up to be engineers and schoolteachers before discovering that they should have been vegetables instead.

They never found any answers. God knows they looked hard enough. I heard they were making some progress, though, before—

Loss of information, Jan says. Limited disk space. She's still smiling at me, insight shines from her eyes with a giddy radiance. But I can see her vision now, and I don't know what she's smiling about. I see two spheres expanding, one within the other, and the inner one is gaining. The more I learn the more I lose, my own core erodes away from inside. All the basics, dissolving; how *do* I know that the earth orbits the sun?

Most of my life is an act of faith.

※ ※

I'm half a block from safety when he drops down on me from a second-story window. I get lucky; he makes a telltale noise on the way down. I almost get out of his way. We graze each other and he lands hard on the pavement, twisting his ankle.

Technically, handguns are still illegal. I pull mine out and shoot him in the stomach before he can recover.

A flicker of motion. Suddenly on my left, a woman as big

as me, face set and sullen, standing where there was only pavement a moment ago. Her hands are buried deep in the pockets of a torn overcoat. One of them seems to be holding something.

Weapon or bluff? Particle or wave? Door number one or door number two?

I point the gun at her. I try very hard to look like someone who hasn't just used his last bullet. For one crazy moment I think that maybe it doesn't even matter what happens here, whether I live or die, because maybe there is a parallel universe, some impossible angle away, where everything works out fine.

No. Nothing happens unless observed. Maybe if I just look the other way...

She's gone, swallowed by the same alley that disgorged her. I step over the gurgling thing twitching on the sidewalk.

"You can't stay here," I tell Janet when I reach her refuge. "I don't care how many volts they pump through the fence, this place isn't safe."

"Sure it is," she says. She's got the TV tuned to Channel 6, God's own mouthpiece coming through strong and clear; the Reborns have a satellite up in geosynch and that fucker never seems to go offline.

She's not watching it, though. She just sits on her sofa, knees drawn up under her chin, staring out the window.

"The security's better on campus," I say. "We can make room for you. And you won't have to commute."

Janet doesn't answer. Inside the TV, a talking head delivers a lecture on the Poisoned Fruits Of Secular Science.

"Jan—"

"I'm okay, Keith. Nobody's gotten in yet."

"They will. All they've got to do is throw a rubber mat over the fence and they're past the first line of defense. Sooner or later they'll crack the codes for the front gate, or—"

"No, Keith. That would take too much planning."

"Janet, I'm telling you—"

"Nothing's organized any more, Keith. Haven't you noticed?"

Several faint explosions echo from somewhere outside.

"I've noticed," I tell her.

"For the past four years," she says, as though I haven't spoken, "all the patterns have just...fallen apart. Things are getting so hard to predict, lately, you know? And even when you seem them coming, you can't do anything about them."

She glances at the television, where the head is explaining that evolution contradicts the Second Law of Thermodynamics.

"It's sort of funny, actually," Janet says.

"What is?"

"Everything. Second Law." She gestures at the screen. "Entropy increasing, order to disorder. Heat death of the universe. All that shit."

"Funny?"

"I mean, life's a pretty pathetic affair in the face of physics. It is sort of a miracle it ever got started in the first place."

"Hey." I try for a disarming smile. "You're starting to sound like a creationist."

"Yeah, well in a way they're right. Life and entropy just don't get along. Not in the long run, anyway. Evolution's just a—a holding action, you know?"

"I know, Jan."

"It's like this, this torrent screaming through time and space, tearing everything apart. And sometimes these little pockets of information form in the eddies, in these tiny protected backwaters, and sometimes they get complicated enough to wake up and brag about beating the odds. Never lasts, though. Takes too much energy to fight the current."

I shrug. "That's not exactly news, Jan."

She manages a brief, tired smile. "Yeah, I guess not. Undergrad existentialism, huh? It's just that everything's so…hungry now, you know?"

"Hungry?"

"People. Biological life in general. The Net. That's the whole problem with complex systems, you know; the more intricate they get, the harder entropy tries to rip them apart. We need more and more energy just to keep in one piece."

She glances out the window.

"Maybe a bit more," she says, "than we have available these days."

Janet leans forward, aims a remote control at the television.

"You're right, though. It's all old news."

The smile fades. I'm not sure what replaces it.

"It just never sunk in before, you know?"

Exhaustion, maybe.

She presses the remote. The head fades to black, cut off in mid-rant. A white dot flickers defiantly on centre stage for a moment.

"There he goes." Her voice hangs somewhere between irony and resignation. "Washed downstream."

// \\

The doorknob rotates easily in my grasp, clockwise, counterclockwise. It's not locked. A television laughs on the far side of a wall somewhere.

I push the door open.

Orange light skews up from the floor at the far end of the hall, where the living room lamp has fallen. Her blood is everywhere, congealing on the floor, crowding the wall with sticky rivulets, thin dark pseudopods that clot solid while crawling for the baseboards—

No.

I push the door open.

It swings in a few centimeters, then jams. Something on the other side yields a bit, sags back when I stop pushing. Her hand is visible through the gap in the doorway, palm up on the floor, fingers slightly clenched like the limbs of some dead insect. I push at the door again; the fingers jiggle lifelessly against the hardwood.

No. Not that either.

I push the door open.

They're still in there with her. Four of them. One sits on her couch, watching television. One pins her to the floor. One rapes her. One stands smiling in the hallway, waves me in with a hand wrapped in duct tape, a jagged blob studded with nails and broken glass.

Her eyes are open. She doesn't make a sound—

No. No. No.

These are mere possibilities. I haven't actually *seen* any of them. They haven't happened yet. The door is still closed.

I push it open.

The probability wave collapses.

And the winner is...

None of the above. It's not even her apartment. It's our office.

I'm inside the campus perimeter, safe behind carbon-laminate concrete, guarded by armed patrols and semi-intelligent security systems that work well over half the time. I will not call her, even if the phones are working today. I refuse to indulge these sordid little backflips into worlds that don't even exist.

I am not losing it.

⚋ ⚌

Her desk has been abandoned for two weeks now. The adjacent concrete wall, windowless, unpainted, is littered with nostalgic graphs and printouts; population cycles, fractal intrusions into Ricker curves, a handwritten reminder that *All tautologies are tautologies.*

I don't know what's happening. We're changing. She's changing. Of course, you idiot, she was raped, how could she *not* change? But it's as though her attacker was only a catalyst, somehow, a trigger for some transformation still ongoing, cryptic and opaque. She's shrouded in a chrysalis; something's happening in there, I see occasional blurred movement, but all the details are hidden.

I need her for so much. I need her ability to impose order on the universe, I need her passionate desire to reduce everything to triviality. No result was good enough, everything was always too proximate for her; every solution she threw back in my face: "yes, but *why*?" It was like collaborating with a two-year-old.

I've always been a parasite. I feel like I've lost the vision in one eye.

I guess it was ironic. Keith Elliot, quantum physiologist, who saw infinite possibilities in the simplest units of matter; Janet Thomas, catastrophe theorist, who reduced whole ecosystems down to a few lines of computer code. We should have killed each other. Somehow it was a combination that worked.

Oh God. When did I start using past tense?

⚋ ⚌

There's a message on the phone, ten hours old. The impossible has happened; the police caught someone, a suspect. His mug shots are on file in the message cache.

He looks a bit like me.

"Is that him?" I ask her.

"I don't know." Janet doesn't look away from the window. "I didn't look."

"Why not? Maybe he's the one! You don't even have to leave the apartment, you could just call them back, say yes or no. Jan, what's going on with you?"

She cocks her head to one side. "I think," she says, "My eyes have opened. Things have finally started to make some sort of…sense, I guess—"

"Christ, Janet, you were *raped*, not baptized!"

She draws her knees up under her chin and starts rocking back and forth. I can't call it back.

I try anyway. "Jan, I'm sorry. It's just...I don't understand, you don't seem to care about *anything* any more—"

"I'm not pressing charges." Rocking, rocking. "Whoever it was. It wasn't his fault."

I can't speak.

She looks back over her shoulder. "Entropy increases, Keith. You know that. Every act of random violence helps the universe run down."

"What are you talking about? Some asshole deliberately assaulted you!"

She shrugs, looking back out the window. "So some matter is sentient. That doesn't exempt it from the laws of physics."

I finally see it; in this insane absolution she confers, in the calm acceptance in her voice. Metamorphosis is complete. My anger evaporates. Underneath there is only a sick feeling I can't name.

"Jan," I say, very quietly.

She turns and faces me, and there is no reassurance there at all.

"*Things fall apart*," she says. "*The centre cannot hold. Mere anarchy is loosed upon the world.*"

It sounds familiar, somehow, but I can't...I can't...

"Nothing? You've forgotten Yeats, too?" She shakes her head, sadly. "You taught it to me."

I sit beside her. I touch her, for the first time. I take her hands.

She doesn't look at me. But she doesn't seem to mind.

"You'll forget everything, soon, Keith. You'll even forget me."

She looks at me then, and something she sees makes her smile a little. "You know, in a way I envy you. You're still safe from all this. You look so closely at everything you barely see anything at all."

"Janet..."

But she seems to have forgotten me.

After a moment she takes her hands from mine and stands up. Her shadow, cast orange by the table lamp, looms huge and ominous on the far wall. But it's her face, calm and unscarred and only life-sized, that scares me.

She reaches down, puts her hands on my shoulders. "Keith, thank you. I could never have come through this without you. But I'm okay now, and I think it's time to be on my own again."

A pit opens in my stomach. "You're not okay," I tell her, but I can't seem to keep my voice level.

"I'm fine, Keith. Really. I honestly feel better than I have in…well, in a long time. It's all right for you to go."

I can't. I can't.

"I really think you're wrong." I have to keep her talking. I have to stay calm. "You may not see it but I don't think you should be on your own just yet, you can't do this—"

Her eyes twinkle briefly. "Can't do what, Keith?"

I try to answer but it's hard, I don't even know what I'm trying to say, I—

"*I* can't do it," is what comes out, unexpected. "It's just us, Janet, against everything. I can't do it without you."

"Then don't try."

It's such a stupid thing to say, so completely unexpected, that I have no answer for it.

She draws me to my feet. "It's just not that important, Keith. We study retinal sensitivity in salamanders. Nobody cares. Why should they? Why should we?"

"You know it's more than that, Janet! It's quantum neurology, it's the whole nature of consciousness, it's—"

"It's really kind of pathetic, you know." Her smile is so gentle, her voice so kind, that it takes a moment for me to actually realize what she's saying. "You can change a photon here and there, so you tell yourself you've got some sort of control over things. But you don't. None of us do. It all just got too complicated, it's all just physics—"

My hand is stinging. There's a sudden white spot, the size of my palm, on the side of Janet's face. It flushes red as I watch.

She touches her cheek. "It's okay, Keith. I know how you feel. I know how everything feels. We're so tired of swimming upstream all the time…"

I see her, walking on air.

"You need to get out of here," I say, talking over the image. "You should really spend some time on campus, I could put you up until you get your bearings—"

"Shhhhh." She puts a finger to my lips, guides me along the

hall. "I'll be fine, Keith. And so will you. Believe me. This is all for the best."

She reaches past me and opens the door.

"I love you," I blurt out.

She smiles at that, as though she understands. "Goodbye, Keith."

She leaves me there and turns back down the hall. I can see part of her living room from where I stand, I can see her turn and face the window. The firelight beyond paints her face like a martyr's. She never stops smiling. Five minutes go by. Ten. Perhaps she doesn't realize I'm still here, perhaps she's forgotten me already.

At last, when I finally turn to leave, she speaks. I look back, but her eyes are still focused on distant wreckage, and her words are not meant for me.

"...*what rough beast*..." is what I think she says, and other words too faint to make out.

※ ※

When the news hits the department I try, unsuccessfully, to stay out of sight. They don't know any next of kin, so they inflict their feigned sympathy on me. It seems she was popular. I never knew that. Colleagues and competitors pat me on the back as though Janet and I were lovers. Sometimes it happens, they say, as though imparting some new insight. Not your fault. I endure their commiseration as long as I can, then tell them I want to be alone. This, at least, they think they understand; and now, my knuckles stinging from a sudden collision of flesh and glass, now I'm free. I dive into the eyes of my microscope, escaping down, down into the real world.

I used to be so much better than everyone. I spent so much time down here, nose pressed against the quantum interface, embracing uncertainties that would drive most people insane. But I'm not at ease down here. I never was. I'm simply more terrified of the world outside.

Things happen out there, and can't be taken back. Janet is gone, forever. I'll never see her again. That wouldn't happen down here. Down here nothing is impossible. Janet is alive as well as dead; I made a difference, and didn't; parents make babies and monsters and both and neither. Everything that can be, is. Down here, riding the probability wave, my options stay open forever.

As long as I keep my eyes closed.

SEKTAR'S WHEEL
Mary E. Choo

It will be difficult for me to record this.

I have decided that I will no longer weave in terms of "before" or "then" when I narrate, unless I must. I will use "now" instead. It should take less plain thread, and make the colours seem brighter, the story more precise. I will also explain things more, so that a stranger might read my work and understand.

I do not think that Sektar will approve.

And so I begin my tapestry.

I am kneeling in front of the monolith, as I always do in the morning. My eyes are closed, and I place my forehead against the base of its cool, tapered mass, its many colours penetrating my lids. I study all the hues—the purples, reds, golds—then try to find the matrix at their core, to read the sky, but there seems little point today. The wind is so cold, and as I braid my coarse hair in the patterns of penance the fine webbed skin between my fingers begins to crack.

I fasten the braid with a seabone clip, but it is untidy. As I raise my head and open my eyes, I can hear Kep and the others talking. I see no change in the stone in front of me, and I look past it, down the long diagonal line of spires that rise like needle trees from the plain. They seem timeless in the early light.

The ground is bright red in the sunlight, and the figures of my fellow-penitents show black against it. They are grouped by the central spire. I cannot hear what they are saying, but the feeling that I get is bad. I wonder if they have made any supplication at all.

I rise and start towards them. Kep's voice is louder than the others, rich, commanding. Though his back is towards me, I am careful not to show how this affects me. The rest of them draw back as I approach, their words slowly fading. Only Kep is talking now, and even he stops, turning to face me. The others genuflect and edge away, their eyes averted as they shuffle towards the path that leads to the city. A few of them call to me and gesture as they make their slow, heavy way across the sand.

Lately, they do not have much use for me.

"You're unhappy," Kep says.

Some of my braids come loose, the bronze tendrils blowing across my eyes, but I can see him through the threads of my hair.

"It's cold," I reply.

"You know my answer to that," he says.

I want to touch him. He senses this, and reaches out, but I move away. This makes him angry, and the dark, shimmering skin at his throat flushes amber. That is not what I wanted, but it is too late now.

"I saw no sign of rain when I searched the spires—not for today, tomorrow, or a long time," I say. My tone is sullen. I have not lead the others well in penance this past season, and I know it.

He spreads his hands, meaning both acceptance and indifference. The webs between his fingers are slick and glistening, but then he does not work with the soil the way I do.

"You should relent, Alikki. It's important to know when to give in, to save something for after..."

I know what is coming, for we have argued about it many times. I push the moment away, shouting at him.

"It will destroy Sektar, if he has to leave his garden! It's his life. You have no right—"

His stride is long, and he reaches me at once. His hand is quick but gentle over my mouth. I permit this, considering what we are to one another.

"It's no good, Alikki. I've arranged the journey. I'm leaving tomorrow, with the others. We can't endure the cold, the rest of it, any longer. Those in the Time Valleys have agreed to let us come and join them."

I thrust his hand away.

"Unbeliever!" I cry. It is an ugly word, the thread I will use to weave it sickly pale. "You didn't try to make penance this morning, to appease the forces we've offended, any of you! You never do! That's why things have gone so wrong!"

"It's Sektar who's wrong, Alikki," Kep says. There is no anger in his voice, like the other times. It is his gentleness that I see now, and this is worst of all. "He's old, and I know it's hard for him to let go."

That is not what Kep usually says about my father. Sektar's harshness, his stubbornness, is a necessary part of being Elder

Maker and leader of our people. Yet he is wrong, selfish to insist that the rest of us stay and struggle against what Kep sees as impossible odds.

It is this stubbornness, and my regard for Kep, that tear me apart.

"What Sektar does is part of my life, my blood too, Kep. You can't ask me to leave!"

He does not ask. Instead, he stands and stares at me. I can see myself reflected in the facets of his eyes. His silence forces me to continue.

"You must do what you think is best, Kep. I can't hold you here. But I'm staying."

He knows this is my final word, but as I turn and walk away I still hope that he will call to me. When I glance back, his lean harvester body shows bronze against the pink sky, and the sun is a fine white point just above his shoulder.

I begin to hurry so I will not change my mind. Unlike the others, my tread is light and I glide across the ground. The webs between my toes are well-oiled and flexible. I save most of my ration of unguent for them, for I must be able to walk if I am to work. Kep deplores the condition of my hands, and has been more than generous with his share of salve, but I cannot ask him for more now.

I refuse to think of him. The path rises steeply, and there are sharp rocks in the coarse soil. The soles of my feet are thick, immune to the cold, but I still pick my way carefully to avoid injury.

At last I reach the crest and look down the incline towards the city. It towers and spirals and curves, elegant, crumbling. It was one of the greatest places on Ursha once, though only my people live in a small part of it now. To my left and down a little, I see traders from the remaining western settlements on the barren road that leads to the plain. Our oceans are mostly gone, though there is still one to the southeast. I am told it is warmer there sometimes, but none of us is certain of this.

I stride out, as I am late for my work. My thin garment winds around my knees. The way down the slope is easier, with fewer stones, and I can see the peaked top of the dwelling I share with my father at the far end of the high-walled city garden a little to my right.

I reach the wall and pass through the gate, closing and sealing it against the wind. The garden is vast, the last space we have where anything will grow. There is a slight upward incline to the land, and the path leads me through the orange and brown of sand and needle trees. Long windows stretch far overhead from one end of the giant sloping walls to the other, supported in the centre by stone pylons. The air here is moist and warm, and as I walk I hear the trickle of water in the irrigation ducts.

I emerge from the grove, crossing into the upper part of the garden. The way to the sky is open here, and I feel the cold.

Sektar is at his wheel. He perches on the small seat anchored in the soil just behind its tourmaline edge. His feet are pumping hard on the pedals which run the mechanism connected to the centre. The wheel is large, and has two sides which are joined in the middle by a broad spoke. Lesser pins run at intervals from one side to the other, each supporting a small trough. The wheel is half-hidden in a cavity in the ground, where there is a well that draws water from somewhere under the city, or so Sektar says. As it spins, this water is scooped up and dumped in the main irrigation duct in front of him. He pumps water every day, but there is less and less, and a number of plants in the shelter are beginning to suffer.

His head is bent, his copper skin slick and glistening. An orange flush burns in the withered folds of his throat. Orange is the colour of an old man's anger.

He must have heard about Kep and the others. Always, it is Kep between us.

"Someone told you?" I ask.

He stops pedalling, braking so hard that precious water slops from the trough and runs down the bright green edges of the wheel. He refuses to look at me.

"Some of them came for their final rations from the garden, when the rest of you were at the spires. They took everyone's share, enough for the whole journey," he says.

He does not talk of the Time Valleys. We would have no freedom there, he says, no garden of our own. We were all meant to remain on the outside, to help him while he grows plants to feed us and to clean the air. He is determined that if we pray and work, we can still bring the rain back.

I will be lonely, when the others leave.

"Father, I think that Kep—" I begin, but it is pointless. He turns his face away, his shoulders stiffening as they do when he makes one of his endless prophecies. The others have gone against his wishes, and he cannot forgive them. Since he will not talk of them, I turn away from him.

"The sun sails farther into the heavens every day," I call back over my shoulder, defiant. As I retreat into the groves I hear the sharp pumping of his wheel.

There is a small lean-to where I keep my tools. I often leave my tapestries here as well, to work on during rest times. I take my stick and rake, and a sack of seedlings. I will plant these today, in the shelter of the sand and needle trees. The soil is moist from Sektar's water, and with luck they all should sprout before long.

I am soon absorbed in my work. I am wearing cloth mitts, but the wet seeps through, irritating my hands. I love the damp, sharp smell of the soil and trees. The light changes into a thousand hues, racing among the shadows. There are flowers too, of my making; silver spike plants and purple sun- discs. They respond as I touch them, beginning to hum and click. All the gardens of Ursha were like this once, before our carelessness destroyed them. It was wet then, and we needed the webs between our fingers and toes.

After a time, I stop to rest and work on my tapestry. I have kept a journal since childhood. I use the eighteen-finger method, which means that both hands are completely occupied and I can work rapidly and in some detail. The seabone frame which holds the cloth is large but light, and rests on two supports.

The boy who helps us comes to speak to me, and my reply is impatient. I apologize. I should not call him a boy, for he is not that any more. But he is the youngest of us, and because of something the harvesters once sprayed on the forests there have been no children for a long time.

This thought reminds me of Kep. I put away my tapestry and begin work again, but my heart is no longer in it. Still, I delve and plant, not noticing how the light has changed. At last there is a hand on my shoulder, and I look up to see Sektar. He has lit the night lamps and smudge pots, and there is dark and a glitter of stars through the glass at the top of the trees. All this is part of a familiar ritual, and for a moment I am in the gardens of childhood once more.

"Enough," he says. "You'll ruin your hands."

I think that if he really cared about my hands, he would give me more unguent. Suddenly, I want to argue, to have it all out in the open. I stand up.

"We must talk about the others leaving, sometime," I say. His throat turns vivid orange.

"They are unbelievers!" he says. It is the same word I used this morning, but object to it now.

"Not unbelievers, Sektar. They just feel differently. They've endured much in the city. The cold grows worse every day."

He is very angry now. He turns and stands with his back to me.

"A long time from now, there will be people on the Water Planet." His shoulders stiffen. He points, as though he can see the Water Planet in the mass of stars just above the garden wall. I have found pictures of it on tapestries in an abandoned knowledge room in the city. "They will discover Ursha, and later they will rename it according to their liking. And when they learn our history, and how we spoiled and abandoned our land, they will know us as fools for what we've done!"

I find all this disturbing. Ursha is a beautiful name. It means "jewel in the sun," and I cannot think of it being otherwise. Besides, he is answering an objection of mine with one of his prophecies. He usually does this, and tonight it makes me angry.

"Our people are afraid!" I cry. I do not know where this word has come from. It is just a sound, really, but I know what it means. Sektar's hands are flexing, trembling. They are thin with age, but still strong, and I see the ridges of white scars on his fingers where he has torn the webs so many times.

"We Urshans have no word for terror, or for ending!" he says, turning. I understand the noises he makes for these strange new words. He looks as though he would like to strike me, now that I have forced him to invent them.

"We had no word for the cold, either, until it came!" I shout. He moves towards me, but I am too quick for him. I dodge away, half-running towards the far corner of the garden.

I feel cold inside, all over. I have lost faith. That is why I cannot call rain from the spires. The others know me for what I am, and because of it they are leaving.

I sink to my knees among some seedlings in the far corner. The boy left the side gate ajar, when he left. Through it, I can see the lights of the inhabited part of the city, close by. They mass like jewels against the night, the dim moonlight tracing the lines of the dwellings. Everyone is up late, preparing. I can hear the long, sliding notes on their redstone flutes as they play to one another through the dark. They are happy to be going.

I cannot bear it. Slowly my lips elongate, flare. I begin to rock back and forth, to croon, but it is not the usual song I sing to my plants to make them grow. It is slow and full of pain. It is a song for Sektar's new word, ending.

A finger traces the edge of my ear.

"Please, Sektar, not now," I say. "Allow me this time alone."

It is not Sektar who kneels beside me, but Kep. It is hard for me to look at him. He is holding out a pot of unguent; a generous portion that will last for some time. He thrusts it at me.

"There will be plenty, in the Time Valleys," he says. He takes my hand, refuses to let it go. "I wish you'd change your mind, but I won't ask any more, Alikki. I'll wait for you there…"

His body is dark bronze in the moonlight, his eyes alight like newborn suns. I feel the power of his presence, his seasoned limbs, the hands that have been idle since the forests disappeared. The plants rustle, click, lean towards him.

He is my strength, all of me that matters. If he leaves, there will be no real tomorrow. I begin to weep, and water runs from the pale membranes at the corners of my eyes.

"You're going away, with people who hate me," I say. "I see it in their eyes."

"That isn't true. They don't hate you. They feel guilty because you and Sektar have tried so hard, and they're abandoning you. There's nothing for them here. Little to eat, nothing worthwhile to do."

"They could occupy themselves, if they wished." As I say this, I know it to be unfair.

"Alikki," he says. He reaches for me, and the unguent pot falls in the dirt between us.

"No," I say. "Please. I can't."

But he has worked his fingers into the sensitive skin behind my ears, just where the large crescent edge rises and folds down over the lobe. I can smell the hot-sand scent of his body, and his skin feels supple and warm.

"Please, Alikki," he says. His voice is like the distant drum of thunder from a childhood memory. "Please."

There is no help for this. I feel my body go slack, begin to flow like the water from Sektar's wheel, and as Kep pulls me towards him, I give in to what we both have wanted for so long.

※ ※

Some things do not bear watching, and yet I cannot stop.

I made no penance this morning. I do not want to see the spires, to feel them or be touched in turn by their beauty. They are a symbol of my failure, and Sektar's. Doing penance at the monoliths of every ruined city on Ursha would not have changed things.

My neck feels bruised where Kep loved me last night. I slept in the garden for a brief time, when he left. I dreamed of people from the Water Planet. They had small mouths and eyes, and strange-coloured skins.

The garden could not hold me today. My weeping disturbed the plants, and I made many mistakes. I have come here, in the afternoon, to a lower part of the rise, where I sit on a jutting rock with my tapestry, finishing yesterday's pattern. I can see the city, the roadway, part of the plain on my left. The air is silent, strangely warm and heavy, and I think it has come from the south. I can hear Sektar in the distance, the clack-clacking of his wheel sounding through the open garden gate.

To my right, and below, the road stretches like some cracked and flattened bone. The last of the city's inhabitants is straggling out towards the plain. She is an older woman, alone and limping, using a bone staff for support. There has never been enough unguent in her ration to soften the webs between her toes, and I can see that they are causing her pain. She was a teacher once, in a vanished settlement to the west. There were farmers, harvesters, lesser Makers among those who left today.

The part of the plain that I can see is beautiful. It glows red in the afternoon light, its surface broken by bright patches of seabone deposit. Our small white sun looks more distant than ever in the pale pink sky. The far hills to one side are shadows, and in my unhappiness I imagine them thick with needle trees, and Kep coming back to me.

He turned to look at me, when he left with the others. We stared at one another for a long time, but I did not change my mind. Some of the rest called out farewell as they passed.

There is a hand at my shoulder, a touch that is light with apology. It is Sektar, and I realize that I no longer hear the wheel.

"You can go if you like, Alikki," he says. "I can manage."

He is looking at me. I see the truth, that he thinks he means this, and my heart fills with pity.

"No," I say. "I can leave, later on, when things are better for you."

This satisfies him, but he looks bent and thin as he turns back towards the garden, his ragged clothes flapping.

I continue weaving, my concentration intense. The characters form rapidly, evenly, though Sektar's new words are difficult. I have enough thread left to do the colours well.

I do not hear anything at first. At last, a sound commands me. The wind tugs at my tapestry, and I look up. The sun is half-hidden by clouds, the air heavier than before. To my left, an ancient stone gong sits at the crest of the rise. Numerous tiny holes pierce its surface from side to side. When there is a high wind coming from the direction of the plain, it rises to a wail as it passes through them. It is doing this now, only louder than I have ever heard it, the gong swinging back and forth on the thick rod which anchors it to two greater stones.

I drop my weaving and run to the top of the rise. The wind is coming in strong gusts, and it is difficult to keep my balance. At last I reach the crest. I can see all of the plain from here; the hills to the right and left, the far horizon, the monoliths in the foreground.

My heartbeat quickens. The penance spires are black, with hard red points that shimmer in the centre. I cannot believe how the sky has changed. It too is red, and massed with angry clouds. The sun is gone, and there is thunder. The sound claps, rolls towards me, and brilliant lightning shoots across the plain.

The gong shrieks behind me. The air near the horizon is a strange, clear yellow. I can see something else now. A purplish-red funnel has formed in the centre, spiralling up from the ground into the clouds above. As I watch, it grows before my eyes. The wind is so strong that I wrap my arms around a large rock and hold on.

"No!" I scream, though there is no one to hear. In the terrible roaring, my voice no longer exists, but I cry out anyway, twice more. "No, no!"

I have been told about the funnels, the red demons, as people call them. They are a thing of nightmares, of stories the old ones tell in the long cold evenings as we seek refuge in our gloried past. The storms used to come in the afternoon, on warm days when the weather was unsettled.

In the time it has taken me to think, the thing has come closer. I have never seen anything move so fast. It is ploughing across the centre of the plain, tearing up the surface and spewing debris. I am filled with terror for Kep and the others. I do not want to look, and yet I watch for too long. The funnel is huge now, a red-black fury that consumes every-thing in its path.

And it is heading straight for me.

I turn and start back along the trail. The wind catches me, slams me into a rock. I rise, start again. The current changes, pushing at my back, and I almost fly over the crest and down the other side, running.

Everything turns a dark, ugly colour that shifts and changes, and lightning streaks above me. The garden gate has been torn away, and fragments are sucked from the ancient wall.

The wind tries to hold me against the stonework, but I claw my way around the edge and into the garden. The trees are thrashing, bent double, the glass that protected them gone. The red demon howls ever nearer behind me, its breath spinning me around as I struggle up the path. There is a lashing of rain, and at last I clear the grove and tumble, sprawling into the upper garden.

Sektar is standing, clinging to his wheel. The house looms frail and crumbling behind him, its shape quickly changing as the wind rips pieces away. His clothes have been torn from his body, and he is naked. He has locked the wheel mechanism so it cannot be moved, and his arms are twined around the spoke, the fingers laced together. His eyes are dark, staring at a fixed point behind me.

"Sektar!" I scream. My effort is futile, for the roaring is all around us now. "Sektar! Get into the underground storage bins! It's a red demon! It's going to go right through us! Come!"

I reach for him, but the wind snatches me away, throwing me to the ground. As I look up at him, he is monstrous, grotesque, and I see that he is mad, an old man trapped by his obsession with his garden and his wheel, and a past he can never have again. Even if he could hear me, it would make no difference. This is his last stand against the wind and the drought and the cold that are destroying us all.

"Father," I am sobbing. I make groping motions towards him as I am forced up the slope. I tumble into the open entrance of the storage cellar near the house. When I get my breath, I brace myself, raising my head until I can just see above the level of the ground.

Sektar and the wheel are directly in my line of vision. He is still hanging on, though his feet are being lifted from under him. Most of the trees have broken away, and I can see the garden wall below.

The red demon is the sky now, all of it, and it howls so loudly that I am beyond hearing it. It jumps the rise, landing and tearing into what is left of the wall, scattering rocks like specs of dust and churning up the path towards Sektar as though it knows that he is there. My hair is being ripped from my head, but I cannot move.

Finally, the funnel confronts my father. It catches his protruding feet and snatches him from the wheel. Then the whirlwind leaps in the air once more. As it arcs high above me, I can see the circle at the bottom, and the brief, dark movement that I tell myself is Sektar as he disappears. There are smaller whirling circles around the inside of the red demon's edge, and I wonder if Sektar is aware of any of this, or if he is able to feel anything at all.

Then I see that the funnel is descending again, right over the house, and I run for the dark underground recesses of the bin. I sink to my knees and cover my ears. Jars and baskets tumble about me as the ground explodes with sound and everything gives in to the fury that is my father's ending.

⁂

I am to blame for much of what happened, or so I have been telling myself these many days.

If only I had gone to the spires that morning. Even if I had done penance alone, I might have seen the storm in them before it came. When I see weather, it always happens. The others would have trusted me and stayed, if I had warned them. We could have sought refuge, if we had the time.

If if if. Such thoughts do no good now.

I found my tapestry and frame undamaged. They were lying by the only untouched clump of flowers, near the wheel. I placed some shards of glass over the fragile blooms, and watered them from the reserve jars in the bins. Then I found enough threads to record things. I am finishing the story of the storm, and will complete the rest tonight. At a later time, I will take my work apart and do a better job.

This will be my last, my ending tapestry. Nothing could

persuade me to do another.

I have cleared things away, preparing before I go. It is dry again, and cold. The webs between my fingers and toes are painful, but I manage. When I can sleep, I find no peace. Last night I dreamed that people from the Water Planet sailed here in pale ships, and that they found my tapestry. I was lying beneath the ground, and I could see them as they walked over my body, my bones. I believe what Sektar said now. Perhaps the name they will give to Ursha will be more suited to what is left of our "jewel in the sun."

I doubt if any of the others survived. I found Sektar's old star-glass in the rubble of the house, and took it to the rise. The monoliths stood whole and bright. The storm cut into the ground around the central spire, and I could see the stones went far deeper than any of us ever thought. When I looked though the glass, I saw some of the others at the horizon's edge, lying still on either side of the red demon's path. The lame old woman was nearest, spread out like a broken tree.

I found Sektar too, outside the far wall. His arms and legs were stretched wide, and there was enough left of his face for me to see that he was smiling. Beyond him, there was a great hole in the city where the storm cut through, leaving the buildings standing on either side. I gave him back to the garden, braiding his hair across his face and wrapping his body in needle tree bark. He lies in shallow ground near the wheel, where I sit weaving.

Yet as I work, I know that all is not undone. There is something new, something wonderful, and as I think of it, the hard knot in my soul unwinds, my heart begins to dance.

I am going to have Kep's child. I felt it stirring the other morning, at the base of my neck. Soon the flesh between my shoulders will begin to swell and glisten. All this is a miracle, considering what I have been through and that I am no longer young.

I do not know what I will do, if I pass Kep on my way to the Time Valleys.

Enough. I have set tomorrow as my leaving day, and there is something I must do. I place my tapestry to one side and rise, climbing Sektar's wheel and settling myself in his seat. The flowers stir under their protective glass by his leaving place. The duct that leads to them is undamaged, and though a portion of the wheel's edge is broken, the mechanism appears sound.

The flowers may survive a few more days.

They must.

My feet find the pedals. I think of Kep and our unborn child. I push, strain, fix the horizon and the sun in my mind. For Sektar and the others, for the plants and trees, and all the vanished gardens of Ursha, I am slowly turning the wheel.

CHIAROSCURO
Eileen Kernaghan

the shadow is always there
dark subtext, dissonance: the mocking laughter
in the fairy wood, the scowling presence
at the birthday feast, the faint suggestion
of warts beneath the velvet coat

this is the page in the book you dare not turn to
the face you see in the mirror
when the light falls at the wrong angle

this is the sly poison under the apple's
smooth red skin, the dark that is not
light's absence, but its twin.

LAIKA
Natasha Beaulieu (translated by Yves Meynard)

She put on the G-string, compressed her heavy breasts in the half-cup bra and pulled the corset's lacing as tight as it could go.

She arched her back and smiled, pleased with the image cast back by the mirror. Her waist was so narrow it did not capable of supporting her bust. The leather undergarments flawlessly matched the curves of her body. Black skins on black skin.

She combed her long hair, stiff and thick as a purebred horse's mane, applied scent and picked the highest heels in her wardrobe.

Then she slid her hands into short leather gloves.

Mr. Rapendish had indicated that the gloves were essential.

// ⦦

"What's your name?"

Black holes, the pupils of Mr. Rapendish, from which all emotion was absent.

"Michelle."

"That's not a whore's name."

She shrugged. "Call me what you like."

She'd never worked in such a repulsive room. A single window, framed by shreds of greenish fabric hanging from a worn rod. Wallpaper striped in brown and ocher, scraped in places. Moth-eaten yellow bedspread, a water-stained beige carpet. Above the sink, a shard of mirror hung from the end of a string tied to a rusted nail. The lone table struggled under the weight of a lamp with a burst shade.

She already regretted coming here. But it was too late. She knew the kind of humiliation she could look forward to. Still, the john was paying triple the normal fee. And after all, it was only for one night. What's one night in a life? Especially a whore's life.

"You'll be Laika."

"Laika?"

"That's the name of the first dog—the first bitch—in space."

At least she'd be a famous bitch. Too bad the doghouse was

so uninviting.

"Take off your clothes. Keep only the gloves."

She was a bit disappointed he didn't appreciate the luxurious undergarments. Nevertheless, she stripped, save for the gloves.

Then she stood and awaited what was to follow.

Mr. Rapendish seemed in no hurry to begin anything. He took off his jacket and settled in the brown armchair, speckled with cigarette burns. He pulled a fifth of whisky out from under the chair. He drank straight from the bottle, then wiped his mouth on the sleeve of his white shirt. His drooping lips grimaced in some indecipherable way.

"Come sit on me, Laika. Like a good faithful bitch. I'll stroke the back of your ears."

She'd have liked to first tell him how degrading she found it to be his bitch for the night. But instead, she went to sit on her master's lap.

He began to stroke her hair. Softly. As if taking the time to appreciate its texture. He picked up one long black lock and pressed it to his nose. He inhaled deeply, with a beatific smile on his lips.

"You smell so good. I won't need to bathe you."

He ran a clammy hand through her thick mane. Found the delicate nape of her neck, began to rub it tenderly.

She yielded to the caress.

Mr. Rapendish tickled the lobe of her ear. She giggled, tried to escape the teasing fingers.

"No, no. An animal doesn't laugh."

He'd made the remark without aggressiveness, in a neutral voice, continuing meanwhile to stroke her.

She decided to play along. She lowered her lids halfway and tilted her head to one side.

Mr. Rapendish kept stroking his pet, for long minutes, in silence. From time to time, he'd drink a swallow of alcohol.

Huddled against her singular john, she almost felt good.

"Are you thirsty, my pretty Laika?"

Since she had no tail to wag, she ventured to utter a brief bark and show signs of excitement at the thought of drinking.

"You're the prettiest and brightest of bitches. That's why I chose you."

He took the dirty glass on the windowsill and filled it with whisky.

She felt her gorge rise.

"Drink."

She reached out with her hand to take the glass. Mr. Rapendish grabbed her wrist. He pulled the black leather-clad hand to his mouth and began to cover it with kisses.

"Oh, what a nice paw. What nice pads you have."

She understood that to quench her thirst, she would have to use her tongue. She began to lap up the booze under her john's fascinated gaze.

"I wanted to bring Windy's bowl, but I'd have looked suspicious, leaving home with the dog's drinking bowl. People would have asked questions. I wouldn't have known what answers to give my wife, my children, the maid…"

She wasn't thirsty anymore. He laid the glass back on the windowsill.

He began to stroke her curly pubic hair.

"I always dreamed of owning a black bitch. Windy's a blonde. I found her old leash and collar in a drawer. I think they'll be perfect for you."

He rose suddenly, careless of her. She fell to the carpet and whimpered. Like a hurt dog.

Mr. Rapendish groped in the pocket of the jacket he'd thrown onto the bed. After a few seconds, he turned back to her, with the expression of a disappointed child.

"I must have left them in the car. That really bothers me. I hate it when things don't go my way."

She didn't doubt it. Fear had begun to seep into her. Her john didn't just want to fulfill a fantasy. Mr. Rapendish had the eyes of a psychopath.

Curled up next to the armchair, she watched him free his belt from the trouser loops.

His annoyed expression suddenly smoothed over. Mr. Rapendish let his belt fall onto the bed. He went to his pet, crouched down next to her, stroked her and affectionately kissed the inside of her paws.

"My beautiful Laika. Don't be afraid, I won't hurt you. Not you. Don't be afraid."

On his knees, he crawled to the bed, reached underneath and brought out a package wrapped in newspaper.

He came back to her. "I've brought you a nice gift. You're gonna be so happy."

She shut her eyes. Tried to make out the smell of canine

perfume. Pictured herself chewing on a doggy biscuit. Shivered at the thought of how a marrow bone would taste.

He yanked on her hair and shook her. "Open your eyes. Don't you want to see the surprise I got for you?"

She made herself open her eyes. Mr. Rapendish held a piece of raw steak before her face.

"Look at that! Now isn't that a lovely piece of meat?"

He waited for a reaction. But she was unable to move.

"You're not jumping for joy? What's wrong?" And he thrust the slab of meat into her face.

Her cry was muffled by the gift. She tried to struggle, but Mr. Rapendish was backing her into the corner of the room, behind the armchair, his hand still shoving the "surprise" against her face.

"You fucking bitch! I bring you the best cut of meat from the butcher shop and you act like it's not good enough for you!"

She was crying, under the raw flesh molded to her face. She could barely breathe.

The torture lasted a few seconds, then Mr. Rapendish stood up. Taking his present with him, he sat down again in the armchair.

Still huddled in the corner, she got her breath back and wiped her face with a shred from the curtain. She remained where she was; better to wait for the master's orders than to displease him.

Mr. Rapendish muttered for long minutes. He seemed to be hard at work on something. She saw only his right arm moving.

Suddenly, he turned to her, a wide smile on his lips. "Come on me, my pretty Laika."

She hesitated.

"Hurry up! Come on me."

He patted his thighs; his gaze was the mild gaze of a happy husband and father.

She approached him on all fours, her limbs aching, and climbed onto her master's lap.

"Good bitch, Laika. Good bitch." He began to stroke behind her ears again. Gently. For a long time.

Then, leaning her head to one side, she let him suckle at her heavy teats and lick the pads on her paws.

The master was nice and kind.

"I don't have a ball for us to play with. I tried to make one out of the newspaper, but that wasn't a good idea. Better to keep it in case you need to go. You understand, don't you?"

She answered "Yes". He stopped stroking her, fixed her with his black, impenetrable pupils.

"Bitches don't talk. They listen and obey."

He pushed her violently away. She tumbled onto the carpet, rolled to the foot of the bed.

"Take my belt."

The order carried no threat. What it did carry was far worse.

She took the belt that lay on the bed, but Mr. Rapendish scolded her: "No, no. In your mouth."

She turned to him, on all fours, her fangs sunk into the leather of the belt.

"Bring it, Laika."

She went to her master. Once she was at his feet, he tore the belt out of her mouth. "Good girl. Good girl."

She watched Mr. Rapendish wind the leather strap around his fist. His black pupils seemed dead. Or sick. Perhaps even innocent.

"I have to train you. You've got to learn to defend yourself against those depraved sickoes lurking everywhere."

He waved his leather-wrapped fist toward the mouth of his pet. She tried to bring it down with her paw. But that wasn't what the master wanted.

"Bite down, Laika! Bite! A bitch is supposed to bite."

The bitch clenched her teeth onto the heavy fist; her head was jerked left and right. But she held on. She growled. Sank her teeth into the leather up to the gums. She could feel a thread of drool running from her maddened mouth, that wouldn't let go.

Her master was satisfied. "Enough! Down, Laika."

She unclenched her teeth but kept growling, her forelegs stiff. Her master seemed upset. "What is it? You want a reward?"

He slipped his hand under the cushion and pulled out a morsel of brownish raw meat, which he waved over the animal's head.

She growled even more and stepped back. The man had cut the meat apart for her. That was what the right arm had been working at, for such long minutes. He must have something sharp on his person. Why did he hide his weapon? Did he mean to harm her? Can a master hurt his beast?

"That's right, I forgot. You're a picky bitch."

He let the piece of meat fall to the carpet. He unwound the belt from his fist and slid the end through the buckle, loosely. He rose and advanced upon his beast, once more huddled in a corner of the room. "I'll break you."

He tried to loop the belt around her neck, but she began to bark, threateningly. He cursed and started to pelt her with kicks.

"You filthy beast! You're like all the others! Nothing but a stupid bitch."

Vanquished by the rain of blows, she allowed herself to be almost strangled by the belt-collar.

Her master tied the belt to one of the night-stand's legs, forcing his bitch into an uncomfortable position. Then he rummaged in his pants pocket and pulled out crumpled hundred-dollar bills. He forced the animal to open her mouth and shoved in the paper pellets, one by one.

"Fucking bitch! This is the only reason you came! But you're the one who's going to pay!"

Suffocating, the bitch nevertheless managed to free herself from her improvised leash. Immediately, she jumped on her assailant, shoved him headfirst against the wall.

Swiftly she pawed out the paper pellets from her mouth. She'd barely spat out the last bill when she saw the blade of a knife shining before her eyes. The knife that had been used to slice the piece of steak.

Laika jumped onto the bed, fangs bared.

Mr. Rapendish rose to his feet. His blade was pointing at the beast. His gaze was a madman's.

"You know what I do with bitches? I disembowel them, I watch them piss their blood away and then I eat their entrails. Afterwards, I throw them in the dump."

Laika kept growling. This man could not be her master. He was an impostor.

"Every day, I have to hold myself back, or I'd do the same to my wife, to my children, to the maid."

Laika was ready to pounce. A good master had no urge to murder his family.

"You're stronger than the others. That's why I chose you. I knew it. I could see in your eyes that you'd be the bitch to save me. The earth must be cleansed of filth like me, Laika! I'm carrion! Do you understand? A piece of shit!"

He'd shouted out the last sentences as he stepped toward the bed, his knife in his hand.

"Kill, Laika! Kill!"

The huge black dog threw herself upon the man. She buried her fangs in the wrist that held the weapon. He dropped the knife, screaming in pain. She went for his throat, mouth gaping wide. Blood spurted. The man collapsed onto the ground. After clawing his face, the beast tore at his shirt and bit into the white flesh beneath.

Some minutes later, his belly slashed open, gurgling, the victim ceased his struggles.

Her mouth bloodied, Laika watched Mr. Rapendish die. He shut his eyes, sketched a soft smile, like a man falling blissfully asleep.

The beast heard the man whisper "Thank you, Laika."

And then she began to howl in grief.

OLD BRUISES
Heather Fraser

The fight had started about art lessons, Midori remembered now. She had skipped out of her aerobic dance class to try out those new art lessons at that trendy little gallery downtown.

Cameron had been furious when he found out. "I got your doctor's report," he raged. "I know how much you weigh. A hundred and twenty-five, Midori. That's twenty pounds over your target weight. What the hell do you expect me to say at the club when they start calling you Butterball?" He had taken her by the shoulders and shaken her. "Butterball, Butterball! They're saying it already. Don't you care about my career? How will you pay for your aerobic classes if I lose my post?"

Midori was lucky, and she knew it. She and Cameron had taken their anger counselling together. "If hitting is your way, that's fine," said the counsellor. "That's what bruise cream is for. But there's no need to break bones. One slap or punch is enough to let your partner know that you're angry. More than that is just a loss of control." Cameron always tried to do the right thing.

Her face hurt. The bruise was just starting to come up, and it was past time she stopped admiring herself and used her bruise cream. If she waited another two or three minutes it would be too late.

Bruise cream, the salvation of her class. However would the ladies cope without being able to remove their bruises? Why, they'd be just like the sluts, wearing their bruises for all to see, all for the lack of a small fortune to keep them in bruise cream.

She dipped her fingers into the pot, and then stopped. She scraped the cream back into its container and wiped her fingers on a cloth. Why did I do that? she wondered, watching her face swell. She had no answer. She just knew that she was tired of the smell of the stuff, the messy cleanup job when the bruise came to the surface, the way it hurt with a sharp, astringent pain instead of a dull ache. She closed the cover and put the bruise cream away.

She stripped before the full-length mirror. Her body was firm and muscled, but her tummy and her upper thighs were showing signs of softening. The target weight Cameron's doctor had set for her was unreal, another of Cameron's fixations. He had to have the thinnest wife in the company, and as long as Julia Baxter kept throwing up in the executive washroom, Midori and Cameron would be having these little fights.

She put on her white satin night-gown, the one he really liked, and went through the connecting bathroom into his bedroom. His light was out, and he snored lightly, his anger spent in one well-aimed punch. She crawled in beside him as he lay sleeping, massaging his chest and his legs. He came awake slowly, reluctantly, his breath smoky with good single malt. "Midori, is that you?" he mumbled.

"Fuck me," she said.

"Oh for Christ's sake, you always do this after a fight," he said, but he sounded more interested than disgusted. He always did, after a fight. She went down on him, and eliminated the rest of his reluctance.

After he had come, he wrapped her satin nightgown around her eyes the way she liked, and held her arms above her head as he made slow love to her. It was good. When she was blindfolded, she could pretend that it was her father touching her like that, and the orgasm went on and on.

⁂

He shook her awake in the morning. "Why is your face so bruised?" He sounded more bewildered than angry.

She shrugged. "I expect because you hit me there."

"That's not what I meant. Are you out of bruise cream? What's the problem? Should I fire your maid?"

"Nothing's wrong," said Midori. "Please don't fire my maid. I have had enough trouble trying to teach the poor slut what little she knows, and I don't want to start over."

"I don't have time to worry about this, Midori. You have to be more careful about the household accounts. I can't be watching over your shoulder every minute."

He left then because he had a breakfast meeting that he couldn't miss. Midori returned to her bedroom to be dressed. This year's styles, with low-cut bodices and short handkerchief skirts on hoops, were inspired by pre-Revolution France, and required almost as many servants to get into.

"I checked on the bruise cream just last week. I know there is plenty there," said the maid, casting respectful, accusing looks at Midori. The girl's own bruises were just starting to fade.

"I take it you saw Mr Robinson on your way in. Did he

threaten to fire you again?"

"Yes, Mrs Robinson," she said sullenly.

"Please don't take him seriously. He says things when he's casting about for someone to blame, and he'll have forgotten about it by supper."

"He's my boss. I have to take him seriously." She ran gentle fingers over Midori's swollen eye and cheek. "You shouldn't look like this, Mrs Robinson. You're too good for this." She sighed. "Should I get an ice pack? That always helps me."

"I am all right," said Midori.

*// *

Her chauffeur drove her to the club, and she watched the faces of the studs and the sluts. There were faces on paintless porches, faces surrounded by rags on sidewalks, faces walking the streets with gritty determination or directionless anger. Some were bruised, some weren't. They took no notice of her car's palpable air of money. None of them looked like they were working, or had worked for some time. It had been like that in the two generations since the restructuring, when the governments withered away and the multinationals became the new overlords, casting aside those who couldn't compete.

It made her crazy, watching all those uncontrolled faces, while she, daughter and wife of company barons, rode imprisoned in her car. Yet she knew that she was the one who was free, while they were trapped by no education, no jobs, no money. Why then did she long to open her door, run out into the filthy streets, let them do to her as they willed.

"Look at me," she would say. "I am bruised also. Will you teach me the places you forage for food? Or will you murder me for my clothes? But I wouldn't blame you, for who could blame you? I would sink into the earth with forgiveness for you on my lips."

Of course she did nothing of the sort, but only rode on as her car began the long climb up the hill to the club. Her eleven o'clock class, called Tautness Aerobics on the calendar but always referred to as Torture by the participants, could not be missed.

Her chauffeur handed her out of the car with her bag. "Shall I return at one, as usual, Mrs Robinson?" His eyes did not so much as flicker at her bruised face.

"Yes, that would be good."

She walked through the grand entrance, where she could just make out the words Faculty Club in weathered stone over the door. "Excuse me, but this is a private club," said the doorman politely.

"I am well aware of that," said Midori, staring him down. "Otherwise I would not have joined."

The doorman examined her face, her swollen eye. Abruptly he looked at the floor. "Of course, Mrs Robinson."

Her fellow participants in the Torture class were, of course, not nearly so ill-mannered to notice anything out of the ordinary. First, they were not saying, you gained weight. Then, they also did not say, you had the gall to show up in class looking like a slut too silly to know better.

"Hello, Midori," said Julia Baxter on the way to the sauna, her splendidly bony frame filmed with sweat. Julia was the only one with enough social standing to be able to speak to anyone, no matter what the circumstances. "May I join you?"

"Of course," said Midori. She noticed that by some coincidence no one else seemed interested. The two of them stripped down and entered the sauna, leaning back against the benches and enjoying the raw heat.

"You haven't been looking yourself for the last little while," said Julia after a suitable pause. "Are things all right between you and Cameron?"

"Things are the same as they've always been," said Midori.

Julia raised an elegant, practised eyebrow. When Midori didn't volunteer any more, Julia sighed theatrically. "Have you seen your analyst? I'm beginning to worry about you two. You've been acting like you're headed for a breakdown, and I'd hate to see that. Your family names are too good for that." Midori remained silent, delicately wiping the sweat from her brow.

"Do you need some bruise cream?" asked Julia.

Midori sat up. "We are well stocked, thank you Julia. This isn't about money. If it were, I would be cooling my heels at home."

Julia nodded slowly, unconvinced. "Take care of yourself, then," she said, getting up with the lithe grace of a cat, a very bony cat, and left Midori alone.

"I am all right," said Midori, to no one in particular.

*// *

"So how do you think the anger you carry towards your father is reflected in your current disregard for your husband's reputation?" asked her analyst, making notes on her laptop.

Midori curled a little tighter into the easy chair. "I think you're making a huge leap to assume that this is about my husband's reputation." She felt cold. Her analyst kept the office much too cold for comfort.

"Are you denying that your bruises will reflect poorly on Cameron's status? You told me that Julia Baxter offered you bruise cream in the sauna. She can't be the only one wondering if the Robinsons have overextended themselves." Her analyst spoke as one would speak to a child. "We established long ago that you aren't harbouring dissolution-level resentments against Cameron. So I want to explore the connection between this acting-out behaviour and your relationship with your father."

Midori sighed, and twirled her hair around a finger, a gesture from her childhood that bothered her mother terribly, that she now only seemed to do during therapy. "All my life, men have controlled me. When my father raped me, the bruises were never visible. Maybe I'm sick of hiding the bruises the men in my life have given me. Maybe I'm trying to tell the whole world how damaged I really am." It sounded like garbage to Midori, but her analyst nodded encouragement, taking more notes.

"Oops, time's almost up." The woman's bristling efficiency softened for just a moment, as it usually did when she was about to give some guiding pearl of wisdom. "Midori, it's too late for this bruise, but the next time Cameron hits you and you can't bring yourself to use your bruise cream, call me right away. It doesn't matter what time. Just call me."

"I will," promised Midori. It amused her to think how her analyst would sound awakened from a dead sleep, how she would struggle to gain her professional composure so that she could be appropriately sympathetic.

"You take care of yourself," said the analyst, putting a nurturing arm around her on the way to the door. "I'm really concerned about this new phase in your dysthemia. If you feel any other unusual urges, just let me know, and we can call Charles to adjust your psychopharmacologicals."

"I am all right," said Midori. *I think I just need to get out of here*, she thought, but you never said anything like that to your analyst, not unless you wanted to spend the next hour analysing from whence came this resentment towards someone who was trying to help you.

✦ ✦

Her children came home while she was painting. Thomas ran up behind her and gave her a sloppy kiss on the bruised side.

"What happened to your face?" he asked, at five quite oblivious to the social implications.

Ariake came in more sedately, and peeked at Midori from under her eyelashes. "Oh Mummy, what have you done?" Nine was plenty old enough to know the difference between sluts and ladies.

"I haven't done anything," said Midori, touching the spot where Thomas had laid his muscular lips. "That's why I'm bruised. When you don't do anything, you get a bruise." She looked critically at the still life. Something about the fruit still wasn't right.

"Can I go play with Albert?" asked Thomas, already forgetting the bruise. "His car is waiting outside. His Mummy is taking him on an overnight to Disneyland for a fitness workout and nutrition counselling."

"Is Daddy terribly angry?" asked Ariake.

"I haven't seen your father since breakfast," replied Midori. It was the shadows. They weren't falling the same way on the fruit as they were on the book.

"Mummy, can I go to Disneyland? I want to go to Disneyland!" Thomas's face was turning red, and he looked like he was on the verge of one of those little tantrums Midori kept hoping he would outgrow.

"Thomas, behave yourself." She reached for her phone and dialled the cellular in Albert's car.

"Hello?" said the chauffeur.

"This is Midori Robinson. May I speak to Katherine?"

"I'm sorry ma'am, but she isn't here. Shall I transfer you to her phone?"

"I want to go to Disneyland!" cried Thomas.

"No thank you," she said, breaking the connection. Thomas was learning to lie almost as well as his father. "You may not go with Albert if his mother isn't with him."

"I want to go to Disneyland!" screamed Thomas. "You never let me have any fun." He lashed out with his hands, and when Midori successfully defended herself, he collapsed to the floor crying and kicking. Midori knew she'd won this round. She returned to her painting, struggling with the shading on that orange.

"I'm going to my room," announced Ariake. "I can't hear myself think in here." She cast accusatory looks at both mother and brother before she flounced out.

Thomas cried and Midori painted for perhaps half an hour before Midori felt a damp head nuzzling against her leg. She took the little boy up into her lap. "I wanted to go to Disneyland," he said, his passion spent.

Midori kissed his dark curls. "I know you did, sweetheart. And we will go. I promise."

That seemed to satisfy him, and after a few minutes he bounded off after his next piece of mischief. Midori sighed, and decided to put her painting away. The shadows on the orange were starting to resemble an old bruise, and her eyes were tiring. Perhaps a day's perspective would help.

◊ ◊

"Midori, I don't know how much longer I can go on like this. Kyle Baxter came to speak to me today. He said Julia saw you at the club yesterday. He wanted to know if everything was still all right between you and me, and then he started recommending some good therapists."

"I could change analysts, if that's what you would like," said Midori diffidently.

"That's not the point. The point is that I could lose my position over this." Cameron downed his drink, and for the thousandth time she saw how much like his son he looked, far more than the other way around.

"Kyle doesn't have that kind of power," she said.

"No, but you know as well as I do that his father does. For Christ's sake, don't be so thick."

Midori winced. "What do you want me to do then, O wise one?"

"Don't get cute with me. Just stay in until your bruise goes away."

"But if I stay in, I'll miss the company formal, where all the company spouses are a must-show. And if I stay in, I won't be able to go to aerobics, and then I'll just get thicker." He was boiling with frustration, she could see. "That was the original point, was it not?"

Cameron slammed the glass against the wall. He took two purposeful steps towards her, right hand clenched, and then he stopped. His brows knit themselves together. "The new bruise cream did arrive, didn't it?"

"Yes, and I put it beside the old bruise cream."

"You will use it, won't you?" he begged.

She said nothing.

"Midori, please, you're making me crazy." He sounded lost,

TESSERACTS[5]

frustrated, not sure what to do with the aggression he had built up.

Slowly, without saying a word, she began unhooking her bodice.

Cameron made love to her blindfolded and bound to the bed. *O Daddy, O Daddy*, she thought, *I'd take it in my mouth for you*. After, as the orgasm faded, she wondered if she'd said it out loud. It was no matter. Cameron often called out the name of his current side dish, and Midori never mentioned it.

He released her from her bonds and sat up beside her, drinking whiskey straight from the bottle. "You can't come to the company formal," he said.

"Why not?"

"Have you really lost it, or are you just pretending?"

"If I stay away, everyone will think we've fallen on hard times," she explained.

"And if you go, everyone will call you a silly slut, and they'll be right." The passion had gone out of his voice. "Midori, I'm trying to help you. Please let me help you." He put his arm around her and began rocking her like a child. "Oh my love, what are we going to do?"

She settled into his embrace, and took a slug from his whiskey, something she rarely did. "I'll be all right," she said.

※ ※

Midori deliberately chose an evening gown in old-bruise green. She made up her good eye and her lips in that colour, the match for her ageing bruise. She thought the ensemble looked rather striking. She dismissed her maid, dispatched her bottle of wine, and called for her chauffeur.

"To the club?" he asked. Midori could have kissed him. Sometimes he seemed to be the only one in her world who understood her.

"Yes, that would be lovely."

They drove in silence through the darkened streets. No sparkling lights shone in this quarter of the city, just the sweep of their headlights and the occasional street fire, with the little children and the bums huddled around for warmth. The children shaded their eyes from the assault of the lights, but the bums didn't bother. Light or dark, it made little difference.

Her chauffeur dropped her off at the door to the club, handing her out of the car like a lady. "Shall I wait?" he asked.

Midori thought for a moment. "No, I'll be coming home with Mr Robinson, I think."

TESSERACTS⁵

"Very good," he said, climbed back into the car, and drove elegantly away.

Midori walked into the club, twirling her skirts like a little girl going to her first formal. The doorman barely flicked an eye at her, but she thought she saw him mutter something into his sleeve as she passed.

Cameron met her, in a rush, before she could get to the ballroom door. "What are you doing here?" he hissed. "I told you not to come." Then more quietly, "You're drunk."

"So are you," she giggled. "I thought that was what we were supposed to do."

"When you look like a silly fat slut, you're supposed to stay home."

"I do not look like a slut. No slut can afford designer originals. I look like a lady. A slightly used lady, but is that really a secret? You use me so well, baby." She held her lips up to be kissed, but Cameron drew back, confused.

Julia Baxter came out of the ballroom, her anorexic frame glittering with sequins and silk. "Let me try, Cameron." He backed off gratefully.

"Midori, let me take you home," she purred conspiratorially. "You're drunk, in a minute you'll be sick, and you're in no shape to stay here tonight."

Midori giggled. "Maybe we should get sick together. That's a bonding kind of experience. Have you eaten enough canapés yet?"

Julia's eyes narrowed, and flashed at Cameron to see if he'd heard. "Midori, you can't stay here. It's not right. Cameron is upset, and he wants you to go home. Can't you think about him for one minute?"

"I think about him every minute," protested Midori. "Can't either of you think about me?"

"I am thinking about you," said Cameron. "If you go in there looking like this, you can kiss you invitations to future parties good-bye, and maybe your club membership too. You'll be *persona non grata* on the social circuit for months. I know these things matter to you. Jesus, Midori, don't blow it on a stupid whim." Julia nodded, taking his arm supportively.

Midori's head spun. Had she missed something? Was it Julia who was Cameron's side dish now? It was so hard to remember. She backed away into the wall, and careened off it, walking crookedly but purposefully toward the ballroom.

"Midori!" cried Cameron.

"I'll call her analyst," said Julia.

Cameron rushed up behind her and took her arm. "Midori, come home."

"No," she said, breaking away from him with a strength she didn't know she had. She looked toward the ballroom. It was brilliant, glittering, multicoloured like a convention of dragonflies on the surface of a pond, insect forms dressed by the pre-Revolution French.

"Why should I go home?" she asked. "We all have bruises, God forbid that anyone should know. God forbid that anyone should look into our souls and see that our husbands hit us, or our wives kick us, or our fathers fucked us every Saturday night when we were six, and we've never figured out how to make bruise cream work on that one. I mean, for God's sake, it's only happened to all of us, how ever could I admit that I'm just like everyone else?" She stepped into the ballroom.

Three club security men burst through the door and wrestled her to the ground, causing her a few more bruises in the process. The man on top of her, Eurasian, greying, reminded her desperately of her father, and she came right there underneath him. She hoped he mistook her thrashing for a struggle.

◢ ◣

The hospital was very nice, and Cameron brought the children every two weeks. It took them a few visits to get used to the institutional setting, but even the first time she was sure they were relieved. Their mother had had a breakdown. That was something that could be understood, could be talked about in the schoolyard, could be usefully explored in therapy.

Cameron came alone on the alternate weeks, and they were allowed conjugal visits. The hospital philosophy was to allow little islands of normality in the hope that the patient would cling to one and eventually pull herself out of her hole of despair. Midori wasn't despairing, but that wasn't the sort of thing you told your analyst unless you wanted to extend your appointment for an hour.

"You're losing weight," said Cameron on one visit, loosening her blindfold and getting up to dress.

Midori shrugged. "Hospital food isn't all that appealing." In fact, she had binged for the first week, and then the novelty of eating wore off.

"Maybe you'll be ready to come home soon." She couldn't

read his expression.

"My doctor says I still have a lot of work to do, that there's a part of me unwilling to give up its secrets, and I can't get better until I am willing to let go." Did she see relief flash on his face? Or was it regret?

"I am all right," she said.

Some secrets were better unshared, and some secrets hid in the open, where someone who could not understand would never see.

When Cameron left, Midori returned to her painting, an erotic portrait of a prepubescent black-haired girl, about the same age she was when her father visited her bed. The teacher wanted to know why she had chosen this subject, and Midori said that it related to her healing.

She could hardly tell her teacher that the five times her father fucked her were the only five times he ever touched her. She cherished them, held to them like a child's rag doll, the only notice she had ever attracted from the man whose name and ruthless image were celebrated in buildings from New York to Tokyo, the only times in her whole childhood she could remember feeling anything at all. No analyst was going to take those feelings from her, turn them into ordinary bruises, and wipe them away with cream and a dirty rag.

So she was going to be here forever. That was all right. They didn't make her do aerobics, and they let her take art classes. She noted by the clock that it was time for class now. Humming contentedly, she packed up her materials and went.

WINDIGO
John Park

There were about thirty in a ragged column, plodding up the bare slope. Their faces were covered in fine brown hair; they wore anoraks of woven fibres, green fur or pebble-scaled leather, fastened with thongs or silver clasps, and they carried packs across their shoulders. In the middle of the column an albino was singing of the receding sun.

As they climbed, the wind rose. The sky was a mass of greenish-grey cloud, streaming before them, and darkening steadily. Over the ridgeline ahead was a faintly brighter patch, where the sun was continuing its long descent towards the horizon. For the last ten watches, they had marched without sleep, and still the sun was too far ahead of them, and always setting.

At the rear of the column, four of the biggest men pulled a laden sled that floated knee-high above the ground. They peered back at the valley one more time, then piled their weapons on the sled, bent their backs and pushed.

At the head of the column, Anil moved to his mother's side. He leaned close to be heard above the wind without raising his voice. "We've lost our guards and gained two haulers."

Gannet nodded and reached to brush snowflakes from Anil's hair. "That's all right. We'll face one threat at a time now. Put your hood up."

"Three more ridges after this one, aren't there, before we see the river? No—four."

"Four, that's right," she said with a faint smile. "You've a good memory." She turned to look at him. Her forehead creased. Absently, her hand went to her throat, where the sun-lizard tooth hung next to the Lar's black oval outside her anorak. "It'll be close, with the sled crippled. We may not make it."

He was not permitted fear. He said, "We didn't lose that much time trying to fix it, and it's always slow in the mountains. When we get down to the river, the rafts—"

"Maybe not this time. The river will be starting to freeze."

"What, then? How can we go any faster?"

"There may be something in the next valley."

"Somewhere we can wait out the whole night?"

"Something I've heard of. We'll have to search."

He wanted to ask more, but she had lowered her head and was striding away from him, no longer his mother but the matriarch again. From the corner of his eye he could see Malachite and Carp, the two conspirators, eyeing him, judging the rift between him and Gannet. He cursed under his breath and lengthened his stride to catch up.

An eighth-watch later, the sled skidded away from its haulers and crashed against a boulder. A rope snapped. Bundles spilled onto the frozen ground.

The albino's song stopped in mid-line.

Shoulders bent, chests heaving, the haulers stood over the sled. Plumes of white streamed from their mouths. One of them, a tall, square man named Pike, gaped at his open hands as though they were alien growths. He was swaying like a sail-tree in a gale.

"Are you going to stare at it until the night catches us?" Gannet shouted, coming back down the column.

Anil strode after her. "They're exhausted," he began. Malachite and Carp were following, ready to support him against his mother.

"I can see that," Gannet snapped. "Sapphire—the rope! Tern, Cerulan—get those bundles."

Forced to stop, the group huddled together, staring out into the dark. Weapons were unslung and levelled.

Knowing Gannet would disapprove, Anil slipped past her and helped steady the sled as it was loaded. His mother said nothing. They began to heave it back onto the path. Another pair of hands pushed beside his. Lazuli's, he recognised, but with Gannet's gaze on his back he pretended not to notice.

Malachite and Carp hovered at the edge of the group, without finding an opening they could exploit.

The sled wobbled over a boulder and almost got away from them. Gannet started shouting again.

"In twelve watches, if we don't get out of these mountains, the night will be on us. Every breath will be like sucking flame into your lungs." Even without facing her, Anil could see her face, the grey skin and beard, frost on her moustache, the dark eyes glaring out of a nest of wrinkles. "Your faces will freeze and split. Your hands will be icicles rooted in your wrists. Your eyeballs will turn to glass!"

Anil felt he was carrying most of the sled's weight himself. The last bundles were fastened down and they started pulling it up the track.

"That's enough, Anil," she said. "Back to your place."

The sled reached the point where it had slipped, and moved on.

"That's better," Gannet said. "Over the ridge we'll stop for food—an eighth-watch. And change the hauling team."

Beside Anil walked Heron and Lazuli her daughter, and Pike the hauler. He must have passed the age when he could afford to let his extremities get chilled. Heron had pulled him off the hauling team, but his eyes rolled in the first stage of cold-rush, as body used up flesh and bones to pour antifreeze into his blood.

Whoever had prepared people for this world, Anil thought bitterly, had cheated them all the way.

"Thrush," Gannet called. "While we march, give us the first stanzas of *Orlando's Descent*."

The young albino lifted his head. His voice quavered at first as his numbed lips formed the first syllables of the chant, then grew strong, telling of the hero's preparation.

Anil sensed that Lazuli was watching him. They had both been tempted towards a forbidden liaison.

Ahead of him, the sunlight was still slipping away from them. Thrush was singing of skycraft burning to cinders in their descent.

With a chance that these were their last watches together, with no hope of meeting another group this late, maybe Gannet would put aside her proscription....

He lowered his head and recited his personal catechism in his mind, trying to visualise the insectlike artifacts in the crippled sled's innards, one by one: red four-legs for amplification, green four-legs for filtering, yellow four-legs...

⁄⁄ ⁊

"Enough, Thrush," Gannet called. They had stopped by the trail and were chewing on dried meat and bread fruit. "All of you—remember that Orlando knew the darkness within him, but still he clung to his true nature. He made sure that his values would be passed on. He did not mean us to be abandoned here. The tale tells us that the Shell of his craft still lies beside our track, in these mountains."

Malachite jabbed his gloved hand at her. "What are you saying?"

"I'm telling you who we are, and what we must do."

"You're giving us no choice. You behave as though no one else had a right to an opinion."

"I'm the leader, and my son will be the next." She touched the Lar at her throat. "If choices have to be made, I'll make them with Lar's help. Think on Orlando's tale. Team three take the sled."

The wind was louder now as they climbed the next ridge. It squeezed their flesh, rasped at their eyes. And its mourning, raging cry seemed to accompany other voices that ached at the edge of hearing.

Pike, the hauler, was sinking into cold-rush, and two others had to help him along. His head lolled; he muttered random syllables.

Lazuli brushed against Anil. "We're going to die, aren't we? She's desperate, talking of Orlando's Shell. She knows we're late." Her gloved fingers gripped his. "Shall we miss our last chance? Because she says so? Because all your life she's said so?" She tugged at his hand. "And it's true about your father, isn't it? She gave him to the Windigo."

"The Windigos are a myth from another world," Anil snapped.

"Even you don't believe that!" she cried, but he had turned away and was walking on alone.

Ochres and greens gradually dimmed into shades of grey. Where the eyes had missed them, patches of whiteness suddenly glimmered—seemed to throb. Behind, the sky was a black vault, hung with webs of trembling light, silver and cold violet, that set phantom shadows leaping.

Malachite shouted. He was pointing into the dark. "Oil fern! A whole grove! Bring the cutter!"

Men were already following him. Anil fetched the heavy beam cutter from the sled and ran, thinking of fuel, food, a few more watches of life.

But when Malachite cracked away the ice over the root-cache and peered in, he froze and then stepped back, hand on his holster. Anil thrust his torch forward. The seeds, large as skulls and armoured against anything less than the beam cutter, had been split open—were splinters and empty shells. Snow whirled through the torch's light.

"Windigo." Anil could not tell who had spoken.

"This close to the dayside?" "They're hungry." "How long

ago?"

A myth, he wanted to shout at them, myth from a forgotten world.

But Gannet believed.

"Do they eat—meat?" he had asked his mother once, unable to put the brutal question directly.

"They eat anything you could eat or burn," she had told him, dispassionate as a leader must be. "You've seen a man's body burn."

"Keep moving!" Gannet shouted at them. "Our lives are blowing away in the wind."

"At least Malachite saw the ferns," said Carp with a glance at Anil as they moved on.

"My son could tell the cache had already been plundered," Gannet answered. Anil met her gaze and squirmed inwardly. He let himself slip back down the column.

Lazuli moved to his side. "Look at her," she whispered. "She pretends she's so strong, but my mother's scanned her. Her joints are wearing out, her lungs are dry as leather, and her heart sounds like a sand-darter with a broken wing."

Anil hesitated. "I've watched her when she thinks no one's looking," he said slowly. "Her shoulders slump, she keeps her leg stiff. And her face looks so—tired."

"Well then?"

"Well what?" he said, suddenly angry. "Do you want to stop and rut here in the snow, like a pair of caprics?...She's old, but she's still leader."

"What are you, then? What will you be?"

Anil turned at the pain in her voice, and gazed at her.

At the back of the column, Pike suddenly screamed. "See!" His arm jerked out, pointing. "There!"

They stared back into the night. There was only snow and the pale spectral shimmering.

"There! There! There!" Pike flung his arms out, started to run. After half a dozen strides he fell, struggled to his knees, tried to crawl.

Carp stabbed a hand towards him. "It's time! For the Windigo!"

Anil knew what he meant, and looked to Gannet.

"A propitiation is mine to decide," she said. Anil could see how she examined the faces around her. Pike was slowing them down, probably would not survive the next few watches anyway.

Gannet stiffened her shoulders. "Anil, get four tent pegs and two mallets, and some rope. Carp and Malachite will perform the staking. The rest of us will go on. You two—be quick and don't lose sight of our tracks."

Anil avoided Lazuli's eyes. He went and fumbled at the sled, stood again. Two mallets. There should have been something extraordinary in the feel of them, but they were just the same implements he used every time they camped. He looked Malachite in the face when he handed the equipment over, but there was nothing he could read in the man's eyes.

Pike seemed unaware of what was happening as the two led him away from the path.

Anil remembered nightmares of shadows with teeth, claws that came out of the dark, and only air to fight against. He found he had put himself between Lazuli and the darkness. Then he stopped, stood staring into the night. A food pack had been left beside the trail, in propitiation.

Gannet turned and snatched a flare from one of the guards. She triggered it and brandished the yellow flame over her head. "In two watches we'll all freeze!" She was a wild figure, seemingly half ice and darkness herself. "March on!" she shouted at him. "March!" Then, in a quieter, urgent voice: *"You will not go back."*

After a sixteenth-watch, Carp and Malachite came panting up with the mallets and Pike's anorak. Thrush began to sing, hoarsely and loud, the chant of transfiguration.

Anil was marching at his mother's shoulder. He tried to find something in her face that he could recognise. She jerked her head towards him, meeting his gaze.

"Your father staked out seven for the Windigo in his time."

"And you staked him."

"Lar's choice," she said, and turned her head away.

Thrush's song ended.

They reached the valley floor. The wind's cold voices swirled around them.

"What was that?" Anil cried, turning.

"The wind," Gannet said quietly. "Just the wind. Keep going."

Anil concentrated on the rhythm of marching, the snow and rock underfoot, the darkness closing around them. Out of the mountains, the air would be warmer....He remembered a blue sky, heaped with golden clouds, and the horizon rhythmically swaying as he hung cradled against a comforting being like a tree patterned with spirals of purple thread; it drooped a foliage of chestnut hair that he reached up and played with.

Now Gannet's hair was grey. Anil saw how his mother held her back rigid; in the flicker of his torch, he could trace the purple spirals dyed into her anorak.

In that remote memory, another tree swayed along beside him, far beyond the reach of his hands. Occasionally it would lean close, and he would recognise the smile among the beard.

He turned to Gannet. "Was my father glad to stake people out for the Windigo?"

"He was the leader," she said. "He could be cruel."

"That's part of being a leader, you mean? What was he like?"

She looked up at him, and her face tightened. "He was taller than you," she said softly, "but not much. You have his eyes."

"What else? Am I like him?"

Abruptly she was the matriarch again. "You'll be leader, after me."

Anil wondered what Gannet's obliqueness meant, and what he would do if he became leader. Instead of just handing the mallets to Malachite, he would give the command, perhaps drive in the stakes himself.

‖ ⟍

They neared the crest of the next ridge. The light was fading from the sky almost uniformly, except for a grey area far ahead that shrank like a sunflake blossom closing against the cold.

At the crest, the group faltered and peered about them. Ahead, the slope disappeared into a void of darkness. The guards unslung their weapons. Impatiently Gannet waved them all forward. Snowflakes played ghostly games with the shadows, stroked their faces with quick, invisible fingers.

"If you were leader, you could change the rules." Lazuli had come up beside him again. "Maybe there's some other way to placate the Windigo." She shook his arm. "Don't brood like that."

"Malachite wouldn't have doubts. A leader has to be cruel sometimes; he has to think of everyone, all at once. I don't think I can do that."

"Not yet. After Malachite has his turn."

"Neither of us may get the chance."

"Then make the old bitch listen to you. If it's one thing you and he can agree on…"

"Don't call her that! Don't ever call her that to me."

"Then you'll never be free of her. What are you going to do?" she asked hopelessly. She slowed her pace and dropped back down the column.

Anil's hands ached. The cold was crushing his fingers because his fists were clenched. He forced them open. But there was a knot of tension behind his breastbone that would not release.

He moved forward along the edge of the column, further from the sled and its haulers. To his right there was just the dark and the snow swirling in the light of their torches. His breathing hurt.

Gannet was at his side.

"She's not right for you," she said. "What if she's with child next time, and due before we get to the rafts?"

"That needn't happen."

"Needn't it? I've got eyes. I know what it feels like. You think you've found a secret to life. You think it's a game you can win, but it's not, it's just trying to keep ahead of the dark, the cold. And in the end you're always alone. She'll destroy you if you let her."

※ ※

They reached the valley floor. The snow was thickening. Gannet shouted back down the column. "Malachite!"

He trotted up, panting.

"We'll keep the sled moving," Gannet said, "but this is where we look for the Shell. If we can open it we may find ways to escape the night. No one has had time to find it, since the first landing, but we'll have to try."

She pointed to a side valley. "Get scouts to explore either side of the way. Ten pairs. Each pair—keep together and don't lose the main track. The rest of us will stop with the sled for an eighth-watch—in the cave at the start of the next ridge. If you haven't found anything in a watch, you'll have to rejoin us there."

Malachite and Carp were one of the pairs, but Carp stopped and whispered urgently to Malachite. From the way he was looking at Gannet, he was urging that one of them should stay to watch her; and from the tension in his face, Anil guessed he was using that as a cover for his fear of leaving the group. Had they seen something when they staked Pike?

Malachite turned to Gannet. "My partner strained his knee

hurrying to catch up," he began.

Before he could think, Anil said, "I'll take his place."

Malachite looked at him quickly, then nodded and turned to go. Anil fell into step beside him.

"Cutting the apron strings, are you, boy?" Malachite said. "Or maybe it needs more courage to stay and wait than come and look for whatever's out there."

"I'm not afraid."

"Then you're a liar, boy, or a fool. I'm scared." Malachite unbuckled his holster flap and pulled out his pistol. "I'll use this on anything I don't like the look of." He put the gun back and turned his blank stare on Anil. "Liars and fools don't make good leaders."

Anil looked away, then said heavily, "No one seriously believes anyone but you should be the next leader."

"Someone thinks it. Doesn't she?"

The way was uphill, over bare rock and through snow that came to their knees. Anil strained to stay at Malachite's shoulder.

"You're panting, boy. That means you're sweating. When you stop, you'll freeze. Better take your own time."

"We've got to stay together."

"Your mother said. You're slowing me down."

Anil squinted at him. Malachite was breathing through his mouth, hard. Clouds of white poured from his lips. His beard was thick with frost. He was probably straining just as hard as Anil was.

They paused at the crest of a rise.

"I remember this area," Malachite said. "There's too much to search if we stay together. We're going to have to separate, whatever your mother thinks." He pulled out his pistol, checked its charge. "I'll take the defile to the left; you follow the slope that way. The valley's not straight, but it's easy enough to stay in."

He was stalking away, with the gun in his hand, before Anil could argue. Anil hesitated, then set off the way Malachite had pointed.

The ground sank, and the valley curved, at first gradually, then more sharply. It divided. He could see rock walls, clumps of shale-leaf, a rock-mole's burrow. Nothing that might shelter them from the freezing night. The wind was still rising. He could not look into it, shielded his eyes with his hand as he tried to check each branch of the valley. Snow eddied around him, leapt up shrieking in wraiths that blew away as they formed. Only exhaustion and the chill in his body kept the fear in check. He was trying to prove something, but he wasn't sure what it was any longer. One more branch, he thought, and he would have to go back.

He stumbled into the side valley. Fifty metres in, he found his own tracks, half-filled with snow.

The valley walls hid most of the sky and channeled the wind. There was nothing to show him which way to go. He choked down a tight knot of terror and began to run. He would have to follow his own tracks blindly, before the wind erased them, through all the detours and windings, back to the ridge where he had left Malachite. Who had told him the valley was easy to follow.

A sound like the wind began to roar in his head. He heaved himself through drifts, the centre of a bubble in a river of screaming white. Once he thought he heard a short bark and voices deeper than the wind. And suddenly there was nothing to follow. He stopped. Above him, the wind was tearing gaps in the cloud, showing the black shimmer of the night sky. The snow around him was featureless.

He walked on again, aimlessly.

His mind found a new place from which to observe the progress of his body. The child in him had always known of the shapes that walked in the shadows, just beyond the reach of lights. Now he saw them. Cowled wraiths loomed like mountain peaks. Their voices uttered the wind's words, and they called to him.

The cold slipped away. The wind fell silent. He saw his body stumble in the snow. He left it and went towards the voices.

The shreds of cloud stopped in the sky. The banners of light beyond them froze into crystal arches. The voices called once more, and grew quiet. Snowflakes hung like hover-moths. A shape was darkening in the air.

It gained definition; he could see the head, though not the face. The shape was taller than him, but not much. It reached out an arm.

Anil.

I'm coming, he cried, in the silent voice this world required. Anil. You know me.

I'm coming.

No. Not yet. Go back. Only—remember what I show you. Remember.

Anil cried out and leapt after the shade.

He fell into his body, labouring on all fours through the snow in the main valley.

Voices came to him. The crack and green flash of a shot split the darkness.

He got to his knees as they ran to him. Lazuli was first, with a torch and a pistol. The others came up slowly, peering beyond him, their weapons levelled, while she dropped the torch, fell to her knees beside him, and hugged him.

"Where's Malachite?" he asked, clutching her, holding her to still the shaking in his body. The others' voices drowned out his: "Didn't you see it? Stalking you. Our lights must have driven it off."

Anil stared at her. "You saw it?"

"Huge and white," Lazuli whispered. "It was right behind you. You didn't see it?"

"I don't know," he muttered. "I thought there was—something. Where's Malachite?"

No one answered for a moment. Then Lazuli said, "They found his coat. And a lot of blood. Why did you split up?"

"Blood?" Anil pushed himself to his feet. He swayed and shook his head. "Later," he said. "I know where the Shell is."

* *

Under snow and ice and a screen of rock-vine, it looked like part of the valley wall—a crumpled cylinder of black metal, lying along the valley floor, with one wing still splayed halfway to the ridge. Gaps as wide as a man's spread arms opened into the cavern within it. Snow was already silting up inside.

They crouched and shuffled into the cavern. The wind's howl stayed behind them and their torches glimmered in a high, arched chamber with ribbed walls. Dimly visible under the ceiling were pipes and girders like limbs of the swamp-tree. On the ground, snow had drifted into heaps that did not hide all the fragments of oil-fern seed, and bones.

"Windigo."

"This is old. From last winter."

There were other things among the snow. Anil went to a grimy mound beside the entrance. He swept the snow away with both arms until he had uncovered what lay beneath. "Another sled!" He put his torch on the ground and sprawled to peer under the housing. "Bigger than ours, and it's got a drive as well as a lifter." He turned on his back and reached upwards, groping.

"Well?" asked Gannet.

"There's no power to the coils."

"Can you make it work?"

"Maybe." He crawled from beneath it, peered at its console. "Some of the dials read." He gripped the side rail and strained to lift it. Lazuli helped and together they rocked and heaved the sled onto its side. Immediately, he dropped to his knees and began unlocking the cover plate from the drive housing.

"How long?" Gannet demanded.

"I can't tell."

"You—this stop is for food." Gannet gestured at Lazuli, who glanced at Anil, then got up and went to set up their stove.

"Carp, Cerulan—watch the entrance, but stay out of the wind. The rest of you—dig through the snow here. Look for anything else that might help us."

The group settled, water was heated, the smell of stew filled the cavern.

Anil crouched, trying to make sense of the new sled's circuitry from what he understood of their own.

A bowl of stew was pushed in front of him. Lazuli smiled quickly from the depths of her hood, and pulled something from her anorak. "My mother found this over there." She nodded to where empty boxes were being pulled out of the snow near the far wall. "Look at it."

It was a flat box with a transparent cover. Lazuli tugged off a glove and pressed a button on the side of the box.

A blue light flickered, then blazed from the transparent cover. They blinked, shielding their eyes, and when they looked again, a figure was looking back at them.

It was a strange figure, thin and beardless, and dressed in loose clothes more suited for a dayside assembly than the flight from the edge of winter. It spoke. The phrases they heard were meaningless, fragments of a speech they barely recognised.

Then the figure vanished. In its place was what Anil realised was a depiction of a world. This world—his world—it must be. There was the river, snaking southwest across the plain.

What was the box trying to tell them? The first figure reappeared, and showed a person like itself, and then a picture of two intertwined ropes, brightly coloured and strung with beads. "The life coil," Lazuli muttered.

The box emptied for a moment, and in place of the coil was a crouched figure thick with white fur, its eyes black pits, its fangs like knife blades. Anil hissed between his teeth.

"It's what followed you in the valley," Lazuli whispered.

Then the first figure reappeared, speaking and flourishing a black pendant—a Lar.

"Are you willfully disobeying me?" Gannet was standing over them. She could have been addressing either one of them.

"Look at it," Lazuli began.

"We need food and, if possible, the sled. Not toys and more luggage. I don't expect to have to repeat my orders. Will the sled work?"

"There's a component missing," Anil said, "probably a green four-legs—"

"Then we'd better be prepared to leave it. If you can't fix it by the time we've eaten, we'll go without it."

At the main entrance, Carp screamed. The sound of a shot crashed through the chamber.

Anil grabbed his torch and ran to the entrance. Carp was crouched trembling, his gun shaking in his hands. Near the edge of the lighted patch of snow lay a crumpled piece of metal that Anil suddenly realised was the remains of a pistol. Just beyond it, hard to see at first, was a shape like a fractured ball of red-black glass....

He stiffened and stepped back, collided with two others.

"They're out there," Carp moaned. "Waiting."

"He was hunting them," Anil muttered, and stepped back again.

Carp's voice rose. "They ate everything but his head."

The others were backing away from the entrance with him.

Gannet screamed at them. "If we stay here we freeze! Move now! Forget the food. Everybody out. Guards, get ready to cover the rear of the column. Now!"

She was afraid, Anil realised: if she couldn't make them leave now, they might cower here until the night was upon them.

Nobody moved.

Gannet coughed. She choked and doubled over, then straightened and drew a long breath. "Anil," she ordered more quietly. "Load our sled. Guards stay at the entrance. Everyone else, go back inside and get ready to leave."

Finally someone answered her.

"How do we hold them off?"

"A sacrifice," Gannet said quietly. "The Lar will choose."

"That worn-out instrument?" asked Heron. "At a time like this?"

"It took my husband. It's the reason my son lacks a father. I'm prepared for whatever it may choose. Are you?"

Heron lowered her eyes. "As you wish."

Gannet hurried them into a circle and pulled the Lar's loop from her neck. "The first to show the sign."

She started with herself, holding the Lar up for them to see, then pressing it to her wrist, so that it tasted her blood. Its pale eye glowed, but did not turn red. She closed her own eyes for a moment, and sighed. Next to her was Carp, and for his blood the eye barely lit. Then Gannet approached her son.

The Lar pressed his wrist and stung. He did not look at it, but he could feel Gannet's hand shaking. He watched her face, saw her eyes stare, then relax, and looked down as the Lar's eye faded.

Gannet turned to Lazuli, who was still at his side.

Heron cried, "Do you know what you're doing?" Gannet looked quickly at her, and her voice fell. "Yes," she said hopelessly. "Yes, you do."

Gannet pressed the Lar to Lazuli's wrist. Immediately, the eye lit. It turned red and began to flash.

Lazuli's face had gone hard. Anil could find no expression he could identify.

"You see!" Gannet shouted. "You all see—the Lar has chosen."

"She can't be the only one!" Anil cried.

"The first, I said. We've no time for more. Everyone, get ready to march." Her voice was high and quavering. "Now—who will drive the stakes?"

This time, Anil did find something in Lazuli's face he could understand. "I will," he said.

Gannet twisted to face him, the Lar clutched against her chest. She stared as though he had struck her. Her mouth opened, then closed. "Drive them in well," she said harshly. "Then hurry; we may still get to the river in time. But be sure the stakes are firm."

"The way you did for my father? You staked him yourself, didn't you?"

"Yes, I did it." Her voice shook. She took a step closer to him, spoke in a thick whisper. "Listen. He was a cruel man in many ways, but I had chosen him. I fastened the ropes and hammered in the stakes and he didn't look at me." Her eyes turned from Anil, stared into the empty night. "I drove everyone away from that place as fast as they could go. But I went back in secret. I nearly died in the cold, running my strength to its limits, because I had to get to him and back, before they knew I'd done more than gone foraging. I was going to let him go, and he would turn up later and say the Windigo had rejected our sacrifice."

"But you were too late."

She bent, and her body was shaken by coughs from deep in her chest. "The ropes had been snapped and bitten," she whispered, gasping. "Two of the stakes were wrenched out. Something was watching me, waiting for my torch to fail. It wasn't human."

"Is that what you've never forgiven him for? Your own failure?"

"You think you understand? You think you know so much you can judge?" She stared at him with a look of anger and despair. "Just do your job," she whispered.

Outside the entrance, Gannet and Carp unfastened Lazuli's anorak. She held herself stiffly and let them pull the sleeves from her arms.

The rest of the party filed out. Gannet waited to the end. She stood and looked at Anil and Lazuli as though she was about to speak, and her shoulders sagged; she seemed to shrink. Then she turned and hobbled away. By the time she had caught up to the others, her stride had lengthened, her head lifted. Almost immediately she coughed and stumbled, but she did not look back again.

The darkness closed around her.

Anil took off his coat for Lazuli. The chill began to bite into his flesh. He remembered the maze of valleys and the voice he had heard in his head. "It's going to be all right, isn't it? The Lar could have been wrong about me."

"I think so," she said. "We just have to wait. Come here."

They lay down together, pulled his coat over them and pressed close. "We've got our chance," she whispered. "At last."

Later she said, "Now you'll never have to stake anybody

else."

He tried to answer, but the cold was squeezing the breath from his body. He hugged her to him. Before his eyes closed, he glimpsed what he had only heard of in legend—the clear sky of nightside. It was full of stars.

He fell into a dream, where he walked the frozen river with Lazuli, under the blazing heavens of the night.

_※ ※_

He was being shaken.

He turned over in the snow, groped for his coat. The hands shaking him went away. His eyes opened, he tried to stand. Lazuli's clothing lay empty beside him, and under a black, shimmering sky, two Windigos were helping a shorter creature to stand. Its limbs were still thin, and its body hair was patchy, white and dark. It turned back once, and gave him a long blank stare Snow whirled up between them.

Then the three had vanished into the darkness, and he was alone.

_※ ※_

His hands would not stop shaking, but he got the main panel off the base of the sled. Something was missing.

The Lar had been right. Or there had only been room for one more of the creatures. Or, somehow, he had failed her

A part in the transfer unit. Green, it would be, with two brown bands. He dared think of nothing else, or the cold inside him would freeze his heart. He got up to walk and beat some warmth into his arms. A part was missing.

Lying in the snow was the box she had shown him, the box that held the Windigos' secret. He snatched it up to smash it against the wall. Then he stopped, imagining wires and coloured units like square rock-bugs. He took his knife to its seals.

_※ ※_

With his breath freezing on the body of the sled, he forced cables into sockets, rammed joints together and began tightening couplings. He hammered the cover-plate on with the hilt of his knife. Then he fumbled with the main switch, and waited for the blue flash that would sear through the icy void in his chest.

The indicators turned green, and the sled vibrated beneath him.

_※ ※_

The fourth ridge, and the sun at last—a crimson smear over

the far horizon where the the river gleamed like a bloodied knife.

In the snow at the crest lay a shape swathed in purple.

Gannet's eyes were closed. Dried blood stained the hair of her cheek and jaw.

"You were right," he whispered, and let the wind carry his words away.

Her eyelids twitched. One eye opened, grey as the eastern sky. It found his face. Her lips parted.

With his face lowered towards her mouth, Anil strained to hear her.

The words sounded in his head, like the words he had heard in the storm, but whether they were made of more than the wind's cries and his own longing, he could not tell.

I shall be near him again. Go to the others. We cannot choose.

"Why?" he shouted, shaking her by the shoulders. "What's the point? I won't do it!"

Her head rolled limply. A snowflake blew across her opened eye.

※ ※

He found the others halfway down the slope. The air was warmer and the wind stripped melting ice from the sides of the sled.

Thrush's song ended in mid-phrase as Anil stopped by them.

Carp was leading the party, as they slogged through freezing mud. They stared, then looked away and shuffled to a halt. Anil stepped from the sled and shoved Carp aside. "Team four," he shouted, "onto this sled. I'm going to ferry you to the river, and you'll starting cutting trees for rafts. I'll bring everyone else in four more trips."

"Boy, you're sounding like your mother," Carp said, pushing in front of him.

Anil was a shell of ice that held the dark's dead voices. A blow, a cry, a flash of sun might shatter him. He looked into Carp's eyes. "We may need a sacrifice while we load the rafts," he said quietly. "I haven't got the Lar now. I'll have to find another way to choose."

Carp swallowed and stepped back.

Anil stared at the others as team four crowded onto the sled. They shuffled from foot to foot, adjusted pack straps, avoided his eyes. But they would follow him. Through the endless, hopeless pursuit of the fading light, they would follow him.

Thrush's voice rose again, singing of Orlando's love abandoned on a forgotten world.

Clouds streamed overhead, purple-black and tinged with the blood of the setting sun. Behind the ridge waited the night, and its creatures. A snowflake brushed Anil's eyelashes.

He could stop now, he thought; he could walk away and offer himself again to the dark, to the relentless, wind-haunted dark. It might bring peace.

He got onto the sled and engaged the drive.

AFTERWORD
Robert Runté

Trouble Down the Mine

One of my colleagues, philosopher and musician Jane O'Dea, recently put it to me that artists are our civilization's canaries. Just as miners used to watch their canaries for signs that the air was becoming unbreathable, we rely on the keener sensibilities of our artists to recognize and articulate the danger signals before the rest of us have even recognized the potential trend. Reading the over four hundred submissions to *Tesseracts⁵* provided me with a pretty good overview of how Canada's speculative fiction writers view the world, and what they seem to be saying is, there's trouble down the mine.

I mean, it's not as if Yves and I deliberately set out to choose the most bleak, depressing, downbeat stories we could find. Quite the contrary. But in contrast to mass market American SF which still largely embraces a belief in technology, progress, and the American Way, Canadian writers seem to have little faith in a bright tomorrow. They have seen the future, and it is run by Westray.

Partly, this underlying gloom reflects hard economic times: More and more citizens are living lives of quiet desperation as rapacious corporations lay off workers and governments cut funding to education, culture, and social programs at the very moment these protections are most needed. Partly, the loss of optimism reflects basic demographics: The baby-boomers— whose disproportionate numbers have for fifty years dictated which themes will dominate popular culture—have now reached middle age and their own mid-life crises. Partly, the growing negativity represents a reaction against the false optimism of the 50s and 60s: We know now that that era's "progress" was premised on unsustainable growth, and a technology that creates more problems than it solves. Perhaps most significant of all has been a growing disillusionment with our civilization's core values: Our view of the nuclear family, for example, has gone from *Father Knows Best* to the talk show's exposé of incest, abuse, and exploitation.

Whatever the underlying cause, Canadian writers seem to have tapped into a particularly rich vein, a seam of coal so dark that it can power the imagination in a way that sunshine and light never could. What is most striking about this vision is that no matter how dark the story, there is nevertheless often a subtle undercurrent of resigned optimism. Canadian writers may tend to start from the premise that things are awful, and about to get even worse, but their protagonists always seem to rise to the occasion—to cope and endure. In Canadian SF, whether our heroes ultimately succeed is less important than that they undertake the struggle, that they find life and dignity in facing whatever confronts them. This contrasts sharply with the usual American motif in which winning is everything, in which the hero is a hero *because* he triumphed over impossible odds. American SF requires a happy ending because only a successful conclusion can justify the adventure's hardships, and erase the pain of struggle. In Canadian SF, the struggle *itself* is what is important; because life is struggle, and when it's over, it's *all* over.

It behooves us, in these dark times, to listen to what our writers are trying to tell us. The appeal of Canadian SF lies in the recognition that things are not necessarily going to get any better than they are right now, but that we have it within us to cope with even worse. Instead of providing us with the easy—and necessarily fleeting—escape from our mundane lives found in most other mass market SF, Canadian SF empowers its readers by presenting us with a dark imagery more appropriate to the modern age: 'participaction' as heroism; the bystander as adventurer; and the decline of civilization as 'interesting times'.

〃 ⦅

Fishing With A Bigger Net

Or at least, that was the trend I saw in this year's submissions. Of course, by the time one has identified the current trend, the artists have already moved on (else what worth their role as visionaries?), so it would not surprise me in the least if future volumes in this series were filled entirely with humorous adventure stories or romantic poetry.

Which is one reason a new editorial team is appointed each year. One of the drawbacks of a continuing anthology is that they often fall victim to a self-fulfilling prophecy: Writers examining the previous edition may assume that the publisher is looking for more of the same, and self-censor their submissions to conform to what they believe is that editor's particular tastes. If *Tesseracts* is to be a true national showcase, however, it must reach beyond any one editor's vision to encompass the full range of speculative fiction produced in this country. By appointing new editors each issue, Tesseract Books ensures that over the course of the series, the reader has the opportunity of samplimg the best of everything Canadian SF has to offer.

This is also the reason the *Tesseract* anthologies are always co-edited. An attempt is made to balance each editorial team for gender, region, and style to ensure that each volume is selected using as broad a net as possible. In the case of the current volume, Yves is from Quebec, I'm from Alberta; Yves is an award-winning author, I'm an academic. True, Yves and I are both male, but that balances the two females (Quebec novelist Elisabeth Vonarburg and Governor General Award winning translator Jane Brierley) who co-edited *Tesseracts^Q*, the anthology of Canadian francophone SF in English translation, so it all comes out right in the end.

Similarly, because neither Yves nor I are particularly comfortable editing poetry, the publishers made a point of seeking out an SF poet as one of next year's co-editors: prize-winning Toronto poet, Carolyn Clink. While that would normally imply her co-editor be from the West, another exception seemed in order, given that Carolyn's husband is none other than Nebula and Aurora winning author, Robert J. Sawyer. As one of Canada's most successful SF authors, Sawyer was a natural choice to co-edit *Tesseracts^6*.

Submissions for *Tesseracts^6* will have closed by the time you read this, so I can also announce that the editors for *Tesseracts^7* will be Alberta author Paula Johanson and Quebec novelist Jean-Louis Trudel.

*// *

But You Should Have Seen The Ones That Got Away

Of course, the *other* reason for having two editors has nothing to do with providing a variety of perspectives: It's so that each co-editor can blame the other whenever we meet one of the authors whose stories we had to reject.

One of the greatest frustrations of editing this anthology was that we could only chose 35 stories and poems out of the more than 400 submitted. Every editorial team since the series began has complained that they had enough excellent material to fill another two volumes; but the page limit must be adhered to, and many wonderful stories turned away. Many of these will find homes in other markets, especially now that Canada has at least three nationally-distributed SF magazines: *ON SPEC,*

Transversions, and *Paradox.* But it really hurts to have to say no, especially when many of the rejects are arguably just as good as those that made it in.

Naturally, the editors try to select the best, but quality is only the first criterion; nearly equal in importance is balance. For example, we received over forty stories (nearly 10% of the total) addressing the issue of physical or sexual abuse. Many of these were excellent, even outstanding, but much as we might have wanted to, one simply cannot fill the entire anthology with stories on a single theme and still present a representative sample of Canadian SF. (I was seriously tempted to organize a separate theme anthology around the issue of abuse, and we certainly had enough quality material to do it, but who would buy it? You thought *this* collection was bleak? My god! You have *no idea* what bleak is!) Thus, having selected three stories from this set that best fit with the rest of our anthology, we had no choice but to send the rest back, even though they were in nearly every respect as good as the ones we finally chose.

This, then, is the corollary of my original point that great writers tap into, and give voice to, current and future trends. While each author's treatment of the theme is unique and original, they are often mining the same vein of ore. What are the odds, for example, that two of the stories that made it into this year's collection would have "Dalai Lama" in the title? Indeed, there were a number of submissions that invoked Eastern religions, but is this just a coincidence, or does it reflect some actual shift towards cultural pluralism in a traditionally Eurocentric genre?

Another apparent coincidence were a couple of fantasies which featured grandfathers sacrificing themselves to save the young protagonist. Then I realized that this was yet another aspect of the abuse theme: As we come to mistrust the nuclear family, grandparents re-emerge as the child's only potential guardian.

Another common theme, though generally less well executed, was a rash of stories featuring some combination of prison and the new virtual reality technologies. I'm inclined to class this one as an instant cliché, one of those ideas whose time has already past, but how can any of these authors be expected to recognize that fact unless they saw for themselves the other twenty-five submissions with nearly identical plot lines? There were even a couple of stories about something else entirely, but whose tone or style or vision overlapped with this group so that they *felt* like more of the same, and were rejected. But how do I explain that to someone who wasn't there?

I mean, other than saying, "That had nothing to do with me, that was Yves!"

≈ ≈

Lessons Learned

So, I at least, will never look at a rejection slip the same way again. I realize now, as no one who hasn't taken a turn as editor ever could, just how big a role luck plays in all this. A writer can never know exactly what else an editor has on his or her desk at any particular time: One month there may be nothing but dinosaur stories, so "Commander Dino in Space" isn't going anywhere; but a year later, a light comedy piece like "Commander Dino" could be exactly what the editor needs to balance out an otherwise overly serious issue. The important thing is to tap into something real, to get there first, and to keep the manuscript in circulation until it sells.

Which is not to suggest that all 400 submissions received were publishable; selecting the top 100 for our initial short list was fairly straight forward. Of the 300 initial rejections, less than 15% were actually poorly written, and even most of these seemed to be by potentially talented but inexperienced writers. A much larger percentage, say roughly half, were adequately written but had some particular flaw that forced their rejection: a good opening and middle, but weak ending; or an excellent plot but a weakly developed setting; and so on.

(An aside to beginning writers: The most common flaw I encountered was expository lump, that annoying interruption in the action where the author feels it necessary to explain every blessed detail of the story's background to the reader. You all know the scene I mean, where the dumb blonde asks our scientist hero how the warp drive works, and he obliges with a twelve paragraph treatise on physics.

(Such expository lumps not only destroy the flow of the story, they introduce an unnecessary challenge to the reader's suspension of disbelief. Most readers could care less about the technical details of the warp drive, but if the writer insists on telling them, they will pick that explanation to pieces.

(It is even worse when a writer tries to fill in some future history, since we all have our own models of the world and will brook no explanations whose politics are opposite our own. Worst of all, to create a situation in which one of the characters has a credible excuse for explaining all this unnecessary background to the reader requires such contortions that the story is invariably destroyed. Why for example, is our hero lecturing the other characters on the history of their own society, when logically they would already know all this themselves? Sorry, it won't fly.

(If you haven't written much SF before, it may be worth your while to track down a copy of Lin Carter's 1957 short story, "Masters of the Metropolis". This brilliant satire has an average citizen getting up and going to work on a normal working day, but is written as if it were a futuristic hard-SF story. The workings of the toaster and the subway escalator are described in meticulous detail, with the oft repeated refrain, "and all this untouched by human hands!" After reading Carter's story, no writer can fail to realize that the characters in their future or fantasy setting would take the world around them just as much for granted as we do ours. Consequently, it is neither credible nor necessary to get the characters to explain the world to the reader.)

For many of the stories in this half of the pile, I might well have been tempted to ask for a rewrite, had the opportunity been available. Unfortunately, the tight timelines for an annual anthology, and the constantly changing editorship, precludes this option, even if we hadn't already had a surplus of top-quality entries. But one cannot help but feel that there is a vast army of talented writers waiting in the wings, just one or two rewrites from adding their voices to the national choir .

Finally, the other half of those that didn't make the short list were the competently written, but routine stories. I can offer these writers little advice, because these stories often had no identifiable flaws, I simply didn't find them memorable. Partly this is a matter of taste and chance, partly that no one writes winners every time. Undoubtedly many of these writers will see publication soon, if they haven't already.

I was frankly amazed that this group made up such a large proportion of the pile. I had no idea that there were so many promising writers entering the field. Twenty years ago I was hard pressed to identify half a dozen Canadian SF authors. Ten years ago, there were maybe 40 publishable SF authors, and another 50 or so developing in the wings. If the submissions to *Tesseracts*[5] are any indication, both those numbers have doubled again. Clearly, Canada has now reached the critical mass of authors necessary to sustain an annual anthology, and *Tesseracts* has adopted the policy that—all other considerations being equal—20% of each volume will be devoted to new authors. If that seems unrealistic, consider that almost half of the stories you have just finished reading are by authors published here for the first time. However dark the vision of our writers, the future of Canadian speculative fiction itself has never been brighter.

Since 1991, Natasha Beaulieu has published a score of science fiction, fantasy and horror short stories in various magazines and fanzines. In 1995, she won the *Prix Septième Continent* with *La Cité de Penlocke*.

Cliff Burns is the author of more than 100 published short stories, as well as numerous chapbooks, a one-act stage play, many reviews and commentaries; has appeared in nine major anthologies, and, not incidentally, is the husband of Sherron Harman Burns and father to two boy children, Liam & Samuel.

Mary Choo's poetry and short fiction has been published in speculative and mainstream magazines and anthologies throughout Canada and the United States. Her short story "Wolfrunner", which appeared in *Sword and Sorceress VI*, was on the preliminary ballot of the Nebula Awards and the final ballot of the Aurora Awards.

Michael Coney says, "Because of the galactic nature of SF, I find it difficult to write a story that is identifiably Canadian. 'Belinda's Mother' is my 50th published short story, and this time I hope I've got it right."

Marlene Dean is a grade six teacher in Fort McLeod, Alberta, Her humour column "Kaleidoscope" appeared in the *Lethbridge Herald* for two years.

Candas Jane Dorsey is a writer of short fiction, poetry, novels and non-fiction. Her latest book is *Black Wine* (Tor Books, January 1997). A 1989 Aurora award winner, she is an editor with, and the publisher of, Tesseract Books, and lives in Edmonton, Alberta.

Ian Driscoll lives in Ottawa, which leaves his evenings free for writing. He was once described as being someone who could "run circles around Barbara Walters", and assumes that this was meant figuratively. He inhales deeply whenever fresh ditto sheets are made available.

Heather Fraser has at various times been a medical lab tech, a high school science teacher, a paid singer, and a student of theology. Her fiction has also appeared in *ON SPEC*.

James Alan Gardner lives in Waterloo with his wife and two badly-behaved rabbits. Half the day he writes SF; the other half he writes computer documentation. Guess which half he likes better.

Teresa (Tracey) Halford, film-undergrad-turned-English-MA, works for now at the CBC and is in deep trouble about the Ralph Benmergui comment in her story.

Jan Lars Jensen lives in Chilliwack, BC, where he works in a library. At press time, little else is known about this reclusive genius.

Jocko is a Cape Bretoner currently living and writing in Edmonton. His poetry has appeared in magazines in Canada, the U.S. and Australia and his first published short story will soon appear in *ON SPEC*.

Sandra Kasturi was born in Estonia, moved to Sri Lanka, New York, Montreal, and eventually Toronto, where she lives with an extremely bad-tempered cat. Her poems have appeared in *ON SPEC*, *TransVersions* and *Contemporary Verse 2*. She is working on a collection of verse and preparing to edit an anthology of speculative poetry. Meanwhile, she avoids poetry readings, gives afternoon tea parties, and is currently not working on a novel.

Sansoucy Kathenor has worked professionally in editing, archaeology and modelling, was the first Canadian to win a Writers of the Future award, and has won other fiction and humour awards.

Eileen Kernaghan's latest book is *Dance of the Snow Dragon* (Thistledown Press). Her novelette "Dragon-Rain" appears in the 1996 Year's Best Fantasy & Horror.

Sally McBride's stories have appeared in *Asimov's, ON SPEC, Matrix, Northern Frights 4*, and others. A 1995 Aurora award winner, she and husband Dale Sproule live in Victoria and publish *TransVersions*, a magazine of the fantastic.

Yves Meynard lives in Montreal. He won 1994 *Grand prix de la science-fiction et du fantastique québécois*, is a three-time Aurora Award winner for the best short work in French, and has won the *Prix Boréal* three times. His stories have appeared in several English-language magazines in Canada and the U.S., and in *Tesseracts 4*. He has published over thirty stories in French, mostly in the magazines *Solaris* and *imagine...*, and also works as an anthologist and editor. He has a Ph.D. in computer science from the Université de Montréal.

David Nickle has had short stories published in *ON SPEC*, the *Northern Frights* anthologies, *Christmas Magic, Tesseracts⁴*, *TransVersions* and *The Year's Best Fantasy and Horror, Eighth Annual Collection*, among others. He lives in Toronto.

John Park was born in England, moved to Canada for graduate studies in science, and is now a partner in a scientific consulting firm in Ottawa.

Francine Pelletier has published over 30 short stories in magazines and anthologies, and has written over 15 novels for young adults. In 1988, her book *Le temps des migrations* won the *Prix Boréal* and the *Grand Prix de la science-fiction et du fantastique québécois*.

Annick Perrot-Bishop is a francophone writer living in St. John's,

Newfoundland. She has published over 30 short stories in Canadian journals and anthologies, and a book, *Les Maisons de cristal* (nominated for *Le Grand Prix de la SF et du Fantastique québécois* and for *Le Prix Boréal*). She has also completed a collection of poetry.

Robert Runté is an Associate Professor, Faculty of Education, University of Lethbridge, where he teaches sociology. He has been actively promoting Canadian SF for over twenty years, as editor of *Neology, The Monthly Monthly,* and *New Canadian Fandom.* He was also editor and publisher of *The NCF Guide to Canadian Science Fiction and Fandom,* which won a Canadian Science Fiction and Fantasy Achievement Award (Aurora) in 1989; he won a second Aurora in 1990 for his promotion of Canadian SF. In 1994 he was Fan Guest at ConAdian, the 52nd World Science Fiction Convention. He is a member of the Editorial Advisory Group of Tesseract Books.

Karl Schroeder lives in Toronto where he is a member of the Cecil Street writers' group. His work has been widely published, including in *Tesseracts3* and *Tesseracts 4, ON SPEC* and *ON SPEC: The First Five Years.* He is currently the president of SFCanada.

Keith Scott lives in Toronto and writes as a member of the Cecil Street writing group. He has appeared four times in *ON SPEC* and his first story in this magazine was republished in *ON SPEC: The First Five Years.* Keith has also appeared in *Prairie Fire*, *Space & Time* and has had three stories read on the CBC.

Dale L. Sproule's short fiction has been published in *Pulphouse: the Hardcover Magazine #1*, *Ellery Queen's*, *Northern Frights 4*, *Northwords, The Urbanite, Into the Midnight Sun* and *Terminal Fright.*; he has also published poems, illustrations and non-fiction including feature articles on SF in *Books in Canada.* Dale and his wife, Sally McBride, edit *TransVersions: New Literature of the Fantastic.*

Paul Stockton is a Reginan living in exile in Toronto. As president of Strawberry Jam Comics he published such comic books as *To Be Announced, night life, Open Season*, and *OOMBAH Jungle Moon Man.* He's the co-administrator of the Comic Legends Legal Defense Fund, which fights the censorship of comics.

Peter Such is a novelist, playwright and poet. He is Associate Dean at Atkinson College, York University where he directs distance education and multi-media learning.

Jean-Louis Trudel, born in Toronto in 1967, holds degrees in physics, astronomy, and history of science. Since 1984, he has published nine books and several short stories, in French and English. He will be co-editor of *Tesseracts[7]*.

Peter Watts, driven mad by long association with some of the sleazier elements of the scientific community, has recently fled the field of marine mammal research. He has since been trying to inflate one of his short stories (the only one, in fact, to achieve a modicum of recognition) into a full-length novel, and hopes readers won't notice that the extra 90,000 words contain few, if any, new insights.

Andrew Weiner has published over 40 short stories in magazines and anthologies including *Fantasy and Science Fiction*, *Asimov*'s, *Interzone, Quarry* and *Prairie Fire*.

ABOUT THE STORIES

"Laika" by Natasha Beaulieu originally appeared, in French, as "Laïka", in *Horrifique #12*, September 1994.)

"RSVP" by Cliff Burns originally appeared in *Grain* (Canada) and *The Silver Web 10* (USA).

"The Stickman Trial" by Jocko originally appeared in the Summer 1994 issue of *ON SPEC*.

"Tortoise on a sidewalk" by Michel Martin first appeared, in French, as "La tortue sur le trottoir" in *C.I.N.Q.*, Les Editions Logiques, 1989.

"The Last Dance" by Annick Perrot-Bishop first appeared, in French, as "Les Yvanelles" in *Solaris 114*, été 1995.

"The Travels of Nica Marcopol" by Daniel Sernine first appeared, in French, as "Ailleurs" in *Québec-Science*, December 1994-January 1995.

An earlier version of "The Paradigm Machine" by Jean-Louis Trudel appeared in *The Hart House Review*, Toronto: University of Toronto's Hart House, Spring 1995.

"Messenger" by Andrew Weiner first appeared in *Isaac Asimov's Science Fiction Magazine*, April 1994.